I0725768

STARFALL

NEGATIVE RETURN

RETURN

DEVIANT

FLUX

JESSIE KWAK

This is a work of fiction. Names, characters, places, and incidents either are the product of the author's imagination or are used fictitiously. Any resemblance to actual persons, living or dead, events, or locales is entirely coincidental.

Starfall copyright © 2016 by Jessie Kwak

Negative Return copyright © 2017 by Jessie Kwak

Deviant Flux copyright © 2018 by Jessie Kwak

All rights reserved. No part of this book may be reproduced or used in any manner without written permission of the copyright owner except for the use of quotations in a book review. For more information, address: jessie@jessiekwak.com

Original book covers by Fiona Jayde

Boxed set cover by Robert Kittilson

Editing by Kyra Freestar

Map by Jessie Kwak

Also by Jessie Kwak

The Durga System Series

The Bulari Saga

Double Edged

Crossfire

Pressure Point

Heat Death

Durga System Novellas

Starfall

Negative Return

Deviant Flux

Standalone Novels

From Earth and Bone: A Ramos Sisters Thriller

Nonfiction

From Chaos to Creativity: Building a Productivity System for Artists and Writers

I learned about the Durga System universe in small glimpses.

I chased leads, followed characters, asked questions, peeked through cracks in doors.

And slowly — so slowly — the Durga System world started to make sense to me.

In the original short story that introduced me to the world, Willem Jaantzen was the villain. I tried writing a draft of the first Bulari Saga book with him still in the villain role, but I was too fascinated by him — and by his crew — to let him stay there for long.

As I worked my way through the Bulari Saga, I found myself delving back into the history of Jaantzen's core crew members: Starla, Manu, Toshiyo, and Gia. In exploring their stories, I ended up writing the three novellas you find in this boxed set. They're meant to be read in any order, but I've organized them in the order I wrote them.

Starla Dusai was the first of Jaantzen's crew to capture my attention. I was fascinated by her relationship with Jaantzen, their individually painful histories, and the deep father-daughter love that had grown — mostly unacknowledged — between them. In *Starfall*, I wrote their origin story and discovered what they both had to give up to get to where they are in the Bulari Saga.

Next, I couldn't stop thinking about Manu Juric, Jaantzen's right hand man and closest friend. He has a quirky wit and a casual ease about him that have made him a fan favorite, and I needed to know how he and Jaantzen met. When I sat down to start *Negative Return*, I found Manu sitting in a bar, getting ready for the biggest paid hit in his young life. With a start, I realized he was planning to kill Jaantzen — and the rest of the book just wrote itself.

Negative Return was one of my favorite books to write simply because I love being in Manu's head so much.

I wrote *Deviant Flux* in part because I wanted to bridge the gap between the scared yet fierce teenager Starla is in *Starfall* and the competent leader she is in the Bulari Saga. Along the way, I gave her the best mentor a girl could have: Giaconda Áte.

I'd written about Gia before, but never from her point of view — and as I worked my way through *Deviant Flux*, she slowly started to open up to me. For years, I'd been trying to crack the nut that was her history, but I couldn't get her emotionally vulnerable enough on my own. That required a visit from a very charming — very unwanted — ghost from her past.

Writing these books has been like solving a puzzle. The entire world is one massive picture, and every book or story lets me shine a light on another small portion — whether that's another neighborhood or another character.

And even when the Bulari Saga is complete, I know I

won't be done with this world. Stay tuned for more novellas, and another series of novels featuring a pair of notorious space pirates in their pre-baby years.

Have a favorite character you hope to see more of? I love to hear from readers. Drop me a line: jessie@jessiekwak.com.

BULARI

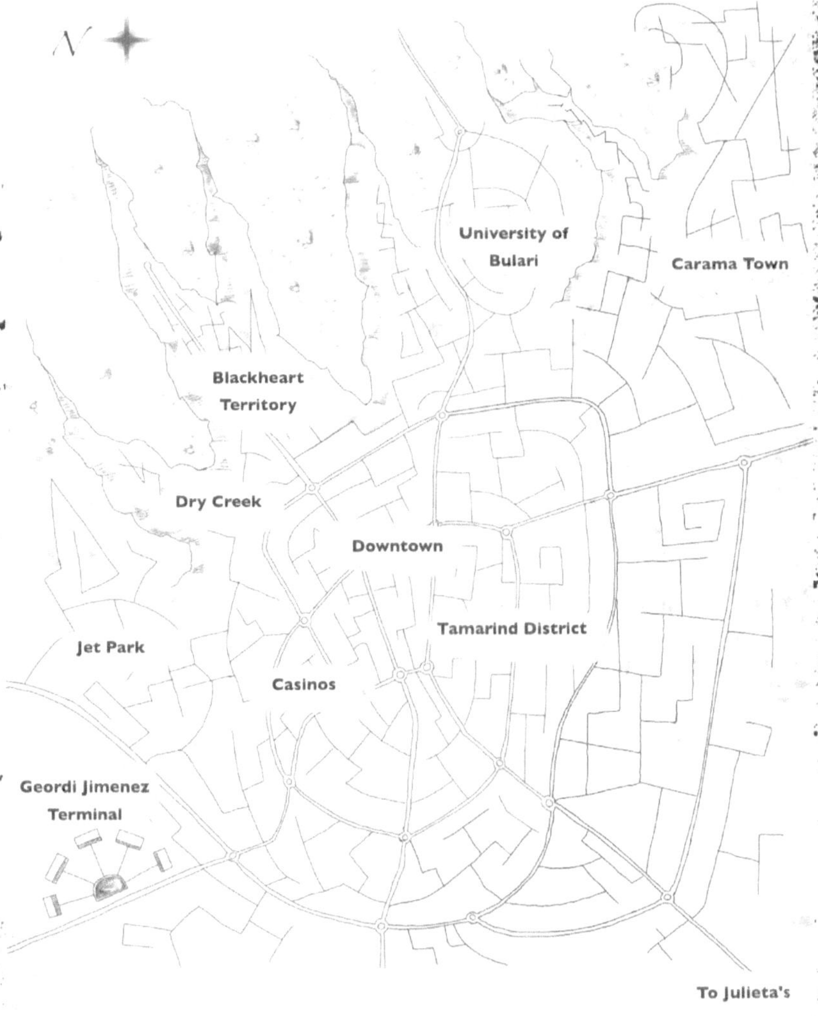
N
University of Bulari
Carama Town
Blackheart Territory
Dry Creek
Downtown
Tamarind District
Jet Park
Casinos
Geordi Jimenez Terminal
To Julieta's

STARFALL

A DURGA SYSTEM NOVELLA

JESSIE KWAK

For my parents,
who raised me strong and curious.

1

Starla

GRAVITY HERE IS CRUSHING.

Starla Dusai switches gingerly from side to back to sitting, the terrible mass of this planet making it hard to breathe, making her joints and bones ache, her heart race at the slightest movement.

Not that she has much opportunity to move.

The cell she's in is about two paces wide and just long enough for the cot — which is not long enough for Starla. At fifteen, she's already shot past her Indira-born parents by a full head, growth spurts set free by the low gravity of Silk Station.

She's tried to sleep the last three nights with legs crooked up and spine curled forward, but the ache in her knees wakes her, the ache in whichever side is being rammed by this planet's gravity through the thin mattress.

The ache in her heart of not knowing if anyone else is still alive.

Cot, sink, toilet. Harsh yellow overhead lights that call out sickly undertones in her pale-colored skin. The

5

walls are featureless but for what looks like a speaker and a camera in the ceiling opposite the cot, where she can't reach. Useless to her, anyway.

Food is dispensed automatically through a slot at what seems like regular times. The lights dim and rise. A cleaning bot scurries through every afternoon and then slips back into its pocket door. On the second day, Starla tried to catch it, but it shocked her so badly the muscles in her hands twitched for what felt like an hour. She lets it do its job in peace now.

The air smells sharp and scorched, like a recycler system gone over-hot and baking its seals. The temperature is uncomfortably warm.

It's what she's always imagined desert-hot New Sarjun would smell like.

Because she's on New Sarjun.

She has to be.

She's in an Alliance prison colony on New Sarjun.

There's no place else she could possibly be.

AT THE END of the third day, guards.

A man and a woman, wearing the same uniform as the Alliance soldiers who'd transported her from Silk Station. They slip through the door, come at her with outstretched hands and careful quiet steps like they're trying to corner a wild animal and they're not sure it won't bite. The man says something to his partner, his pudgy lips mashing the words into meaningless shapes.

They don't bother trying to speak to her.

Starla pushes herself into the corner of the cot, feet digging into the mattress. She's snarling as they pounce, drag her to her feet — she's panting with the effort of moving on this stupid, stupid planet — and wrench her arms backwards into cuffs. They push her through the door. She's barefoot.

Starla tries to stay calm, but for as badly as she has wanted to leave the cell over the last three days, now the metallic, vibrating hallways and branching corridors close in on her. She cranes her neck to see down the corridors they pass and is rewarded with a shove between the shoulder blades.

The two wrestle her through hallways, keying regularly through double-thickness glass doors to enter less secure — or more secure? Starla doesn't know — areas of the prison. Into a dingy metal room, bigger than her cell, a single metal table bolted to the floor, a bench on one side, a chair on the other. They fold her kicking and struggling and panting onto the bench, uncuff her, and slam her hands into new restraints on the table before she even realizes she had a brief moment of freedom.

Job done. The two leave.

Starla twists, cranes her neck to see the door they left through, trying to learn anything she can about this new prison.

Brushed aluminum walls and a floor scuffed with shoe rubber — some of the marks scraping high up the wall as though someone had been testing the strength of it, or kicking out in anger. The walls are battered, with dents and dings that catch the harsh light and pool it into tiny craters. The room stinks of something acrid, a mix of cleaning solvent and welding fumes that seems to be cycling through the air vents.

Starla coughs.

She's waiting only a moment before two women enter. One's short, even for planetborn, with a blunt gray bob and glasses, wearing a plain purple dress suit. The other's tall and thin, with a square jaw and thick black hair cut close to her scalp. She wears an Indiran Alliance uniform. They remind her of something, a split second of recognition that fades the more Starla tries to grasp at it.

The short woman wrinkles her nose and says something to the tall one, too fast for Starla to catch.

"Hi Starla," the short woman says then, speaking and signing. "My name is Hali." She spells it out, then makes her hand into an *H* and taps it against her left shoulder. "This is Lieutenant Mahr." Mahr doesn't get a name sign.

Starla lifts her chin a touch, but makes no show that she's understood. The short woman, Hali, frowns at her.

"She's a child," Hali says to the Alliance woman, Mahr. She's speaking more clearly now than when she first entered the room. Starla stares at her lips, greedy for information. "You can't keep her like this. There are laws."

The lieutenant shrugs. "Figure out what she knows," she says — or, Starla thinks she says. The lieutenant's lips barely move, her scowl permanently carved into her dry, angry mouth.

Hali turns back to Starla, speaking and signing again. "Have they treated you well?"

Starla frowns. What is she supposed to answer to that? Everything's fine, thanks for asking? The amenities could be a bit more posh, but they're serviceable?

She raises a hand to sign something rude, but she's cuffed to the table.

Her hand comes up short with a jerk.

"We can't communicate if she's restrained," Hali says to Mahr.

If Mahr replies, Starla can't tell. The lieutenant turns

to knock on the door, looks like she shouts something through it, and one of the original guards returns with leg restraints, locking Starla to the crossbar of the bench before releasing her hands. "Thank you," Hali tells him. He ignores her.

Hali sits in the chair across from Starla; Mahr leans against the wall with arms crossed, one hand resting on the stunner in her hip holster. Hali sees this and frowns. "She's a child," she says again. Mahr just raises an eyebrow.

Starla sits with hands folded. Trying to look like a child, whatever children look like on Indira. She's heard her entire life, from newcomers to Silk Station, from people born on either planet — Indira or New Sarjun — that she and her asteroid-born cousins look years ahead of their age because of their height. On some, like Mona, it looks graceful. On Starla it just looks boyish and scrappy. One of the uncles told her that once. She thinks he meant it as a compliment.

A stab of panic pierces Starla's heart.

She tries not to worry about her cousins. About Mona. About Auntie Faye. About her parents. She saw escape pods, shooting like torpedoes; she saw ships peeling away from docking bays and flashing out of view before the Alliance missiles tore through the station and set Starla's home blazing bright as Durga herself.

1, 4, 9, 16, 25 . . .

Starla forces herself through multiplications to redirect her thoughts.

She's missed something: Hali signing to her. Starla furrows her brow, and Hali repeats herself. "I'm here to decide what to do with you. Do you understand?"

Starla finally nods. She's found that if she refuses to

respond at all, some people write off communication for good. This might be her only chance to get answers.

"Good." The woman's still speaking aloud while her hands dance, probably for Mahr's benefit. "Do you know where you are?"

Starla considers. Is the woman gauging her knowledge of geography, or her intelligence in general? Probably both. "Prison," Starla signs. "New Sarjun."

Hali frowns at that last sign, and Starla fingerspells it. She can't remember the standard USL sign for New Sarjun — she and Mona had their own slang for so many things.

"Yes," says Hali. "That's right. You're under Alliance protection."

"My parents: what happened?" Starla leaves the last sign hanging in the air a moment before resting her hands back on the table.

Hali looks at Mahr, who's apparently said something to her — Starla sees only the last few syllables slicing out of Mahr's sneering lips. "She's asking about her parents," Hali says. Mahr just shakes her head.

"We'll get to that," Hali says and signs to Starla. "But for now I have some questions. Can you tell me about life on Silk Station? Were you taken care of there?"

Starla wrinkles her nose. "It was home," she signs, confused. Was she taken care of there? What the hell was that supposed to mean?

"Who raised you?"

Starla glances from Hali to Mahr, who is watching her coldly. What are these questions?

"My parents raised me," Starla signs. "Where are they?"

Hali ignores her question. "I'm confused. Did your

parents take you with them on their raids? On the *Nanshe*?"

"Of course not," Starla signs. She'd wanted to go for years, but they hadn't let her. Not until this year, until her fifteenth birthday, when they'd finally agreed she could start training as crew. If not for that, she wouldn't have been on the *Nanshe* when the Alliance attacked Silk Station. Wouldn't have —

Hali is waving to get her attention. "Then who raised you when they were gone?"

Starla shrugs. What, did this woman want a list? Any number of aunts, uncles, older cousins, station mechanics, and cooks had done the job.

Starla and the other children had stalked Silk Station, hurtling through the corridors as if propelled by rockets, chasing after older cousins in the peculiar game they played in the figure-eight hallway near the bioregenerative gardens, screaming and reversing directions on a toe, arms flinging out to correct over-exuberant spins in the low gravity. They were legion, underfoot, existing continuously on the verge between play and being snatched up by one of the station crew and given a chore.

Dinners were the same chaos, a gaggle of children descending on the commissary at any hour, whenever they were hungry. School was TUTOR, an AI that came preloaded with courses from Hypatia Educational Facilities Corporation that students could work through at will, with full knowledge that their progress data was being reported to the aunts and uncles. Curfew was a word from the novels she downloaded from TUTOR.

Who had raised her?

"Whoever was around," Starla signs.

"Whoever was around," Hali says, and she and Mahr

share a look full of meaning that Starla can't decipher. "You're very thin," she says and signs to Starla. "Did they feed you well?"

What the hell did that mean?

Starla glares at her. "Where are my parents?"

"We're just trying to understand your life," Hali says, hands fluid and defensive. "You're on the edge of what the Alliance considers a child. Your parents chose to become criminals, but you had no choice. You've had a hard life. Do you understand?"

Starla feels a chill. Raj and Lasadi Dusai chose to live life on the fringes, managing their glorious and infamous empire from an asteroid station hidden deep in the debris of Durga's Belt. Starla Dusai, on the other hand, could tell a sob story about being beaten and neglected and starved at the hands of her horrible pirate parents, and win a free ticket into the open arms of the Indiran Alliance. A free ticket into the society her parents had fled years ago.

"Where are my parents?" Starla snarls the words on stiff, angry fingers.

Hali looks sad. "I don't think she's ready to talk yet," she says to Mahr.

Mahr knocks on the door and the two guards come back in, hands and stunners raised to subdue her.

"Where are — "

Starla gets only those words out before her hands are grabbed, her arms cuffed, her ribs slammed into the hard metal edge of the table.

They drag her back to her cell.

Jaantzen

———————————————

WILLEM JAANTZEN IS FIFTEEN BREATHS AWAY FROM
pulling the trigger. He's counting them: One, two . . .
The bulk of the pistol feels like a living thing nestled
against his chest.

Ahead, Mayor Thala Coeur of Bulari is shaking
hands with the Cormoran ambassador, welcoming him
to New Sarjun's capital city, her teeth gleaming white in
that picture-perfect smile as she turns to the cameras.
She's changed little these three years, rust-colored skin
still glowing and taut, hair plaited into a cascade of tiny
braids — not bound brash with gold as she'd once done
when she controlled only the Nova neighborhood, but
more classically styled these days. Appealing to all her
voters.

Three, four.

It's hot today, baking. Mirages shimmer up from the
sidewalks, and all through the crowd fans are snapping
open and shut, misters floating above, wafting down
cooler breezes on their turbine gusts.

Jaantzen glances up at one of the misters for a split

second, catches the gold glint of the surveillance cam in the center. Wonders if this is one of the Bulari Police Department's, or one of Toshiyo's. He can't tell the difference, and he doesn't care. That's why he hires the sharpest people he can find — to ensure that moments like this go off without any hitches.

To say that Willem Jaantzen has spent three years dreaming of this particular moment would be misleading. He's thorough, not excessive. Dedicated, not single-minded. He's spent three years preparing, yes.

Three years obsessing, no.

Ahead, Coeur exchanges a joke with the ambassador, claps him too heavily on the shoulder. The man flinches, and Jaantzen feels a hint of pride for his city, almost. Coeur may be wearing the veneer of civility, but the fierce woman who styled herself Blackheart when she ran Bulari's most powerful crime organization is still there beneath the surface.

Good.

Jaantzen gets no pleasure from slaughtering sheep.

Jaantzen's earpiece crackles and he hears Toshiyo's telltale clearing of the throat. "What is it," he snaps.

"Boss. Julieta Yang's calling."

Jaantzen blinks. Twice.

Breathes.

"Have her speak with Manu." That's the plan, not Toshiyo calling in to interrupt him after she's given him the all clear. Manu Juric is the executor of all that comes after this moment.

"Boss, I tried that."

Not a surprise. In Bulari's underground, Julieta Yang is one of his fiercest rivals and oldest friends, yet they rarely speak about business. If she had a petty business matter to discuss, she'd have had one of her daughters call.

No. Julieta Yang called because she, Julieta, has something to say to him, Willem. Right now.

Coeur turns for another photo op, holding her million-mark smile only slightly longer than the camera before turning towards the entrance to the Indiran Alliance Embassy. Her security guards scan the crowds, their eyes skimming over Jaantzen.

Nine, ten.

"Boss?"

Right now, Jaantzen should be making his peace. He clenches his jaw and tries to blend in, another face in the crowd. He'll look into Coeur's eyes in the moment, but if she recognizes him too early, the game's over.

And she will recognize him. She will know it's Willem Jaantzen who finally got his revenge.

Eleven, twelve.

He wants to ignore this call, ignore Toshiyo and get on with his plan. Since Toshiyo gave him the go-ahead he's seen only one face in his mind's eye: Tae's.

He wonders if Coeur ever thinks about Tae and his children.

He wonders if she ever holds her own family close in the dark and marvels that their fragile little lives have lasted this long in the bloody wars of Bulari's underworld.

"Boss?"

It's time, but his hand isn't reaching for the gun.

"How long is the mayor's speech slated to be?" he murmurs.

Toshiyo's relief is evident in her voice. "Thirty minutes. They'll be leaving out the Commerce Street entrance."

Coeur offers her arm to the ambassador, and they both walk up the stairs.

Willem Jaantzen melts back into the crowd.

"What in sweet damnation does Yang want?"

JAANTZEN FINDS a corner table in a cafe he trusts and Toshiyo patches the call through to his earpiece. Julieta Yang won't answer a video call, only voice. She's convinced video calls are easier to track, no matter what anyone else tells her. One of the mister drones has followed him from the plaza; it dips its wings twice, Toshiyo's signal.

Willem Jaantzen doesn't relax.

"Madame Yang," Jaantzen says, waving away the waiter, the owner's son. The boy hovers, watchful yet discreet and visibly nervous. He's not used to being alone around Jaantzen. "How may I help you today?"

Julieta Yang's voice is cool and aloof, gone papery around the edges with age in the years since they first met. He'd been a fool child just getting started in the game, and she'd come herself to deal with him for poaching on her territory. All these years later, and she can still make him feel like a fool child with the right tone.

"My people have intercepted troubling news about mutual friends of ours," she says. Never for the small talk, Julieta goes straight to the point — "Life's too short to pretend to care how someone is doing," she'd told him once.

Jaantzen doesn't ask; waits for her to tell him. He's sweating more than usual — he can smell himself through the expensive suit and the nice cologne: the sharp bite of adrenaline. His body had prepared itself for the inevitable hail of bullets and is having trouble adjusting to the fact he's still alive.

"The Alliance attacked Silk Station three days ago," Julieta says. "By all accounts, they destroyed it."

An echoey silence in Jaantzen's head; the restaurant seems hushed. There but for the grace of God go we all, one fiery explosion away from having no family, one volley of torpedoes away from having one's entire organization, everyone one cares for and protects, completely destroyed. He signals to the owner's son for a glass of wine.

"Any survivors?" he asks once he's sure the horror won't color his voice.

"Yes," she says. "There was enough warning for some of the family to flee before the Alliance began firing. Reports are still coming in."

"Raj and Lasadi?"

"The *Nanshe* was apparently mobile when the Alliance attacked. It was boarded and prisoners were taken. We haven't been able to learn whether Raj and Lasadi were among them." A pause. "I was hoping you could do that. It's more your expertise."

"I can connect you with Toshiyo — "

"I don't need your surveillance team," Julieta snaps. "My surveillance is the best. I need your political connections."

Jaantzen checks the time on his comm, takes a sip of the wine. He has ten minutes to get back in place by his count; as if on cue, Toshiyo sends an update: *She's wrapping up. 10min to exit. You good boss?*

Jaantzen's not good.

Raj and Lasadi Dusai have taken care of themselves and their family for decades. If the Alliance got them this time, it's because they stretched past their limits, picked the wrong pocket, slit the wrong throat.

They'd nearly done it seventeen years ago when they tried to turn over a ship containing one Willem Jaantzen. Fortunately, the result of that encounter had been life-long friendship.

Julieta Yang's business would be taking a dip with the loss of the Dusais and their steady supply of pirated goods, but he knew that wasn't the only reason she was upset. Raj and Lasadi Dusai, once you'd met them, were infectious. Their business partners often found themselves unexpectedly becoming friends.

If Raj and Lasadi planned right, their family — their daughter; he thinks of her with a pang and moves on — will be taken care of. Like Jaantzen's people will be.

Jaantzen has taken care of everything. His legitimate businesses are all shielded from backlash through layers of red tape, his illegitimate ones dissolved and the assets put into a fund to be distributed by Manu Juric, who will ensure that everyone is comfortable during the transition.

Right now, Jaantzen should be thinking about Tae and his children. Preparing to see them, should that be his option in the ever-mysterious afterlife.

He doesn't need to be thinking about the Dusais.

"I'm in the middle of something right now," he says. He's not telling Julieta what. He doesn't need her blessing — or her chiding.

A sharp breath on the other end of the call. "Ah, yes. I heard what you've planned for today, and I think it idiotic."

He doesn't ask how she knows, and in seven minutes it won't matter. He drains the glass of wine and authorizes a hundred-mark transfer to more than cover the bill. He stands, nods to the owner's boy. "I thought you'd appreciate the chance to soak up some of my territory," he tells Yang.

"Those idiots in the Sendera Dathúil would get there before me, you know that, Willem. Things are good in Bulari now. Balanced. Don't toss the lot of us into the churn."

"That's not my concern, Julieta. I'm taking care of my people. You can take care of yourself, Raj and Lasadi can take care of themselves, and the Sendera can go to hell. I'm paying my own debts today."

The mister is trailing behind him, veering from hanging plant basket to hanging plant basket like a working drone would. His comm buzzes: Toshiyo. *5MIN BOSS.* Ahead, he can hear the noise of the crowd; he starts to slip into the outskirts, blending in.

Julieta Yang is still in his ear, but he's already gone, scanning the plaza to check the guards, check the misters. He's working his way to the front of the crowd.

"We have learned one thing," Julieta says, and his attention snaps back to the conversation, caught by her tone. She's been holding back a card, and she's ready to play. He tenses. "We know they've captured the daughter."

Jaantzen doesn't answer, but he's doing the math. How old is the girl now? He hasn't seen her since she was just starting to walk, when Raj and Lasadi brought her with them on one of their many trips planetside. She'd been about the same age as his daughter Sora had been when —

Now she'd be fourteen — no, fifteen.

Now the Alliance has the girl, will they treat her as a child, or as an adult, a traitor?

"Raj and Lasadi made you godfather, didn't they?" Julieta asks, but it isn't a question, and again he doesn't bother wondering how she knows. Julieta Yang's specialty is expensive luxury goods and even more expensive information — both of dubious origin.

"She's being held in Redrock Prison," Julieta says, like she's telling him tomorrow's weather forecast. "Here. On-planet," like there might be other Redrock Prisons. He can almost hear her examining her cuticles with feigned disinterest.

Two minutes.

"You know people who could help, don't you," says Julieta, and for a moment he thinks he hears worry in her voice. "There's nothing I'll be able to do about it."

The last time he saw the girl, she was all gangly limbs and graceless toddler exuberance, that same glorious joy and innocence as his Sora and Mikal, yet so different in her fierce desire to break free from her parents' orbit.

There's a flurry of activity in the guards by the door; the moment is here. He hasn't seen Starla in years, but he's seen Raj, he's gotten updates on his goddaughter, he's made renewed promises over business dinners to take care of her if anything ever happened to Raj and Lasadi.

Ahead of him, Coeur is walking out, flashing that smile and a palm-out wave to the crowds below her. Her gaze dances over him, and the pistol in its holster burns hot and fierce. He buttons his coat.

"Dammit, Julieta," he says.

"Let me know what you find out," she says. "I'll help where I can."

3

Starla

Starla's back in her cell, door slammed and lights
flicked off to pitch black — even the dim lights that had
glowed through the other nights. A spike of fear in her
chest. Starla wonders if lights-out is punishment for not
telling Hali and Mahr what they wanted to hear. Sensory
deprivation to make her afraid.

1, 4, 9, 16 . . . She counts her squares like Deyva
always told her to do, whenever she was angry at a
mechanical problem whose solution was eluding her. She
gets as high as 17 times 17 before she feels the panic
subsiding.

Starla lies back on her cot with knees bent.

It's just darkness. It's not a punishment, it's just a
reminder of the deep black, of that inky, starry night
she's been plucked from. She belongs among the stars,
not here.

She realizes her eyes are still open, and closes them.

She remembers.

STARLA'S HANDS were clumsy in the EVA suit she'd stolen from her mother, but she'd been practicing making her gestures bigger so that Mona could read her signs even through the unsubtle suit. Of course, they wouldn't always have visual communication, so Starla had reprogrammed the heads-up display on her mother's helmet to show her what Mona was typing. She had programmed a glove to recognize what she was finger-spelling and transmit that to Mona.

Starla carefully removed the right glove from her mother's suit, replacing it with the one she had modded herself. She stared at the lower left corner of her screen, waiting for the glove to patch into the system.

GLOVE_TEST_3 DETECTED, blinked the screen. Starla suppressed her delight. It was working.

She glanced over at Mona, who looked nervous. "No backup system," Mona signed. Starla nodded. She knew. But this was a trial run, just to make sure she could communicate. Eventually, they would get a backup system in place. She certainly wouldn't be comfortable relying only on her modded glove to pass messages back, not if she ever got to go out on the skin of the *Nanshe*.

Starla slowly began to fingerspell the alphabet, watching as each letter appeared in the lower corner of her screen. *A – B – C* . . . She glanced over at Mona, who was staring at her comm. Mona nodded, signing the letters she saw back to Starla.

Starla felt a thrill of excitement.

Should work like a charm.

"Ready," signed Starla, and Mona grimaced nervously.

Her scaredy-cat cousin was as ready as she'd ever be.

Starla's mother's suit was snug, but Starla had been

nervous about stealing a suit from a taller cousin. Her mother's would just have to do.

Mona glanced up at the ceiling in that gesture Starla had learned to recognize: an announcement was coming over the intercom. For some reason she couldn't fathom, everyone looked to the direction the sound was coming from like it helped them hear it better.

As expected, Starla felt her comm buzzing in her pocket — three short jabs. She couldn't reach it, not geared up as she was, and she hadn't had time to patch her incoming messages into her mother's helmet where she could read them.

Starla waved to get Mona's attention. "What is it? Comm in pocket," she signed.

"Shuttle docking in the bay right next door," Mona signed back. "Maybe we should wait until tomorrow."

"No."

No way was she getting this close without testing the glove outside. After years of waiting, Starla's parents had finally agreed to let her join one of their training runs with the new recruits. She would show them that she was ready, that she was resourceful. That she should join their crew permanently.

Starla punched the button for the airlock, and the door slowly began to open.

She felt a tap on her shoulder — the sensation muffled through the suit — and turned to see Mona shaking her head. "We know the glove works," she signed. "Try tomorrow?"

Starla shook her head again. "Mom's already going to yell at me," Starla signed. "Might as well earn it."

Mona looked resigned. "I'll get yelled at, too."

"Tell them I made you do it."

"That doesn't work anymore."

Despite her nerves, Starla grinned. They had been getting into trouble for years together, and Mona had almost always been able to talk herself out of trouble by saying she was just watching out for Starla. It never bothered Starla — even on the times Mona had come along willingly, Starla had always been the instigator.

They were as opposite as could be. Mona was curious about books and history, spending hours on her own with TUTOR learning about the harsh early days of settlement on Indira, about life on the *Ark Matsya*, about old Earth. Starla had put in the required hours with TUTOR, trying to get the AI to teach her what she was really curious about: electronics, programming, mechanics, weaponry. She soon found that TUTOR's curriculum was annoyingly theoretical, and although she continued to work her way through the calculus and physics courses just so the AI wouldn't ping her mother that she was skipping lessons, Starla began spending more time down in the mechanics bay learning about the daily operation of the station and getting her hands dirty in its wired guts.

"I'm going," she signed. Mona's shoulders slumped. "Now."

Fear, delicious and electric, thrilled through her as she stepped through the airlock door. Starla took a deep breath. She could feel the pressure change as the door slid shut, and she deliberately turned away from the window separating her from Mona.

Behind her were the familiar corridors of Silk Station. Behind her were generations of a tangled family tree and many friendly transplants — all too quick to step in and help out whenever she had trouble with something.

In front of her was the black, glittering with stars.

She took a step forward, tentative, though the outer airlock wasn't even open — the thick glass still seemed too thin — and startled when the broad, scarred side of a shuttle lumbered across her view. The shuttle that was docking in the bay next door. Right. She took another deep breath.

A message from Mona popped up on her screen. *You OK?*

Starla almost turned around to give her a thumbs-up, but she had to break herself from relying on visual communication. She made a fist and signed yes, instead, and to her delight the glove captured the movement. *Y-E-S*. Starla beamed.

She had never been outside the station in an EVA suit, but she'd done the drills, and she'd read about it. She'd watched TUTOR's instructional videos and gotten one of her older cousins, Amit, to talk her through it one day when he was in the middle of a passionate anti-Alliance diatribe and too distracted to wonder why she was asking.

She waited until the shuttle was past the window before starting the sequence Amit had given her. Next time she would have to figure out how to patch her comm into the helmet — she felt naked without her connection to the rest of the station — but that wouldn't be hard.

O-P-N-N-I-N-G-N-O-W, she fingerspelled, and the glove translated each letter. One typo. Not bad, but still some fine-tuning to do.

CHECK BELT CLIP, Mona typed back.

Starla sighed and checked her tether, then she did turn back to give her cousin a thumbs-up and a grin. Mona looked terrified.

Starla hit the button.

She could feel it, the sensation of the vacuum a subtle thing yet phenomenally alien. Starla self-consciously checked the belt clip again, feeling the reassuring tension of it tethering her to the station. She wouldn't be going anywhere. She would be fine.

Starla stood at the edge of the airlock, gripping the handrail on the left side as she stared out into the expanse. Blackness, washed with stars and studded by the ever-shifting vista of the asteroids that made up Durga's Belt.

It was the same view she'd seen every day of her life, but today there was no glass between her and the void.

She realized the lower left corner of her screen was blinking, annoyed. *O-O-O-O-O*

She let go of the handrail and the *O*s stopped.

There was a bug she would have to fix.

WHATS WRONG, came Mona's response, predictably. *N-O-T-H-I-N-G-S-T-U-P-I-D-G-L-O-V-N*

Starla frowned at the glove, annoyed.

She could still feel the thrumming of the station around her, the minute vibrations and shifts, the way it shivered from time to time like a living creature. It was more intense at the core, but here, out at the edge? Silk Station felt like a distant memory.

Starla fought the wild urge to let herself float free towards the heavens.

She could feel the gravity of the station still, feel its life and energy through her feet. The place she'd known her whole life, the energy she'd experienced for fifteen years. The same old people with their same old stories and complaints and dramas.

The black expanse beckoned her with its tantalizing unknowns, and damned if Starla was going to stand on the edge of it and not taste it.

GOOD TEST RUN. COME BACK IN?
N-O-T-Y-E-T

Starla hadn't gotten this far just to open up an airlock and stand at the threshold.

Starla stepped out.

IT'S STILL dark in her cell, but Starla is smiling, the memory of floating soothing the ache in her bones, the memory of Mona soothing the pain in her heart.

And the scent that had lingered on her suit when she'd reentered Silk Station, that faint, metallic scent like the fumes from a welder, or the antifreeze Deyva used to flush the systems. The smell of space.

Starla can still remember it, if she tries.

She'll fly again.

Alliance be damned.

4

Jaantzen

JAANTZEN STEEPLES HIS FINGERS IN THE GLOW OF THE screens, trying to ignore the rat's nest of tangled cables and gadgets and drifts of unlabeled data sticks littered over the tables, keeping his attention on the data streaming across the central monitor.

"How much longer?" Jaantzen asks.

It makes his skin crawl to be down here in the clutter and chaos, which Toshiyo navigates with deftness. She plucks data sticks out of their disorderly piles without looking, mutters epithets beneath her breath at each flicker and stall of her computers. She slaps a monitor on the side and Jaantzen winces.

It does no good to remind her who is paying for all this equipment she so haphazardly scatters throughout her lair, and Jaantzen has stopped doing so. He's hired people at the top of their game and given them what they need to do their jobs. And he's learned the best thing to do is sit back and stay out of it.

Besides, buying out Toshiyo's indenture was a costlier investment than any of these pieces of equipment, and since he's given her — and all his people — the choice to stay or go, the smartest thing he can do is make sure she's happy working for him.

She's been almost drunk with relief since he returned to the office this morning, her words tumbling over each other and attention flung recklessly throughout the room. Jaantzen finds it charming to know just how much she would have missed him.

Manu Juric is happy to see him, too, bustling about the office like a mother hen to make sure Jaantzen has everything he might need. Jaantzen isn't sure what Manu would have done had Jaantzen gone through with his plan to kill Coeur; Jaantzen would have left him enough money that he wouldn't have to work, but Jaantzen can't imagine the man sitting back and doing nothing.

Toshiyo's black-lacquered nails clatter against the keyboard, and after a long moment, Jaantzen begins to suspect she's forgotten he asked her a question.

"Ms. Ravi?" She looks up him and blinks, her glossy black ponytail catching the light of the screen. "How long?"

"Oh. Five minutes," she says, turning back to her keyboard.

Five minutes. It seems like an eternity, one in which he can only sit and curse Julieta Yang. She was right about there being nothing Toshiyo could do for her — Julieta's information was the best. Which is why he doesn't believe that she doesn't know whether Raj and Lasadi were among those captured from the *Nanshe*. She'd known about the girl. Why wouldn't she know about the parents?

Jaantzen finishes the dregs of his green tea, grimacing — he's trying to quit coffee today. His doctor, Gia, has given him any dozen number of things he should quit if he wants to live a good long life, which Jaantzen has been ignoring given his circumstances with Coeur.

But now that this chance — so perfectly choreographed — has been destroyed, he's thinking again. "You wanna live to kill that bitch, you gotta start skipping dessert, boss" — those had been Gia's exact words. The little luxuries — cigars, red meat (as rare as that was on New Sarjun), anything else that raises blood pressure — were to be plucked one by one out of his arsenal of foods until only blandness remained.

Rice and beans. Even just the words conjure up memories of the tasteless, watery, pale brown glop that was the staple of every homeless shelter and food bank he'd eaten at as a child. Bland food has long been linked in his mind with those starving years. At least the Willem Jaantzen of today can afford any spice in the galaxy, if he likes.

At mealtimes, this may be a consolation. Right now, he just wishes he could buy a few minutes' speed out of Toshiyo's servers.

"You want, I can let you know when I have an answer," Toshiyo says, not looking away from her screens. Her drawl is pure rural New Sarjun; he picked up her indenture from a mining conglomerate out in Ruby Basin after hearing stories about a young ops tech with an uncanny ability to glance at a spreadsheet and pinpoint a motherlode. Streaming data pools in her black eyes.

"Am I bothering you?"

She spares him a frown. "No," she says, too quick.

"Then what is it?"

Deep sigh, her thin shoulder climbing and dropping. "I'm not supposed to stress you out," she says. A quick sideways glance, flash of green catching in her irises. "Gia's orders."

Jaantzen's doctor is enlisting help from his staff. Lovely.

"I promise I won't die of a heart attack on your watch, Ms. Ravi."

She doesn't look convinced. Gia is formidable, but Jaantzen likes to think of himself as more so — and he'll be even more so as soon as he loses a bit of the girth he's allowed to accumulate around his waistline since Tae —

Willem Jaantzen shifts in his chair. "How much longer?"

Toshiyo's attention snaps back to the monitors, her mouth quirks into a smile. "Got it." But it's another full minute of tap-tap-typing until she sits back. Jaantzen feels like he's about to explode.

"The lists for Redrock Prison show one Starla Dusai," she says. "Maximum security wing, isolation cell."

Jaantzen relaxes at that. Isolation means she won't be at the mercy of the worst of the worst to be found in maximum security. It may not be comfortable for the girl, but at least she's not in with the general population.

"And her parents?" he asks.

Toshiyo frowns at her screen. "They were picked up from the *Nanshe*, but they haven't been recorded as entering any Alliance prison on New Sarjun."

"So, they're being kept elsewhere, they've been checked in under alternate names, or they're dead," says Jaantzen. Toshiyo nods slowly. "Find me every suspicious name in the timeframe," he says.

He's not ready to entertain the possibility that they're dead. Not when their daughter is waiting for them to come for her.

Jaantzen stands, almost bumping his head on a low-hanging shelf. He's got nearly half a meter on Toshiyo. "And find me someone in that prison who can be bought or convinced."

"Yeah, boss."

Jaantzen can't quite turn away; he's been dancing on the edge of his last request. Toshiyo senses him there, fingers going still. She glances over her shoulder. "Boss?"

"And find out Mayor Coeur's schedule for the next month."

She doesn't look at him. Cracks a knuckle on each hand. "You got it," she finally says.

She's typing away, back in her own world. Jaantzen stands in the doorway, watching. He wonders what she would have done if he'd killed Coeur. Gone to work for Julieta, maybe? Or pivoted straight and narrow to work for some corporation indenture-free? He likes to think she would have found some place to be happy and live a more normal life. He makes a note to ensure her employment with someone trustworthy before he takes his next chance at Coeur; he'd been remiss in this, last time.

His stomach growls. It's time to follow his next lead.

***

SEVENTEEN YEARS AGO, Willem Jaantzen took to the skies to protect his cargo from the scourge of the shipping lanes: the *Nanshe*. Part favor to himself, part favor to Julieta Yang, who had agreed to fund the trip and had sent one of her daughters along to negotiate her own terms with the infamous pirates.

Jaantzen mostly remembers being miserable. It's the

only time he's left New Sarjun, and he never intends to again.

But face to face with the famously rakish captain Raj Dusai, negotiations ended with guns at each other's heads, the tension shattered when Raj broke into his huge belly laugh and tossed away his weapon, inviting Jaantzen and his crew to share in a meal of New Manilan delicacies obtained from an Alliance cruiser.

Raj and Lasadi primarily preyed on Alliance ships, a habit Jaantzen warned them about repeatedly. They claimed it wasn't political, but Jaantzen knew better — the Dusais hated the Alliance with all the fire of Durga herself. And that fire burned them in the end.

Even so, Jaantzen can understand. In the early days of his operations, Jaantzen had been full of anger and rage at those whose politics had thrown him to the dogs. He flaunted himself at police, took pride in destroying petty politicians' lives. The stronger he got, the less care he took.

But as he grew older, he began to understand the value of highly functional relationships with strategic people in power — even if he didn't agree with their politics.

Particularly if they were people with whom he shared a certain civic pride, and a desire to keep New Sarjun free from the Alliance's yoke.

People like Youssef Tabari.

JAANTZEN WALKS TO THE ARCADIA, something that will make Gia proud though it gives his security fits. His organization is back to normal operations now, which means Manu Juric can once again insist on setting guards even this deep within Jaantzen's territory.

The Arcadia is a classy establishment just outside the tourist district — a place Youssef Tabari certainly can't afford on his government salary. It's a good way to keep the balance ever so slightly in Jaantzen's favor. A good number of the staff owe Jaantzen their loyalty, plus, the hostess keeps a pistol in her stand. She's a crack shot; he's seen her use it.

Jaantzen's men clear him to enter the restaurant; the hostess shows him to his favorite booth near the kitchen. On the other side of the pass-through window, the head chef raises a hand in greeting.

Jaantzen orders a bottle of wine as Youssef walks through the door, then stands to greet his old friend with a hug.

"I have to get back to work after this," says Youssef predictably as Jaantzen pours the wine, but he picks up the offered glass anyway. As he always does.

It's small talk as they order, Jaantzen going through the motions of putting Youssef at ease. Tedious, but Youssef is a prize associate. Over the years he's become very highly placed in the Trade Commission of New Sarjun, on track to the top job of commissioner within another election cycle or two. As a man who specializes in imports and exports, Jaantzen will do what it takes to have Youssef on his side.

Jaantzen clinks glasses again after the waitress brings out their meal: chickpeas and dumplings swimming in a spice-laden sauce. It's not on the menu — Jaantzen prefers the surprise, lets the head chef choose.

"I hope you don't mind me treating you to dinner today," he says. "I have something that I need to ask you." Youssef leans back, spoon hovering over his plate. Wary. "What do you know about the Dusai family?"

He can see Youssef judging his answer, deciding how to proceed.

"Surely you heard Silk Station was destroyed a few days ago," Jaantzen says, prompting.

Youssef blinks. "That was highly classified," he says. "I barely have clearance to be told myself."

"The Alliance is coy with their information," Jaantzen says smoothly. The Indiran Alliance and their withholding of information involving New Sarjun is a constant thorn in Youssef's side, and Jaantzen prods that thorn gently, a reminder that they're both playing for the same team, regardless of which side of the law they're currently on.

It's the thing Jaantzen likes most about New Sarjun. A deft manipulation of political tensions can erase many a criminal record. Hell, it had gotten Coeur elected mayor.

"The Alliance didn't need to tell us anything," Youssef says. "Durga's Belt isn't New Sarjunian space." He chews, slowly. "The Dusais were suppliers of yours, weren't they?"

"Not suppliers," Jaantzen says. "But we had an amicable arrangement."

"I can't say many but you will be sad to see them gone," says Youssef.

"Perhaps not. But I do have certain obligations that need to be fulfilled. I know their daughter is being held at Redrock Prison. I need to find out what happened to Raj and Lasadi."

"I'd assume they'd have been taken to prison, as well."

"Then I'll need to call in a favor. How quickly can you get me credentials to fly in to Redrock?"

Youssef's jaw tenses. "I can't do that."

"Yes, you can, old friend," Jaantzen says. Youssef can do any number of things; Jaantzen has seen it. "I need to get the girl out of prison. Possibly her parents, too."

"Why would I help you with that?"

"Because without Silk Station, without the *Nanshe*, the Dusais aren't a threat to New Sarjunian commerce, any more than I am." Youssef's eyebrows rise at that. "And the girl's only a child. Fifteen. The Alliance can't hold her for her parents' crimes."

"They can hold her for whatever they want," says Youssef. "They're the Alliance."

Jaantzen tilts his head, spoon halfway to his mouth. "Isn't this our planet?"

"I'm not starting a political war for you," Youssef says.

"I'm not asking for a war. But I'd guess others might feel as we do about the Alliance kidnapping children — particularly when they're keeping them in maximum security prisons on *our* planet. I'd guess there might be a few key people who find this something to be irked about. I just want to reward them for doing the right thing."

Youssef's fingertips tap at the table. "How much?" he asks.

"I think you're familiar with how much I value assistance of this magnitude — and how much I value information," answers Jaantzen. "Particularly something like the classified Alliance records of the attack on the *Nanshe*."

Youssef nods slowly. "I'll see what I can do." He mops his plate with naan. "And fast. If they decide the girl's involved with the OIC, they can do whatever they want with her."

Jaantzen frowns at that. "The Dusais weren't OIC."

"It doesn't matter. If the Alliance decides they need to get rid of someone, all they have to do is prove that person is reasonably likely to be OIC."

"Even a child?"

"Old friend, she's not a child to the Alliance," Youssef says. "They've locked away younger than her, if they thought they were terrorists."

"Then let's work fast," Jaantzen says, dropping his napkin to his plate and standing to offer his hand. Youssef's smile is wary, his hand slightly clammy. Nervous. Jaantzen lets his smile grow more generous.

His comm buzzes as Youssef is walking out the door: Toshiyo.

Found a contact. Alliance officer named Ximena Nayar. But you're not going to be happy about this one.

Jaantzen frowns at the name, trying to remember if he's heard it before. *I'll be back shortly*, he types. *With lunch.*

He sits back down and signals the waitress for a to-go order of chickpeas and dumplings. He feels suddenly very tired.

OIC.

No matter what happened to Raj and Lasadi, he won't be able to fool himself into thinking their daughter's age will guarantee her safety in Alliance custody.

————————————————————

5

Starla

————————————————————

STARLA'S BEEN WRESTLED INTO THE INTERROGATION
room again, feet restrained, hands free. She shifts on the
metal bench, back aching from holding her spine straight
in this gravity without a backrest. She slouches. Straightens. Rolls her shoulders.

After what seems like an hour, the Interrogation
Twins return: Hali and Mahr.

Mahr looks like she sleeps standing up in her uniform
so it — and she — won't wrinkle. Hali's in green today,
with a fake flower pinned on her lapel. She's obviously
not military. Some civilian contractor flown in to help
with the deaf girl. Starla wonders if there's more call for
that sort of thing on backwater New Sarjun than on
Indira.

She's remembered now what they remind her of: it's
an old children's vid she and Mona used to watch, with a
family of clowns living aboard a spaceship. Mahr and
Hali are the two moms, one stiff and militaristic, one
round and matronly. Starla can't remember the names of

the characters, but it gives her satisfaction to have recalled this much.

"How are you today?" asks Hali, signing and speaking for Mahr's benefit.

"Water," Starla signs back.

It's been the most pressing thing on her mind. The heat of this stupid planet is sucking her dry, her knuckles cracking and lips flaked to bleeding; she can't stop picking at them.

"Can we get her some water?" Hali asks Mahr, who says something out the door. The water comes in a flimsy plastic bottle that wrinkles under the slightest touch. Starla takes it with both hands to keep it from spilling.

She thinks of Deyva, who had boasted he could make a weapon from anything and had tried to teach her to do the same.

Can't make this piece of garbage bottle into a weapon, that's for sure.

She doesn't look at Hali until she's done drinking, even though she can tell the woman's trying to get her attention. Starla sets the bottle aside, nearly empty, and wipes her dry lips on the back of her hand.

"We have some other questions today," Hali signs and says when Starla finally makes eye contact. "But I'm still here to talk about your home life, if you need someone."

Starla's been thinking. It's obvious Hali and Mahr aren't going to tell her where her parents are, or what happened to the rest of her family on Silk Station and to the crew of the *Nanshe*. Not until they get some answers of their own.

She's considered trying to act feral — she's read about feral children, raised away from society, raised without parents; she thinks maybe that's what Hali wants to hear. Poor thing, can you imagine, raised in a situation like that? And deaf no less. It's a blessing we got her away . . .

"How often did you travel with your parents on the *Nanshe*?"

Starla blinks. It takes her a moment to process Hali's signs; she hasn't been paying attention.

"Never." Not since she could barely walk, and they'd brought her here to New Sarjun. But she doesn't remember that, not more than flashes.

"But you were rescued onboard the *Nanshe*."

Starla bridles at that word, *rescued*.

"That was my first time. Training voyage."

"She says it was a training voyage," Hali repeats aloud to Mahr. "Her first time on the ship."

"So she was training to be part of the crew?" Mahr asks.

Starla waits to answer until Hali's interpreted the question. She doesn't want to let on how much she's able to understand. Nor does she trust herself to get all the context without Hali's help, and she doesn't want them to start thinking they can just yell at her and be understood.

"Not crew," Starla answers, and Hali looks satisfied as she repeats Starla's answer for Mahr. "Just training."

She's decided to play the innocent card for now — not the feral card, not the abuse card; she'd never forgive herself for that — but maybe she can distance herself from the more anti-Alliance actions of her parents and the *Nanshe*.

"Did your parents ever talk to you about their trips?"

Starla senses a landmine here. Probes at it. "Their trips?"

"Did they talk to you about what they did when

they — " Hali fumbles in her signs, here, thinking. "About where they went on the *Nanshe*? Either before, or after?"

Starla seizes on the last, sensing a distinction she can take advantage of. "Sometimes after. Never before." Again, Hali looks satisfied, and Starla takes a deep breath. "They liked to talk about the places they visited. They would bring me presents."

Hali is repeating Starla's sentences as Starla signs them, and a tension flinches around the room at the last. Starla feels a spike of panic. Presents. Not all of them purchased — and even those that were purchased were certainly not with legitimately earned credits.

She remembers the last gift they brought home from a trip to New Sarjun. Here. Before, Starla had always thought it sounded exotic, but now she wonders how her parents could stand to visit such a horrible place.

It had been at breakfast, a week before that last day.

Raj Dusai was already wearing his shipping-out clothes. The crew of the *Nanshe* didn't have a uniform as such, just a pewter-gray jumpsuit with twin stripes across the chest in some sort of glossy black biofabric that glimmered whenever the crewmember was aboard the ship. Raj was wearing the jumpsuit with his many-pocketed flight jacket and a pair of yellowing white socks that looked out of place. His gravity boots sat beside the door.

He wouldn't wear those on the station, of course, and there they sat whenever the *Nanshe* was in dock. Starla stared at them, ignoring her father, knowing that their familiar spot by the door would soon be vacant — and he would be gone.

And she would be left behind, again.

Lasadi Dusai came in a moment later, holding a package in her arms.

"Oh, good," she said, in response to whatever Raj had said behind Starla's shoulder. "This is for you, sweetheart," she said to Starla, handing over the package to free up her hands. "We love you," she signed.

The package was wrapped in one of the brightly colored New Sarjunian scarves her mother favored. They were too flashy for Starla, but that never stopped her mother from picking them up and then gifting them to her whenever they'd stopped on New Sarjun. Starla unwrapped it carefully. This one was a livid lime green shot through with turquoise and gold, the pattern feathered out from the center. Her mother waved her hand inside Starla's vision. "Peacock feathers," her mother told her, fingerspelling the bird's name.

The scarf was pretty, but once unwrapped, Starla didn't even notice it slide off her lap to puddle on the floor. Inside was a jumpsuit, just like her father and mother both were wearing. Starla gasped in delight and let the whole mess fall off her lap, leaping up to hug both Raj and Lasadi at once, all awkward angles and knobby elbows. She could go on the training voyage. They were going to give her a chance to join the crew.

Starla blinks. She takes a sip of the water. 1, 4, 9, 16 — She's missed whatever Hali is saying to her now.

"What kinds of presents?" Hali signs and speaks, repeating herself.

Starla shrugs. "Scarves," she signs. "Toys," she signs, because it seems like it'll help them keep thinking of her as a kid even though she hasn't been one for years.

"Did your parents ever discuss politics with you?"

Starla considers this new line of questioning, wary. What does Hali mean, politics? As in, who did they think was going to win the presidential election in Arquelle? Starla wrinkles her brow, not sure.

"Did they ever talk about the Alliance?"

Oh. Politics.

Starla strains to see a clear path to navigate through this one. "Not really," she signs. It's mostly true. Her parents may not like the Alliance but they aren't overly political about it. They keep to themselves. Maybe they target Alliance ships more frequently than those that call Durga's Belt their home, but that was just being neighborly. No one throws a dead rat in their own air recyclers.

"Are you very close with your cousins?"

Now another non sequitur. Starla frowns. "Some of them," she signs. "The ones that are my age. And . . ." She shrugs. "They're cousins," she signs. "I like some of them, I don't like others. Doesn't everybody?"

Hali doesn't answer this. Starla has been given to understand that not everyone has as many cousins as she does, and not everyone lives as closely with them. And that not everyone calls every kid they know who's about their age "cousin." If she's honest, she has to admit that she doesn't actually know which ones are related by blood, and which ones are related by virtue of being part of the family on Silk Station. No one at home cared, and she doesn't care either.

"Do you know Amit Dal?"

Starla gives her a look that says, Of course, I'm not an idiot. Amit is her Auntie Faye's oldest son. Auntie Faye is her mother's sister. He's blood relations for sure.

"Did he ever talk about politics with you?"

Oh, yes, Starla thinks, but does not sign. And now she begins to realize where this is going. Amit has been deeply involved with the OIC — the Organization of

Independent Colonies — and he's tried to convince her parents to get involved, as well.

Starla wonders if she should pretend not to know what the OIC is.

She's been thinking too long.

"Did he ever talk about politics with you," Hali signs again.

Starla shakes her head, gives a bemused little shrug. "I'm just his little cousin," she signs.

Mahr barks something at Hali when Hali repeats Starla's words. Hali nods. "I think we're going to talk about this some more tomorrow," Hali says and signs. She gives Starla a smile.

This time, when Starla is taken back to her cell, the lights stay on. She wonders if she's done well today.

She can't tell.

STARLA LIES on her cot staring at the ceiling and wonders if Amit made it. If Auntie Faye made it.

If Mona made it.

She wonders if the Alliance blew up her home because they thought her family sympathetic to the OIC.

They aren't — weren't? — except for Amit and a few of the cousins his age. Her parents despise the Alliance, but it hadn't seemed to be in a political way. More in a predatorial way.

The Indiran Alliance doesn't get out to Durga's Belt so much, anyway, there at the flickering far edge of New Sarjunian space.

Indira and New Sarjun are next-door neighbors, and the only two inhabitable planets in the Durga System. That was the bright point in the sky Starla's ancestors had picked as their most likely seed system over a thousand years ago, and Indira had had the distinction of seeming a more likely choice to support a fragile race. The generation ship, the *Ark Matsya*, was still in orbit over Indira. Starla would love to see it — she can't imagine tech that ancient crossing galaxies — but catching even a whiff of Indiran atmosphere would have been risky business for her parents, and so for her.

The other planet in the system hadn't been colonized until centuries later, when rugged, contrary types who bridled under civilized rule decided to see what sort of living they could eke out on New Sarjun's sun-baked crust. The centuries since had put a polish on New Sarjun's rough edges, but it was far from gleaming.

Indira had been a bickering collection of petty states until a few decades ago. By force or by guile, the diplomats from Arquelle, Indira's largest and most powerful country, had talked the rest of the planet into a treaty.

That would have been all well and good, but the Indiran Alliance, led by Arquelle, wasn't content staying planetside.

Colonies on the Indiran moons were pressured to join next. Then colonies farther out. And that might have been successful, but the planetside alliance on Indira was starting to crumble, and countries who'd been amenable at first got to feeling the wrong end of the deal, feeling over-trampled and misused while Arquelle got stronger and more powerful.

And as the cracks began to show, Arquelle became more insistent that the entire Durga System join the Alliance, stretching fingers out to New Sarjun and into Durga's Belt, the asteroid chain just beyond, a rat's nest of unaffiliated asteroid stations and colonies that Arquelle insisted should be registered and taxed.

Arquelle and New Sarjun butted heads more than once about that, while most out in Durga's Belt merely scoffed and ignored Arquellian tariffs.

And those who didn't scoff? Like Amit? They joined the Organization of Independent Colonies, and started planting bombs.

Starla had gotten most of her gossip about Amit from Mona.

Mona was like a sugar cube set in a spilled pool of tea, soaking up every drop of scandal until she was full and bursting, then running to Starla desperate to spill everything she'd heard to the one person she could count on not having overheard it all first.

Starla found glimpses into this world fascinating. She'd mastered the world she experienced immediately, and was passing knowledgeable about the world she was taught about on TUTOR. But although her family, most of them, had no difficulty communicating with her, she couldn't overhear the sharp words her aunts and uncles exchanged, the slipped secrets older cousins forgot to keep closed-lipped.

Mona gave her a glimpse into this intriguing silence, flipping salacious signs from her lithe fingers, her facial expressions and posture so perfect that Starla always knew exactly who she was mimicking. Scribbled diary conversations, giggling late at night, rapid-fire texts teasing out secrets about the rest of the family —

The family.

Her parents.

Starla doesn't realize she's crying until the water spills from her eye sockets, streaming into her ears. She jams the heels of her hands into her eyes, knowing they must have her on surveillance and ashamed to let them see her weak.

Starla knows she's never going back to Silk Station.

She's on her own, now, just as her parents, wherever they are, are on their own.

She can't sit around forever.

But she can plan.

6

Jaantzen

"MAJOR XIMENA NAYAR IS PERFECT," SAYS TOSHIYO.
She's starting with the positive news, as is her preference,
but Jaantzen can tell by her forced optimism there's bad
news, too. He glances at Manu, who's watching Toshiyo
with over-eager interest. Jaantzen guesses Manu knows
what the bad news is.

Jaantzen braces himself and waits.

They're sitting around the conference table in the
upper office; Toshiyo pulls up Nayar's file in the center
of the table. There's no picture.

Manu leans in. His hair is an electric orange today,
glowing against his midnight skin — he's darker even
than Jaantzen — and his nails are painted an opalescent
sherbet to match. He's been draped in black for weeks,
and Jaantzen suspects this return to vividity is in honor
of Jaantzen's failure to kill Coeur.

"She's a requisitions officer, stationed at Redrock
Prison and overseeing the supplies," says Manu.

"Where's the picture with this file?" Jaantzen asks.

Toshiyo ignores him and swipes to the next page.

"We have reason to suspect she's turnable," says Manu. "She was born here in Bulari, but her father was Arquellian, an officer in the Indiran Alliance stationed on New Sarjun. That gave her dual citizenship, and she eventually joined the Arquellian navy, then the Alliance forces. Because she was born here she's primarily been stationed on-planet, though she's seen combat, too." Manu scrolls down. "Most notably the slaughter at Teguça. After that, she put in for a transfer back to New Sarjun. She took a command cut to take her current position, though she's retained her rank and security clearance. This suggests that Teguça soured her for fighting."

"And according to my contact at Redrock Prison, it soured her against the Alliance," says Toshiyo. "She's not bold about it, of course."

"High enough rank and clearance status that she can command even the prison warden," Manu says, "and enough connection within the prison that she can pull some favors if she needs to. But enough out of the main chain of command that she can act without as much suspicion. We think with the proper persuasion she would help us."

Manu's nodding as he says it, eyes wide and trustworthy like a waiter bobbing his head as he asks if you want dessert.

Jaantzen steeples his hands over his lips, leaning back. "She sounds ideal," he says. He waits for the bad news.

Manu and Toshiyo exchange a look. Toshiyo swipes at the desk, and an image of Ximena Nayar fills the screen.

That rust-colored skin, those high cheekbones and fierce black eyes, and even though she's not smiling in this image, he's certain that once she does he'll see a ferocious flash of gleaming white teeth, that million-mark smile aged by ten years.

"Coeur," Jaantzen says.

Toshiyo clears her throat. "Nayar is Thala Coeur's older sister."

Jaantzen's processing this. "Does she hate her sister as much as I do?"

"They have the same mother, different fathers," says Manu; it's not an answer to Jaantzen's question. "We think she'll work with us."

Jaantzen's staring at that face, marking the differences: it's all steel and grit where Coeur's is elastic and mirthful, but they have the same bones, the same eyes. "And does she hate her sister as much as I do?" he asks again.

Manu clears his throat. "By all accounts, they're friendly," he says.

"Then we're not working with her," Jaantzen says. "What are our other options?"

Manu and Toshiyo share a look. "They're slim, boss," Toshiyo finally says. Her nails click against the desk keyboard and another three files show up, replacing Ximena Nayar's face. "Gia's still friendly with some of the guards from when she did time there, but none that have maximum security clearance."

Jaantzen scrolls through the guards' profiles, frowning. They may come in handy, but none have the clout they'll need to pull off either a release or a rescue. He's never bothered to cultivate a relationship with anyone at the Alliance prison colonies. He assumed he'd never need it. He'll die before he ends up there, and if he's smart he'll be able to protect his people, too.

As Raj and Lasadi should have been able to do.

Jaantzen remembers laughing over wine with Raj and Lasadi — and Tae. Talking safety nets and fortresses — "We'll set up a child exchange," Lasadi had said, "We'll let you take her when she's a bratty teenager," and Tae, laughing, "Be careful, we've got two bratty teenagers in training to send your way."

Over the years Jaantzen had understood that the Dusais weren't just networking with business partners outside of Silk Station, they were engineering a safety net for their family to land in should the inevitable come.

Jaantzen hadn't understood, then, that Silk Station wasn't their fortress. Even when Raj had shown him diagrams, the way whole wings were actually spacecraft ready to launch at short warning, the escape pods in every home. The Dusais had never meant to hole up there and fight, they'd meant to scatter to the breeze and land soft as they could.

If Jaantzen had understood, he might have spent more time building safety nets and less time building his fortress, his stronghold, which in the end was so easily pierced.

He may not have understood in time to save his own family, but he can still do something for the Dusai girl.

"Who else?"

It comes out angry, and Toshiyo and Manu both tense up. Toshiyo's fingers are hovering over the keyboard like she's thinking, but he's seen this before, her freeze response triggering at his anger. Some self-preservation technique built up during her indenture, maybe.

He takes a deep breath. "Manu?" he asks to give her time.

"We've learned they have a civilian social worker seeing her. A woman named Hali Fernanz. Tosh?" he says gently.

Toshiyo's fingernails clatter again, and another file appears in the center of the desk, a doughy woman with steel-gray hair in a short, harsh bob.

"We think she's a weak point," says Toshiyo, back in the rhythm. Jaantzen takes a deep breath. "She's got a spotless record, and by all accounts seems to be a good advocate for children in the Alliance's prison systems. I doubt she'll do anything illegal, but she seems the type who won't want to see a girl locked up for her parents' crimes."

Jaantzen nods slowly. A woman like that could be useful, but her conscience makes her slippery. It's much easier to work with someone whose loyalty he can buy.

"The officer in charge is Lieutenant Mahr," adds Manu, and Toshiyo flicks Mahr's profile onto the screen. "Reassigned to Redrock Prison seven years ago after misconduct charges in the regular Alliance forces."

"What did she do?"

Manu shrugs.

"I haven't been able to break the classification around that yet," says Toshiyo. "But I did find something else. I broke into her bank accounts on a whim, and the Alliance isn't the only one giving her a paycheck."

"Who else?"

"I'm not sure," Toshiyo says, obviously annoyed by her inability to give him an answer to that. "I've got a trace out on the account, hasn't turned anything up yet. Too many layers. But it's always the same amount: five thousand marks. And it's irregular. Every few months or so."

Jaantzen is intrigued. "What service is our Lieutenant Mahr performing for a mystery party every few months?" he asks. "Can you cross-reference that with records at the prison and see if anything comes up?"

"Already did it, boss." It's why she's worth every penny he's spent on her — her and her arcane equipment.

Toshiyo pulls up yet another screen. "There's a couple things that match," she says, drawing up the highlights as she talks. Manu leans in, curious — apparently they haven't discussed this yet. "There's four deposits. Three match with the prison's grain shipment, and two match with interdepartmental sensitivity training seminars, but I'm guessing both of those are pure coincidence. Because all four match with this."

She pulls up another screen and Jaantzen leans in, deciphering the list of names. "Death records," he says, and Toshiyo nods. She's highlighted four, each of them one day after the date of a deposit into Mahr's account. Each of them listing the cause of death as "Unknown." They are the only four records to do that in an otherwise well-documented list.

Something else about the four gives Jaantzen pause. All are juveniles.

"Inmates who die at Redrock Prison are cremated," Toshiyo says. "But these four are missing cremation records. And" — she swipes at the screen with a flourish, her excitement bubbling over — "I checked into the prison undertaker's bank account."

Four dates are highlighted. Four transfers of one thousand marks each.

"Who's buying these kids?" Jaantzen asks.

"Working on it, boss."

Jaantzen nods. "Is there anything else?" Toshiyo and Manu both shake their heads, glancing at each other for confirmation. "Good work. Figure out how we use this thing with Mahr, and keep at the social worker. She seems useful, but I want to make sure we're solid before we approach her."

Jaantzen stands, buttons his coat. He'll go for a walk, try to make sense of all this. Something here is tickling the back of his brain, and if he can just clear his head he'll understand it.

"Boss, what about Ximena Nayar?" Manu asks.

"Find me more options," Jaantzen says, and he sees the flash of frustration in Manu's face.

He doesn't care. He will not be negotiating with Blackheart's sister.

7

Starla

STARLA WAKES IN THE MORNING AND DOES SQUATS, TEN of them before she sits with a gravity-heavy thud back on the cot. Only two full push-ups before her arms give out.

She tries to remember all the resistance exercises her mother tried to get her to do back on Silk Station, and comes up with tricep dips off the edge of the cot. She manages three.

Jumping jacks: fifteen.

Sit-ups: six.

Starla collapses panting on the cot until she's caught her breath, then does the whole routine again.

She's been picked up and slammed back down, shoved into restraints, marched down hallways at will, and she's done with it.

After today, she's never going to be weak again.

She's made it five rounds and her muscles are shaking with the effort when she finally slumps back on the cot.

Starla knows that Hali believes her. She's not sure

what Mahr, that pinch-faced dirt-kisser, thinks, but she's certain that if the Alliance allowed fifteen-year-old girls to be tried as enemy combatants automatically, Mahr wouldn't be bothering with any of this.

She's starting to feel safe. It's time to push her boundaries.

It's time to try for a weapon.

She has no possible weapon but the afternoon cleaning bot. It shocked her, last time she tried to capture it, but today she has a plan. She's been running scenarios in her mind all night, riffing on things Deyva taught her about electronics, about dirty fighting. About making weapons with whatever was at hand.

Deyva.

She hopes he made it out of the station alive.

He was the only one who would teach her anything, at first. She'd been ten years old, swarming the hallways of Silk Station with the rest of her cousins, that day he yelled into the melee that he needed a volunteer.

It was standard that passing mechanics would pluck a kid or two from their games whenever they needed someone small enough to squirm inside the ventilation ducts and smart enough to thread the right color wire. Starla's hand always went up first, even though her lipreading as a child was abominable and she often had no idea what would be required of her. She only knew she could do it.

And Deyva, the first mechanic who, finally, picked her, soon learned it.

Deyva was stocky — he hadn't been born on-station — with deep bronze skin and eyes shining like the brightest stars.

"You," he said, finger pointed at the top of her head, past the others. "What's your name?"

"Starla," Starla said, and was annoyed when she saw Mona repeat it for him.

He said something else, face turned so she couldn't see his lips, and Mona answered, speaking and signing both so Starla could see. "She can't hear you, but I can interpret."

Deyva shrugged, pointed his index fingers at both girls, and jerked his thumbs for them to follow.

Deyva didn't need to talk much, Starla learned over the years. He preferred machines to chatter, and he had a concise way of explaining things that didn't require half the words other people seemed to need. He never tried to learn USL, just developed his own system of nonsense signs that always made the same perfect, economical sense as his explanations.

It was to his bench in the engineering station that she'd disappear whenever she was fighting with her parents, or shirking her lessons with TUTOR, or just bored. Her parents must've suspected where she went — for all she knew, Deyva probably told them — but they never came looking for her there.

She and Deyva hadn't talked much about his past, but she knew it had been quite different from life on Silk Station; he always seemed bemused by the gaggles of cousins and the complete lack of supervision. He had grown up on New Sarjun, she knew, in the capital city of Bulari, and she got the impression that he'd grown up on the streets, like in the entertainment vids she and Mona watched sometimes about the city's crime bosses and gangsters. He had snake tattoos on the backs of his wrists, and a wicked-looking scar on his cheek. When she asked about it once, Deyva just laughed, as he always did. "Kids do stupid things sometimes," he said.

She'd asked her father about it, too, but he provided

no more insight. "Deyva's story is his own to tell," her father had said. "But you aren't going to find many out here in the black who like talking about the past."

Starla doesn't think Deyva was just fond of snakes. He has — had? — an OIC tattoo, too. Her parents might not have wanted to talk about him, but as usual Mona was a fount of snooped information, gossiping, during their frequent sleepovers, long after either of their parents had gone to bed.

"He was in the OIC." Mona'd signed the last letters in her lap, low and secret. "On the run from the Alliance."

The official sign for the Alliance is two clasped hands, but between them the girls had used their own sign, cast harshly down to the side with disdain, like a rotted piece of fruit.

Starla reminds herself not to use that one in front of Hali.

NOW STARLA'S watching the cleaning bot's hatch, afraid she'll miss it if she doesn't keep her eyes peeled.

She has no idea what time it is, but she hasn't seen it yet today, and so she tells herself it must be coming soon. She has her blanket clenched in her fists — she doesn't know why they bothered to give her a blanket when it's so horribly hot here — and she hopes that the insulation from it will keep the cleaning bot from shocking her too badly. She has the flimsy water bottle, which no one seemed to care if she kept. She's not sure what she'll do with that, but it seemed wasteful to pass up the opportunity to try something.

After what seems like ages, the little door slides open and the cleaning bot scurries out.

Starla knows from watching it for the last few days that it will make a sweep of the floor clockwise before scuttling up to do a quick swipe of the toilet seat and hopping down to disappear back into the wall. It hasn't seemed to be programmed to notice her movements, as though its makers assumed its electric shock would be enough protection.

And maybe it will be. Starla will find out.

She tenses, launches herself with squat-tired thighs across the room as it scurries onto the seat of the toilet, her blanket folded in front of her like a shield.

Her plan works — she knocks the miniature robot into the bowl, where she expects it to short-circuit in the shallow water. It's not ideal, but she'd rather have the metal parts than the electronics.

It doesn't short-circuit.

The cleaning bot explodes beneath her hands, throwing her back against the wall with a force that seems completely impossible for such a tiny little machine. She thinks she must have screamed.

The synthetic blanket ignites with a rush of heat that she can feel on her cheeks. She flings it away from her; smoke roils off it to pool on the ceiling.

The cleaning bot scurries out of the toilet and escapes through its hatch, trailing sparks.

Smoke chokes the room, and Starla's lungs are burning. Where are the fire-suppressant foams? There's water in the little plastic bottle, still, and Starla flings it in a spray at the blanket, sending up clouds of steam with the black, toxic smoke. She turns away to pound at the door, shielding her stinging eyes.

The door slides open and Starla falls through, retching, into the arms of her two guards. They immediately wrench her singed hands behind her and into cuffs.

Busted.

62

8

Jaantzen

"It seems you have a problem with directions," Jaantzen says. "And I'm not sure how to make this point to you any more clearly."

The whites of the skinny rat thug's eyes are splashed with red — not anything Jaantzen or his enforcer, Kobe, did to him, but something he did to himself by dipping too frequently into the stash of shard he's been peddling in the southern reaches of Jaantzen's territory. The skinny rat thug's eyes are bulging with fear. As they should be.

Willem Jaantzen is getting back to work. Rolling his sleeves up. Taking the bull by the horns.

It should feel good, yet crackling at the edges of everything he does is the tentative, crystalline sense of a world just on the verge of breaking.

He's used to living in a world of sudden shifts and changes, but this feels different. Off kilter. It makes him want to move cautiously.

He can sense it in his crew: an inability to focus on priorities, a lack of decision and dexterity.

He doesn't blame them — none of them know what they'll be able to expect tomorrow. When he made his plans for Coeur, a period of transience had been set in motion. Now his entire crew — and he himself — are caught in that moment. Caught midway between coming and going, between living and dying.

None of them know if they can relax back into the roles they once had.

"This is the third time I've heard about you selling shard in my neighborhood," Jaantzen says. He picks up one of the blister packs off the table, holds it up to the light. Inside, a waffled black tab coated with white powder: slip it under your tongue and press down, and the waffle-like razors slice through the delicate skin to wash the drug directly into your bloodstream without a physical trace. Jaantzen turns it in his hand; the powder glimmers in the light.

The thug's gaze follows Jaantzen's hand, hungry.

"Who are you working for?" Jaantzen asks.

Kobe cracks his knuckles, a smile creeping onto his boxer's face as he senses a moment of action. The shard-pusher whimpers.

They're in a warehouse south of the Port of Bulari, an area no one bothers to police these days. Honestly there's not much need. For the last few years Jaantzen and his crew have had the area on lockdown, and the neighborhood's improved quite a bit. Restaurants stay open later now. The city buses have stopped routing around it. Real estate values are rising, thank you very much.

He's fended off an incursion or two from Sendera Dathúil, and he stays vigilant against scum like the pusher he's got chained to this chair.

Scum like this have been getting bolder lately,

though, and it's only a matter of time before the bigger of the second-tier gangs start testing the seals. No rumors of Jaantzen's vendetta against Coeur seem to have gotten out, but jackals still scent death in the air.

It's what Julieta Yang is worried about.

"I ain't working for no one," the pusher says.

Jaantzen nods to Kobe, and the big man's fist drives into the pusher's stomach. "Where are you getting your supply?" Jaantzen asks. The man chokes on a cough in response. Kobe hits him again.

Jaantzen folds his arms, frowning. "I guarantee whoever keeps you supplied with shard isn't paying you nearly enough for your loyalty," he says. "Kobe — " His comm buzzes: Toshiyo. "Please excuse me for a moment," he says, and he turns away from the mess to answer.

Toshiyo clears her throat. "Boss, we have a problem."

Jaantzen glances over his shoulder, motions for Kobe to continue without him. Always more problems. "Go ahead."

"I put an alert on the lieutenant's account," says Toshiyo. "I wanted to make sure we were the first to know if she had any other big transfers."

The warehouse suddenly seems very cold. "And I take it she has."

"Yeah, boss." He can hear her typing. "And there's more. I finally traced the owner of the account. It's Sendera Dathúil."

Jaantzen takes a sharp breath. Sendera Dathúil is the second largest of the crime syndicates in Bulari, having taken over many of Blackheart's seedier operations when she took her talents into politics. They check off many of the more mundane categories of crime — protection rackets, smuggling, drugs — but they're also rumored to dabble in darker places, like kidnapping street kids to sell as illegal indentures to the mining corporations.

If they're buying kids from the Alliance prison, it isn't as a charity project.

"We have no way of knowing if the money transfer is for the Dusai girl," Toshiyo says, breaking into his thoughts.

That's true, but it doesn't matter. "I'm not interested in learning that the hard way," he says. He turns back to Kobe. "Finish up here, then I'll see you back at home." Kobe gives him a bloody thumbs-up.

"Toshiyo, please coordinate a phone call between myself and Major Nayar."

WILLEM JAANTZEN SCHOOLS his face to business-like, eases the tension out of his shoulders and jaw. Resists the split-second urge to put a bullet through the screen.

"Major Nayar. It's a pleasure to make your acquaintance."

Jaantzen gives her a brief smile.

Ximena Nayar inclines her head, not agreeing, not disagreeing. Watching,

Jaantzen revises his estimation of her. She lacks her sister's aggressive charisma, and if ever she does smile, it won't be her sister's million-mark grin. Nayar has a certain seriousness about her — a certain trustworthiness — that Coeur couldn't mimic if she tried.

She hasn't yet spoken, but Jaantzen is considering doing business. He reads people quickly; he's had to, to survive for so long.

"I don't just help out with jailbreaks," Nayar says

flatly. Another woman who despises small talk. She's sizing him up, too, frowning slightly at what she sees.

"Yet you agreed to speak with me," Jaantzen says.

"Curiosity," says Nayar. She doesn't elaborate. Jaantzen assumes this is her way of asking what he wants.

"Starla Dusai," he says. "She's being held at Redrock, and I need to get her out."

Nayar reaches out to tap at another screen; her gaze flickers back and forth as she reads. "Starla Dusai," she says. "Is this political? Business? Leverage?" She looks up. "What's in it for you?"

"The girl's my goddaughter," Jaantzen says.

A subtle shift in the way she's watching him, just for a moment, then her attention moves back to the other screen.

"She's being held in isolation in maximum security, which means they haven't figured out what to do with her yet," Nayar says after a minute. She frowns. "But it doesn't look like she'll stay that way for long."

"Stay what way for long?"

"In isolation." Nayar doesn't look pleased. "A girl that young, they shouldn't be putting her in with the general population. Not in max." A tiny line appears between her eyebrows as she swipes at the screen. "It looks like they've ID'd her as OIC. She'll be treated as an enemy combatant."

Jaantzen bites back a curse. He should have swallowed his pride faster. "Is she in max now?"

"Not yet," says Nayar. "But the move will probably be soon."

"What about her parents?" Jaantzen asks. "Are they in max, too?"

Nayar taps a few more buttons on her screen, and he

sees it in her face before she even speaks. "Raj and Lasadi Dusai were killed during the attack on the *Nanshe*," she says.

It's officially gone, now, that clinging hope that the girl would be fine without his intervention, that Raj and Lasadi wouldn't need him to play his part in their safety nets.

The girl has no one, now. No one but him.

Jaantzen takes a deep breath.

"There's something else," he says. "I have reason to believe that the officer in charge of Starla Dusai has been selling juvenile inmates to Sendera Dathúil. My people detected a large sum of money transferred into the officer's account this morning. I worry that the girl is in immediate danger."

Nayar's attention shifts back to her other screen, pulling up information. "Mahr," she says, and her tone of voice says it all. "Always thought that woman was shit."

"I can get you evidence, in exchange for your help with the girl."

Nayar scowls. "Said I thought Mahr was shit. I didn't say I cared."

"It would be quite the coup for you to take her down," Jaantzen says.

Nayar's full attention is back on him, coal-black eyes evaluating and serious. "I think you're mistaken, Mr. Jaantzen," she says. "I don't care what Mahr does. I'm not looking for a feather in my cap. If you come out here and I help you with the girl, I name my price."

"And what is that price?" But he knows it already, he can sense it.

"I'm fully aware of your vendetta against my sister,

Mr. Jaantzen," she says. "I want you to promise her safety."

Silence. Jaantzen has been preparing for this moment, for this request, he's told himself he'll do what it takes — the answer will not release his tongue.

"I'll call back," he says instead. "Fifteen minutes."

Nayar nods. She cuts the feed.

Willem Jaantzen's hands are shaking with rage.

A CUP OF GREEN TEA. Sitting in his room with the lamps off, the glittering night constellations of Bulari's skyline illuminating the space. A faux-leather couch, expensive and comfortable. A triptych of paintings by his favorite artist hanging above the dining table; Tae bought them for him the week before she died, they stab at his heart every time he looks at them, but he can't bring himself to take them down.

Jaantzen sips the tea; it's too hot, it scalds his tongue. He barely notices.

"Call Julieta Yang," he tells his comm, and it's only seconds before she picks up.

"Willem?" She's been waiting for him.

"Did you know that Raj and Lasadi were dead before you called me?" he asks. No small talk for Julieta.

"Yes." The reply comes immediately, and without explanation.

Jaantzen doesn't need one. Her aim had never been to save the Dusais; she had never cared about the girl. All along she's been worried about the balance of power in Bulari's underworld, should he kill Coeur.

Jaantzen isn't surprised, but he's startled to find himself wounded nonetheless.

"What are you going to do about the girl?" she asks.

"I'm not sure," he says, but it's not true; if he's honest with himself, he's already made his decision. He made promises to Raj and Lasadi that he'd take care of their daughter if anything happened to them, and he made promises to himself that he would have his revenge.

Since meeting Tae, his promises to others have always taken precedent over those made to himself. Killing Coeur went counter to that, but he'd convinced himself it was the right thing to do.

It was time.

He'd fucking earned it.

"What would Tae want you to do?"

The question stings, as she meant it to. "Good-bye, Julieta," Jaantzen says.

He disconnects the line.

JAANTZEN KEEPS HAVING THIS DREAM, though not as often as he would like. In it, he's sitting at a table by himself in that shady kebab restaurant he frequented in those days, which has the same seasoned soy doner on the rotisserie as every other kebab joint in Bulari — only difference, the garlic sauce at this joint is to die for. He's drinking alone.

It's a time before Toshiyo, before Gia, before Manu, before everyone he works with now.

It's a time when his crew isn't a family — it's a collection of strange characters held together by mutual anger. People he'd grown up with in orphanages, people he knew from the streets. People he trusts only by virtue of the fact that they haven't yet sold him out.

He's alone, until one of the waitresses comes to sit at his table. Thick mud-red hair and skin the rich topaz of a full moon hung low on the horizon. He's startled. They've spoken only briefly; she's never served him. He doesn't come here often, though he's been here more, recently. It feels familiar. He needs somewhere familiar lately.

"You seem lonely." It's a line he's heard from women who want his money, but he doesn't think she means it that way. Something in the way she looks at him is anything but seductive. He can't put a finger on it.

"I've been watching you," she says, matter-of-fact. "And you seem lonely."

Jaantzen smiles politely. It's obvious she doesn't know who he is.

"Tae Boroma." She holds out her hand to him, and the way she does it is so charming, he'd like to give her a false name, see how long this moment could last before she learns he's a monster. But he could never — and already her co-workers are gathering near the pass-through window, stealing glances as if unsure what to do, whether to break in and snatch her away.

"I'm Willem Jaantzen," he says. He doesn't take her hand. He doesn't want to feel the recoil when she realizes her mistake.

"I know," Tae says. The hand stays there, waiting, and finally he shakes it. Her handshake is firm. She smiles. "You wanna get out of here?" she asks, and after too long a moment he finally nods, raises his hand to call over his server.

Tae just shakes her head and stands. "I already got your tab tonight," she says. "C'mon, I got something to show you."

And it's the lights display down by the river, a neutral

spot among Bulari's gangs, and she instinctively finds a space for them to sit in the hot New Sarjunian night that's out of the way, safe and secure. She has a flask of cheap whiskey in her bag, but they only take a few sips.

They're still talking when the sun comes up.

JAANTZEN CHECKS HIS WATCH. It's been fifteen minutes, and the tea is finally cool enough to drink without scalding. He takes another sip and calls up a connection with Ximena Nayar. She doesn't greet him, just lifts her chin. In that gesture she looks as fiercely defiant as Coeur in the height of her Blackheart days. He pushes away the thought.

"You have my word," says Jaantzen. "On my honor, all vendetta between myself and your sister is cleared. So long as I return alive and free from Redrock Prison, she no longer has anything to fear from me, or from any member of my organization." He takes a deep breath. "But believe that nothing in the world will save her if you double-cross me."

Ximena Nayar only nods, precise, seeming impatient at his caveats. "How soon can you get here?"

9

Starla

STARLA FIGURES THEY'LL JUST PUT HER IN ANOTHER CELL, but they only let the smoky air out and toss her back in. The air looks clear now, but it stings her eyes and scours her sinuses.

Starla surveys the damage.

The thin mattress is scorched and soggy on the far end, and the blanket — and her pillow, she notes sourly — are both gone. The brushed aluminum wall above the toilet is licked by a rainbow sheen. The toilet itself is a misshapen hunk of scrap metal now, but somebody's put a bucket out next to it for her to use. Starla wrinkles her nose.

She sits on the damp mattress for a moment, but the smell of scorched metal is giving her visceral flashbacks of the *Nanshe* —

Strapped in against the maneuvering and helpless while on the screen Silk Station is disintegrating, shuttles and escape pods spiraling away in glittering trails while Alliance torpedoes slice after them, whole wings she never realized are actually parked spacecraft breaking away in fiery cascades, their engines demolishing their berths, the life she knew as a child vanishing before her eyes, the gut-wrenching shudder of the Nanshe *taking a hit, the acrid, roiling smoke and then the visual panic as the ship is boarded, black-helmeted Alliance soldiers screaming orders —*

Starla squeezes her eyes shut to block out the images, then stands.

She starts another round of exercises — squats, push-ups, jumping jacks. This time with a vengeance.

STARLA'S just fallen back on her cot, too exhausted to care about the singed mattress, when Hali and Mahr enter. Starla pushes herself to sit, frowning.

Hali is looking around the cell, eyes wide with horror. "What happened?" she asks Mahr.

"Your sweet little deaf girl got some big ideas about the cleaning bot," Mahr says — Starla thinks Mahr says.

"Are you all right?" Hali signs and speaks.

Starla nods. She knows the woman means "Are you injured?" and not "Are you still being held in an Alliance prison?"

"What do you want?" Starla asks. She's not in the mood for the Interrogation Twins' stupid questions.

"We want to move you out of isolation," Hali says and signs. Starla glances at Mahr, who seems unhappier than ever, something Starla hadn't thought was possible. When Hali moves again, her speech doesn't quite match her signs. "If you cooperate, you'll be moved to a different wing," say her lips, but her hands say, 'It's dangerous for you here."

Starla frowns at that. "Cooperate how?" she signs.

"You're too young to legally be kept here. I can get you assigned to a lower security ward," Hali signs, as she says, "We just have a few more questions about your life on Silk Station."

Starla is grudgingly impressed with her dowdy interpreter. That can't be easy to do.

"What do you want from me?" she asks.

"They need to believe you've been mistreated," Hali signs. "How old were you when your parents first started leaving you behind?" she asks.

Mahr curls her lip. "This is useless," she says.

"She's a troubled child," Hali says. "The Alliance has to take that into account." She turns back to Starla. "We know you don't belong in maximum security prison," she says and signs. "Just cooperate with us."

"And be put where? With my parents?"

Hali falters at this. "I'll see what I can do," she signs

"What did she say?" Mahr's eyes are narrowed — Hali may be smooth in her subterfuge, but she's not a natural liar. Her tension is thickening the air, and Mahr scents it like a jackal.

"She's willing to talk with the child psychologist," Hali says, with a glance at Starla. She has to know Starla can read her lips by this point. "Please, sweetheart," she signs, low and away from Mahr.

"Only if I can see my parents," Starla signs, and Hali's face goes white.

Starla forces herself to stay calm — 1, 4, 9, 16 — and wills Hali to just fucking say it. To just tell her.

"I'll see what I can do," Hali signs and speaks, and Starla pushes herself back against the wall, drawing her knees up between herself and the lie.

"I'm not going anywhere." Starla forces her stiff fingers into the shapes, forces herself not to cry.

Her eyes burn with held-back tears, but she still sees the way Mahr's shoulders relax. She doesn't know why, doesn't care. Hali's trying to say something to her; Starla looks away. She stares at the wall until the Interrogation Twins are gone, then she buries her face in her arms.

HOURS LATER, Starla on her singed cot, grieving.

Hali's been lying to her about her parents all along — even if they're still alive, Starla knows now she'll never be reunited with them. Even if she takes Hali's bait, spins horror stories about her tragic, neglected childhood, she'll get the pass back into society alone. Her parents will be executed, or be sentenced to work in Alliance mines, or at the very best rot in this prison forever.

The least she can do is not betray them by giving Hali the poor-little-Starla story she's looking for.

The lights have cycled to night and she's finally beginning to drift off in the near dark when something jolts her awake.

Her door is open, a figure is standing there with arms crossed — she can tell even in the dark that it's Mahr, the way she stands, the angry, angular bent of her hip.

The lights come on, blinding bright now, and Mahr thumbs for Starla to follow her.

Starla sits up, dream-drunk, tear-drunk, confused — what is this? — and holds up a hand to mean *just a minute.*

Mahr shoots her in the chest.

———————————

10

Jaantzen

———————————

New Sarjun's northern hemisphere is in summer, and even after sunset it's stifling hot, crackling dry. They've crossed over the desert along with the last light of day, the low sun knifing shadows over the parched sands and highlighting the rims of the craggy canyons with gleaming rays.

Jaantzen has never flown over the desert except once, leaving the planet, and this close-ish proximity to it is at once fascinating and disturbing. It's not a place meant for human habitation; he's grateful to land at Redrock Air Force Base, where he gives the Alliance soldiers fake credentials supplied by Youssef Tabari. Tonight he's Rosco Kudra, CEO of R.K. Refrigeration & Coolants.

Refrigeration and coolants. Jaantzen wonders if it would be an interesting industry to invest in, with the cash he got from dissolving his more illegitimate operations.

Ximena Nayar meets them on the runway. Her handshake is solid and her demeanor trustworthy, but Jaantzen can't stop comparing her to her sister; every

77

gesture and expression conjures up ghosts of Coeur, which in turn conjures up ghosts of Tae. It's a vicious cycle he doesn't need, and he looks away, pretending to take in the security as Nayar explains how this will work.

"Getting her out for questioning shouldn't be a problem," she says. "There's a note in her file already about potential OIC involvement. Sooner or later that means she gets treated like an enemy combatant just to see if we can scare her into spilling anything. The guards won't think twice about a major calling an OIC combatant out for questioning in the middle of the night."

Jaantzen glances back at her. "Would that bother you? If she was involved with the OIC?"

"That's not why we're here," Nayar says, but he can tell the answer is no. Interesting. An Alliance officer sympathetic to the OIC? Toshiyo has found a goldmine in this woman. He makes a note to buy Toshiyo another fancy gadget when he gets home.

He's brought one of Gia's meditech prodigies with him, a lanky boy with a shock of red hair and a complexion wholly unsuitable for New Sarjun; Jaantzen's never seen him without a sunburn. Gia's assured Jaantzen that the boy is her best; Jaantzen never really trusts anyone but her, not when emergency medical aid could be needed. But bringing Gia — an ex-resident of Redrock Prison's maximum security ward — through a possible Alliance checkpoint posed too many risks. The boy, who'll wait with the pilot back at the plane, will have to do.

Jaantzen's going in alone with Ximena Nayar.

The prison sprawls out in front of them a few kilometers from the base, a collection of low brick-and-steel buildings, their roofs slick with solar arrays. There's a fence stretching out between the prison complex and the air force base — no one wants escapees thinking they can hijack an Alliance Air Force plane — but it doesn't surround the complex.

Security is next to nothing apart from a checkpoint in the fence; he's surprised. "Where would you go if you escaped?" Nayar says with a shrug. She's driving a rugged personnel transport with a closed cargo compartment just big enough for a person to fold herself up into; she swerves absently around a familiar pothole. "There's nothing else up here — and no one's crossing that desert on foot."

They park far from the main entrance, near a loading dock that's stenciled with the number 16. "There's a surveillance gap here," Nayar says as she backs the jeep up to it. "Camera's out. I've actually been bitching about it for the last six months since this is my main loading dock for max security kitchen deliveries, but nobody's bothered to do anything." She shrugs. "Might as well take advantage."

Nayar shows her credentials to no one as they enter the prison's main office building, though she exchanges words with the guard — Patch, she calls him — in the control room. He barely looks up from his computer monitor as she tells him she's showing around a vendor.

"I also need to see one of the prisoners," she says, and he does look up at this; Jaantzen tenses. But the guard's broad face shows only brief annoyance, not suspicion. He'd hoped for an obligation-free graveyard shift, apparently.

"Starla Dusai," she says, spelling out the name as he hunts-and-pecks it into the computer.

"Got her," he says. "Where do you want her?"

"Is Interrogation Room 3 available?" Nayar asks. "Good. Set her up there and ping me when she's ready to go. I'm going to show Mr. Kudra around the commissary, but I'll want to see her as soon as I'm done."

The guard's attention flickers to Jaantzen, but only briefly. This must not be out of order, either.

The guard keys them through, into the prison. "This is the general-population facility," Nayar says when they're out of earshot. "Low-risk prisoners only in this building. A lot of them work here, too, in the kitchen or whatever. Reduces the cost of running the place. My main head of purchasing is an inmate. You'll be working directly with him if you sign on."

Jaantzen's half-listening to the patter, picking out the parts that seem relevant and ignoring the parts she'd be telling a potential vendor. She's giving him an actual tour, he realizes, talking about supply chains and fulfillment processes, the electricity usage rates of their current refrigeration systems, and Jaantzen keeps thinking it's taking too long. Shouldn't they have gotten the call by now?

Nayar must have been able to sense his unease. She checks her comm, like she could have missed the guard's message, slips it back in her pocket and keeps talking.

They're as far as the storehouses when he can't take it anymore. "This is taking too long," he finally says, breaking into her tour patter. "Something's wrong."

She doesn't answer, just dials up a number. "Patch, I'm wrapping up here. What's with the girl?"

She's listening, and though her stony expression doesn't change, Jaantzen can read the problem in the tiny flare of her nostrils, the twitch in her jaw.

"The girl's not in her room," she says, switching off the comm. "We need to go."

11

Starla

STARLA FALLS HARD ONTO RIBS AND JOINTS ALREADY aching from the hellish gravity, the wind *whooshes* out of her lungs. She gasps for breath while footsteps march away, the vibrations getting fainter then stopping abruptly. Whatever Mahr shot her with makes her chest burn like hell.

Starla rolls onto her side, forcing her eyes open to see two uniforms walking away down what looks like an alley between two buildings. They're not the guards who took her to the interrogation room the past few days. Different ones. Mahr's bony hip casts a shadow across the asphalt from the mouth of the alley.

Mahr's talking to someone else Starla doesn't recognize, someone skinny, scruff-faced. Not in an Alliance uniform. The man is gesturing at Mahr as he speaks, but it's just random, punctuative. Unhelpful. Starla gets nothing, except he doesn't seem too happy.

The ground vibrates occasionally in long slow growls — fade in, fade out — that Starla would have guessed were vehicles going by except that there's a pattern to it. Two long, one short. It reminds her of something, she can't figure out what; her head feels like it's stuffed with fiberfill.

When she realizes no one's really watching her, she risks raising her head to look around.

No one's watching her, but there's also nowhere to go.

The alley dead-ends behind her. There's a ladder at the end, but Starla's not strong enough to climb it as fast as she'd need to, to get out of range of Mahr's stun weapon.

Or the other, much more deadly looking weapons carried by the other guards.

Beyond the guards, the alley opens up into a vast paved lot with nowhere to hide; she can just see a fence beyond. Starla fights to keep herself calm. Now isn't the time to panic. Now she needs to figure out what to do.

A change in the vibrations in the ground — it's a vehicle approaching, a van backing into the mouth of the alley. She acts groggy when they come back for her. It's not hard; she's exhausted from the stunner Mahr zapped her with. Mahr barely looks at her, she's still talking with the scruff-faced man. He's sleeveless in the heat, ink scrawled up his scrawny forearms in a pattern that reminds her of Deyva and his snakes.

She can smell his cologne, mingling with baked asphalt and engine oil.

Her heart's racing. She wills herself to stay calm.

Now that they're at the mouth of the alley, she can see that the pavement stretches out beyond the van, see the buildings on either side, lined with loading docks, parked trucks, cargo containers. The inside of the van is smooth molded plastic with no doors.

Once she's inside, she'll have no more options. If she

runs now, she might be able to find cover long enough to evade them.

Maybe.

Just as the two guards hoist her to the back of the van, Starla twists in their grip, kicks with all her might towards the left, aiming for the man's groin. Her bare heel connects and the guard drops her, toppling the other guard off balance.

Starla's expecting this; the other guard is not. She lands and drives her elbow up into the soft spot below his sternum as he falls.

She's panting, but she scrambles free, risking only a split-second glance over her shoulder to see Mahr and the scruff-faced man shaking off their surprise.

She runs as fast as she can.

12

Jaantzen

"YOU'VE GOT TO BE SHITTING ME."

Nayar is raging at the guard, Patch. Jaantzen's glad to be on this side of the desk.

"You don't know where she is? Who's been in charge of her questioning?" she asks, as though she doesn't already know. She's reading over his shoulder as he pulls up that information. "Alert Lieutenant Mahr that she's missing," she says.

Patch nods, grateful for something to do. He's braced against the brunt of her anger, shoulders tense and jaw clenched.

"She's not answering," he says.

"It's late," Nayar says. "Try again."

"She always answers," the guard says, but he tries again.

"Trace her comm. Is she in her quarters?"

Patch shakes his head. "Her comm's off."

Jaantzen can see the brief moment of thought, flashing through Nayar's eyes. "Keep trying to trace her, and tell me what you find," she tells Patch. "Come with me," she says to Jaantzen, which gets him a slightly longer look from the guard than before. Jaantzen gives the man his most innocuous Rosco Kudra smile.

"Yes, Major," Patch says after a moment's hesitation. "Should I put the base on alert to find the girl?"

"Not yet," Nayar says. "I'll call you if we need backup."

Patch glances back and forth between Nayar and Jaantzen. Jaantzen can see it in his eyes when he decides it's above his pay grade and security clearance to wonder why a refrigeration and coolants executive is joining Major Nayar in the hunt for a teenage OIC terrorist.

"I'll let you know what I find out," Patch says, settling back into his chair.

"IF I WAS GOING to try to offload human cargo in the middle of the night, and didn't already know about the faulty security camera on Dock 16, I'd use the area by the generator building," says Nayar. She's jogging comfortably; Jaantzen is struggling not to pant. "There's an alley there that's secluded and fairly unsecured, and close to the max facility." She slows as they reach a corner, checks the safety on her sidearm.

"So you think that's how Mahr's been smuggling out these kids?"

"It seems the most likely. If we get in a sticky spot, feel free to shoot to kill," says Nayar. "Particularly if we're talking about Sendera Dathúil."

"You don't need witnesses to prosecute Mahr for kidnapping?"

Nayar shrugs. "Mahr's not my problem. I don't care

if she walks free." She glances at him. "But quieter is better," she says.

They round a corner and there's a van parked by the loading dock, no windows but the driver's compartment. Nayar swears. "That's one of my supply vans," she whispers. Jaantzen can see her scowl in the wan light. "That bitch is using my van."

"You're sure it's not your people?"

"If it is, they're still where they shouldn't be with a van that isn't checked out."

Jaantzen can hear humming coming from the far side of the van, catches the faintest hint of kosh smoke wafting their way. It smells cheap, acrid. He wrinkles his nose, and Nayar nods and pulls out a knife. "Now," she whispers.

She's around the corner of the van before he can react; he hears a strangled gargle and follows to see a man sprawled on his back. His chest is rising shallowly, but he's not conscious. Apparently being head of requisitions isn't all sitting at a desk.

"I'm faster with a gun," Jaantzen says.

"Smarter if nobody sees you anyway," Nayar says. She passes her ID badge over the reader at the rear of the van and there's a faint hiss of pneumatics as the doors open. It's empty, as Jaantzen suspected. He wouldn't be caught standing around waiting if the cargo had already been loaded.

"Help me with this," she says, and together they load the man into the back of the van. He's wearing a guard uniform; Nayar taps her comm over the ID badge and frowns at the name.

"Anyone you know?"

She shakes her head. "He's in maintenance," she

says. "Nobody who should have access to a requisitions van."

She shuts the door, makes sure it's locked to her ID badge only. "Now I guess we wait until they bring her out," she says.

13

Starla

STARLA'S CROUCHED ON A LEDGE ABOUT TEN METERS UP,
panting. She's figured that hiding and thinking will be
smarter than running aimlessly. Whatever Mahr is doing,
she seems to be trying to fly dark. Starla suspects she'll
have at least a few minutes before Mahr decides it's
worth alerting the entire prison.

Beyond the buildings there's a huge swath of asphalt
and packed gravel, and beyond that she can see what
looks like a launchpad and airstrip. A fence stretches out
between the two, but it can't go on forever.

To be honest, Starla barely sees the fence. Despite
the pressing need to focus and plan, she's having trouble
not gawking.

Overhead, the sky is gaping wide, space stations and
super-massive cargo haulers tracing lumbering paths
between glittering stars. A blue-tinged star hovering just
above the horizon can only be Indira — Silk Station isn't
close enough to make Indira out so clearly, so she's never
seen it in real life before. Beyond everything, the first of
New Sarjun's two moons is starting to rise; right now it's

just a sliver, shading the black desert landscape
blood red.

The whole scene's alive in a way she's never experienced, the gradients of the atmosphere and wisps of
clouds and the burst of some distant electrical storm
embroidering it with depth and texture.

It's breathtakingly beautiful.

Starla forces her attention back to the task at hand.
She's heard stories of this desert prison. She knows that
making a run for it isn't an option — there's nowhere out
here to run *to*. But she thinks she doesn't have to escape
the entire prison in order to survive this night; she just
has to escape from Mahr.

And then?

Then she's back to square one. Say she turns herself
in. She's still trapped here answering Hali's questions, no
way home, no way of knowing what happened to the
rest of her family.

Starla crouches, looking past the fence, out over the
airfield.

That would be her way out, if she knew how to fly
one of those things. She wonders if she could stow away.
They'll need to send in supplies, from time to time, and
surely not every plane that lands here is Alliance. Surely
there's some that aren't so well guarded.

Starla thinks through her options.

Right now they'll probably be searching any plane
that leaves — it only makes sense, with a newly escaped
prisoner. But a week from now? They'll assume she ran
out into the desert and died. That would be her time to
try to get past the fence and stow away.

Through the wall against her back she can feel that
same rhythmic vibration, two long, one short, and she
realizes it reminds her of the generator back on Silk

Station. A generator building will be relatively unvisited, she guesses, and full of places to hide. So now all she has to do is figure out how to get inside this building, and then live there for a week.

Starla ignores how absurd this plan sounds.

She might be able to get in through the roof, she thinks, but first she'll have to get onto the roof. The ladder she climbed stops at this ledge.

The ledge, though, wraps around the building to Starla's left. It's narrow and exposed, but she hasn't seen anyone come by yet. She might be able to risk it, if she inches along.

Starla stands, shuffles away from the safety of the ladder. She tries not to look down.

She's never needed to be afraid of heights before.

SHE'S TRYING to move as seamlessly as she can, hoping that translates into silently, and she's just turned the corner when she sees movement. It's one of the guards. Starla freezes; he doesn't look up.

He's walking softly, as though trying to be secretive — and limping, Starla notes with satisfaction. Starla hopes this means she's right about Mahr not calling in reinforcements just yet. He passes right underneath her, and she stays as still as possible, trying not even to breathe until he's out of sight around the corner.

Starla counts to twenty, let that be enough time for him to pass by, then begins her slow shuffle. Now that she's around the corner, she can see another ladder ahead, leading off a small balcony. If she can —

She feels her bare foot hit a loose brick, watches in horror as it skitters along the ledge and plummets to the ground below. Is the guard far enough away? How loud a sound did it make?

Starla shuffles faster along the ledge now, as fast as she can stand, keeping her gaze on the balcony ahead. She's ten meters away. Nine. Eight.

Movement below: the guard has returned to investigate. She's loud now — she must be with how fast she's moving — and he looks up. His face registers shock and he says something, with lips tight and close. Whispering, not yelling. Still trying not to attract attention, she hopes, and she ignores him, keeps moving. She's two meters away from the balcony when he raises his gun.

Starla feels the energy sizzle past her as she makes a final leap, desperately judging the amount of force she needs to bridge the gap.

Her open palms slam against the lowest rail of the balcony — not the top, as she'd been hoping — the grotesque weight of her New Sarjunian body threatening to tear her grip loose. She swings wildly for a terrifying moment, then manages to hook her heel up onto the balcony and pull herself in.

Another bolt of energy sizzles past with a blaze of blue light, leaving a slice of pain along her upper arm in its wake. The small hairs on the back of her neck are standing on end, and she can smell burning. The sleeve of her jumpsuit is scorched, the bricks behind her are cracked and smoking.

Starla has miscalculated. She'd thought they wouldn't kill her. Apparently she'd been wrong.

14

Jaantzen

Jaantzen doesn't like waiting, and something feels wrong in this night. The man in the back of the van, Jaantzen wonders what he'd say if he could be asked — whether he knew who he was waiting for, or if he'd merely been given a routine task with no explanation.

And what if Nayar hadn't wanted him, Jaantzen, to be able to ask anything? The thought whips through his brain like a flash at the corner of his vision: fleeting, yet leaving an uncomfortable smudge of uncertainty in the spot where it had been. He glances over. She's looking out into the darkness, forehead creased in thought.

"How do we know they'll bring the girl here," he says. He doesn't like all this uncertainty. Doesn't like being surrounded by Alliance soldiers. Doesn't like being at the mercy of Coeur's sister.

"We don't," Nayar says. "It's the most logical place, but we have no way of knowing for sure what Mahr's up to." She shrugs. "This is all conjecture."

"I don't like conjecture."

"I imagine not." Her attention has slid off him,

93

though, into the shadows around the buildings. The flat darkness is reverberating with tiny noises: the hiss of ventilation systems kicking on, the slow *WUB-wub-wub* of a generator deep inside one of the buildings.

Nayar moves suddenly, and Jaantzen's hand is on his pistol, aiming it at her head as Nayar's own weapon leaps up to match, a split second too slow for it to have mattered. Her lips break into the ghost of a smile; she pulls up.

Jaantzen slowly lowers his pistol.

"Touchy," she says, sidearm dropping back to ready as she turns away from him. "I'm just here to help. And if you — "

Somewhere, not too far away, the night sizzles with the charge of a plasma carbine set to its maximum. It echoes in the alleyway; to Jaantzen, it sounds like it's coming from every direction at once.

"C'mon," Nayar hisses, and she's sprinting forward, away from the direction they'd come from.

She's nearly out of sight when a figure flashes out from behind a pile of crates, launches itself at her. They roll, grappling. She's strong, but the man's scrappy and tough, all wiry ropes of muscle and street-fighting technique — dodgy and dirty. He's not in uniform, he's just wearing a close-fitting biosilk shirt cut short to show off tattoos, and baggy pants that give his kicks better range. Nayar's military-trained blows aren't landing. Jaantzen catches the glint of a knife the second before it plunges downwards.

Jaantzen fires.

The skinny thug drops to the ground, the knife clattering to the asphalt beside him. Nayar stands, wincing, and kicks the knife away from the man's reach.

But he won't be reaching for anything.

Jaantzen nudges one ropy arm open, sees the familiar Money-Beauty-Death symbols intertwined with nudes on his forearm. "Well, there's your evidence," he says.

"What is?"

Jaantzen stabs a finger at the tattoo. "Sendera Dathúil," he says. "Anyone else caught with this tattoo is killed."

Nayar nods slowly. "Thanks," she says.

Jaantzen's looking around, doesn't see anywhere the familiar clunky shape of the carbine they'd heard. Besides, if this thug'd had one, he'd've probably used it instead of going hand to hand with Nayar.

For a brief moment he wonders if it was a decoy, a lure to get them away from the van so the delivery can finish, but then the sound comes again, twice, and a flash of electric blue reflects off a stack of oil barrels a hundred meters away.

"Let's go," Jaantzen says, breaking into a run.

15

Starla

STARLA SEARCHES FOR A WEAPON. SEES THE CRACKED bricks where the guard's blast hit, grabs one. Takes careful aim and hurls it — again she miscalculates the force needed, and the brick shatters at his feet. She's rewarded by another blast from his gun — it hits the ladder behind her and energy crackles up the metal tubing. Starla stares at it, wide-eyed, hairs rising on her arm where it's inches away from the metal. Apparently climbing to the top of the building while hoping he doesn't hit her won't be an option.

She throws another brick, deliberately aiming this one at his feet to test the force she'll need, and as it shatters there, he looks up with a cocky grin. He says something to her, his torso jerking in a laugh, and in the second he looks down to check the charge on his gun, she throws a third brick.

True aim, this time. It hits him square in the ear and he nearly drops his weapon, throwing his hand up to the wound. His fingers come away black with blood. He dodges her fourth brick, and Starla flings herself back against the wall as he raises the gun. Part of the balcony crumbles away as he shoots. Starla pulls her feet back from the edge, panic rising as she readies herself for the next shot.

It doesn't come.

She risks a glance, brick in hand.

Mahr is here, now, yelling and waving arms, and obviously furious with the guard. Starla relaxes a fraction. Maybe she'd been right, and the plan wasn't to kill her after all. She watches Mahr yell for a few seconds, then makes her decision.

Starla starts to climb.

Her hands are claws on the rungs, her heart racing with both the effort of the climb and the terror she feels waiting for the blast that will electrify her molecules into the metal.

When it comes, it's not the electric shock she's expecting. Instead, the ladder shudders and shards of brick rain down on her from above; Starla ducks her head and closes her eyes against the ferocious hail. She can feel the metal of the ladder shrieking as it twists under her weight, looks up in horror as the struts attaching it to the brick above pop loose one by one and the ladder slowly peels away from the wall.

Starla tries to climb down, but her feet slip off the rungs as the ladder tips backwards by degrees, faster and faster until it's gone horizontal with a crash against the balcony. The impact breaks the last of her grip.

Starla falls.

16

Jaantzen

Jaantzen's yelling as the Alliance woman — she can only be Mahr — takes aim at the ragged figure on the ladder. But he's too far away, and his shot skims past her when the charge from her own weapon jolts her out of its path. He ducks for cover as the guard beside her turns and fires. Nayar's ended up on the opposite wall, taking cover behind a stack of crates.

The plasma carbine leaves a smoking black char on the asphalt beside him — apparently the Alliance version of this weapon has gotten a boost beyond what Jaantzen is familiar with. Nayar leans out from cover and fires, but her shot goes wide, and she's rewarded by a charge from the carbine that ignites the contents of the crates she's hiding behind.

Someone is screaming. High above the battle scene. And Jaantzen watches in horror as the lanky teen girl who can only be Starla Dusai clings to the shrieking wreck of a metal access ladder as it rips from the building and twists on itself with a stuttering pop of rivets. The slow fall picks up speed until her grip is torn free and she falls a full story to the ground below.

He fires at where Mahr had just been standing, a second earlier, and hits nothing.

A minor avalanche of crumbling bricks and twisted metal is raining down around the girl. He can't tell if Starla is moving.

He also can't tell where Mahr ducked to hide, but the guard with the plasma gun is in a doorway, and he's raised the weapon to fire at Ximena Nayar once more.

Jaantzen can't get a clear shot from his corner.

He bellows and charges out from hiding, only faintly aware of Nayar following his lead.

The guard pivots, squeezes the trigger, but one of Jaantzen's slugs catches him in the shoulder and it jerks the carbine off target, the blast sizzling past Jaantzen's sleeve with a stench of charred wool. Jaantzen's next slug goes between the guard's eyes.

Searing agony catches Jaantzen in the ribs, left side, and he bites down on the pain, whirls to face Mahr, her hiding place betrayed by the shot she took at him.

Somewhere through the rush of blood in his ears he hears Nayar yelling, and in the split second before he pulls the trigger he hears her and drops his aim from chest to belly.

Lieutenant Mahr falls back against the wall, hands clenched and bloody around her gut.

"I've got her," Nayar says behind him. "Get to the girl."

Jaantzen glances at his comm. An alert from his biosilk chest armor tells him that he's been shot — Thank you, technology — and that he's broken a rib. It also tells him he doesn't seem to be experiencing any internal bleeding. Gia's meditech prodigy back at the plane is getting the same alert. He'll be ready for triage when they get back.

And Starla — her eyes are open and blinking rapidly in shock; she's lying on her back with her leg bent at a sickening angle, but shielded from the largest chunks of debris by the twisted skeleton of the ladder, which is propped above her. A fierce, protective place has opened up in Jaantzen's chest, drowning out the searing stab of pain through his ribs as he flings the debris off her.

Her eyes focus on him and widen in panic, and somewhere in the adrenaline flooding his mind he pulls up a few of the signs Raj taught him the last time Jaantzen met his goddaughter, so long ago.

"Hello, Starla."

He hopes he has her name sign right. "You're going to be safe," he tells her, trying to speak clearly. "You're going to be safe."

The panic in her gaze ebbs slightly, and she doesn't try to fight him as he checks her for injury. The leg seems the worst, and she grunts as she pushes herself up to sit, face a mask of pain. Jaantzen's surprised she hadn't shattered like a stick of hard candy at the fall. She's gaunt, unsubstantial, skin nearly translucent with shock and from growing up in the black.

She signs something to him, and he shakes his head, not sure what she's said. She scowls and jabs at his broad chest, then opens up her hands in question.

In the distance, an alarm is going off. He can hear shouting, getting closer.

"It's time to go," Nayar says behind him. "Can she be moved?"

Jaantzen nods. "I think so," he says to her. "I'm a friend," he says to Starla. She frowns at him, and he's not sure if she's understood. He holds out a hand. "We have to go. You'll be safe."

She takes his hand, and he ignores the pain in his ribs as he hoists her up to stand on her good leg. She cries out in pain.

Behind them, Mahr is still lying against the wall, gasping for breath. Her eyes widen with recognition as he turns, her expression shifting from fear to surprise. "Willem Jaantzen," she says. Her gaze darts back and forth between Jaantzen and Nayar. "Major Nayar, what are you doing with — "

Jaantzen winces at the crack of Nayar's pistol. Mahr slumps back against the wall.

"During a routine tour with a vendor, I came upon the lieutenant in the process of illegally selling an inmate into indenture," she says quietly. "Unfortunately, Lieutenant Mahr resisted arrest. Equally unfortunately, the vendor has chosen not to do business with the Alliance."

She reholsters her pistol. "A shame, but I'll get over it. As for the girl, she ran off in the confusion. I doubt we'll find her — and certainly not alive." Nayar straightens and tosses him the key to the jeep. The shouting is getting closer. "Head back through this alley and take a left to find Dock 16. Keep the girl out of sight, and if anyone at the checkpoint asks, tell them I stayed late to take care of some business."

Her expression is fierce as she takes his offered hand.

"Pleasure doing business with you, Major," he says. "Until next time."

A brief snort of a laugh quirks her lips into an exact image of her sister, but Jaantzen just turns away, arm supporting his goddaughter.

He has family to take care of, too.

Starla

THE MAN WHO KNOWS HER NAME SIGN MOTIONS FOR
Starla to get into the coffin-like crate in the back of the
jeep, and she does, trusting, screwing her eyes shut
against the sight of him putting the lid over the top. He's
the biggest man Starla has ever seen, tall as her station-
born cousins but bulky, too, in a way that's hard to get
out in space. His expensive-looking suit is tailored
perfectly around his broad shoulders and barrel chest.
His skin is a rich, deep brown. Diamonds glitter in his
ears.

Something about him feels familiar, she thinks. She's
not sure why, but something about this ferocious, gun-
toting man feels right.

And he knows her name sign.

The engine of the jeep thrums through her chest,
each bump and stutter sending waves of pain and nausea
sloshing up from her leg. They stop once, for a long time,
and she tries not to panic though she's desperate to know
what's going on.

Finally the jeep starts moving again, and a moment

later the engine is off and she feels her crate moving, bites her lips, can only hope she's kept herself from screaming out in pain. Feels herself resettled, and then searing light slices through the gap as the lid is removed.

She blinks, pushes herself to sitting. She's *inside*, but she can't tell inside what. Something narrow like a cargo shuttle; there are stacks of crates just like hers strapped against the wall.

The big man is here, too. He pauses, takes a deep breath.

"Hi, Starla," he signs again. It's clumsy, mechanical.

"Who are you?" she asks, but apparently that's it for his bag of sign language tricks. He grimaces, looking embarrassed, and pulls out his comm. Speaks to it — she catches "My name is," she thinks — and passes it to her.

My name is Willem Jaantzen. I'm a friend of your father's, and I'm here to get you away and safe.

"Where are my parents?" she signs

Starla signs the words frantically, and Willem Jaantzen — she knows that name, her parents had talked about visiting him — furrows his brow, gestures at the comm. She types the question and thrusts it at him.

And then he meets her gaze, his own holding none of the pity that was in Hali's expression, none of the softness or the fear to tell her the truth. Willem Jaantzen's gaze holds nothing but cold anger. "Your parents are dead," he says softly, passing the comm back, but she doesn't need to look at the words blinking there to understand what he said.

Starla isn't surprised, not any more.

"Thank you," she signs, and he nods.

He glances over his shoulder, says something to a smaller, younger man with bright-red hair and a duffel bag. Together, they hoist Starla from the crate and onto a reclined chair with a flight harness, and for a brief moment she thinks they're going home, they're heading back to the stars. But this isn't a shuttle, it can't break the atmosphere, not without tearing itself apart and scattering them across the surface of New Sarjun in a spectacular, fiery hail.

Jaantzen hands her the comm. *WE'RE GOING TO MY HOME*, it says. *YOU'LL BE SAFE THERE. THIS IS NOLE, HE'S GOING TO LOOK AT YOUR LEG. IS ANYTHING ELSE INJURED?*

Starla shrugs, staring at the last sentence. Everything aches, but it has for days. And nothing's screaming at her worse than her leg.

Nole's already got scissors out, the metal is cold against her calf as he slits the material of her jumpsuit. Jaantzen reaches across her to snap the harness in place, then sits, wincing, in a seat beside her. She wonders if he's been shot: there's a hole singed in his expensive jacket, but no blood.

Jaantzen shouts something to the pilot and the plane begins to roll, faster, faster, she's pushed back in her seat with the motion, like the *Nanshe* under thrust — like, but not the same. She can feel the moment the wheels peel away from the planet's surface, the smooth glide tilting upwards, with a rush of adrenaline in her gut that's almost euphoric.

She relaxes against the chair, lets her head roll to look out the window. She expects to see stars; instead she sees the second of New Sarjun's moons cresting the horizon in a glimmer of cold fire. It's a view Mona would have loved to see. *Would* love to see.

Starla waves to get Jaantzen's attention, makes the sign for *comm*, which he probably doesn't understand, though he hands her the device.

NEED TO FIND OUT WHAT HAPPENED TO MY FAMILY.

His broad brow furrows at that. She can see him wondering if he needs to tell her again what happened to her parents.

COUSINS. AUNTS. WHOEVER.

She has to find out if she's alone. She has to learn what happened.

Jaantzen takes back the comm to respond, but his speech is slow and clear. "You have my word."

Starla turns to stare back out the window. The moon has risen fully now, liquid gold flowing over the crumpled-paper landscape of the desert. It's unlike anything she's ever seen: raw, surreal. Stunning.

NEGATIVE RETURN

A DURGA SYSTEM NOVELLA

JESSIE KWAK

For Robert,
for always pushing me to write my best.
And for watching all those gangster movies with me.

$$\rule{3cm}{0.4pt}$$

1

Bad Jazz

The lounge singer is in over his head.

He has a decent voice when he stays in the right register, Manu Juric thinks, but every song he's chosen tonight has been a challenge — a touch too high, the notes fraying around the edges. The Bronze Room is too cheap a bar to filter it through an autocorrect unit.

Manu'd chip in to buy them one, but he'll never get invited back after what he's about to do.

The singer's crooning in a mismatched suit, his hair and makeup done expertly but cuticles scuffed and shoddy, nails flaking underneath the cheap lacquer. Not just overreaching his vocal chords — he's overreaching his league.

Manu tipped him anyway, earlier this evening, his tagged one-mark token tumbled in with all the others in the jar.

Manu's drinking whiskey, the bar's cheapest over plenty of ice to water down the flavor of engine oil. He's sipping it slow, taking his time, and already he's starting to get looks from the bartender.

Nobody nurses shitty whiskey at the Bronze Room. The bartender is one poorly sung verse away from calling his boss and reporting his suspicions.

Manu knocks back the whiskey, tags the bottom of the glass, then raises a finger to the bartender. The bartender slides another whiskey across the bartop; Manu thanks him with a wink and a bit too lingering of a smile — it's not faked, there's plenty to admire, and the bartender's tight shirt doesn't require much of the imagination. Manu transfers him a generous tip from Sylla Mar's expense account.

The bartender just turns away with a polite service-industry smile and drops Manu's empty glass into the sanitizer without noticing the tag at the bottom. Let him come to the wrong conclusion about why Manu is camping at his seedy bar just outside the posh, touristy Tamarind District.

Manu can't even remember the last time he came to this part of Bulari. He thinks it was when he was still a kid, just dropped out of third levels to help his dad with the business, barhopping on cash stolen from his dad's till with some of his buddies from Carama Town, tallying up who could get the most colorful cussing-outs from tourist girls and toss-outs from bouncers. If he remembers right they got kicked out of six bars before the cops got called.

It was a good night.

Manu gives the Bronze Room another scan. This may have been one of those bars; he can't remember. The end of that night's a bit of a blur.

Manu taps a fingernail against the side of his glass, waiting. His nails are a poison acid green tonight, same as his hair. The color pops nicely against his black skin.

He goes over the dossier once more.

The mark tonight's on the meaner end of the Bulari thug spectrum; he's the type almost everybody'd like to see gone, though nobody but Manu's been stupid enough to try. Small crew of riffraff, each uglier and crueler than the next. Got himself a live-in lady, a clean-looking type who must have a pretty low opinion of herself to end up with scum — but she's hardly alone in this city. Manu'll be doing her a favor, killing Willem Jaantzen.

Manu's been gathering intel on his mark for two weeks, long enough that Sylla Mar's started dropping hints that maybe his heart's not really in it, that maybe Manu's all talk and no action.

Those are the exact words she used, too, last time her goons brought him in. Lounging on that black velvet like she styles herself a goddess, smoke from her laced cigarette spiraling through her neon purple and pink locks. Dry, overpainted lips and eyelids weighed down with pigment, Sylla looked a caricature of a vid crime lord, right down to the thick-jowled musclemen who flanked her divan.

Even now, Manu tries to imagine those men as his co-workers, Sylla as his boss. Tries to imagine himself taking orders spoken in that husky undertone, punctuated by the cartoonish cracking knuckles of her goons.

Wonders if he'll ever stop watching his back with them as his crew.

No. Joining Sylla's crew isn't ideal, but who ever said life was perfect? The city's getting tight, lately. Strangling out the independent operators, choking out the way Manu used to exist. Too many petty alliances between the bosses, too many turning snitch on the little guys to build up their credibility with the government. Sometimes a freelance hitman needs a friendly crew to weather out the storm of crackdowns and backstabbings.

And Sylla's crew will do.

Better than getting himself an indenture. Manu'd rather be free and hungry than owned by some corporation.

Provided he can handle this initiation she set out for him.

Killing Willem Jaantzen.

It's a terrible idea, and Manu's been thinking of walking away all week. He actually can't decide if Sylla's messing with him — maybe she's one of those women who hates saying no outright, and this is just a convenient way to get rid of him for good rather than taking him in. She sure didn't seem to think he could actually do it.

If he's honest with himself, he hasn't been thinking he can do it, either. He's taken out his fair share of lowlifes and deadbeat ex-boyfriends, but he's never had a mark this big.

You don't know if you don't try, though, right?

Because if he makes this hit, it doesn't even matter if he sticks with Sylla and her band of shifty thugs. Killing Jaantzen will get him a job wherever he wants.

Killing Jaantzen with style might even get him a job with Thala Coeur, Blackheart herself. Now there's a scary bitch — but she's got a crew that actually watches out for each other. Joining Blackheart's crew, now that's a proper life goal.

Manu doesn't need Sylla, but he does need this win.

The singer stops crooning to a smattering of applause that seems more grateful than appreciative, and he disappears into the back with his tip jar. Manu notes that with a frown. It's not a big deal — Manu's tags have been thoroughly seeded. Just, Manu hopes the singer hasn't put all those tokens in his pocket.

Nobody deserves that, even for botching show tunes this badly.

Manu takes another sip of shitty whiskey.

He's gonna have fun busting this place up.

MANU DOESN'T NEED to be watching the door to know when Willem Jaantzen walks in. The whole energy of the place shifts, gets thin and sharp as a razor. There's two Arquellian girls a few seats down the bar, laughing too loud to hide their nerves, racking up stories of slumming it in Bulari to tell their friends back on Indira. They notice the hush but don't mark its meaning; the one closest to Manu glances towards the door and raises a catty eyebrow before turning back in a cascade of black ringlets to whisper in her friend's ear.

Manu shifts like he's checking her out and sees Jaantzen walk past, all broad shoulders and barrel chest. He's dressed more stylishly than Manu's used to seeing, like a man taught young which social cues others respect and who's now able to afford it. He's got two silver earrings in his right ear, two silver rings on each hand — bright glimmers against his rich brown skin.

Jaantzen ensconces himself at an empty table, though he doesn't seem possessive about it, not like Manu expects from a man at the head of one of Bulari's most up-and-coming crime rings. It's not the best table in the house, but it's in the corner with a decent view of the door. And a proximity to the stage Manu's sure Jaantzen will regret when the singer comes back for his next set.

Jaantzen's not traveling with bodyguards, this deep in his own territory, but he does have companions. Manu recognizes them: a brother and sister pair a lot of

Bulari's bosses work with, the Lordeurs. They're bankers, kind of. Laundering big takes and fencing stolen goods. Tossing money out and reeling it back in with fat fish like Jaantzen attached.

He hesitates now. You never know when you might need a loan — plus, the Lordeurs've got a lot more friends than a loner thug like Jaantzen. Manu wonders if he'll ever need their services, decides probably not. And anyway, the whole bar is tagged at this point. If he walks away now he's never getting another chance — and he's out a small fortune in hornet tags.

Manu ignores that nagging, rational voice telling him that the smart thing to do is to walk away.

The singer's gone back up onstage; Manu catches Jaantzen's frown of annoyance at the first warbled notes, catches the singer's furtive glances at Jaantzen's nearby table. The boss is in the house tonight, and this guy knows he's not getting invited back for another gig.

Manu pushes his glass back towards the bartender and waves off the raised eyebrow asking if he wants another drink. He slips his little transmitter underneath the bartop and clicks the sequence to arm it. Feels it pulse faintly under his fingertips to tell him it's good to go.

No safe return now. Not until he kills Jaantzen.

Manu pushes off to the bathroom, a touch of whiskey sway to his shoulders and a sloppy nod to one of the Arquellian girls. She gives him a dirty look.

He's counting, and as he draws level with Jaantzen's table — a fraction of a second after he hits twenty — the bar shatters. The front of the glasses case blows off its hinges in a rush of smoke and fire. The long mirror beside the bathroom hallway and the picture window beside the front door both shatter, cascading shards of glass hitting all the high notes over the sound of screaming. At the back of the stage, the singer's backpack explodes. That's where that tagged coin ended up; Manu lets the thought slide past.

His attention is entirely on Jaantzen.

The Lordeur siblings have ducked to take shelter below the table — the little blasts from the hornet tags sound like gunshots, and all around people are diving to the floor.

Willem Jaantzen is not diving to the floor.

He hasn't registered Manu as the enemy yet — Manu dropped like the others in the chaos. As Jaantzen turns away to scan his bar, weapon in hand, Manu takes his shot.

Jaantzen must have heard something, seen a flash. Anyway, he's fast for such a big man, and as Manu squeezes off a second shot, Jaantzen kicks the pistol out of his hand.

No worries, Manu's got a backup gun.

He draws it, springs back to his feet and away as Jaantzen charges him, feeling the situation slip. Had to be flashy to impress Sylla, he thinks. Had to be an idiot.

His third shot is an inch too low, hits square in Jaantzen's body armor rather than in the throat, and Jaantzen only grunts, catches him with an elbow to the sternum, a meaty hand to the throat. Jaantzen lifts him off the ground by his collar, those dead shark's eyes searching his, and all he can think is that he's seen this scene in gangster vids, and it does not end well for the guy with his feet dangling over the glass-strewn bar floor.

Jaantzen lifts his chin to someone behind Manu, and a blast of pain hits him between the shoulder blades.

Game's over.

———————————————

2

Botching the Job

———————————————

MANU IS SURPRISED TO WAKE UP.

That he's bound to a chair in an empty basement, single bulb sputtering overhead — that's not so much a surprise. Jaantzen hasn't killed him, so this is definitely the sort of place he'd find himself.

The floor around him is covered in tarps, a bad sign. But he's still dressed, and he's not gagged, so . . . Manu scents the possibility of negotiation in the air.

Footsteps behind him, two pairs. "I'll answer anything you want," he says, conversational. Let's start off on the right foot here. Let's be helpful.

"Giving up so easily?" He's been studying that voice for weeks: Willem Jaantzen.

Manu shrugs. "Nothing to give up," he said. "I ain't got nobody to protect."

"Working on your own, then," Jaantzen says.

"I don't like working with others," Manu says. "I end up pulling all the weight, but you still gotta split the profits with the team. Or one of the other guys pulls a gun." No point in mentioning Sylla Mar —

she's not big news enough to get him out of this mess, even if he could live with himself for snitching. He may not give a shit about her, but he's got morals, dammit.

"You could pull the gun first." A footstep, crinkling in the tarps.

"Guess I never think of that."

"Shortsighted."

"Or longsighted," Manu says. "Could be I'm building up a rep as somebody folks want to have around. I hear I'm easy to work with." He wants Jaantzen to step out in front of him. Partly to look the man he couldn't take down in the eye, partly to read what chance he's got of getting out of this alive. "You got a gig?"

A long pause. "I'm sorry?"

"A gig. You need some work done?"

"You think I'm going to hire a man who just tried to kill me?"

"Papa always said I had too many big ideas for my own good," Manu says.

"I'd say your father was right," Jaantzen says, but there's a hint of amusement in his voice that Manu reads as a good sign. "What's your name?"

"Manu Juric."

"Manu. Juric." Jaantzen rolls the words around on his tongue like he's tasting them. "How much am I worth to you dead, Mr. Juric?"

"Five hundred thousand marks," Manu says. It's not what Sylla would've paid him — she's too stingy — but he's seen that number floating around the bounty boards. It's a mouthwatering amount, but it hadn't been enough to get Manu to jump into this mess earlier.

Should've kept that cautious mindset, it seems.

Jaantzen whistles low. "A tempting sum. I can see why you let it make you careless."

Manu bridles at that, but bites his tongue. You don't get very far mouthing off to the bad guy when you're chained to a chair in his murder dungeon. Manu may have been dumb to try for this bounty, but he's not an idiot. Not normally.

"Five hundred thousand marks has a nice ring to it," he says.

The tarps rustle again; a footstep to the right. Jaantzen appears in Manu's peripheral vision.

"Tell me about yourself, Mr. Juric. I don't believe I've heard your name around."

Manu licks his lips. "I'm a bounty hunter. Freelance hitman. You got a job needs done?"

"Depends. Do you normally botch your hits so badly?"

"Touché, man."

"How's your résumé, Mr. Juric? Anyone I've heard of?"

Manu's thinking hard about the string of lowlife scum he's taken out over the years, but he's coming up blank in regards to notoriety. "The list is long, but it's not very distinguished," he finally says.

Jaantzen just tilts his head; the light from the sputtering bulb glints off his silver earrings. "How long can the list even be? You're what, eighteen?"

"C'mon, man. Twenty-four. But I seen your rap sheet from when you were eighteen, so I'd guess you know what even a teenager can accomplish with the right attitude."

Jaantzen's eyebrow arches. Manu tries to act like he didn't mean it as a challenge, like he's just making conversation in a charming murder dungeon. His shoulders are starting to ache, a low scream he's doing his best to ignore. The way Jaantzen's watching him, Manu can't tell if he made a serious tactical error there.

Finally Jaantzen looks past him, nods sharp to whoever's waiting over Manu's left shoulder. Manu tenses, but no blow comes.

"You're a middling hitman, Mr. Juric," Jaantzen says, but it's not an insult — Jaantzen's musing something over. "But you do create an impressive distraction. And I can be more valuable to you alive."

"You'll pay me half a million marks? For what?"

"Let's not start with the sum. After all, I still need to pay for repairs on my bar." There's a speculative chill in Jaantzen's eyes. "Let's start with me not killing you."

"Pretty valuable, that." Whoever's waiting over Manu's left shoulder takes a long, deep breath through his nostrils; Manu can't shake the feeling that the man's scenting his fear. Manu tries harder to force his heart rate back down. "My life's a good start."

Jaantzen tilts his head, watching. He's lit from behind, only the stern curve of his cheek, the regal angle of his nose lit by glancing light. "Excellent."

A footstep to Manu's left; the second man finally comes out from behind him. Manu's been picturing a clone of Jaantzen, but while the man's just as huge, he's uglier and fair-skinned, his mane of black hair glossed back into a ponytail. Manu fights the urge to laugh inappropriately, but this hunk of muscle is just the spitting image of the disposable, bad-tempered goons Jaantzen's known to run with.

"Meet Kai," Jaantzen says. "He's running the team."

Kai cracks his knuckles like he read it in the Ultimate Manual of Intimidation Tactics. Dammit, Manu hates working in teams. But beggars can't be choosers — not the way the game's being played these days, and not when a goon with fists the size of your head is looking for an excuse to use them.

"Nice to meet you, Kai," Manu says.

"That's the spirit, Mr. Juric. Now. Are we doing business?"

Manu nods, wrists burning. "You got it, boss."

"Good," says Jaantzen. "Kai?"

And he turns and walks out of the room, nonchalant. Manu takes a deep breath. He supposes he deserves this.

The big man steps forward with a smart punch to the ribcage, another to the gut, Manu doubles in the chair, retching. A fist to the jaw snaps his head back, and for a dizzying moment he's about to black out. A thick hand grabs him by the back of the neck, shakes him roughly out of the fog. "You listen to me," the man says. His voice is close in Manu's ear, his breath is a patina of mint over halitosis.

"Listening." Manu's aware that the word comes out as an embarrassingly frantic gasp.

"You answer to me, you got that?"

Manu nods. He thinks this has been abundantly clear from the beginning. The theatrics weren't necessary, but he understands the intimidation game.

Or, he thinks he understands the game.

A knife flashes into Kai's fist, and for a moment Manu thinks he's dead. That all this talk of jobs and money has been a weird sort of foreplay to the main event. What else could he expect? He's heard the rumors about Jaantzen. The man attracts only the sickest lowlifes too unbalanced to find a home in any other crew.

Kai tilts his head, raises the knife. "When you look in the mirror, what do you see?" The knife presses the length of Manu's cheek, a thin, biting line.

Manu's stomach clenches in fear. He can't answer.

"What do you see?" A touch harder on the blade. Manu's thinking about nothing but his left eye, that gleam of metal bisecting his vision. His left eyelid is squeezed shut tight like that scrap of flesh would do anything to protect the eye beneath.

"Just a kid from Carama Town," Manu says carefully, trying not to move.

"Not anymore." The knife slips — just a hair's breadth — and Manu feels something warm and wet trickle down his jaw. "You look in the mirror now, you see somebody belongs to me," Kai says. "You got a question about this gig, you talk to me. You get an order from Jaantzen, you check with me first. I find out you didn't, I kill everyone you have ever cared about. We clear?"

Manu nods, as carefully as he can.

"We clear?"

"We clear."

Another flash of the knife, and the ropes around Manu's arms fall free. He resists the urge to touch his stinging cheek — it doesn't feel deep, though he can feel the trickle of blood slowly dampening his collar.

"Good," says Kai. "Now let's go meet the rest of the crew."

3

Motley

Manu's new friends are waiting for him inside a
cavernous warehouse. Kai blacked out the spinner's
windows on the way here, but they're somewhere near
the docking yards, Manu thinks. He can feel the building
shudder as one of the larger cargo haulers takes off
rumbling into orbit. It's midday — Manu wonders just
how long he was out — but he can't see a thing out the
warehouse windows. They're all too high and smoky,
light filtering thin and miserly through them.

The warehouse is set up like an ops center: screens
and desks, cots lined up like they expect everyone to
settle in for a few days. Manu can feel his neck cricking
already as he frowns at the narrow beds.

"Make yourself at home," Kai tells him.

"Where's my gear?"

Kai just walks away from him, and Manu doesn't
press it. Kai's twice again Manu's weight, and he didn't
get that way by sitting around eating fritters. Jaantzen
hasn't followed them up the stairs, and Manu isn't sure

whether he feels more comfortable with Kai alone or with the mob boss around.

Neither, he decides. Definitely neither.

Fortunately, now he's got more options when it comes to dance partners.

There are four others in the huge space. A hook-nosed man is squinting at his comm like he's working, but the jerk of his shoulders and faint grin on his bruiser's mouth betray his game. When the man sees Kai, he pushes himself off his cot and calls out; Manu can't hear their conversation, but it sounds like they're arguing.

Another man has taken possession of an empty stretch of floor for his impressive martial arts practice, sweat luminous on his gold-white skin. He's bare chested and graceful, his glorious model's abs marred by a wicked-looking scar that traces the jut of his left hipbone before veering south below the waistband of his loose trousers.

There's a girl in the far corner. Mousy and small, she's picked a cot nearest the wall and is keeping to herself, absorbed in the glare of some type of hand terminal Manu's never seen before, glossy black hair falling in a curtain to obscure her face.

And there's the reason she's chosen that cot: a tall woman, a slice of muscle with blue-black skin and well-toned shoulders, prison tattoos stamped behind her ears and tracked down her inner arms. The women aren't talking, no sign to show they mean anything to each other except that the tall black woman looks up from her comm and gives him a glare when she catches him looking at the girl behind her.

There's a third cot on the near side of the black woman.

Manu walks over.

"Manu Juric," he says, thrusting out a hand. She regards him coolly, then takes it. He expects a power play, but her grip is just firm.

"Gia."

The girl behind her doesn't look up. Gia ignores her, so Manu does, too.

"This cot taken?"

Gia shrugs, and he drops his jacket. The heavy denim hits the barely-there mattress with a sorry thud, and the space between Manu's shoulder blades twitches in anticipation.

"Man, what a job," he says, and gets nothing. "Be a trip, yeah?" It's poor bait and Gia doesn't stoop to it, just goes back to reading on her comm. "You been waiting around long?"

"You gonna keep talking all day?" Gia scrolls down without looking up.

"Probably not."

"Glad to hear it. Washroom's that way, you wanna clean yourself up."

The blood from the shallow cut has dried itchy on his cheek; he can feel it flaking as he gives Gia a smile she doesn't look up to see. Probably best to take care of it sooner rather than later.

"Thanks. Nice meeting you," he says, and gets no response.

He takes as long as he dares in the washroom. He looks like he spent the night chained to a chair in Willem Jaantzen's murder dungeon, and he decides it's not the most flattering look he's ever sported. He gingerly scrubs the blood off his cheek — though he can't get it out of his collar — and splashes cold water on his face. It'll have to do.

"Everybody round up," Kai's yelling as Manu comes back out.

With how many cots are in the warehouse, Manu expects "everybody" to be a few more than what it actually is. So far they are six: Gia, her little mouse, Kai, the martial arts model, the surly hook-nosed bruiser, and Manu.

Shitty team, is what he's thinking. He looks around to see what everyone else thinks. The answer is unclear.

The shitty team gathers around the desk. It's one of those cheap ones: disposable, self-destructive if things don't go well. Or if they do, and you just don't feel like hiring a crew to move it. Or if the power surges. Or somebody accidentally spills a cup of coffee down the circuitry.

Kai powers it on, thumps it with his fist when it blinks. It's showing a map. Manu's on the wrong side, but this city's an old friend. They're looking at the Tamarind District — there's that swanky bar his ex, Marisa, kept insisting they go to and he had to pay for.

"The job's this." Kai zooms in on the map, mumbling curses under his breath as the grainy hologram flickers, the graphics pulled kicking and screaming through the wiring of the cheap desk. The image finally snaps clear. "Smash and grab, more details on the target to come. But for now, know that what we need's here." The stubby finger points at an address across the street from the swanky bar. Manu recognizes the hotel, the Blue Falcon.

He lets out a low whistle. "Only Bulari's finest," he says, and Kai gives him a look.

The mousy girl has ended up beside him. She glances at him as though seeing him for the first time, then leans forward to see where Kai's pointing. "Where is that?"

"Posh hotel," Kai says. "Place's called the Blue Falcon." He glances at Manu. "You been there?"

"I never stayed there or anything, but yeah, I've been." To the lobby. During that night trying to get kicked out of bars with his buddies. They hadn't made it past the first set of doors.

"What's the target?" This from the martial arts model. Manu looks up, taking the chance to appreciate the man close up. He's rangy, with brassy, shaggy hair. He brushes it off chiseled cheekbones as he waits for Kai's answer.

"Details to come," Kai says. "It's a fast job. We're expecting a courier to pick up the goods. Our job is to intercept. Easy money."

"Famous last words," says the bruiser. Red-earth skin on this one, cracked through with years of too much sun and too many drugs. His black eyes hold challenge for Kai. "How do we know you've got our back?"

"Because I already gave you my word, Beni," a new voice says. Manu doesn't need to turn to look to see who it is.

Willem Jaantzen walks into the room. He's changed into a new suit since Manu saw him last, this one smoky gray. Manu didn't get any blood on Jaantzen's last suit, but he must've put a few bullet holes in it. Or maybe the man just likes a good costume change. Manu can appreciate that.

Jaantzen takes up a position at the head of the desk; Kai steps to the side, but there's a moment's hesitation Jaantzen doesn't seem to notice. Manu's going to have to be careful not to get in between those two.

"Let's all get to know each other, shall we?" boss man says. "My name is Willem Jaantzen. I'll be running this operation."

"And who are you?" asks the bruiser Jaantzen called Beni.

Manu expects fury, from what he's heard of Jaantzen's temperament, but the man only hits Beni with a mild, evaluating look. Manu might even say it bordered on amusement. He glances around the table to see who else doesn't know who's hired them; sees only the white-gold man with a guarded look. The two women are staring at Beni like he's just said New Sarjun was flat. Kai looks . . . Kai just looks like Kai. Kinda murderous, kinda dumb.

"I'm the one who's running this operation," Jaantzen says again.

"And who are *you*, man?" Manu asks of Beni. He gets a look of distrust from the red-earth man, smiles back.

"Name's Beni Chav. You need to get somewhere quick, I'm your man."

"Mr. Chav is quite skilled," Jaantzen says. "He spent a decade racing Flat Creek, and a few more years on the pro circuit here in Bulari. I believe he has — and correct me if I'm wrong, Mr. Chav — two gold medals and three silvers. Very commendable, though not a complete surprise given his family's history on the track. He'd probably still be there now, save for certain money problems brought on by his penchant for gambling. Which might not have been a problem, except that his mother developed Matiz's syndrome, and his father had to start dealing in shard to pay her medical bills." Jaantzen fixes him with a stare. "Shall I go on."

Beni's nostrils flare, just a touch, and Manu can see

the same thought in everyone's expressions: What does he know about me?

"I got this job through a contractor," Beni finally says. Grudging tone, slouching in his chair. Manu notes the way he tends to lean — to the left — and judges the shots he may need to take accordingly.

"Still, it pays to do a touch of research on the people you'll be working with," Jaantzen says mildly. He turns one hand out to the martial arts model, the other to Manu. "Oriol Sina, meet Manu Juric. You two have similar skill sets. You'll be working closely with Kai."

"And what exactly are the skill sets?" Gia's watching him with narrowed eyes.

"Ballroom dancing champions, us," says Manu. Across from him Oriol cracks a smile, the corners of his eyes crinkling. Manu wants to keep watching him forever — and not just because he's easy on the eyes. He's one of the most relaxed-looking humans Manu has ever come across. It's soothing.

"They're both excellent at killing people," Jaantzen says, holding Manu's gaze for the briefest of seconds. Mostly excellent, thinks Manu. Gia rolls her eyes. A stitch appears on the mousy girl's brow.

"You'll both especially want to play nice with Giaconda," Jaantzen says. "She'll be sewing you up if you get yourselves sliced open." He gives Manu a long look. "Particularly if you step on your partner's toes."

Manu ignores the jab, but doesn't try to hide his surprise at the rest. He'd taken Gia for a hired gun herself, with those lean, muscular arms and prison tattoos. "You're a doctor?"

"Gia coordinates," Jaantzen says simply. "When we're done here, let Gia know what you need."

Only one left unintroduced in this little crew. The

mousy girl has been watching the proceedings with a look of wariness, a flutter of anxious knuckle cracks that only pause when she's watching Jaantzen. Manu notes that with interest. Something about the way she holds herself reminds him of someone, some ghost from the past he can't quite put a finger on. For a minute he thinks it's Marisa — that serious little downturn to the mouth — but that doesn't quite track.

"And what's she do?" Beni gets a second wind of gruffness and jabs a finger in the girl's direction like a dog that doesn't understand it's lost the fight. Good to know.

"Toshiyo will be our eyes in the sky," Jaantzen says. "She will be working closely with me. That means if you hear her give an order, you obey it instantly."

That little slip of a girl, giving orders? Manu can see the thought reflected on the faces of everyone around the table — even Gia. Toshiyo's hand creeps up to cover her throat.

"Understood," Manu says, tapping his fingers to his forehead in a quick salute to her. She gives him a faint smile, shoulders relaxing slightly. "What's our target?"

Jaantzen nods to him; it almost seems appreciative. "You're to retrieve something important. That's all you need to know for today." Manu barely holds back a snort; he's only been brought in for a couple group contract gigs, all back before he had enough of a rep that he could make a living on his own. They were always the same: We'll tell you what you need to know, when you need to know it. Like every mob boss had gone to the same crime leadership seminar.

"We'll spend tomorrow gathering supplies, so tell Gia what you need," Jaantzen says. "I'll speak with you all then."

And with that the big boss man tugs a cuff into place and walks out the door.

The shitty team stays, staring at the grainy hologram — and at each other — with suspicion.

This is going to be terrible.

4

How To Make Friends

TIME TO MAKE THE ROUNDS.

Manu decides to start with the model martial artist, on account of if he's going to get shot down, it might as well be by the prettiest face in the room.

Oriol's sitting on his cot alone, brassy hair falling into his eyes as he types something into his comm. Wiry tendons dance in his forearms as his fingers move; when he sees Manu approaching he slips the device into his duffel.

"What's your deal, man?" Oriol says, but it's curiosity, not a challenge. He leans back on his elbows, feet crossed at the ankles. He's still barefoot.

Manu sits on the cot across from him, trying self-consciously to match Oriol's casual pose. "My deal?"

"You an assassin? Hired gun? What's your deal."

"Bounty hunter, these days."

The look on Oriol's face, that raised eyebrow and a smirk. "Bounty hunter." Manu waits for commentary; it doesn't come.

"How about you?" Manu asks.

"My deal is I don't like to talk about myself," Oriol says. But the way he holds himself says enough. That faint hint of an Indiran accent — Arquelle, probably — the reflexes and the moves he was showing off earlier. Oriol's been well trained, and Manu'll be damned if it wasn't by the Indiran Alliance. Manu wonders what's got an ex-soldier doing crime on the wrong planet these days.

An uneasy feeling pokes at the back of Manu's mind. Whatever the job is, this crew is too odd a mix. He'd expected thugs like Beni and Kai to be running with Jaantzen, and Gia with her prison tats isn't a stretch. But Oriol seems too sophisticated for this kind of mess. And the girl, Toshiyo . . . He wonders if she's been kidnapped, somehow. Brainwashed.

"Job seems rushed, yeah?" he asks. "What's your take?"

"I don't have one."

"Not into speculation?"

"I get the job done, then get out."

"You're not the type likes to draw out the fun? I'll keep that in mind."

Oriol shoots him a wry look. "I take the money that's offered."

"I'll keep that in mind, too," Manu says with a wink.

The response he gets is a raised brow.

"You worked with the man before?"

It's the subtle kick of his foot that tells Manu no, though Oriol only shrugs.

"How'd you get the gig?"

"Man, anybody tell you you ask too many questions?"

"Just Gia so far today. Oh, and Kai."

Oriol's gaze slides to the cut on Manu's cheek. His

expression is dark, but it's gone so quickly most would've missed it. No love lost between Kai and Oriol, then. Good to know.

"Well. Manu Juric, you ask too many questions," Oriol says. "Another man might tell you that with his fist."

Manu knows who those other men are — he was raised by one — and he knew Oriol wasn't one of them when he started his pestering. But Oriol just lays back on the cot, one knee bent, eyes closed, one arm folded under his head. His shirt's riding up just enough for Manu to get another glimpse of the jagged scar scrawled over his hipbone.

Gia catches his eye from across the room; she's typing into a hand terminal, one hip cocked against the desk, Kai at her side. She jerks her chin, a summons.

"I'm gonna go talk to Gia. You got everything you need?"

Oriol doesn't open his eyes. "I'll talk to Gia myself," he says.

KAI PULLS himself taller as Manu walks up; if Gia notices the display, she's ignoring it. Manu gives the big man his deference in a quick nod — his pride has never been dependent on pissing contests. Kai's chin lifts in satisfaction.

"Everything I need's in my gear bag," Manu says, and Gia looks up from her comm. "But I could probably use some more of those hornet tags."

Gia arches an eyebrow. "What for?"

"They're distracting. And fun."

"Nobody's blowing up anything," Kai growls.

Manu shrugs. "You got it, boss. Then I just need a change of clothes."

Gia's gaze flickers to the blood soaking into his collar before she gives him a once-over. "I think my sister's got pants in her closet would fit you. Want me to pick up some eyeliner from her, too?"

Manu flashes his teeth in a smile. "Nah, I got some in my gear bag. Along with several guns I think you'll find quite impressive."

She's giving him a look, chin down and eyebrows raised like is he for real.

"Several," he says again, and now he can see Gia can't decide whether to laugh or tell him to fuck off. They're making baby steps.

Kai's just giving him a glare — the big man's standard expression, Manu's starting to think. He wonders if the glare softens when he's kissing a lover. Or being snuggled by puppies. Manu wonders what it would take to make Kai laugh.

"You *are* gonna give me my gear bag back, yeah?" he asks the big man, gets a reluctant nod. "And my comm? Good." Turns back to Gia. "Then I just need the change of clothes. Thanks, Giaconda." A flare of nostrils. Ah, noted. That's not the name to use in the future.

"Gia, I sent a list to your comm," says a voice from behind him; Manu lifts his chin to greet the mousy girl. Toshiyo. She blinks at him, like she's trying to remember where she's seen him before.

"How did you know my — " Gia's comm buzzes. She frowns at it. "What's a Lumar lens?"

Toshiyo launches into an explanation while Gia scrambles to take notes.

Manu tunes it out, more amused by watching Kai try to follow along. "What's our objective?" Manu asks him.

The big man blinks. "Ain't important."

"I'd say it's pretty important, if it's worth whatever you're paying us all," he says, and he hears Toshiyo's explanation stutter and loop, just the once; she's listening. Gia's stylus is paused over her comm, but she's still got her eyes on Toshiyo. "I'm sure we didn't all come out of the bargain basement like yours truly."

A muscle's twitching in Kai's jaw. "Ain't important," he says again, and Gia starts typing along with Toshiyo's explanation once more.

"Thanks, boss," Manu says with a smile so wide it stings his cheek.

As he turns to go, Kai grunts something; Manu turns back in time to catch the object Kai's tossed to him.

His comm.

There's that, at least.

IT'S nice to have his comm back, but Manu'd really kill for his gear bag right about now. Not for the weaponry — Manu isn't stupid enough to give that a try, not until he knows the lay of the land. But he has a toothbrush in there, a change of underwear. The basics.

And some not-so-basics: a tiny bottle of good face wash, eyeliner, deodorant. He won't try to get the word from Oriol again today, but Manu still smells like old blood and fear-sweat from the murder dungeon and he's certain it'll be wafting over to Gia and Toshiyo tonight. Sorry, ladies.

Still, the comm is something. He thumbs it on, is gratified to see that they haven't managed to break his encryption, though they've obviously tried.

A single message is buried in his secret inbox, from Sylla's number, from hours earlier: *CALL ME.*

Manu lies back on his cot and gives the screen a few taps. *CAN'T TALK NOW JOBS STILL ON.*

He waits. Fifteen seconds, maybe twenty before his screen flashes.

SO YOUR STILL ALIVE. CALL ME.

CAN'T TALK NOW.

CALL ME.

Manu sits half-up on his cot. Kai and Beni are arguing in the corner, Oriol appears to be trying to sleep, Gia is cleaning a gun — Manu'll have to watch where she stashes that, it could be his chance — and Toshiyo is back on her cot exactly as he first saw her, hunched over her strange hand terminal behind a curtain of silky black hair.

There's a door across from the washroom that leads to a balcony. Manu strolls towards it, and except for a brief glance from Kai no one goes after him. Good to know: Kai doesn't think there's any escape this way.

Kai's right. It's just a narrow overhang overlooking nothing but other warehouses, with a long and messy fall to the pavement below. They're not far from the docking yards, and the rumble of magtrucks on the shipping lanes is loud and close. If they're bugging conversations out here they probably can't pick up much.

Manu taps out Sylla's number. Leans back against the low wall surrounding the balcony so he can see the door, the sharp edge of the concrete biting into his lower back. His cheek feels swollen and fever hot in the cool night air; it aches to put on the fake smile he affects even though he's only initiated a voice call.

Sylla's fast to answer. "Manu. Hon." Her husky voice

is two ragged steps past sultry, but she still wields it like a diva. "Thank God."

The sentiment's feigned, he knows, but it still hooks him sharp right below the sternum. When's the last time he came through a bad job and had someone care he'd made it? Not since Marisa — well, not since before he told her what he actually did for a living.

Although even in the good days, Marisa had really only cared that he'd made it to dinner on time.

"I'm all good," he says, half to Sylla, half to himself. "I'm fine."

"I was so worried about you."

"No need to worry." But Manu spikes to attention. Sylla doesn't worry about full crew, much less a loner like him. And as much as he'd like to flatter himself, she's not that interested in anything but his potential as a crew member.

And if she's not worried about him, that means she's worried about what he might say to Jaantzen.

"Coulda got yourself hurt," Sylla purrs.

"Nobody knows a thing," he says, hoping that's enough to reassure her.

"Mmm?" Muffled, she's talking to someone away from the mic. There's a familiar noise in the background, something he can't quite place, like a wind chime. He tries to remember if Sylla has any wind chimes in her lair.

"Nobody here knows about us."

"Of course not. Where are you, hon?"

"I'm still on the job. I'm safe." Not that he believes that. But she needs to, or she'll think he's a liability.

He hears that muffled voice again, wonders if they're trying to track him. That should be impossible with this comm, but still he won't bet his life on it. That familiar chiming comes again from the other end of the line, along with a sound like a magtruck shuddering on a patch of bent track. He frowns. He doesn't think Sylla's lair is on a magtruck line.

"You going back to your place?" she asks.

"I'm still on the job."

Sharp sucked-in breath, a snip of clicking teeth. "You with him?"

"Undercover, like."

She snaps a command to whoever's out of range of the comm. "Like hell, undercover. I heard about the circus you put on at his bar — word's been spreading thick, Manu. Old folks' homes is buzzing with the news. Babies talkin bout it, hon. You think you're undercover with him, you being played." A wet cough. "And you being played, *I* being played."

"Don't worry about it. It's under control."

"Don't worry? I don't just have your sorry ass to take care of. Hon, I got me a whole crew I gotta keep safe. Come on in. I'll protect you."

But he's not crew, and he never will be after this botched attempt. Not unless he can make amends, pass the attack at the bar off as Phase One of the Flashy Secret Plan. Sylla wants him to come in, but not so she can protect him. She wants to protect her own.

And Manu isn't one of her own.

"Manu? Hon? You there?"

Manu's been listening to the silence beyond her voice. He knows that familiar shuddering magtruck catching on the bent track. He knows that wind chime.

Marisa bought it for him for his birthday last year.

Sylla Mar and her thugs are inside his apartment.

"Manu?"

"I'm still on the job," is all he says. "Trust me."

He thumbs off the call.

Sylla's hunting him already.

He rubs the back of his neck and stares at the bright maw of doorway he just came through. It dawns on him that the safest place for him to be right now is inside that warehouse working for Bulari's most hated thug.

He comes back to Sylla without this kill, he's a dead man.

5

Easy Peasy

WHEN HE COMES BACK IN, EVERYONE'S AS HE LEFT THEM. Beni and Kai both look up as he enters; Gia's with them now, too, and someone's pulled out a pack of holocards. The three are playing a surly game of mystix; Beni plucks a card from the table and barks out profanity as it shifts from red to green and spoils the flush he thought he'd drawn.

Toshiyo's still sitting crosslegged on her cot, attention buried in her hand terminal.

Manu drags his feet as he approaches, scuffs his heel. Coughs. Toshiyo doesn't seem to track his approach. "Hey," he says when he's standing at the foot of her cot.

Toshiyo jumps, startled. She blinks at him a moment as though placing him. "Manu," she says, and he's not sure if it's a greeting or she's just jogging her own memory.

"Yeah, hey." He jerks his chin over his shoulder at the card game. "Not much for mystix?"

Toshiyo blinks over at the others. "What are they playing?"

"Seriously? Where you from?"

"Korin. Ruby Basin. I don't play a lot of games."

"Everybody here's playing some sort of game." He tries to say it lightly, like it doesn't mean anything.

"I'm not playing a game," Toshiyo says, tilting her hand terminal towards him. Misunderstanding. "I'm getting into the security feeds at the hotel."

"Yeah? Anything good?" She's scooted over on her cot, so he sits, assuming it's an invitation. She doesn't seem to notice.

"They have three video systems," Toshiyo says. "I've only gotten into the first one." Her hand terminal's screen is a sandstorm of letters and numbers; Manu can't make heads or tails of it. "This is the main feed — it looks like it covers most of the hotel, except for the lobby. The two other feeds cover various parts of the floor, but they're a lot harder to break into."

"Lemme guess. We need eyes in the lobby."

"It's not fun without a challenge."

Manu glances at her, but the girl doesn't seem to be saying it ironically. "You try saying that when you're the one might have to walk in and shoot up the place," he says.

Toshiyo blinks at him as though considering if she'd miss him. Or any of them. "What happened to your face?" she asks instead.

"It's a new part of my beauty regimen," Manu says. "Do you think it's working?"

Toshiyo just laughs. "I bet Gia could fix it up quick so it doesn't scar," she says. "I've seen a lot of that in the mines — medtech is expensive out there, but plenty of people are willing to pay if it's their face."

"I'll ask her about that," Manu says, but he won't — not until after. Until this job's done, he's got a reminder every time he looks in the mirror. Thing is, Manu's still not sure what he wants the cut to remind him of. That he screwed up bad, or that he owes Kai a scar of his own. A bit of both, he guesses.

"What's your deal?" he asks.

"My deal?" Toshiyo frowns at him. "Oh — I analyze data for Blacklode. Analyzed, I mean. I'm a — was an ops tech."

"How do you get in with this crew? It's an awful long way from Ko — from the Ruby Basin." He already can't remember the name of the shit little town she just said she was from.

"Oh." Toshiyo blushes, stares down at the device in her hands. "Jaantzen paid off my indenture."

"He bought out your indenture?" But that isn't what she said, is it. Manu's eyes go wide. "He *paid off* your indenture? Like, just so you'd do this job?"

"I don't think I'm supposed to talk about it," Toshiyo says, wincing, and for a split second Manu feels guilt at pressing her so far — but that's the game, isn't it? Get the information? He's not on anyone's side here.

"I tried to collect a bounty on Jaantzen," he says. Change the subject, give her some quid pro quo to make her comfortable again. "But I guess I managed to both underestimate him and impress him at the same time. He convinced me to join his crew instead." None of the crew seem the type to gossip, but if Toshiyo isn't tight with her stories — and she's clearly not — this is the version he'd rather get around. None of this "He tied me to a chair and Kai beat me to a bloody pulp" nonsense.

"He's a very impressive man," Toshiyo says, then presses her lips tight. He's spooked her, now.

The gesture seems familiar — and Manu finally

places it. Toshiyo's got a way about her that reminds him of a cousin, years ago.

His only cousin, she was about his age. He remembers years of rambunctious laughter getting shushed in their grandmother's house, how those years faded just like her color as she and Manu got older and both their daddies got meaner. Siggy, everybody called her. Sigmaria was her real name, just like that Arquellian pop star who was making the rounds on the music feeds at the time.

What happened to cousin Siggy, he remembers being told by his father with a backhand, by his grandmother with a pinch to the arm, was none of his business. None of his business that Siggy stopped speaking, stopped playing, turned gray and frozen when her own father came back to their grandmother's to pick her up each night.

Just like whatever happens to Toshiyo or Oriol or Sylla or whoever is none of his business.

Manu's not on anyone's team but his own.

"Hey, you got a map of the area around that hotel? There's this bar, right across the street. My old boyfriend used to love that place." It had actually been Marisa's favorite, but Toshiyo sits up straighter, and whether it's the distraction of the work or the assumption that he won't be hitting on her, he's not sure. Whatever it is, she snaps back into herself.

"Yeah, I got that right here." Again, Manu can only see streams of numbers on her hand terminal. "I'll send that over."

She's easy peasy, which is good. If Toshiyo is working close with Jaantzen, being tight with her might just be his key to getting close to his target without arousing suspicion. Because Jaantzen certainly isn't going to let him into killing distance on his own.

"Great. My number is — " His comm's screen flashes. Manu frowns at it. "How'd you get this number?"

Toshiyo's eyebrows knit together like the question doesn't make sense. He thinks of the attempted break-in on his comm.

"Did you try to get through my comm's encryptions earlier?"

"No, do you need me to? It's easy." No guile in that face. He's suddenly absurdly grateful that Kai hadn't thought to ask her.

"Nah, I'm good. Thanks for the map." He stands, holds out a hand that Toshiyo doesn't notice; she's gone back to her terminal.

He frowns down at her. The curve of her neck looks just like Siggy, and it gives him a queasy sense of guilt he can't quite quell. "Hey, Tosh. A bit of advice," he says, forgetting the game for a moment. She looks up, blinks. "You can't trust any of us."

"I don't," Toshiyo says defensively. "I mean, not the others. But . . ."

"But I seem nice." She nods, and Manu gives her his best smile, brushing off the tiniest part of him that feels like shit. "Being friendly's just the way I get what I want. But you gotta have just as much of a guard up for friendly as you do for mean."

"Sorry," Toshiyo says.

Manu laughs. "You and me don't have no debt with each other, but ain't everybody here's on the same side."

Toshiyo frowns at him. "But aren't we all working for Jaantzen?"

"I hope so."

Toshiyo just squints back down at her terminal, but Manu looks up to see Gia watching him, unfriendly. He feels Gia's eyes on him the whole time he saunters to the washroom. Like she knows what he's thinking. He winks at her, shuts the door behind him. Gonna be a long night, he thinks, baring his teeth to the mirror and rubbing them half-clean with the meat of his index finger.

Gonna be a long night.

6

Fun at the Terminal

Morning.

Manu wakes coughing from a dream of thick cigar smoke to a smothering cloud of fabric over his face. He claws at it, gasping, and finds pants. Shirts.

Across the room, Beni and Oriol are laughing over mugs of coffee. Gia's standing at the foot of his cot with a faint smile. A pecking order is clearly being established.

Manu takes a deep breath.

He doesn't care about pecking orders. They just keep you from noticing who you should really be paying attention to.

He examines the garments to find mediocre fabrics, modern styles. Boring colors: grays and blues. "Looks like they'll fit," he says. He swings his legs over the side of his cot, makes no note he's annoyed.

His foot hits something familiar — his gear bag. He unseals it and paws through the contents. No weapons, what a surprise, but the rest of his stuff is there. It'll do.

Manu locks himself in the washroom and checks his comm, but there's no message from Sylla. No message from his landlady, either, so maybe Sylla hasn't yet torched his apartment in anger. That's a good sign.

For a fraction of a second he thinks of messaging Sylla to see if she'll water his jadau plant, but the impulse towards self-destruction flames out as soon as it strikes. Don't push her buttons, Manu. Don't make her think you're joking about this job.

Don't let on you know how serious the stakes are.

He can't get the cloying reek of cigar smoke out of his nostrils, and he sniffs at the clothes Gia brought him to see if it's something there or if it's just a trick of the brain, lingering from his dream.

He knows the smoke — it's his grandma's, the brand she used to smoke during the long hours of his childhood he spent under her care. The brand's old-fashioned, but he still catches whiffs of it sometimes and is transported back to her house in an instant, heart dropped out of his chest like he's nine again and he and Siggy are tiptoeing through that magical wonderland their grandmother called home.

He remembers it as a maze: every garment Grandma ever owned folded neatly in teetering piles when her closet became too full; the packaging materials for every item she might want to return someday shoved in the corner, though those items had worn out years before; dusty glass bottles stacked in crates to exchange at a corner store long gone out of business.

It was stuffed with the fascinating odds and ends she'd brought home, no rhyme or reason but that she might need them someday. She had seven brooms, three electric tea kettles, fourteen obsolete comms. A complete set of a child's novelty luggage printed with tourist scenes from Indira and slapped with slogans: Visit the Green Planet. No place to sit.

He understood now that she'd been future-proofing her life, clinging to anything and everything she might need, clinging to her sons and her grandchildren with a death grip. And the same blind eye that meant she couldn't be convinced to throw out the coat with the torn-off sleeve meant she couldn't see what her sons were doing to her grandchildren, no matter how Siggy started to vanish and Manu to go surly.

She couldn't choose between two broke-down armchairs, let alone choose between her drunk-ass sons and her crimeless grandchildren.

Manu's not a hoarder — not of things, not of people.

You can't keep hold of anybody. He'd learned that trying to keep hold of Siggy. Trying to keep hold of Marisa. People won't choose you, so why bother choosing them?

He washes up in the sink, brushes his teeth, changes into the new clothes. Reapplies his eyeliner, adding a streak of cobalt blue along the upper lash line just to annoy Gia.

Grins into the mirror until the cut on his cheek cracks faintly.

Everything about this job feels like a death trap — including the memories it's dredging up.

Let's get this done and get out.

GIA WAVES him over as he drops his bag on his cot. "You'll come with me to pick up the gear," she says.

Across the room, Beni and Oriol are conferring with Toshiyo. "What're they up to?" Manu says.

"Reconnaissance. Toshiyo's hacked the hotel's main

security feeds, but there's a secondary system she hasn't been able to patch into. Needs a man on the ground. C'mere. Let me fix that cheek."

"Maybe later."

Way she's watching him, Manu wonders if she knows where he got it. Wonders if she's in with Kai. Wonders if she got the same threats from Kai and Jaantzen to get her cooperation, or if she joined up willing and able.

For a moment there's a hesitation in her expression that borders on genuine compassion, but the moment vanishes. "Yeah, I ain't walking around the terminal with you looking like that. Come here."

And he finds himself sitting on her cot while she rummages through her gear. A cool smear of knitting gel, and he can feel the local anesthetic kicking in to numb the sting as the gel dissolves the scabs. Gia swabs his jawline to catch a rolling bead of new blood.

"You grew up in Bulari, yeah?" she asks.

"You tell that by the accent, or my charming disposition?"

"I can tell by how full you are of yourself. Just like every Bulari boy I ever met."

"Glad I live up to expectations."

Gia ignores him and pulls a device the size of her thumb out of her bag. She twists it and the end glows blue; it's soothingly warm when she presses it against the cut. His cheek begins to itch. It's maddening.

"How good a surgeon are you?" Manu asks.

Gia's fingers are strong and sure, holding his jaw. "Stop talking, Manu."

"Like, you can reattach nerves with your eyes closed? Or mostly battle-trained?"

Battle-trained is his working theory. She's got a tattoo in the crook of the elbow: two bars across a half circle looks like a setting sun. Redrock Prison. It's the prison the Indiran Alliance has north of the impassable Jupari Desert belt, where they mostly take terrorists and other riffraff they capture off-planet and don't want to ship all the way home to Indira. They got the concession from New Sarjun a century ago somehow, and no amount of fuss these days will make them give it back.

Tattoo like that from Redrock, this Giaconda probably fought in an anti-Alliance skirmish or two. Some slum kid like himself, radicalized against the man.

But:

"I trained at Sulila," Gia says, like it's nothing. She tilts his head with her fingers, examining her work. "I've never tried to reattach nerves with my eyes closed, but given how many times I've done it with my eyes open, I'd trust me blindfolded over most anybody else you could find."

Manu lets himself look impressed — it isn't hard, and Gia deserves it.

Sulila is ridiculously elite and hardcore religious — though the latter is nothing he's sensing off Gia. There aren't many who can afford to pay for Sulila Corp.'s medical school on their own, and it's expensive enough that few of their graduates ever earn out their indentures. Whoever bought Gia's could still be looking for her, time spent in Redrock or no.

At least once a day, Manu finds himself grateful that he dropped out of Hypatia's Carama Town school and started working for his dad the bookie. God only knows what kind of trouble he'd be in if he'd gotten himself an indenture.

"I suppose you'll do in a pinch," he jokes, and Gia only raises an eyebrow and begins to swab off the wound.

"The scar's still visible, but it should heal up to nothing so long as you stay out of the sun and stop pissing people off," Gia says, stepping back to look at him critically. "Though that seems like a long shot. You need to work on your game with the ladies."

"My game with the ladies is just fine," Manu says.

"Well then I just ain't your type."

He shoots her a glance. "What, you don't like guys?"

"I'm not gullible."

"You just ain't learned to like me yet."

Gia pulls her comm out of her pocket, starts typing something in. "Just a sec," she says. "Gotta make a note to pick up an extra case of bandages. Might need it, you keep annoying me."

Manu kicks back and stretches his arms up high overhead; he catches her quick glance at his abs before she turns away.

"Worthwhile investment," he says.

GEORDI JIMENEZ TERMINAL is in a fairly seedy part of town, near the warehouses and the shipping yards. Manu hasn't spent much time here, apart from the occasional need to get a specialty weapon or two. In fact, the last time he was here was to pick up the gear he used to tear up the Bronze Room.

Those had been fun.

"You know what this plan is missing," he says. "Explosives. We can still get me a dozen of those hornet tags. I know a guy."

Gia gives him side-eye. "You know what I really hate doing?" she asks. "Fixing up people who've been exploded."

"I've never gotten myself exploded."

"Yeah? In my experience, most idiots haven't until it happens to them." She steers him around a drunk passed out in the stairwell.

"What are we picking up, if not explosives?" Manu asks, acting incredulous.

Gia shoots him a look. "There are so many other things," she says. "Besides explosives. Neural stunners, for example. Simple. Effective. Don't require a lot of cleanup on the doctor's end."

"Neural stunners don't make a loud bang."

"Stealth. Look it up."

"Neural stunners are boring."

Gia rolls her eyes. "Sometimes boring is a blessing, kid."

They've gone down to level C, and it's like a carnival down here: loud and echoey, the sounds of laughter, slamming doors, shouted curses pinging off the high metal walls and cavernous ceiling. Gia says something he can't hear. Manu leans towards her. "What?" he shouts.

"I said it's all the way at the end," she shouts back.

He follows her, threading through the throngs of people. It's the middle of the day, which is one of the better times to do business in level C of the terminal. Get out of the heat and the dust of Bulari's midday scorchers, get underground where it's naturally cool.

And, at midday, the lunch stands are running at full speed. Sizzling fat and clinking silverware, the shouts of vendors hawking fried noodles, samosas, anticuchos. Manu's stomach grumbles. There's nothing to eat at the warehouse but a pile of military-grade ration packs and coffee substitute with no sugar. Maybe they'll have time to sample the food carts afterwards.

Their destination is almost all the way to the end of

the terminal, where you find the businesses that don't rely on foot traffic. It's quieter here, the crowd orbiting mainly around the food carts and other services near the entrance.

Here are the shipping companies, the small cargo brokers, the salvage ops who don't need a more visible spot in the terminal because their commerce comes from word of mouth spread through Bulari's underbelly. Most of the stalls at this end are shuttered, metal grates rolled down and locked.

Gia's checking numbers on the stalls; she pauses in front of C-746. It's shuttered, but she knocks on the grate. The silence goes on for too long.

"We got the right time, yeah?"

Gia nods, but doesn't answer. She's tense, fingers itching towards the holster on her hip. Manu checks his own weapons — she gave him a pair of pistols once they were on the road — then scans the room around them. Yawns.

"Who are these guys?" He hadn't bothered asking earlier; he didn't think she would tell him. But now he can scent her nerves and it's put her off-balance. Opened up just the slightest chink in her armor against him. It's times like these when people find him helpful.

"Contacts I was given."

Given. That explains some of her unease. "By Jaantzen?"

"You ask a lot of questions."

"I get that a lot," Manu says.

A metal *snick* sounds from the other side of the grate, and the door rolls up with a clatter.

There's three people inside. The one who rolled up the grate, and two others, a man and a woman, both casually armed with vicious-looking pulse carbines.

Manu smiles and opens his hands, nonthreatening. Gia lifts her chin at them in greeting.

"Good morning," she says. "I trust the weapons aren't necessary."

The man who rolled up the grate just shrugs. He's scrawny, shaved head, metallic-ink tattoos winding around his wrists. "We ain't met you before. Ain't gonna take chances."

"We're not here to make trouble," Gia says. "We already gave you half the money. Soon as we see the goods, the other half is yours."

The man purses his lips over his shoulder. "Goods are over there."

The other two stand back to let them pass back into the stall. Back into a death trap, Manu thinks.

He glances at Gia; she's thinking the same thing. "I'd like to take a look at it here in the light, if you don't mind."

She wins the staring match. The two thugs put down their weapons and bring forward a crate, set it near the entrance to the stall.

The tattooed man leans forward to type a code into the lock, and the top of the crate slides open. Manu stands back to cover Gia while she checks the contents. She pulls out two empty duffel bags, roots through the rest. "It looks like it's all here."

"Of course it is," the tattooed man says.

While Manu keeps an eye on the thugs, Gia piles the contents of the crates into the two duffels. She pulls out her comm. "I'm having the money transferred."

The tattooed man nods, waiting. A soft chime; he pulls out his own comm. "I see it."

"So we're good, then," Gia says. She hands one of the duffels to Manu. Easy way she lifted it, he wasn't prepared for just how heavy it is. He shoulders it with a huff. Tattoos gives him a smirk; Manu ignores it. Let them think he's weak. More opportunities that way.

He shifts the duffel so his hands are free and the weight is good.

"Of course," Tattoos says. "Wouldn't wanna hold you up. I hear you got plans."

Gia stills. "What kind of plans have you heard about?"

Tattoos breaks into a long, slow grin. "Hear you got plans with the queen bee."

The queen bee?

"I haven't heard anything about that," Gia says, dismissive, and it's so casual Manu can't tell if she's lying.

Tattoos just raises an eyebrow. "No worries. May fortune smile on you," he says, and even before he's finished the sentence Gia's dropped her duffel and has him in a headlock, a pistol digging into his temple.

Manu and the two hired guns are slower to move, but he's quicker than them both and has his pistols out and pointed before they've quite caught on.

"Gia," Manu says.

"What the fuck's your problem?" Tattoos gasps.

"Why did you say that?" Gia asks, pistol digging harder. Tattoos puts his hands up. The hired guns have their attention on Manu's weapons. This is not going well.

"Gia," Manu says again. "What is this?"

"I want to know why he said that."

"Just a saying." Sweat is beading up on Tattoos' scalp; a trickle runs down his nose and splashes onto the concrete. "Just a thing you say, someone you know's going into battle."

A beat, then Gia slams her pistol back into its holster,

lets Tattoos rise. But she keeps hold of his wrist, pushes his sleeve up to see his forearm.

One of the tattoos glimmers with microscopic opalescent beads embedded in the ink. The bulk of the image is clinging strands of red-blossomed devilweed, drawn so that the thorns seem to pierce his arm and draw blood. Three symbols are scrawled there in among the vines — Manu doesn't recognize them.

"'Money, beauty, death,'" says Gia. She lets go, shoulders her duffel bag again. "Come on," she says to Manu.

He covers her until she's out of the storage unit, then takes a few steps back himself. Tattoos seems mad, yeah, but mostly just confused. He doesn't look like he's about to kill them.

Manu hopes.

He's been wrong more than once this week.

"Sorry about all that, folks," he says. "Definitely owe you a drink next time."

"Get out," Tattoos spits, and Manu gives him a rueful smile, holsters his right pistol, keeps the dominant left ready to go.

But Tattoos just slams down the rolling door. Manu breathes a sigh of relief. He's sweating now, the scent sharp and raw.

Gia's on the move.

"What the fuck was that?" Manu says when he catches up with her. The way Gia is walking, heads are raising in Manu's peripheral vision, jackals scenting adrenaline on the wind. Manu grabs her arm. "You're calling attention," he says, and she glances at him. Slows.

"Sendera Dathúil," Gia says, like he should know what that means.

"What?"

"Dathúil," she repeats, like maybe he just hadn't heard her.

"And what the hell are they?"

"Redrock gang." She's walking fast again. Manu catches her arm and forces her back into the moment. "Started in Redrock, at least. Religious nuts. Believe some crazy shit about the end times."

"And they run weapons, too."

"Apparently."

Manu doesn't know what Jaantzen's getting them into, but he doesn't care. Right now, they just need to get out of here with the gear, and without a firefight. Gia's walking calmer, now, and everyone's ignoring them. The Sendera-whoever idiots aren't following them, but he can't know if they've called ahead, so he's scanning the room for anything he can find. For any body language out of place.

He's scanning, and he sees a lone woman taking her lunch at a noodle counter, twirling her ramen daintily with a fussy gesture Manu recognizes even before he sees her face.

He whirls, pivoting on his heel to dive deeper in the crowd, but it's already too late. Those wide, fox-brown eyes meet his in surprise, and she's fumbling for her comm, sloshing noodles over the bar in her hurry.

Jaxie, Sylla Mar's third in command.

Manu's melted into the crowd, but Jaxie spotted him for sure.

This is shaping up into a bad day.

7

Pickup Lines

BACK AT THE RANCH, GIA STOPS THE SPINNER BUT doesn't move to get out. Manu gives her a look. The sharp line of her jaw is tense, a cord of muscle taut under her midnight skin. "We getting our stories straight first?" he asks when she doesn't seem ready to say anything.

Gia gives him a long, slow look. "Let me say my piece about Sendera Dathúil. I'm the one's got a problem with them. You just stay out of it."

"If they're so bad, why haven't I heard about them?"

Gia's quiet a minute. "You have," she says. It's a long time before she speaks again, but Manu waits.

"You know that ambassador's kid that got kidnapped last spring?" she asks. "That was them."

Manu raises an eyebrow. Of course he'd heard about that — everyone had. The kidnappers had taken the ransom, but still nobody'd found the kid.

"You think Jaantzen knew who they were when he set you up with them?"

He's using "you" deliberately, pushing her buttons.

Trying to gauge the depth of her loyalty to Jaantzen. Toshiyo is clearly on the man's team, Beni and Oriol are clearly in it for the cash. Kai's in it for the power, but Manu can't figure out why Gia's here. She's putting on that mercenary vibe, same as Beni and Oriol, but there's something in the way she watches Jaantzen when he's in the room that makes Manu wonder if she doesn't owe him something deeper than work for hire.

Maybe she's got a debt to pay off, just like Manu.

"You think he knew you had a problem with them?"

But she only holds out a hand for his pistols. "I'm not here to think," Gia says, sharp and angry. And just like that her armor's back on.

Armor's on, but the way she slams the spinner into its dock shows he's hit a nerve. Some core of trust she used to have with Jaantzen has been broken.

A deep one, too, by the way her anger's got her seeing short, her attention only on what's in front of her nose — and what's raging in her mind.

Isn't that just perfect.

Gia's got her back to him for only a second, but it's all Manu needs to slip his hand inside the bag and grab a knife. He sticks it sheath and all down the back of his pants and shrugs his jacket into place before Gia turns around again.

The handle's awkward, digging painfully into his spine, but he doesn't care. He has a weapon.

It's all part of his brilliant plan:

Step One: Find a weapon.

Step Two: Find a way to be alone with Willem Jaantzen.

Step Three: Kill Jaantzen, earning the wrath of the very dangerous people involved with this job.

Step Four: Head home to Sylla Mar, who might be so angry she kills him anyway.

Step Five: Fame and glory.

Or something like that.

Manu shoulders the bag and leads the way towards the door, feeling Gia fall into step behind him. Killing Jaantzen was a terrible idea when Sylla suggested it to him, and it's an even more terrible idea now.

Manu has a sinking feeling about his plan.

But at least he has a knife.

———

INSIDE THE WAREHOUSE, Toshiyo's sitting in front of one of her monitors; she glances in their general direction as Manu and Gia enter, but doesn't acknowledge them. "That's it," she says. "To the left."

Willem Jaantzen is there, arms crossed, standing over her shoulder. If one of the most notorious criminals in Bulari had been standing over his shoulder like that, Manu would have been jumpy as hell, but Toshiyo's relaxed. Or just absorbed in her work.

Jaantzen glances over at Manu and Gia. "Success?" he asks.

"All good," Manu answers. He sets his duffel on the table and stands back as Kai shoulders in to look things over.

"No, to the left," Toshiyo says.

She and Jaantzen are watching a POV camera on one monitor — it must be Oriol, judging by the ritzy interior of the Blue Falcon's lobby. On the second monitor, a shaky feed is jostling as Oriol adjusts a miniature camera. On the side of the screen, four of the six camera angles are already turned on, showing them nearly everything that Toshiyo hadn't been able to hack into.

"Right there," Toshiyo says, and Oriol clicks his tongue against the roof of his mouth twice in acknowledgement. The feed on the second monitor stills as Oriol adheres the miniature camera into place. Toshiyo leans in to study the feed. "Perfect," she says. She taps a button and the newest feed fills the fifth slot on the side of the screen.

"Last one is the entrance cam," Toshiyo says. "I need you to position it — right, you see that girl with the purple hair?" Two clicks. "Put the camera under the bartop, just below her elbow."

"I hope you've been practicing your pickup lines, Mr. Sina," Jaantzen says, and Oriol just sighs.

Manu grins. This oughta be good.

Jaantzen turns, mutes his mic. "And did everything go as planned on your end, Mr. Juric?"

On Oriol's POV feed, the purple-haired woman's face fills the monitor. She looks up, annoyed. Oriol's off to a good start.

"No problems," Manu says. Depending on your definition of problem, at least — they got away squeaky clean, though who can tell what will come down the pipeline as a result of Gia's little altercation and Jaxie spotting him.

Doesn't matter. The knife digs into his back as he shifts. "Got the goods, hit the road."

"What was your estimation of our contacts?" Jaantzen asks.

Is this a trap? Manu's working it through. Does Jaantzen know the men were Sendera Dathúil? Would he have cared? Probably not — he's got a reputation for using the worst and darkest crews.

Anyway, who Jaantzen uses for supply is not his problem. His problem is getting out of here alive and without getting on the shit list of every powerful person in Bulari: Jaantzen, Sylla, this new Sendera gang, whoever.

"Weapons smugglers." Manu shrugs. "Seedy, but I never met one seemed honest. It's just the business."

"Would you use them again?"

"Nah," Manu says. "Bigger chip on their shoulder than I normally like. Seem the type that business could get personal too quick. And that ain't my style."

Jaantzen nods thoughtfully. "Thank you for your input, Mr. Juric."

"Course." And because he will never learn to stop nosing around, he adds, "Friends of yours?"

Jaantzen gives him an evaluating look, and Manu assumes he won't get an answer. But, "No," Jaantzen finally says. "They came recommended by the financier."

The financier. Fascinating. Well, at least Gia wouldn't have to be pissed at Jaantzen for picking those assholes to deal with. Not that he should care, he reminds himself.

Oriol's voice comes soft from the monitors. "Oh, you're from Arquelle?"

"Shit, she's from Arquelle," Manu says. He leans closer to the screen to watch Oriol get destroyed, and to break eye contact with Jaantzen. The man's giving him a searching look — not like he knows what Manu's got planned, but something different. Something Manu can't put his finger on. It's making him uncomfortable.

"My sister just moved to Arquelle," Oriol says.

"Nonono," Toshiyo says. "More to your right."

Oriol's POV feed shifts as he leans in; on the screen, the purple-haired woman rolls her eyes, goes back to reading on her comm.

"You on-planet for long?" Oriol asks.

"Please leave me alone," the woman answers without looking up. "Or I'll call security."

"A little back to your left," says Toshiyo, leaning in to the feed with a frown. "No, left. Left left. There."

"Supposed to be a dust storm coming tonight," Oriol says, and Manu groans.

The shaky feed stabilizes at the entrance.

"All right. Get out of there, Oriol," Toshiyo says.

"Well, it was good talking to you. Enjoy your stay." Oriol's feed turns away from the woman just as she gives him another glare.

"Beni, he's on his way out," Toshiyo says.

Jaantzen steps back. "That was well done, thank you, Ms. Ravi," he says. "I'll be back shortly to go over the rest of the plan."

The knife is itching in the waistband of Manu's pants.

"Can I get a word with you, boss?" he asks. As far as pickup lines go, it's an oldie but a goodie.

Jaantzen turns to him, slow and measured like he sees all the way through the little charade Manu is trying to play.

But he nods. Buttons his suit jacket. Holds an arm out to the balcony.

The same door Kai wasn't worried he'd escape out of, the one with no exits.

Showtime.

8

Team Player

Last time Manu was alone with Jaantzen, he wasn't standing on his own two feet like a man. He wasn't armed. He was at Jaantzen's entire mercy.

Maybe he still is, but at least he feels like he's got a better control of his destiny right now.

They walk out onto the balcony. Manu hasn't had a chance to evaluate it by daylight, but it looks like his initial examination from last night still stands: There's no way off this balcony without a fifty-foot drop to the pavement below. Kai and Gia are back in the warehouse, and neither of them will hesitate to take him out if they think he killed Jaantzen.

The only way he makes it back through that warehouse and out the door into freedom is by doing Jaantzen's job, or through some pretty fancy lying.

Fortunately, Manu's a pretty good liar.

"Mr. Juric." There's no follow-up, and Manu assumes that's Jaantzen's way of asking him what the hell he wants.

"Just wanted to ask about pay," Manu says. It's the

first thing that comes to mind. "We never did go over a number."

"You'll get a cut, same as the rest of the crew."

Manu's making calculations. He's seen how fast Jaantzen is. Manu thinks he might be faster, but Jaantzen has a gun — and Manu's not sure he'll be so fast Jaantzen couldn't squeeze off a bullet. And even if Manu doesn't get hit, the second a bullet gets fired, Kai and Gia will be at the door to see what's going on.

If he wants to make his move, he needs a stronger element of surprise.

"Like a percentage, or what's the deal?"

"Flat sum," Jaantzen says. "One hundred thousand marks."

Manu lets out a low whistle, impressed in spite of himself. His suspicion from studying Jaantzen's operation has been that Jaantzen's rates are mediocre at best. The sum must be coming from the mystery financier.

"Will that be sufficient, Mr. Juric?" Jaantzen asks. "I understand it's not the half million marks you were expecting to collect, but if this job goes well there's the possibility of ongoing work."

"Sure thing," Manu says. All these numbers are meaningless to him anyway — it's not like he'll see a dime if his plan goes through. And it wasn't about the money in the first place. It was about getting into a crew. Even one as shifty as Sylla's. Had to be better than the increasing risk of getting washed out as an independent.

But the phrase "ongoing work" snags his fancy a moment, and he lets himself consider a future alongside Kai and whatever other Kai-like nasties Jaantzen has in his pocket. Manu's feeling desperate, but is he desperate enough for that?

Jaantzen still hasn't given him an opening. Manu

looks out over the balcony, tries a casual position he hopes Jaantzen might imitate. The other man is still watching him like a hawk. It's like Jaantzen doesn't trust him. Big surprise.

"You aren't still considering other offers, I trust, Mr. Juric."

"Course not. But money talks."

"Are you saying that money can't buy loyalty?" Jaantzen raises an eyebrow, and in a brief moment of shock Manu realizes the big man's making a joke. "My faith in humanity is shattered," Jaantzen says, and then the eyebrow falls, the attempt at humor darkening. "I'll beat any offer your former employer made you, I promise you that. And I also promise you that if you incite a bidding war, I will kill you and anyone you love."

A chill down Manu's spine. He doesn't have many left, and if Marisa was smart she burned all ties to him once she found out what he really did. "Got it." He flashes a smile that Jaantzen does not return.

"Who put you up to the hit on me?"

"I told you I was working on my own."

"What if I told you Sylla Mar is staking out your apartment?"

Then Manu would say she has no sense of self-preservation, spreading their connection around like that. The woman has no brains. "I'd tell you she's pissed cause she asked me out and I told her no."

The corner of Jaantzen's lip quirks upwards; it takes Manu a moment to realize he's smiling. The expression is alien on Jaantzen's face, and there's something else behind it, something Manu doesn't know how to read. He's being evaluated, he can feel that. But no longer for his threat level.

"I appreciate loyalty," Jaantzen says.

Manu doesn't have a quip for that.

Talking with Willem Jaantzen all up close and personal is disconcerting. Manu's perception of the man's been turned on its head — there's that reputation for viciousness and unfairness, which Kai embodies so well. But the way his people react to him — Manu realizes he's starting to think of Toshiyo and Gia as Jaantzen's people, even if the rest are mercenary — is not what Manu expected.

Toshiyo is a mystery of a human being, and her devotion to Jaantzen seems wildly out of character given the man's reputation. Gia seems the sort of hired tough not to care, but somehow she's fiercely protective of Jaantzen.

It's all giving him pause.

Maybe the live-in lady is mellowing the grizzled gangster after all; Manu brushes the thought away. Now isn't the time to think about Jaantzen's girlfriend. Or about Toshiyo, or about Gia.

Manu is missing his chance.

Jaantzen is stepping back, out of Manu's range.

"Hey, can I give you some advice, man?" Manu calls, and it's probably a bad plan, but Jaantzen turns slowly. "Tosh is good, but she's not like the rest of us. You're gonna have to be careful with her, you think she's worth keeping around."

"I'll take your point, Mr. Juric."

He starts to walk away, and Manu knows he should shut up, but it's never been a strong point — and in the middle of a job isn't the time to pick up new habits. Plus, he's about to lose his chance. "She likes you and respects you," he says, and in Jaantzen's profile he sees a flicker of a confusion. "She'll be a good crew member."

Of all the people he's met, Willem Jaantzen is one of

the hardest to read. The man's face is carved like rock but for a muscle twitching at his jawline. A wash of adrenaline floods Manu's chest and gut; the handle of the knife is digging into his kidney, and if Jaantzen turns in anger, maybe, his judgement blown by Manu's overstepping his bounds, Manu might just have the opening he needs.

But Jaantzen just turns back to study him. "Thank you," he says finally. "And would you?"

"Would I what?" Manu frowns, the moment he was supposed to have struck now lost.

"Make a good crew member."

"For the right crew, maybe."

A flurry of activity through the door, and Jaantzen turns to see who's just entered. Beni and Oriol, probably — they wouldn't have been very far out.

Jaantzen's back is broad and open, the perfect target. Manu palms the knife, steels himself to pounce. He's a heartbeat away when Jaantzen shifts and Manu can see the tall woman who's just entered the warehouse.

It's Thala Coeur.

Blackheart herself.

Manu's crisp, action-oriented adrenaline buzz drains into the high, shaky whine of catastrophe averted.

He slips his sweaty palm off the handle of the knife just as Jaantzen turns back to him. "Well, Mr. Juric. Shall we go meet the financier of this little expedition?"

Blackheart is financing this job.

"Sure thing, boss." Manu hears himself say the words, feels his face form an automatic smile. But he almost killed Blackheart's showrunner right before whatever big job she had planned.

He has a long list of people it'd suck to piss off — and a very short list of people it would be fatal to piss off.

That list is Blackheart.

Manu watches Jaantzen's broad, knife-proof back walk away.

He's not going to get another chance — and not just because of Blackheart. Manu knows, without putting a finger on exactly when it happened, that he's lost the ability to do Sylla's job.

Manu takes a deep, shaky breath and goes in to meet his newest new boss.

9

Blackheart

COEUR'S RUST-RED FACE IS IMPASSIVE AS SHE SURVEYS THE warehouse. Half her jet-black braids are woven into a crown; the tips of the rest are capped with gold and jingle as she turns her head. She's wearing slim red trousers and a black blouse that looks like real silk, light catching in soft halos where the fabric pools at her elbows and waist. She's wearing a pair of those silent bioleather training slippers, the kind worn by dancers, or boxers. Or professional thieves.

It's a deceptively soft look. Manu's never seen the woman up close, but she's famous for joining her crew in the boxing ring where they train — and for coming out on top more often than not.

The pale skin on the woman on Coeur's left is the perfect canvas for a tapestry of ink and technology that blend in an unsettling tableau. Gold-coated wires twine from ports in the right side of her shaved scalp, snaking through channels in her metal collar to their terminus in a panel set between her shoulder blades.

She's the greenest thing on New Sarjun: tattoos of

jungle vines and serpents cover every exposed inch of skin on her right side, long-limbed spiders peeking from behind leaves, a wild-fanged monkey leaping from her shoulder. Her mechanical right eye seems to peer from between lush foliage.

Oh. And they're not alone, Manu realizes with a sinking heart. One last depressingly familiar face has followed Coeur in.

Jaxie. Sylla Mar's third in command.

Jaxie catches his eye, grinning.

Manu swears under his breath, but he knows true danger when he sees it. And Thala Coeur is the most dangerous thing in this room. Jaxie and Sylla will just have to wait their turn.

Before anyone can say anything, the door opens again, and it's Beni and Oriol this time, voices raised in the heat of an argument.

The jungle woman at Thala Coeur's side puts her hand on her pistol.

"It's fine," Coeur says, her voice a laughing sing-song.

Oriol lets out a string of curses.

Manu's watching the others to see if they were expecting Blackheart. Oriol's barely muffled profanity marks him as a no. Beni's jaw's on the floor — turns out he recognizes someone in the Bulari underground after all. Kai wears his sourest Kai face. Gia's scowl gets scowlier, but not in surprise. She and Coeur share a measured look, then Coeur looks past, dismissive. Manu's drama radar pings. Damn, he loves a good feud.

Toshiyo doesn't seem to register Blackheart, but she's biting her lip like she's barely holding herself back from asking the tattooed girl if she can play with her tech.

Manu tears his gaze away from Toshiyo, pushing

down the sudden, nagging guilt he feels for how he used her to take down Jaantzen's guard.

Coeur's gaze skims past Manu — skims past everyone else in the room, even Jaantzen, like nobody here's worth caring who they are. He's heard that about her. You gotta prove to her it's worth bothering to learn your name.

Being beneath Blackheart's attention isn't the worst thing that could happen, though — getting her attention for the wrong reason is far, far deadlier.

Getting her attention for the right reason could be gold, though.

"I wasn't expecting a skeleton crew, Willem," she says, finally meeting Jaantzen's gaze. "Or do you have others hiding in the closet?"

"This is the crew. They'll get your job done."

Your job, huh? With Coeur in the equation, the sum Jaantzen's willing to pay makes more sense. Coeur's an extravagant spender, and her money's always good.

She shrugs, and the gold caps on the ends of her braids tinkle softly. "Then it's a good thing I brought reinforcements," she says with a half smile, like she thinks the thunderclouds gathering over Jaantzen's head are funny. She jerks a thumb at each of the new crew in turn. "Jaxie. Sarah."

Manu hears Beni's soft snort. The girl with the tech does not look like a Sarah.

Jaantzen gives Coeur a measured look. "It would have been nice for them to be here for the initial planning," he says mildly.

Coeur just smiles, easy and bright. "Why don't you show me what you've got."

"Everybody gather around," Jaantzen says.

Manu finds a spot around the big, cheap desk in

between Oriol and Beni, away from Toshiyo, and across the table from Jaxie and the other woman so he can watch them less obtrusively. Jaxie slouches into place like a regular thug, but the woman with all the tech has some element of military training to her. Could be the stiff way she holds herself, like maybe her spine is fused with robotics, too. The tattoos, Manu sees now, are there to hide a mass of scars.

She scans the table, her mechanical right eye whirring slightly as it moves. It skims past Manu, pauses on Oriol, who gives her a slight nod of respect, if not recognition. One soldier saluting another, Manu thinks, and files it away for later.

Coeur and Jaantzen stand on opposite sides of the desk, and Manu can feel the dominance game crackling through the air between them. Coeur may have hired Jaantzen to crew this job, but Jaantzen won't be acting like a hired thug.

Manu makes a mental promise not to step in between these two.

Kai, Manu notices, is mirroring Coeur's pose, though he's locked so stiff he's practically vibrating, like a mystix player trying too hard to keep from giving away a good hand. At least someone here is happy to see Blackheart.

"Good to have you all," Jaantzen says. "Ms. Ravi?"

A few clicks on the cheap desk, and Toshiyo brings up a schematic of the neighborhood, complete with the new video feeds Oriol got them.

"We've got a better idea of what's going on in the hotel," Toshiyo says in her charming country drawl. "With our own cameras set up, we'll be first to know when the target is moving. Should be first thing tomorrow morning."

She zooms in on the hologram map; it freezes in a

blur of pixels for a moment, then refreshes. "Normal couriers pick up from the side door," she says. "Word is, what we're after is getting hand-delivered out the front." She sticks a finger in the hologram. "Here."

"And where's it headed?" asks Beni.

"Along a set route," Jaantzen says, and Beni scowls at the nonanswer. Toshiyo types in a code and the route blazes green through the miniature cityscape, vanishing off the edge of the desk without revealing its terminus. Manu's not the only one frowning at the incomplete route line. Who the hell are they stealing from?

"Beni, you'll be positioned here to intercept," Jaantzen says. He sets a location pin in the hologram map, then glances up at Coeur's two new recruits. "With Manu and Jaxie. Kai will follow the courier with Oriol and Sarah. Basic smash and grab — Beni, you run him off the road. Kai pens him in from behind. Disable the driver, take the goods. Rendezvous back here."

"How do we know what to take?" asks Jaxie.

"There's only one crate," says Toshiyo. The hologram sizzles and pops. Toshiyo hits refresh. "Sandstorm's coming, sorry," she says as a loading bar appears above the map of the city. She cracks her ring fingers in unison; they sound like gunshots. Manu glances at the high windows, but of course he can see nothing.

"That's it," says Coeur. Or is she asking?

She's got an airy way with her words, like every sentence is simultaneously a jab and a challenge, her lips constantly on the edge of smiling. Like she sees what's funny and the rest of you haven't got a clue.

"That's it," says Jaantzen.

Manu expects another dominance game between them, but Coeur just steps back from the cheap desk and rolls her shoulders, nice and relaxed.

"Go get 'em, team," she says.

"Everybody rest up," Jaantzen says. "The target's moving early tomorrow, and I want you fresh."

The little crew — Manu can't decide if they're more or less motley with the addition of Sarah and Jaxie — dissolves into the vastness of the warehouse. Kai and Sarah stalk off to confer in the corner, Oriol peels off his shirt again and stakes out a section of floor for his martial arts routine, and Jaxie is watching Manu with a bald-faced "gotcha" grin. Manu turns his back on her — he's not ready to deal with that now.

"You up for a game, man?" Beni's got his deck of holocards out, shuffling them in midair with a snap. The colors shift in a rainbow blur as he bridges the deck. "C'mon. Keeps your mind sharp. And your hands."

"Not tonight," Manu says, and Beni's face falls. "Next time, yeah?" he says apologetically, even though he'd rather spend another night in Jaantzen's murder dungeon than sit through a card game. Just the thought triggers memories of his grandmother's cigars, the claustrophobia of her house, Siggy's gray face, the pointless hours wasted with incomplete decks.

"Your loss," Beni says with a shrug. He cuts the deck with one hand, and heads off to corner Gia.

Toshiyo's the only one still standing by the desk, staring at the frozen loading bar with her hands braced on the edge. Her knuckles are white.

"Hey, Tosh." Manu hovers between staying and leaving when she doesn't answer. This situation is already tangled enough without getting emotional, and the last thing he needs tonight is to indulge in his guilt. But something about the curve of her neck won't let him walk away.

He sighs, and raps his acid-green fingernails against the desk's surface. "Tosh. You doing all right, kid?"

She finally breaks eye contact with the loading bar, blinks up at him. "I'm fine," she lies.

"This isn't your type of crowd."

"Worse types out in the mines." Her accent's stronger when she says it, memory triggering the stamp of the place on her body. She crosses her arms; Manu hears the faint crack of a knuckle out of sight.

Manu frowns at that. "These are some pretty bad types."

"Not all of you. Oriol seems nice." She's got a hint of a smile in her eyes — he almost misses that she's teasing him. He wouldn't have expected it of her, not with her mind seemingly always in her devices.

He likes her, but any friendly feelings she has towards him are just going to lead to trouble for her down the road. He wants to tell her to run, to get out of this mess before it gets her killed, or locked up. Or — worse — breaks and misshapes her into any one of them.

"What are you doing here?" is what he asks instead.

"My job." It's firm. Decisive.

"You don't belong with us," Manu says. "Oriol seems nice, but he's a mercenary. Just like Gia. Just like me." He jerks his chin over his shoulder to where Sarah is locked in a menacing match of scowls with Kai. Even Beni's avoiding them for now. "Just like them."

"You're not all bad. Jaantzen — "

"We're all bad," Manu cuts in. He doesn't want to hear what she thinks about Jaantzen; it tightens the knot in his gut to know what it would have done to her if he'd finished the job an hour ago.

"I feel safe around you," Toshiyo says. "You wouldn't hurt me."

That stabs straight to the core.

"Remember what I told you about not trusting anyone here?" Manu asks, and if the words come out harsher than he intended it's because he's mad at himself more than anything. "That goes double for me, kid."

Her cheeks flame red — whether with anger, with shock, or with sadness he doesn't wait around to find out.

He feels the burn of her gaze between his shoulder blades as he walks away. Directly above the spot where the hilt of the stolen knife still digs into his back.

———————————

10

Professionals

———————————

Manu decides to talk to Oriol. For a break — not business, just conversation. After all, he's the only one who doesn't seem to have three agendas at once. Plus, he's easy on the eyes.

He doesn't get ten steps away from Toshiyo before Jaxie catches him on an intercept course. "Fancy meeting you here," she says.

He keeps walking — Destination: Out of Earshot — and she follows along beside him. "I found you," she says, grinning like she's won first place in an amateur detective contest. Her mass of thin brown dreadlocks is tied in a messy knot at the base of her pale neck; her eyeteeth are lacquered in turquoise and trimmed with gold, filed to have just a bit more point than usual. She's dressed in casual black fatigues and prickly with her usual collection of weapons handles. Manu wonders if he can get one or two away from her.

"Surprise for sure," Manu says.

Jaxie has the presence of mind to make sure no one's listening, though her stage glance around the room

183

screams conspiracy. Fortunately, no one's watching, either. "Word's got around the boxing gyms that Coeur and Jaantzen were looking for some people for a job. Sylla figured this was where you ended up, and when I saw you with her" — a jerk of the chin at Gia across the room — "I figured that's what happened." Jaxie grinned. "So here I am to make sure you finish your job."

Manu gives her a look. "How do you know who Gia is?" He'll stick with polite questions, but really he's dying to ask how she got to be so stupid. She'd kill Jaantzen now, with Coeur in the picture? Risk bringing that wrath down on Sylla? Blackheart'd burn Sylla's entire operation to the ground and be back home by dinner to enjoy a nice glass of wine.

"Nice reward on her head from the Alliance," Jaxie says, and Manu keeps himself from glancing over his shoulder at Gia right now. "Only reason nobody's collected it is she's thick with Jaantzen and he's tough to get through. And ain't many people want to work with the Alliance." She shrugs. "And she's a tough bitch. Hard to take her in a fight."

"That's three reasons."

Jaxie frowns at Manu like she's not sure if he's giving her shit or not.

He is.

Manu only really knows Jaxie by face and reputation — she is a predator, but slow. Sylla doesn't have much in her organization by way of brains, and Jaxie certainly doesn't add to the balance. She's not just in Sylla's crew for looks, though: Manu's seen her fight in a friendly sparring match — "friendly" in quotations. Her opponent had to be carried away.

"Coeur know you normally work for Sylla Mar?"

"Course not," Jaxie says, but Manu doesn't believe it.

Coeur didn't get to the top by being unobservant. And speaking of, she's probably observing right now. Noticing that Manu seems awfully friendly with Sylla's lackey.

Last thing he needs is for Coeur to think he's working with Sylla, because he's not — not anymore. Coeur's fortuitous arrival at the warehouse didn't just spare Jaantzen's life, it gave Manu a second chance.

Because forget Sylla Mar and her excuse for a crew.

If Manu does this job right, he could have a shot at joining the best crew in Bulari. Coeur may be scary as hell, but her crew's known as the tightest family, folks who've actually got your back so long as you do your work well. Unlike Sylla's band of opportunists.

If he can just ignore that knot in his gut.

"I'm here to make sure you finish the job," Jaxie says again, like she can sense he's slipping and the repetition will help reel him back in.

"I'll do it. After this gig is finished."

She frowns at him. "Sylla — "

"Sylla gonna pay you what this job's gonna pay?" That twitch in her cheek says no. "Then we do this job, and I make good with Sylla. All right?"

He doesn't care if she believes him or not. He leaves her standing in the middle of the room, head cocked and frowning.

ORIOL IS GLIDING EFFORTLESSLY over his stretch of the warehouse floor, long, lean muscles giving an impressive display as he moves through his poses. Manu crosses his arms and leans against the wall, appreciating.

Oriol kicks out in a slow, graceful arc, spinning on the ball of one foot, his chiseled abs supporting the stance. "Did you want something?" he asks. He lunges and holds, wrists snapping into place like a dancer. His skin glistens.

"You ever get tired of flying solo?" Manu asks.

Oriol raises an eyebrow and flows into his next form. "What's there to be tired of? The independence? The not having to do shit you don't want to do?"

"The hustling for gigs. The watching your back all the time."

"I been watching my back since before you were born, boy."

Bullshit. Oriol can't have more than a decade on Manu. "How old do you think I am?" he asks.

Oriol holds his new pose just long enough to give Manu a slow smile and an appreciative look. "Old enough."

"It's the eyeliner, isn't it." Manu sighs dramatically. Oriol laughs. "Mama said it made me look older."

There's a tiny pause, and Manu almost wants him to ask: Your mama still alive? Your mama know what you do for a living? Your mama a good cook? Anything so Manu can bare a sliver of soul, say, I never knew the old lady.

But Oriol doesn't ask.

Professionals don't ask.

"You thinking of joining a crew?" is what Oriol does ask.

Manu shrugs. "Kinda have to these days. What do you know about Coeur?"

Oriol gives him a level look; Manu can't tell if he knows the dramatic adventure tale of how he was press-ganged into this little heist. "Know she prefers her people to call her Blackheart," Oriol says. "Working for her would be bread and butter." He drops into a plank, holds it effortlessly with sculpted shoulders and sinewy forearms.

Working for Coeur would be more than bread and butter — it would be a meal ticket for the rest of Manu's career. Granted, there wouldn't be anyplace to go up to, working for her. His career likely wouldn't be too long.

But it's not going to last even another month if he doesn't find himself some sort of crew. Not with the dust storm he's been stirring.

"What are you thinking?" Oriol asks, flowing into another sweeping kick. Manu catches a whiff when he moves: burnt cinnamon and gun solvent.

"That it's not fair. You ain't even breathing hard."

Oriol laughs. A leap, a handclasp, a bow, and he's finished his cycle. He grabs a towel off the edge of his cot and begins a lovely show drying off. The scar over his hipbone stands out like a rope. "I've trained since I was a kid."

"Well, your form's not too bad. There's hope for you yet." Manu pushes himself off his casual stance against the wall. "Military? That why you're so good?"

For a second he doesn't think Oriol is going to answer him — professionals don't talk — but, "Indiran Alliance," Oriol says after a moment. His attention's caught by something past Manu's shoulder, and Manu glances behind him to see the techno-thug, Sarah, talking with Kai and Gia at the other end of the warehouse.

"You and Sarah both, huh?"

Oriol frowns, as though he's not sure how Manu knew. Most people aren't aware of a fraction of the information their body language broadcasts, Manu's found.

"Yeah, looks like," Oriol says. "Tech like what she's

got isn't normally civilian." He tosses aside the towel and pulls on a shirt, then sits on his cot. Manu sits across from him, not waiting for invitation.

"You serve out your indenture?"

"Disability discharge. Then an old buddy needed some security and I needed some cash. And now?" Oriol doesn't say more, just waves a hand around the warehouse as if to say, And this is where I ended up.

Manu doesn't have to ask about the injury. The way Oriol's thumb started rubbing his hip, it must be whatever intriguing scar runs below his waistband. Maybe after all this wraps up Manu will get a chance to learn more about it. He sincerely hopes so.

"How about you?"

"Me? Nah, no military for me."

Oriol rolls his eyes. "I can see that, kid. I meant how did you get into the business?"

Marisa's the only person Manu's ever told the truth to. They'd finally had the "This is what I do, this is how I got here" conversation, which ended with her begging him to get out of the business, him refusing, and her parents calling the cops. Good times.

"My cousin got in with this abusive asshole a few years back," he says before he regrets not saying it. "She got pregnant and tried to leave him, so he killed her." Manu clears his throat. "He was my first hit."

Oriol whistles, low. "Good for you."

Manu hasn't told this story enough to dull it up yet, and he didn't expect the stab of pain, like the moment's still fresh-cut and razor-sharp. Those guilty feelings about Toshiyo must be dredging up company; Manu's having trouble pushing back the memory of Siggy's papery palm cooling in his hand.

For one wild moment he wants desperately to turn

Oriol into a confessor. To peel back a little of the bandage and show the wound — like he tried to do with Marisa before that all blew up in his face. *I tried to tell her he was no good*, he wants to say, or, *I figured if she could handle her dad all those years she could handle him*, or, *She told me she loved him.*

But Oriol? Oriol's a professional.

Manu's a professional.

"Too little too late," is what Manu finally says, with a wave of his hand. "Anyway, turns out the asshole was in deep with a local gang and they had a bounty out on him. They paid me off and asked if I'd work another job for them. Not like I had anything else going on, so I said yes." He spreads his arms. "Almost five years later, look at me. Working with the best."

"I'm flattered."

Manu winks. "I was talking about Blackheart."

Oriol doesn't return his levity. "I know you were," he says, and for a moment there's something weary behind his gaze. "Tell you what, kid. You wanna join a crew, that's your call. Just don't do anything stupid to get on some boss's good side."

Way too late for that.

Manu wants to ask why, pry at that tiny chink in Oriol's armor. For a moment, the way Oriol's watching him, Manu thinks he might even just answer.

But that kind of intimacy isn't just frowned upon by professionals — it's dangerous. Distracting.

"Thanks for the advice, old-timer," is what Manu says, and the moment is gone.

Oriol shakes his head in faux outrage. "Old-timer? How old do you think I am?"

"Not too old." Manu glances over his shoulder. "But

old enough to see we're not being told everything about what's going on."

A shrug. "Of course we aren't. Name of the game. Here." Oriol reaches into the duffel at the foot of his bed, pulls out a clear bottle filled with brown liquid. It's a familiar label — not the cheapest whiskey, but not the priciest, either. Something Manu himself would have bought.

He takes the offered bottle and Oriol's fingers brush up against his companionably. Oriol's watching him, those honey-gold eyes catching the light.

Manu smiles. Sips. Hands it back. "What's next for you?" he asks.

"I never think about the next job in the middle of the current job," he says.

"That's not true," Manu says. "Everybody's always got the next plan brewing. You got somebody waiting back for you, or what's next?"

"Thought I might lie low for a while. Get some relaxation on somewhere."

"That sounds good."

"I know it does. You oughta think about the same."

"Is that an invitation?"

Oriol just shrugs, but the way he tilts his head says yes.

"I'll check my calendar," Manu says.

Manu almost doesn't hear it when she calls, that tentative alto not quite rising above the rest of the group's clamor. He lifts a hand, and Oriol falls silent beside him.

"Uh, guys?" Toshiyo calls again, a little louder this time. She hasn't left the cheap desk, and she's hunched over her strange hand terminal, eyes wide with worry. Manu's halfway across the room before he realizes he's moving; across the warehouse, Jaantzen shoulders past Kai.

"What is it?" Jaantzen's voice booms where hers is timid, and the rest of the chatter in the warehouse fades away.

"They're on the move," Toshiyo says. "It's showtime."

11

We're a Go for Trouble

"Now?" That's Kai.

Toshiyo just blinks at him. She's thumbing commands into her hand terminal with her right hand, cupping her left over her ear to help her listen in better to whatever she's got going on.

"Now?" Kai growls again.

"Let her work," Manu snaps, and Kai rounds on him with teeth bared.

"Let her work," a voice echoes, and Manu's surprised to see it's Coeur. She glances at him only briefly as she turns to study Toshiyo. Kai falls silent beside her, chin dropping.

Well.

Manu glances at Jaantzen, but he doesn't seem to notice his bulldog's come to heel for Coeur.

"The courier company's moving the package," Toshiyo says, ignoring everyone except for the voices in her earpiece and whatever she sees on her hand terminal.

"Have they changed routes?" Jaantzen asks.

"No, boss. Just delivery times."

"Why?"

"Not sure. Could be because of the storm coming in."

"You find out, you let me know."

"Yeah, boss."

"Then the job's still on as discussed," Jaantzen says. "Kai, Oriol, you're with Sarah in the truck. Manu, Jaxie, you're with Beni."

Manu catches the earpiece Gia tosses him — they're all getting one, except for Sarah, who taps a sequence into her gauntlet. Oriol's popped a caffeine tab under his tongue; he sees Manu notice and offers up the package. Manu shakes his head. Caffeine doesn't play well with his natural adrenaline, and he's got plenty of that going at the moment.

"Where's she going?" Jaxie says, thumbing over her shoulder at Gia.

"Gia's either making sure you don't get shot up, or fixing you if you do," says Jaantzen. "Your choice."

"I'll take the former," Manu says.

"Then you best stop testing me, boy," Gia answers. She tosses the last of the earpieces to Jaxie and grins at Manu; she looks like the goddess of war on the eve of battle. How this one was ever accepted to a religious academy like Sulila is beyond him. "Here," she says, and hands him a thumb-sized neural stunner. "I been saving this for you."

Manu turns it over in his palm: it's a matte-black rubber bracelet with a pair of nodes on the side about fifteen millimeters apart. It's the type off-planet women wear discreetly on their wrists when they go out slumming in Bulari. Manu lifts an eyebrow at Gia. "Gee. Thanks."

"Less mess when you deal with the driver," she says. She's got one on her own wrist, like she couldn't just knock any asshole out with one good punch from her well-muscled arms.

No one asks where Coeur is going to be — far away and out of the line of fire is what's understood. Manu's surprised she even bothered to show up at the warehouse, and wonders again just what's in this shipment.

None of his business, is what.

Manu pops in his earpiece and has a strange out-of-body sensation as Toshiyo speaks both in his ear and across the desk.

"Testing," says Toshiyo, repeating herself as they gear up. She frowns at Sarah. "Do you — "

"I gotcha," Sarah says, tapping a finger on the panel behind her right ear. "Loud and clear." Toshiyo stares at her in naked fascination.

"All right. I'll be keeping an eye on the transport from here and direct you where to go."

They break apart into teams; as Manu's waiting for Jaxie and Beni to finish suiting up, he spots Coeur standing by herself, the light pooling in the soft drape of her black silk blouse to highlight the topography of muscles beneath. Her arms are crossed; the long, scarred red-brown fingers of one hand tap an impatient rhythm.

Manu licks his lips, makes the move. "Wanted to say thank you for the opportunity," he says, and Coeur's gaze drifts onto him like a feather, light and impermanent; he's no threat to her.

She's drinking him in, filing him away, and Manu stays relaxed, lets his body fall into the same casual stance as hers, mirroring the angle of her hips, his hands in his pockets. Not a troublemaker — he's useful. Friendly.

"Good to see new talent," she says finally. "You and me, we'll talk when this is all over. I like me some fresh blood from time to time."

"Sounds good," he says, with little bow of his head to show he appreciates she's doing him a favor.

His pride should be buzzing — he's getting the green light from his dream boss — but it's not untying that knot in his gut.

He glances back at the desk and sees Toshiyo watching him, disappointment clear on her face. When he meets her gaze, she looks away and does not turn back.

Manu shakes it off. It's not like he was on her side, or Jaantzen's side, or even Sylla's side. Maybe Coeur's side's a bit rotten, but it's no worse than any other.

And if so, then why does he feel no better than his grandma? Choosing poorly by failing to choose at all?

Goddamn this job and what it's dredged up.

"Manu."

He spins to find Gia, grateful for the interruption of his thoughts.

"I grabbed this from your gear," she says, and slips a package into his hand. He pockets it without looking, knowing by touch that familiar roll of adhesive-backed tags and miniature remote controller. The last of his hornet tags. Manu grins.

"I already regret giving you this," Gia says. "You look way too happy."

"I'll do you proud," he says, and gets only a shaking head in return.

"Just keep yourself off my table."

"Got it, Giaconda."

He winks and walks away before she can answer.

Jaxie and Beni are waiting for him, now; Beni shouts at him from the door to hurry up.

"Good luck," Coeur calls to Jaantzen, and her brilliant smile beams a fraction of a second too slow. No love lost there, Manu realizes. But then, what he hears, there's no love lost between anyone in the business and Jaantzen.

Except for Toshiyo.

And except for Gia; Manu sees her solemn nod to the big gang boss as she walks past.

Manu gives him a deep nod, too. Respectful. He means it, no matter what brought them together and where their paths may go from here.

"Good luck," Manu says to Toshiyo, and gets only a cool look in return.

He tells himself it's a good thing. That he's only helping sour her on a business she shouldn't be in in the first place.

He tells himself that no matter what he's heard about Jaantzen, the man seems to honestly care about Toshiyo. And anyway, Gia's got her back — and she's the fiercest woman he's ever met.

He feels like shit.

12

Heisting

IT'S DARK OUTSIDE, DUSTY, A SANDSTORM BLOWING DOWN
from the desert and into the Bulari Valley so that the
whole city is blanketed in a faint haze. It probably made
for a romantic blood-red sunset from the decks of high-
rise tourist bars earlier this evening, but now it's got plans
for mischief. Manu can't tell if the constant rumble of
cargo shuttles and magtrucks out of the spaceport is shut
down, what with the wind. Probably.

Manu coughs; beside him, Jaxie sneezes in a series of
short, ridiculous bursts. When she gets herself under
control she gives the rest of the group a feral glare, light
glinting off her turquoise-and-gold incisors. No one
comments.

Manu's got a nice breathing mask back at his apartment, one of the better biosilk ones, but he hadn't
brought it with him to bust up the Bronze Room. He
hadn't realized he was going to get into such a fun new
adventure.

He'll be better prepared next time.

He gives Oriol a salute, then lets Jaxie shoulder past

him to take the front seat in Beni's spinner. He'd rather be in the back keeping an eye on them, anyway.

Out into the road, and Beni's driving fast and loose while Toshiyo's voice echoes through their earpieces with updates on the courier's route. Beni handles the spinner like the pro Jaantzen said he was — Manu guesses all those games of cards must indeed be good for the mind and the hands.

Jaxie lets out another round of the ridiculous sneezes, bitches about hating sandstorms. Manu ignores her.

Their position is marked by a glowing green dot in the faint hologram of the city superimposed over the windshield, but once Manu gets his bearings he doesn't need to follow it to know where they are.

This is his city and he's in the zone, following their route in his mind even as his vision glazes at the flashing images outside the window. Store lights are soft glows in the haze.

Manu's never been off-world — hell, he's never left Bulari — and he's not sure he wants to. But something about Oriol's soft accent, and the idea of emerald rice paddies and actual oceans sending in storms and hurricanes rather than the whirling dust storms sent in by the Jupari Desert — it sounds awfully nice right about now.

"He just reached Pioneer Plaza, turning left onto Mahti Drive."

Toshiyo's voice comes staticky through his earpiece, bringing him back to the moment. They're getting close — he blinks to refocus his eyes and lets the blur outside resolve into familiar scenery.

Beni takes a sharp right into an alley; Manu sways with the motion of the spinner. In the front seat, Jaxie is muttering to herself as she checks her weapons.

"Hold tight," Beni says, and Manu digs into the

handholds. Beni skids the spinner around the corner, drifting into the path of the courier van. Manu braces himself for impact, but the van skids to a halt, swerving to miss Beni and crashing into a low retainer wall with a screech and a spark of electronics.

Beni dances the spinner out of range as a second crash sounds — Sarah's vehicle smashing into the back of the van.

Manu's first out of the spinner, guns up to cover the driver. Smoke is pouring out of the engine, out of the cab, and the man stumbles out hacking. He's got a lightweight pistol in his hand, but he's too disoriented by the smoke and the crash to do more than wave it through the air in front of him.

"Drop it," Manu yells, and the man's eyes widen as the smoke clears enough for him to register Manu's guns and Jaxie's hefty stun carbine. He sets the pistol carefully on the ground; Jaxie scoops it up, shoves it in her belt.

The area is secluded, mostly warehouses and industrial businesses, but it won't be long before someone comes to investigate the noise. Manu hopes Gia had enough time to get in position and warn them if she sees anything.

"He alone?" Manu shouts to Jaxie, who's prodding at the smoke boiling out of the cab with the glowing tip of her stun carbine. "You alone?" he asks the driver.

The driver coughs, refusing to answer.

"He left alone," Toshiyo says in his ear; he thinks she says — the static is getting worse as the storm intensifies. "Secure him . . . back help the others."

"All clear in here," Jaxie yells, hopping down from the cab.

Manu zaps the driver with the neural stunner — it's got a bigger, more satisfying kick than he expects — then he and Jaxie each grab one of the driver's arms, hauling him away from the smoldering ruin of his courier van to prop him against a warehouse grate.

Manu reaches across his chest to cuff him, and the man's jacket falls open. Manu can see the edge of what looks like a badge: concentric circles on a blood-red background. He shoves the jacket open the rest of the way to be sure.

Alliance.

Shit.

"Shit!" Jaxie's eyes are wide. "Should I kill him?"

"How are you such an idiot?" Manu says.

He ignores the daggers she's glaring his way. Trigger-happy psycho has no sense of how consequences play out no matter what the game, apparently. He snaps the cuffs into place and frisks the man for weapons, electronics, anything. Not that it matters much what he finds — the call was probably sent automatically as soon as the van crashed. And a whole swarm of Alliance special security ops will be on them in a minute.

"We need to tell the others," Manu says. He's on Jaxie's heels as they jog to the back of the courier van. Kai and Oriol are securing a bulky crate in the back of Sarah's van.

"Driver's down," Manu shouts. "But we gotta go. He — "

He's interrupted by screeching tires and whirls, pistols out. But it's just Beni's spinner, speeding away to the rendezvous like he didn't have passengers he was supposed to take with him.

Manu swears.

"I guess we're riding with you," he says to Sarah, and she just glares at him and thumbs at the narrow, hard benches lining both walls of the van.

Dammit, Manu hates this job.

Sarah's starting to pull away before Manu even has a chance to close the back door.

"Drive!" Jaxie growls. "The driver had a fucking Alliance badge."

Well, Manu no longer needs to decide if he's going to mention that or not. He manages to get one arm through a safety harness before Sarah lurches the van into her first corner. "Did you know we were hitting the Alliance?" Manu asks Oriol and Kai. Kai just ignores him.

"I don't ask," Oriol says with a hint of impatience.

Manu clicks his microphone on. "Tosh? Did you know we — "

Something clicks out on his feed. He frowns at Kai, but it's Sarah who's tapping something into her gauntlet.

She hits a button and his earpiece comes back to life with a dry pop. He can hear Toshiyo on the other end: "Manu? Manu, what happened? Come in."

"Tosh, the courier was Alliance. Get out of there." But he can tell his words aren't getting through.

"Manu?"

"He's good," says Kai, and Manu can hear Toshiyo's sharp intake of breath. "Communication troubles. Sandstorm."

Sarah clicks off the connection again.

"What did you do?" Manu asks.

"Time for radio silence," Sarah says.

"What the fuck is going on?"

"New plan," Kai says. "Alliance got told where the base was."

"Told by who?" Manu asks.

Kai doesn't answer. "Change of rendezvous. Beni, come in." He taps at his earpiece. "Get me back with

Beni," he tells Sarah. "Chump took off too fast. And hail Gia. We need her to meet us."

Jaxie makes a face at Manu, but then just straps herself into the harness without a word. She's game for anything.

Oriol says nothing, but he meets Manu's gaze with a small frown. This is all news to him, and he's not happy about the change in plans.

"Base needs to know," Manu says. But Kai and Sarah have obviously hijacked this job — whether they're going out on their own, or working with Coeur to double-cross Jaantzen. He wants to live, he needs to keep his mouth shut. "If the Alliance is on their way to the warehouse, we have to tell base."

"Not your problem," Kai says.

Oriol's shaking his head, Shut up, kid written all over his face.

"Yes, ma'am," Sarah says in answer to some call only she can hear. "We have the crate. Heading to the second rendezvous point."

Coeur it is, then. They're heading to the second rendezvous to meet with Coeur, who has set Toshiyo and Jaantzen up to take the fall with the Alliance.

And his first job as her new potential recruit is to let them.

"You can't leave them to get picked up," Manu says, even though that's clearly what Kai and Sarah intend to do.

"We got orders," Kai says, his voice barely more than a growl.

Manu doesn't care.

"What the hell is in this box Coeur wants so bad?" he asks, slipping out of his harness.

Kai lunges for him, but Manu's already pried the lid

off the box. It comes loose more easily than he expected, and he lurches back, spine cracking against the bench.

"You guys knock it off back there," Sarah yells, swerving — out of necessity or emphasis, Manu can't tell which.

Manu pulls himself gingerly into a crouch, but Kai isn't coming after him — he's staring at whatever's in the box, his face a mask of fury. A flush of red seeps out from his collar and hairline, and Manu'll bet he's about to see real-life steam pouring out of the man's cauliflower ears.

"What the hell?" That's Oriol, his professional expression fractured into confusion.

Manu pushes himself up to see.

What's in the box is Beni: limp, but breathing, folded up like a rag doll, his neck cricked at an uncomfortable angle.

And on that neck, two welts, about fifteen millimeters apart — like the marks Manu's neural stunner just left on the neck of the courier driver.

"I saw Beni driving away," Jaxie says, brow furrowed in confusion.

Manu also saw Beni's spinner tearing away. He never for a minute thought Beni wasn't at the controls.

"So who was driving?" Jaxie asks.

Kai lets out a deadly growl.

"Gia."

13

Backing Up the Backup Plans

"Which way did she go?" Sarah yells, and Manu grabs a handhold just as she swerves to the right. He tumbles onto a bench and grabs at the harness, trying three times to get the buckles to catch. Oriol's done the same across the way.

"Hail her!" Kai yells back.

"I'm trying. She's not answering."

"Of course she's not answering," Manu says, and for a split second he gets a face full of Kai's red-eyed fury. Oriol's giving him a warning look. "If she and Jaantzen were planning to double-cross the rest of us the whole time, you think she'll answer now?"

Sarah spits out a string of profanity and veers to the left.

"She'll have a backup plan with Toshiyo and Jaantzen," Manu says. He's staring down the bull; he can feel Kai's breath hitting his cheek in hot, angry blasts, but he doesn't care anymore: *Cut me again, asshole,* he thinks. He's over these games.

"They're the only ones who can bring Gia in, now," Manu says. "Unless they get taken by the Alliance."

Kai and Sarah share a glance.

"Unless you think I'm wrong, and Gia's actually working with Blackheart. You think Blackheart was planning to leave us all out to dry all along?"

That gets results. Manu's gratified to see righteous fury on Kai's face, and can't believe Jaantzen got taken for a sucker by this one. Everything about his body language screams traitor. He wishes now that he'd said something, but how could he have known?

Thing is, it's not a matter of whether or not he could have known — he knew the whole time. Knew by their body language that Kai was loyal to Coeur and that Coeur wouldn't think twice about throwing Jaantzen to the wolves. Knew in his gut that Marisa would leave him the second she found out what he did. Knew by reputation that Siggy's deadbeat boyfriend would kill her if she tried to leave.

He just hadn't done a damn thing about it. Just like his grandma'd never done a damn thing about what her sons did to either of her grandkids.

Oriol's trying his best to stay out of the argument. Checking his weapons, reloading a magazine. Jaxie's hanging with one arm hooked through her harness, watching Kai and Manu like she's at a boxing match but doesn't have money on the line. Nobody's paying any attention to Beni. Poor bastard's gonna have a bad day when he wakes up.

The Alliance is closing in on Toshiyo and Jaantzen, and nobody else is going to help them out.

"You wanna get Blackheart her due, you better track down Gia," Manu says. "And Jaantzen and Toshiyo are the only ones who can do that."

A long beat. Kai's glare slowly morphs into frustration as he realizes Manu is right.

"Pull over," he barks at Sarah. "Base, you copy?"

Sarah screeches to a halt in an alleyway, then taps something in her gauntlet. The maneuver makes Oriol drop a bullet. He gives Sarah a mild-mannered look that on another man might be fury, then reaches long golden fingers to pick it back up, snap it into the magazine.

"All right. You're on," Sarah says.

"Base, you copy?" Kai asks again.

Toshiyo's voice crackles through all of their ears. "Kai! What happened?"

"Target was Alliance — I think we got played. You two get out of there."

A faint hesitation. Manu shouts at Toshiyo in his mind: Listen! Get out of there!

"Copy that," Toshiyo says finally. "Rendezvous two."

"Good," Kai says. "Gia, you copy? Rendezvous two."

"I'll make sure she and Beni know. I'll still be — shit — "

Toshiyo cuts out in a staccato of gunfire.

Manu's heart sinks.

<hr>

RENDEZVOUS TWO IS EVEN DINGIER and less impressive than the original warehouse, and about twenty minutes away. They pull into an oversized garage, the sort of place you could strip down and refurb an entire orbital cargo hauler. Given the stink of oil and jagged piles of thruster parts stacked haphazardly around the room, that's probably exactly what it's been used for.

Manu's the first one out of the van — he's been having trouble breathing since they lost Toshiyo, but the stench of mechanics and dust in the garage isn't making things any easier. He scans the room, sneezes. Scans the room.

Sneezes.

"What the fuck is this place," he mutters. He's aware how pissy he sounds. He needs to dial it back.

Oriol steps out beside him, and Manu can feel his evaluating gaze. Oriol's deciding if he needs to distance himself. They share a brief glance, but Oriol just goes back to scanning the room. He's chosen sides from the beginning, and that side is Team Oriol. Manu shrugs it off.

"Help me get this guy out," he says to Jaxie. Beni's still crowded into the box, and nobody's thought to do a thing about it. Not even Manu, until just this second, so he doesn't give himself any hero points, either.

Beni wakes up as they pry him out, head lolling and muscles loose. "It's okay, big guy," Manu says. "You're gonna be fine."

"Zheeee."

"It's okay."

Manu and Jaxie stretch him awkwardly on the floor of the van, stand to go. Beni grabs for Jaxie's arm, misses, grabs again and claws his fingers in her sleeve. She looks like she might hit him. "Zheee," he says, his speech a blur of vowels on his stunned tongue. She tugs away and he lets out a desperate, frustrated moan.

"It was Gia," Manu tells him. "We know."

Beni slumps back, message delivered. He doesn't try to move again as Manu and Jaxie leave him lie.

"What now," Manu snaps at Kai as he climbs back out of the van. He can't keep the anger out of his voice, even though he knows he'll be no help to Toshiyo and Jaantzen if he pisses Kai off so much the man shoots him before they even get here.

If they're even still alive.

"Now we wait," Kai says. He gives Manu a long, evaluating look. "You got a problem with that?"

"No problems," Oriol answers for him. Manu swings his head to meet the other man's gaze, and those honey-gold eyes pierce sharp. "Do we?" Oriol says, quiet.

"No problems," Manu says.

None that'll do him any good to bring up now, at least. He shrugs on his jacket. "I'll check out the perimeter," he says, and walks away before anyone can stop him. Behind him, he can hear Oriol murmuring something to Kai, defusing the situation. Whatever it is, it makes Sarah laugh.

Rendezvous Two is all fourth-wave architecture, around the era when prefab warehouse panels were first being constructed on New Sarjun instead of being slung across the void from Indira. Got that signature gray-yellow patina from the early industrial metal composites corroding over time. Replicas of this look are popular in bars in the tourist district — the more dedicated to colonist kitsch the bar, the pricier the shots of imported Indiran liquors.

Nobody's setting up a swanky bar in this place, though — not without some serious bribes paid to the Bulari health department. Manu slaps his palm on the cracked glass beside the door and feels it shift. It's been covered over in a peeling, yellowing film. Probably the only thing keeping it together for now.

Someone's been living here, though they're not home now. There's a pile of trash in the corner, picked through and sorted into careful piles. A few moped frames stripped of their parts. Nothing to indicate that whoever normally lives here is into anything bigger than petty theft and dropping shard.

Manu tries a light switch. The archaic electrical system doesn't seem to be working, but Manu pats the side of a circuit box as he passes.

"Anything to report?"

He turns just as Jaxie exhales a cloud of cigarette smoke. It doesn't improve the warehouse's general eau de dusty oil fume.

Manu points at the pile of blankets in the corner. "We have a fellow trespasser."

Jaxie's pulse carbine snaps to hands, the cigarette dangling from her lips.

"Relax, psycho. He's not here."

She shoots him a dirty look and lowers the gun.

"We just supposed to meet them here?" he asks, and Jaxie shrugs. He tries to ignore the elephant in the room, that Jaantzen and Toshiyo are probably in the custody of the Alliance as they speak. Best say your goodbyes, if that's the case. Get caught stealing from the Alliance it's a trip to Redrock, for sure — and Manu doesn't know anyone who's ever gotten out of Redrock.

Except for Gia.

He desperately hopes she's out there doing something heroic.

A glass sign over the door reads Office. Manu gives a little hop and slaps it as he walks past. Jaxie gives him a look. "For good luck," he says.

"I didn't know you were superstitious."

"Learned it from Grannie."

"Grannies don't always teach the best lessons," says a man's voice behind him. Rich baritone, and Manu spins with weapon in hand, not sure what sort of reception he'll be receiving. Across the room he hears safeties clicking off, Kai's grunt and swear. Beside his shoulder, the faint whine of Jaxie's pulse carbine.

It's Jaantzen and Toshiyo; he's carrying a briefcase in each hand, she's clutching a backpack clunky with bulky angles. His expression is dark.

"Nice to see you all, too," he says.

14

Kill Shot

Manu lowers his weapon a fraction, sees the others do the same. Guns don't go back in holsters, though, and Manu doesn't think anyone is fooled by the faux civility.

He honestly didn't expect Jaantzen to show up here — the fact that he'd been betrayed must have been painfully obvious, and he's not an idiot. But here he is, playing right into Coeur's hands. Manu has a sick feeling about this.

Jaantzen walks slowly through the room, Toshiyo trailing behind him with wide eyes. Her grip slips on the awkward backpack and Manu has to stop himself from grabbing it from her and shouldering the load. He needs his hands free for whatever's about to happen.

He needs her out of here.

"We've got to track down Gia," he says. "She — "

"She knocked Beni out and took the goods," Kai cuts in. His glare makes it clear he doesn't trust Manu not to let something slip.

Everything has slipped, asshole.

"Why would she do that?" Jaantzen asks in mock surprise.

"You told her to," Kai growls, and Jaantzen doesn't deny the obvious. "You double-crossing us?"

The slight hint of amusement on Jaantzen's face hardens. "I'm doing the job I was hired for, Kai. I'm not sure I can say the same for you."

The veins in Kai's thick neck are pulsing hard. Manu clears his throat before speaking — he doesn't want to get a bullet in the head.

"There's a table here where Tosh can set up her gear," Manu says, pointing to a workbench away from the van, away from the action. Away from trouble. Kai and Jaantzen both glare at him.

"She can call Gia where she is," Kai says. Toshiyo starts to set down the backpack, and Kai swings his gun back to cover her. "Slow," he says.

Manu sighs. "Seriously, man, she — "

"Shut up or I kill you," Kai says.

There's an edge in Kai's voice beyond the anger, and even Sarah's glaring at him now, her mechanical eye scanning him independent of the biological one. Manu wonders what she sees.

The edge in Kai's voice is a sort of dizzy power that Manu has heard over and over in his life from people who believed they were finally throwing off some sort of imagined oppression. It's the same sort of fever pitch his dad's voice would take on when he'd been drinking, just before the blows began to land. But Manu doesn't think Kai's been drinking. And that just makes this moment even more dangerous.

Toshiyo's bag meets cement with a heavy clatter as the equipment inside shifts against itself. She slides her fingerprint along the seal and a faint heat trail follows behind. Unlocked.

"Show me," Kai says, and she looks confused for a second, starts to reach in.

"Show him what's in the bag," Manu says. He'd like to say more, but Kai shoots him a dangerous look.

Manu's mind is racing. Everybody has triggers: say the right word and they'll smile at a shared memory, laugh at a joke, or fly into a rage. It's how he kept Marisa around for so much longer than she should have stayed, even though they were terrible for each other — knowing just how to defuse an argument, how to make her smile again. It's how he worked his dad's anger to shift his attention when all the body language screamed danger. How he knew exactly when to ask his grandma for a favor.

And how he's learned when to get the hell out of the way.

Every cell of his body is screaming that now is one of those times.

Manu doesn't know Kai well enough to know his triggers, but he can tell he thinks he's on the edge of something big. The way he's peacocking on power, chest out and chin up, the lazy way he's swinging the weapon back and forth, Manu guesses he's been waiting to get the upper hand on Jaantzen a long time.

Two days ago, Manu Juric would be standing back to see where the bullets landed, then walking out with the winners. Today, he's choosing sides.

And the side he's choosing is the one currently having the guns pointed at their heads.

Marisa was right: He makes terrible decisions.

Toshiyo yawns the mouth of the bag towards Kai, whose expression goes all brow-overhang and pursed lips; he can't make heads nor tails of the mess inside. Neither can Manu, but it's clearly not a gun or a bomb. Kai waves her on.

Toshiyo pulls her complicated-looking hand terminal out of the bag and thumbs it on, touches her earpiece as though waiting for it to pair, which it certainly should have done already. She cracks both ring fingers.

Manu frowns.

Seriously? Is Toshiyo Ravi acting?

He starts to interject again, give Toshiyo that extra second before Kai wonders why things are taking so long, but Jaantzen speaks first.

"What is it you were unhappy with, Kai?" Jaantzen asks. "The pay? The hours?"

Kai's weapon is still trained on Toshiyo, though his attention swings to Jaantzen. Sarah frowns at him. Jaxie shifts her weight. Oriol's standing loose and ready. Though for what, Manu isn't sure.

"What?" Kai asks.

"You and I, we've worked together for years. What did Coeur offer you that I couldn't? Better pay? Benefits?"

"She didn't have to offer me anything," Kai says. "You think you're so smart, but I know you came from Brightby orphanage just the same as me. You think you're so posh in your suits and your fancy wines, but you ain't nothin more than what I am. Then you think you can buy me like I'm some indentured goon."

"I never tried to buy you," Jaantzen says. His gaze is level, even. His hands are out straight, but his right hand wants badly to slip under his coat. Manu can tell by the angle, by how much closer he holds it, by the ever-widening gap between the thumb and the forefinger while the left stays still as a statue. Kai doesn't seem to notice. "I don't do indentures."

"'I don't do indentures,'" Kai says, mocking. "You never done an indenture, you don't know what it's like to make that choice. Lookin down on the rest of us who've done it like it's dirty. It's the fuckin way of life."

Jaantzen frowns slightly at that, and it's genuine. "You would've preferred I put you under contract?"

Not the time for this conversation. Manu screams at him in his brain, because he can see Willem Jaantzen is genuinely curious about Kai's employment preferences, and Kai is only curious about how good it'll feel to finally pull the trigger.

"Making decisions like you're a god, like you're so fucking smart, when what have you done but wore fancy clothes and send others to do your dirty work?"

"Didn't I pay you well?"

"Fuck you." Kai swings his weapon up for a kill shot.

Toshiyo cries out.

Manu pulls his trigger.

15

Too Much Drama

Kai falls, a slow topple back, a stray bullet squeezed from his gun past Jaantzen's leg, a shower of sparks as it ricochets off the bag of machinery in front of Toshiyo.

Manu waits for the bullet that will take him, from Sarah, behind them — he hears her swear — but Oriol is faster. He lets a spray of bullets fly as he dives for cover. Manu spins to take her out, but it's Jaantzen's shot that catches her straight between the eyes.

Manu aims his pistol at Jaxie's head. "You do and you're dead," he says.

She lowers her pulse carbine, raises a hand. "We good, man."

It's over as soon as it began.

Oriol stands carefully, scanning the room behind them, his weapon at the ready. "Shit, man," he says. "This is too much fucking drama."

"I'll split Kai's and Sarah's cuts between the three of you if you stay on my crew until we're through," says

Jaantzen, pistol still in his hand, evaluating Oriol's trustworthiness. Evaluating all their trustworthiness.

Oriol lifts a golden eyebrow. "Cut of what? This deal gone south, man." But he's not casing Jaantzen, he's turned and is watching the room, body language tense but casual. He'll take the offer, even if he doesn't like it.

"My crew gets paid," Jaantzen says. His hand's on his pistol, his finger on the trigger. His eyes are painting a target on the back of Oriol's neck.

"He's good," Manu says. Jaantzen glances at him. Manu gives him a nod. "And Jaxie's good."

"She's one of Coeur's."

"She's with Sylla Mar," Manu says, and Jaxie lets out an angry yelp. Jaantzen doesn't look surprised, and Manu wonders if he's known all along, or if he's just not that easy to rattle. He suspects the latter. "We're in." He gets an irritated side-eye from Oriol, but no argument. "Tosh, you all right?"

There's no answer. Behind him, Jaantzen lets out a curse.

Manu spins to find Toshiyo slumped on the floor, hands pressed to her side, covered in blood. Her eyelids flutter weakly. Manu grabs an extra shirt from his gear bag and kneels beside her, carefully peels back her fingers to press it over the wound. "Stay with me, Tosh," he says. "Gia's on her way."

A quick glance up at Jaantzen to confirm — he's already on his comm.

"Blackheart knows where we are," says Oriol. He's kneeling beside Sarah's body, checking through her clothes. "Thousand marks says she got an alert when cyborg-gal bit it. We need — ah, here." He tugs something free from her shoulder and holds it up to the light: a hard plastic vial half filled with silvery liquid.

"What is that?"

"Coag nanites. Part of the automatic tech system."

"How do you know?"

"You ain't seen me naked yet. Get me a vein, man."

"Boys." Jaantzen holds out his hand for the vial; Oriol hands it over, then opens up his small medkit and pulls out a syringe. He holds out his hand for the vial, but Jaantzen is still staring at it. "What will this do to her, Mr. Sina?"

"Fix her enough that we can move her." Jaantzen's still waiting. "I ain't working for Blackheart, I'm working for a living," says Oriol. "Your name's on my contract, and Tosh's the one who's gonna get us payday." He shrugs. "Plus, unless any of the rest of you've patched up a bullet wound in the middle of combat . . . ?"

Manu has her sleeve rolled up by the time Oriol's gotten the vial back from Jaantzen and kneels beside him. The heat off his shoulder is a stark contrast to Toshiyo's cool arm.

"Press your thumbs there, Manu. K, Tosh, I need you to squeeze your hand," says Oriol. The silver liquid swirls like smoke as Oriol finds the vein and depresses the syringe. "Good girl. Manu, hold her tight a sec. The first minute can be pretty shitty." Oriol grabs Toshiyo's legs, leaning his weight down just as she starts to kick. "Sorry, Tosh."

Manu spares a glance up at Jaantzen, but he's scanning the room, apparently deciding to trust them after all. "Get on the door," Jaantzen says to Jaxie. "Gia's on her way."

"So's Blackheart," says Oriol again. "We're gonna sit you up, kiddo." Toshiyo's tremors are starting to subside, and Oriol's got a miniature spray can of wound sealant to replace Manu's blood-soaked shirt. The foam stiffens into a pliable shield, but he winds a sterile wrap around her torso to hold it in place anyway. "Your color's better. How's your pain?"

"Fucking hurts," Toshiyo says, the words rasping tight between her teeth.

"Yeah, that happens. Only thing I got in my kit's gonna knock you out. And I don't think we can afford you knocked out just yet."

"I'll be fine," Toshiyo says. Oriol smiles back, but it's only for show, Manu can tell. Oriol isn't sure about that at all.

Jaantzen is listening to something through his earpiece. "Get her in the van," he says. "Gia's meeting us here."

"Boss?" Manu shares a quick look with Oriol.

Jaxie clears her throat. "But Blackheart — "

"Coeur is meeting us here, too."

Manu's sharing a look with Oriol. What the hell? Dueling with Blackheart isn't the way he'd been hoping to spend the rest of today.

"Let's get her in the van," Manu says.

In the van, Beni's slumped on one of the bench seats with his chin on his chest. He looks up groggily as Oriol and Manu lift Toshiyo in, and raises his hands.

"I'm on your team," Beni says. "Whoever the hell your team is now."

"Good to hear it," Manu says. "I think we're gonna need a good driver soon."

Beni sighs. "You all done shooting each other out there?"

"Probably not."

"I hate this job."

"Tell me about it. Keep an eye on her, and get ready to — "

Beside him, Oriol swears and spins back to face the main door to the garage. Manu hears the soft click of Oriol's rifle, the faint whine of Jaxie's pulse carbine. The sharp clack of Jaantzen's machine gun. He turns back to face the open door, aiming with his left pistol and handing his right back to Toshiyo.

"The red button on the side is the safety," he murmurs. "Don't shoot if I'm in the way."

"I can shoot a gun," she says, but her voice is shaking. He doesn't risk a glance back to see how she's doing.

A pair of burly bodyguards stalk through the door first, then the slim, dark silhouette Manu will never mistake.

Thala Coeur stares down the barrels of a quartet of weapons and smiles.

16

Payout

"WILLEM."

Coeur waves back her bodyguards and steps into the center of the room. A half dozen barrels follow her. And she may be three to four and look unarmed herself, but Manu recognizes the assault carbines her bodyguards are carrying. Those bullets are made to pierce powered armor. A van door isn't going to do much to stop them. Nor will the light body armor he saw Oriol putting on back at the warehouse.

Coeur takes a slow, deliberate scan of the room, ignoring the pair of bodies but holding each person's gaze in turn. Her head's high, her shoulders loose, like she's walking into a bout she's planning to win. Thing with Coeur, though, she's not brash, she's not cocky. She wins because she plans to, not because she expects to. Manu gives her a faint nod when she meets his gaze, and he sees her nostrils flare, evaluating whether or not she can count him friend or foe.

Foe, bitch.

She turns to Jaantzen last. The gold-tipped ends of

her braids clatter together as a handful of them slip off her shoulder.

"I thought we had a nice plan," she says to Jaantzen. "Didn't you think so?"

"Up until the part where you were planning to hang me up for the Alliance."

"Sorry about that, Willem. And I apologize for underestimating you."

"I don't expect you'll do it again."

A long, slow smile. Her gaze sweeps the room once more. "I misjudged your ability to inspire loyalty."

"Money can do that."

Money did that for Oriol and Jaxie, certainly — but Manu can hear Toshiyo's labored breathing behind him, thinks of Gia out there somewhere. Thinks about how he's just sided against the most dangerous woman in Bulari. No amount of money could have gotten him to make such a misguided move.

"Speaking of money." Coeur presses a button on her comm. Jaantzen's own chimes in his pocket. "You've got your cash, so bring in your gal and let's do some business." Her gaze cuts briefly to Sarah and Kai. "What do you say, we're even? Looks like we both lost people on this one."

"I'm not sure Kai was one of my people," Jaantzen says.

Coeur just shrugs. You don't get as far as she has and still have a sense of shame, Manu figures.

"But I would say we're even, Thala. I was in it for the job, you were in it for the goods. We've both gotten what we came in for. Except you didn't get a fall guy to distract the Alliance."

"That's fine. I have a plan B."

"Glad to hear you'll end up all right."

"My goods, Willem."

Her hand's at her side, drumming on her thigh low and casual. It might be an unconscious gesture on someone else, but both her guards are keeping one eye on it.

Manu does, too.

"Ms. Ravi," Jaantzen says. "Can you please ask Ms. Até to join us?" Coeur's nostrils flare at Toshiyo's name like she's scenting for hidden prey; her attention falls on the van behind Manu. The guard at her left is tuned to her motions like an augment mech on a factory line; he shifts to sweep his weapon over the van. His right eye is a mercury swirl and he's blinking strangely, like information is feeding into a contact lens. Could be his scope doubles as a scanner.

"Got it, boss," Toshiyo calls from the van. Manu can hear her tapping on her hand terminal, faint under the sound of her labored breathing.

"Giaconda is on her way," Jaantzen says.

And by on her way, he means she's been waiting in the wings for her dramatic cue.

"Got your goods, Thala."

Gia's voice comes from the doorway that leads farther into the office complex. She's got an iridescent case on a wheeled cart that looks like it was stolen from a hotel lobby.

Coeur breaks into a slow smile. "Thanks, sugar," she says. Manu thinks he could live to one hundred and never again hear someone call Giaconda "Sugar."

"We'll just be on our way, and you can have your goods," says Jaantzen. "As you suggested, I think we can say we're even. But please take me off your list of available contractors in the future."

"I'd say I'll be taking a few people off my list," she

says, gaze sweeping the room again. Again, her gaze stops briefly on Manu. He gives her another slight nod and she looks satisfied. Manu's attention is on the hand on her thigh. "You're free to go," Coeur says. "You have my word. Pleasure working with you, Willem."

"Wish I could say the same."

Jaantzen raises his chin to Gia, and she gives the cart a kick. It glides, clattering across the cracked cement floor.

Thala Coeur grins. She reaches for the handle with one hand; her other hand cuts a sharp arc. Her guards snap their rifles to squeeze out the rounds that'll end them all.

Manu squeezes his fist on the detonator hidden in his palm.

The room explodes.

HORNET TAGS ARE BRILLIANT.

They're practically invisible to the naked eye, just a piece of explosive resin the size of Manu's thumbnail on a patch of transparent adhesive. A bit of ignition, a minuscule receiver. They're no grenade, shredding through the room with shrapnel. They're no dynamite. Really, the only way they'll kill you is if you have a bad heart and don't know they're coming.

But they're distracting as hell — especially when you've slapped a bunch up on big glass panes and shoddy electrical boxes.

He's timed the first wave a fraction of a second apart, so it sounds like a spray of gunfire coming from outside the building.

Coeur has a pistol in one hand, and her own round

of bullets sends Manu and Jaantzen ducking for cover. Her bodyguards are slower to react — one has turned to the entrance as though to face a new threat from that direction. Jaxie drops him. Oriol drops the other.

"Don't shoot the case," Jaantzen bellows, and Manu pulls up at the last minute so his shot goes wide and shatters one of the plate windows he hadn't tagged. Coeur and her mystery case are silhouetted in a glittering hail of glass as she sprints back out the door.

Outside, Manu hears voices yelling. Coeur's guys? Police? He's not interested in finding out.

"I'd be a lot happier about the future if we'd gotten her, too," Oriol mutters.

"Time for a long vacation," Manu says.

"Goddammit, Manu," Gia yells.

"Wasn't that fun?" he yells back. "Handy, too."

"We can talk about fun later." She shoulders past him into the van. "Hey, Tosh. Hold on, babe. Beni, how you feeling, buddy? You ready to drive?" Beni stares at her with naked fear.

Outside, the voices are getting closer. Manu runs to cover Jaantzen as he limps towards the van. Jaxie's joined him, driven by her natural lackey's instinct to protect the alpha, whoever that alpha may be. "Lotta guys out there," she says.

"Then let's head out the back," Jaantzen says. "I'm sending coordinates to your nav."

They pile into the van. Beni's in the driver's seat, eyes on Gia like she's a feral scrub hyena. Gia's got Toshiyo strapped to one of the benches and is waving some magic medical wand over her abdomen. "Nice job on the coag nanites, whoever thought of that."

"Oriol," Jaxie says. "How bulletproof is this thing?"

"Not very," Jaantzen says, checking his gun. "I hope your reflexes are recovered, Mr. Chav."

Beni just snorts. "Bitch can't steal my touch."

Gia laughs.

"Good to hear. Now let's drive."

Manu sets off his second round of hornet tags as Beni peels out of the garage, and just as a swarm of Coeur's thugs come piling in. This time — and he's proud of this one — a pair of tags have just enough power to sever a wire cable suspending a hoist. It drops, sags against the remaining cable, then twists free in a shriek of rusted metal-on-metal.

Beni swerves out of the way just in time, throwing them all against the wall of the van. Jaxie and Oriol are first to recover, firing out the windows at the gunmen who are still standing.

Gia hoists herself back to Toshiyo's side. "How many more of those do you have, asshole?" she growls at Manu.

"Zero more," Manu says. "Somebody wouldn't buy me any."

"Please add hornet tags as a permanent item on Mr. Juric's supply list," Jaantzen says.

"Noted with fucking objections, boss," Gia says. Permanent item.

Oriol gives him a look, perfect eyebrow raised, and Manu almost says something to brush it off. But he doesn't have anything to prove to Oriol.

Jaantzen's watching him, and Manu gives the man a nod.

"Got it, boss," he says.

17

Never Say 'Ain't Ever'

B∃NI'S HANDLING SKILLS SEEM TO HAVE RECOVERED AS quickly as he said they would, and within a few minutes they're in a nondescript office complex in the bad part of the North Bulari industrial district. Manu feels his soul shriveling just being in this part of town, which during the day is full of indentured office workers and the humming of official business: trade, infrastructure, construction. He doesn't understand what they do here, and he doesn't care.

Cheap adobe walls make the street feel like a desert canyon, cut off the view to the businesses behind, differentiated only by the address numbers and occasional business name stenciled on the sheetmetal gates. The better-kept businesses have painted their section of the wall, stopping sharply at the property line as if to say, Unlike those guys, we take pride in our business.

The wall around the old-fashioned accordion gate that Jaantzen directs Beni to stop in front of is clearly owned by one of those guys, with paint scored back by sandstorms so badly that a lattice of cement blocks shows through the adobe in places. But when Jaantzen gets out to palm the lock, the gate sparks faintly as the invisible energy shield around the place shimmers to off.

A pack rat scurries out of the wall.

Inside is a short driveway and a soulless office building.

"We're safe here," Jaantzen calls, and Manu jumps out to help him secure the accordion gate once more. His scalp tingles as the energy field sizzles back on.

Gia seems to know the place — she directs Oriol and Jaxie to carry Toshiyo into the office building, orders Beni to come with them so he can lie down. No one barks orders at Manu, so he steps back to the van to start sorting through the chaos of gear this little adventure has produced.

"Mr. Juric, if you have a moment."

Manu gingerly brushes shards of broken glass off his gear bag, which is mercifully sealed. "Yeah, boss." The word comes out without him meaning it to.

Last time Manu was alone with Jaantzen, he was plotting how to get a knife between the man's shoulder blades and get out alive. Now?

Manu's not sure where they stand now.

"What is your estimation of me?" Jaantzen asks.

It's not the question Manu was expecting. He frowns at the man. He's studied him for weeks, spent plenty of time watching for weaknesses these past few days. His estimation has shifted, but he's not sure when. Probably before he even made the decision not to kill him out on the balcony.

"You're not what I expected," he says. Jaantzen waits, watching him. "Kai, that's more who I expected based on what I heard about you. You've got a reputa-

tion for being someone who hires disposable crew —
who is disposable. Which I guess is why Coeur thought
she could hang you out to dry.”

Manu's thinking. He's not sure how to say all this.
“Where'd you find Toshiyo?” he asks instead.

Jaantzen's expression darkens, a storm hovering over
his brow. “By reputation,” he says. “I was looking to hire
a permanent ops tech to handle security and
surveillance, and word came about a tech genius at a
mining corporation.”

“So you bought her indenture.”

Manu says it wrong, deliberate, and sees Jaantzen
balk like the idea is distasteful.

“I paid off her indenture,” he says. “Then I hired
Ms. Ravi on retainer to help me when I need it.”

“Retainer?” Manu asks, frowning. Most bosses in
Bulari run their crew as indentures or pay them per job.

“I don't work with anyone who can't walk away, but I
don't want to scrounge for my team each time.”

Jaantzen's watching him now, gaze steady and even.

Manu breaks first; he nods and shifts as though he's
scanning the compound. “And Gia? She's a trip.”

“Gia and I have a long history,” Jaantzen says. “I
don't require her services often.”

“And Kai?”

“Kai was from the old way of doing things. Someone
I'd contracted with many times in the past, but never
trusted. I need people I can trust, Mr. Juric.”

“Understood.”

“I can offer you a monthly retainer, plus overtime
and a bonus for the more dangerous jobs. In exchange I
would prefer you work solely for me.”

“Join your crew.” Manu tilts his head. “Your crew's
got a bad rap. That's the other thing I know about you.”

"It does, and for understandable reasons." Jaantzen clears his throat. "And I would like you to help me change that."

Manu blinks, not sure at first if he's heard correctly. "Me?"

"I've been watching you. You read every person on this job like a book, and you played them just as well as you needed. I'd planned to kill you during our first conversation, yet by the end of it, I'd hired you."

"I appreciate that."

"I saw you bolster Toshiyo's confidence when we needed her. You've defused Kai and Beni." He gave a faint smile. "You've even made Gia laugh. You're a decent fighter, but I can find a dozen of those on any street corner in any slum. What I need is someone who can help me build a team."

Somewhere down the line, Manu's already made the decision. He shrugs. "Course."

"You're not going to negotiate?"

"We can talk about money later."

"Coeur will probably try to kill you if you work for me."

"I'm already on her shit list. Probably got a better chance working with you than wandering out on my own."

Jaantzen nods slowly. "What about the others?"

Manu knows who he means: Oriol, Beni, Jaxie. He takes them in order of easiness.

"Jaxie's bad news on a good day," he says. "I wouldn't trust her to water my jadau plant while I was on vacation without sniffing around to find somebody who'd pay her more to let it die instead. But let her run back to Sylla with her cash and she'll be too embarrassed at taking the pay to bring any fight back to you.

"Beni'll do the job well, but he won't put his life on the line for you. You knew that. The thing I'd watch if I were you is I get the sense he holds a grudge, and he's not happy about what Gia did to him. And you, by extension."

Manu feels bad saying it, knows it's probably a death sentence. "Let me talk to him and be sure," he adds. If he senses that Beni will be a threat to his new crew, he can take care of it himself.

Jaantzen nods slowly. "And Mr. Sina?"

Ah, now there's a blind spot, if Manu's not careful. "Oriol doesn't seem interested in anybody else's drama. He's not curious, and he doesn't talk if he doesn't need to. The man's a pro."

"Would he make a good addition to my crew?"

"Oriol?" He's the type of no-nonsense person with a put-together life that Manu has always been drawn to. It would be nice to keep working alongside him, but Manu has to be honest with Jaantzen — and himself. "Nah, boss. He plays for his own team. Keep his number, though."

Jaantzen nods, and his gaze shifts past Manu's shoulder. Manu turns to see that Oriol has come back out of the office building, is leaning lazy shoulders against the adobe wall.

"I presume you'll have it," Jaantzen says. He claps Manu on the shoulder. "I'm going to go see Toshiyo. Keep an eye out."

"Sure thing, boss."

Manu watches him walk away, then crosses the driveway. "Hey, man."

Oriol tilts his head to look at him, a faint smile on his lips. "Hope you asked for what you're worth," he says.

Manu shrugs. What he's worth is a relative number.

What Jaantzen's worth to him is even more so. He's not worried about cash. Besides, he doesn't want to talk about it, not with Oriol. "What are your plans?" he asks. "You got your pay, did your job. On to the next adventure?"

"Gonna lie low," he says.

Manu's watching, wondering if he's been put out of the picture now that he's chosen sides. Now that he's not so cool and smooth.

And as though he can read Manu's mind, Oriol's sardonic smile cracks briefly into the genuine thing. "I ain't ever working with you again, man."

"Never say 'ain't ever,'" Manu says, and Oriol just shakes his head. "And besides. You just said you don't have plans to work for a minute, anyway. Not until this whole thing blows over." He tests his luck, leans against the wall a couple inches from Oriol. "I heard you were planning a little vacation."

"Could be."

"Need some company?"

Oriol smiles. "Could be." Oriol's gaze trails downwards as though considering, then his thumb hooks into Manu's waistband, tugging him a fraction of an inch closer. His other hand reaches into Manu's pocket to pull out his comm. Manu's hip is on fire.

Oriol types his information into Manu's comm, hands it back.

"Now you know how to get ahold of me."

"I was born knowing how to get ahold a person," Manu says with a lift of an eyebrow. "I'll show you if you want."

"You can't come if you're gonna make a joke out of everything," Oriol says, then reddens. Manu starts to laugh. "Dammit, man. I already regret giving you my number."

"I'll make sure that regret's short-lived," Manu says. He pats the comm in his pocket. "When we go on vacation," he adds.

Life's about to get good.

DEVIANT FLUX

A DURGA SYSTEM NOVELLA

JESSIE KWAK

For my cousins,
I love you all.

1

Starla

THE AIR HERE IS THICK WITH MEMORIES.

Starla Dusai breathes deep the sharp tang of oil and sweat, the sweet musk of antifreeze and unwashed bodies passed through the recycler too many times to count: Maribi Station smells like home.

At least, it's the closest she's found since she watched Alliance missiles shatter her family home into stars five years ago.

There are differences, of course. For one, there are too many people here, bodies crowded into every corner, in every corridor and doorway, brushing past her from every direction. The air is more electric than in her childhood home of Silk Station, too, geared towards entertaining the thousands of travelers who arrive here to catch shuttles deeper out into the black or farther into Durga's Belt, or who are waiting for the bigger transports to shuttle them back to the surface of one of the two sunward planets, Indira or New Sarjun.

On Silk Station there was breathing room — even when her parents' ship was in port and Silk Station

swelled with crew, it was all family. And in her new planetside home on New Sarjun, Starla can go for hours
without seeing another soul if she wants. In a way, her
godfather's home ebbs and flows just as Silk Station did,
especially in the past few years with his soldiers and hired
mercenaries flooding in and out, thudding footsteps and
the tang of blood in the dry air waking Starla more than
once in the middle of the night.

She's taking the long way to meet Gia at the boxing
gym, through Terminal A, which is doubly packed with
people this close to the shift change. Starla hopes this will
give her better odds of finding the one person she's
desperate to find — even if the press of people is making
it more difficult to actually pick an individual out of the
crowd.

She hadn't counted on the newcomers. Terminal A
isn't just packed with station inhabitants today. A ferry
from elsewhere in Durga's Belt has just docked, judging
by the glut of travelers shouldering duffel bags and stopping in the middle of the passage to frown at the station
transit maps and mouth questions to each other.

Starla slips through them, ignoring the few that seem
to ask her for directions.

Her comm buzzes with a message from Gia.

YOU SKIPPING TRAINING?

Starla's beginning to regret coming this way. She
thought heading through a large swath of the population
would give her a better chance of spotting her target, but
it's just chaos, a constant swarm of people.

It's hard to take it all in.

The terminal's length is lined with shopping and
entertainment, callers beckoning from the neon-clad
doorways of casinos and brothels and bars — a heady
pulse thrums through Starla's chest as she passes one,

and she catches a glimpse of a room packed with bodies and smoke and flashing lights, the mass of people dancing. For Starla, it's just after lunch. But in such a transient place, you can choose your own time.

So long as you keep moving, it seems. In the stream of Terminal A, she can't find a single spot to just stand for one second and type out a reply to Gia without being in the way. Somebody always needs to get by, or set something where you're standing, or open the door you didn't notice behind you.

It makes her skin crawl. Silk Station didn't use to make her skin crawl — it fit like a glove. Is it this station in particular? Or is it that she's become used to wide open spaces after five years living on New Sarjun?

Gia's message blinks insistently at the edge of her field of vision.

She sidesteps a hawker in religious headgear who clutches at her arm and tries to hand her a saint token, saying something to her around blue-painted teeth. Starla brushes the woman back and slips into the lee of a pile of crates for a second's breather, grabs her comm.

BE THERE IN 5.

She pushes Send; Gia's message disappears from her heads-up.

Gia has a thing about timeliness that Starla should probably try to emulate, but she can't be bothered this trip. Despite being comfortable with the station's layout, she keeps misjudging the time it will take her to get through Maribi's labyrinth — and she's always hesitant to leave off her search.

Because her cousin Mona is here, she knows it. And in her imagination, every instant she turns away from an open doorway, Mona walks past. Near misses, it has to be — she's been all over this damned station.

And she's running out of time.

BE HERE IN 2. HAD ANY LUCK?

Gia's response blinks on the bottom of Starla's heads-up. Starla swipes it away without responding, because, no, she hasn't had any luck. Anyway, Starla can tell Gia in person when she gets to the boxing gym. In five.

Starla stops to scan the terminal, turns to find a woman in a forklift suit yelling at her. Probably to get out of the way so she can get to the crates; words blink at the bottom of her heads-up, the unit's attempt to transcribe the forklift operator's diatribe. It's coming out garbled — maybe she's got an accent, maybe it's too loud for the unit to work properly.

Or maybe she's using too many expletives. One thing Starla has realized on this trip with Gia is that the software isn't programmed to transcribe swear words. She'll have to fix that.

Starla waves both hands at the forklift operator — *All right, all right.* — and ducks back into the throng. She keeps scanning the people passing, out of habit, but doesn't see anyone who looks like her cousin.

After five years of searching, she's seen nothing of her family but obituaries. Auntie Faye's ship was shot down shortly after the attack on Silk Station. Amit was picked up by the Alliance and has since disappeared. Uncle Ro was cornered on the volcanic moon Pele, shot himself before he could be arrested. Deyva hasn't been heard from in years and is presumed dead.

Her parents and countless others died in the initial attack.

So when one of her godfather's smuggling contacts saw someone matching the description of Starla's cousin,

Mona, working on Maribi Station, Starla had to see for herself — and fast.

There are still a few bounties on the boards for missing members of the Silk Station diaspora, and others are out there hunting her cousins, her aunts, her uncles. It's what worries Starla the most, that maybe the reason she hasn't found any of them is because they're being snatched up by bounty hunters first, trundled into cargo holds and whisked off into secret Alliance prisons.

Like she'd been shipped off to Redrock Prison right after the attack. She'd had the help of her godfather, Willem Jaantzen, to escape, and now she'll do anything she can to help the others.

If she can find them.

But there are dozens more Alliance prisons throughout the Durga System.

And a hundred more hub stations like Maribi bored into Durga's Belt and Bixia Yuanjin's moons.

It doesn't matter. Starla will find Mona, even if she has to open every door in this place.

A change in the current of foot traffic catches her attention. Somewhere up ahead, the crush of people is getting more packed on the edges, and individuals are looking up and turning back around, slipping into open doorways, making themselves scarce.

Starla's been paying so much attention to the faces of the people around her that she's nearly in the middle of it before she realizes what's going on: an Indiran Alliance squadron marching through the center of Terminal A, five soldiers with hands on weapons like they think Maribi is theirs to police — or like they're expecting to stir up trouble. Their riot visors are down and scanning the crowd, and Starla's mouth goes dry.

She knows what they're scanning for. Known criminals. Terrorist group members. Exiled freedom fighters. The daughters of notorious pirate families.

She tries not to look frantic, tries to blend in, but she's caught at the edge of the crowd — even those who aren't on an Alliance wanted list aren't too keen to mix up with a troop like this. If she runs, if she pushes through, she'll only attract more attention.

But in a second she'll be face to face with the soldiers, and that close, their facial recognition will uncover her for sure.

She'd rather run and look suspicious than get caught — but as she tenses, someone grabs her from behind, pulls her through an open doorway and out of sight.

A hand clamps over her mouth, though Starla doesn't think she's cried out. Gia's been training her well, though, and Starla breaks free in seconds, spins to meet her attacker.

She doesn't recognize the woman's face at first, not with the wild mane of magenta hair and the scar slashed across her nose and cheek. But she would recognize the way those hands formed her namesign anywhere.

"Starla," she signs, "it's okay. It's me."

Mona.

2

Gia

GIACONDA ÁTE IS NOT A FAN OF SPACE.

She admittedly doesn't get out much back home, but
after two weeks either in a transport or on Maribi
Station, she's realizing how nice it is to know that she
can. To know that she could go hiking in the desert
plateaus around Bulari, or even hop on a train and head
out into the hinterlands around the capital, visit some
podunk town or other whose name she's only seen
stamped on shipping crates and freight trains. Get wild
and drive out to the family farm, see if anyone from the
old commune is still alive and kicking around.

Here, it's like living in a coal mine, all tunnels and
cables and tight spaces and too many sallow people.
She's never realized how necessary it is to have a horizon — combine that with the knowledge that if you walk
too far up, down, left, or right, you're through an airlock
and drifting.

Gia feels the loss of possible directions like a missing
limb.

She checks the address on the doorway to the

Manilan coffee place, notes with disappointment that she's still a few numbers shy. She'll have to come back later, because she could use the caffeine boost and this place smells amazing — coffee, cardamom, orange, honey. It looks like the sort of place that would help her unwind.

She can't even remember what being unwound feels like.

In a way, that's part of this trip. Head off-planet to keep Starla out of trouble, take in the underwhelming sights of Maribi Station, and forget for a minute about how she's spent the past few years digging bullets out of her friends and putting them into her enemies. After a mess like an all-out war, a girl needs a getaway. Needs to drink a cup of decent coffee without worrying that it's too quiet, too crowded, an ambush, a trap.

Back home on New Sarjun, it's a fresh new world. The losers of Bulari's underground civil war between the crime families have been killed or pushed into exile, and the rest of the families are licking their wounds and sniffing at new opportunities. The lingering atmosphere of grief and opportunism is almost as exhausting as the war had been, so when Jaantzen needed someone to go with Starla to find some long-lost cousin on Maribi Station, damn sure Gia had leapt at the chance.

The next stall in this row of restaurants is a respectable-looking empanada joint: sweet corn pastries stuffed with vat shrimp and curry. It also smells amazing. And the address is also a few numbers shy. Dammit.

She's on one of the lowest levels of Maribi Station, and despite the bustle of people and heat from the kitchens, Gia can't shake the chill. Mentally, she knows there's no difference between the heart of an asteroid and a spaceship, but it feels like being buried.

Maribi Station wasn't founded by a corporation like most of the larger outposts in Durga's Belt. Instead, it began as a scrappy claim settlement, with prefab units glued to the asteroid's surface while miners tunneled below, eventually fortifying the tunnels they dug and boosting the number of services and amenities on offer until it became the unmatched transit and shipping hub it is today.

Because of this, it's not a slick company town like so many of the others are, impossible to break into for business unless you have an ID number with the Alliance. Instead, control of Maribi has fallen into the hands of one main family, which acts as an umbrella organization for a whole host of smaller operations on the station. Want to start a competing operation? You'll find yourself out an airlock in no time. But if you have an idea for a complementary business, you're welcome pay tribute to the Maribi Cartel.

Problem is, when a group like the Maribi Cartel has no competition — either for control of the station, or from other nearby shipping hubs — they start to think they can do things like double tariffs and docking fees. Maybe that worked while the families of New Sarjun were occupied trying to murder each other, but now things are back to normal, and something's got to be done.

That's the second reason Gia is here: to be Jaantzen's representative at tomorrow's meeting of interested stakeholders from the planets of New Sarjun and Indira, and a smattering of other outposts in Durga's Belt. Some of the biggest names in organized crime throughout the system are here to do a little collective bargaining.

But first, she's got a one-on-one with a local shipping operator who's not with the cartel. It doesn't hurt to gather other allies, in case the cartel isn't interested in negotiations.

She finally matches the address to a deli two doors down from the empanada restaurant. Its plastic backlit menu is cracked in half, the lower half unlit, and reads like a mugshot lineup of humanity's most uninspired sandwiches. Skimming through the options, Gia can almost taste the wilted lettuce and flavorless soy shawarma.

"What do you want?" growls a young tough leaning in the doorway. Literally nothing about the deli is a customer magnet, but this guy and his buddy, who's playing solitaire at the bistro table just outside the door, ensure that no one could possibly mistake it for a dining option.

"I'm here to see Lorn," she says, and that sparks a round of cagey glances from the toughs.

"That right." The solitaire kid slaps another card onto the bistro table.

Gia crosses her arms, gives them both a look that says she doesn't have time for shit and neither does Lorn, whoever he represents.

"I can come back later," Gia says. "Got all the time in the world, only it seems like Lorn thought it was urgent. I guess you can explain this to him, though."

That gets another look, and finally the tough in the doorway pushes off his lean, lazy like he's been planning to get up at this particular moment anyway. He's half her age and lanky as a string bean — they all are out here — but it's clear he's been training those low-G muscles.

Gia's not here to fight — and looking for a fight in every gesture is another relic of the past few years of civil war she needs to let go of.

Chill, girl. Be chill.

The lanky youth pushes open the door and pauses halfway in, mumbles something to someone on the other side. Glances back at Gia as though evaluating her. Says something else through the doorway.

Finally he turns, pushing the door all the way open with a whipcord arm. "You can go in," he says.

"Thank you kindly." Gia gives him a tight smile, then steps past; he hasn't left her much room and she wrinkles her nose at the reek of his cologne. If she catches a whiff of that on her shirt later, she's gonna be pissed. He grins down at her. She rolls her eyes.

The restaurant is empty. When Gia walks in, the cook behind the window gives her a quick look, then suddenly remembers he needs to be elsewhere. Something's sizzling, smells like burning onions and rancid fryer oil; Gia feels the cloud of it sinking into her pores. Forget the cologne. She's gonna smell like *this* place for the rest of the day.

The inside of the deli is claustrophobic, just like everything on this station. She'd suspected she was in the outskirts of this level, and since the far wall of the kitchen is literally dug-out rock, her suspicions are confirmed.

The thought makes her shudder.

There's a lunch counter outside the kitchen window, a row of booths across from the lunch counter. Only one of them's doing business: a single man, a pair of chipped coffee mugs, and a carafe.

"We're all just on a ball of rock hurtling through space," the man says; he's seen her reaction to the dug-out asteroid wall in the kitchen. "Some of us are just forced to acknowledge it more than others. And as far as I understand, getting tossed out into your Jupari Desert will kill a person almost as fast as getting pushed out an airlock here."

"You're most comfortable with what you know, I guess," Gia says, shoulders relaxed, guard up. It's not the most pleasant conversation opener, but is it a threat? Or just what passes for small talk on Maribi?

The man waves a hand for her to join him.

"Coffee?" he asks, palming the carafe as if to pour.

A rainbow of oils swirl on the surface of the brown liquid in his cup.

"I'm off the stuff," Gia says. The stuff he's got in his cup, at least. "You Lorn?"

"That's right."

Gia slips into the booth across from him and takes a good look.

Lorn is an olive-skinned middle-aged man with a paunch and a receding hairline, looking more like a bookkeeper than the surly soldier she was expecting. He's got that sallow cast to his face that says he lives in space and can't afford a VitD bed, the pinched look she's beginning to suspect comes from the constantly seeping chill you feel on Maribi Station, no matter what the temperature actually is.

Doesn't help that the booth is little more than a metal bench, the paint peeling off. Not designed to sit in for long; Gia's been here thirty seconds and the bones in her ass are already complaining. Good thing this guy Lorn has some extra padding there to help him out.

"I appreciate your time," he says. "My apologies about the secrecy."

"I take it you don't work for the Maribi Cartel."

A tight smile, so fast she's not sure she saw it. "No, Ms. Áte. I don't work for anyone. But I belong to a group that can help Mr. Jaantzen achieve his goals."

She hates this kind of cryptic talk — she's not Manu, Jaantzen's silver-tongued lieutenant — but she forces herself to relax. "Tell me more," she says, figuring polite is always a good move at the beginning. You can always escalate from there if you're feeling feisty, but it's harder to get back to civility if you start off cranky.

"I understand you're here to negotiate a better shipping deal with the cartel for Mr. Jaantzen," Lorn says. "What tariff rate did your boss pay on his last shipment?"

Gia lifts an eyebrow. "No offense, but I'd like to know a bit more about you," she says.

"Thirty-seven percent," Lorn says. "Up from twenty-five percent on the one before. Did you know the cartel charges a different rate to everyone who ships goods through Maribi?"

This is news to Gia, and apparently Lorn can see it on her face because he nods, satisfied. "And that's not even just a number handed down from the cartel — it all depends on who in the docks wants to take their cut, figuring your boss is too far away to complain and doesn't have any other good options when it comes to shipping his goods. It's greed, of course. And prejudice."

If Lorn is expecting her to ask whether the cartel's lackeys are prejudiced against Jaantzen for being from New Sarjun, being lowborn, or just being a newer player to the game, he'll be disappointed. Gia just raises an eyebrow.

"If you don't believe me, just ask some of your fellow delegates, if you have any you trust. The Yangs paid thirty-two percent last time, the Demosgas only eighteen."

"Prices get negotiated differently," says Gia, though the discrepancy is sharp — and it's no wonder Julieta

Yang is so fiery pissed about this whole thing if she's paying nearly double what Aiax Demosga is. "And I'm here to take it up with them directly."

"Not to mention the docking fees," Lorn says, like he didn't hear her. "Or, rather, the bribes certain crew bosses in the docks skim off the top for themselves." He drinks his coffee; the nerve-grating slurp is a negotiation tactic all its own.

"What do you have to say to me?" Gia asks.

Lorn just sets his mug back down. "I expected Mr. Jaantzen to come to Maribi himself."

"He doesn't like to leave the planet," Gia says. And even if he did, with all the reconciliation and restructuring necessary in the wake of the civil war, he's got his hands full.

"Or maybe his lieutenant, Mr. Juric."

Gia tenses at that, not sure if he's probing for information or simply making conversation. "He's busy," she says. Though in truth she's not yet sure if Manu will ever walk again. The last few months of the war did their damage.

Lorn takes another sip of coffee; the rainbow oil slick swirls.

"We've been hearing rumors of trouble back in Bulari."

"We've had some disagreements. Seems to be cleared up now."

"We've heard that Willem Jaantzen is a troublemaker."

"He's a trouble solver," Gia says. "Tell me why I'm here."

Lorn nods slowly, runs a pudgy finger around the rim of his coffee cup. "If we're going to be making deals," he says, "we want to be sure we're making them with the right person."

"Glad to hear it. Because if you want to keep chatting I can go find you a therapist. You want to make a deal, spit it out."

"Ten percent, no dock fees. Guaranteed for five years."

Gia raises an eyebrow. "Who are you to offer that? You're not with the cartel."

Lorn shakes his head, slow. "The cartel is yesterday's news," he says. "We're the next wave of power on Maribi. And we're offering Mr. Jaantzen the best deal he'll get on this rock. Or in Durga's Belt."

"In exchange for?"

"We need funds to finish what we've started. All we're asking is a year's estimated tariffs, prepaid."

Gia laughs. It would be a fantastic deal if there was any chance of it being true. The Maribi Cartel rule their station with an iron fist, and have done for as long as she's been alive. Its leaders have lived through riots and backstabbings and attempted coups and have come out stronger than ever, time after time. And this accountant-looking fellow is going to take them down?

He's furrowed his brow, offended, and she waves a hand: *No offense.*

"Man, I don't mean nothing by it. But we're not gonna just give you a hundred thousand credits and see if it works out. Even if you put your neck out by meeting with me."

Lorn tips back the rest of his oily coffee. Grounds cling to the rim; he grimaces and wipes his mouth with the back of his hand. "I'm a ghost, Ms. Áte; you won't find me again unless I want you to. Tell the cartel someone's plotting against them and they'll yawn — it happens all the time. You have until first shift tomorrow to talk with your boss and get his answer. If you gamble and we win, it's an eyewatering deal. If you keep your cards off the table and we win, you'll want to find another shipping hub."

Like there is another shipping hub this convenient.

"Jaantzen doesn't take kindly to extortion and threats."

"I'd much rather it be an investment offer."

"And that's all there is to the deal."

Lorn gives her a small, private smile. "Only that when the disruption goes down, you remember who your boss placed his bets with, Ms. Áte."

Oh.

He wants her to fight for him, whoever he is. There's not even a chill in Gia's gut at the thought, not after the routine horrors of the past two years. It's just a dull, aching sickness, like bad vodxx on a stomach gone too far past the point of hunger.

If he's done even a touch of research on Jaantzen he'll know she's one of his best fighters and his most skilled surgeon — an asset anyone would need on their side during a war.

An asset she very badly does not want to be.

Every fiber of her being screams to get on the first boat out of here — doesn't matter where it's going, so long as it's not another war zone, so long as she's not just another hired gun in just another never-ending fight. But she tamps that down as a trick of the oily stench of this place. She may have taken Sulila oaths to do no harm when she earned her doctor's badge, but Jaantzen doesn't pay her for her flawed conscience or cloudy, cracked morality. That path forked years back, and Gia took the wrong turn.

At least this time she's not going to be expected to watch everyone she loves be carved up and broken. At least this time it's just strangers.

"I'll talk to Jaantzen."

She holds out a hand to shake, then rises. She needs to get to the gym before Starla misses her, and out of the deli before the oil-impregnated air causes her face to break out like a teenager. This place seems smaller even than when she walked in — it clamps around her like a vise and she's half hoping one of the young toughs at the door gives her enough lip that she feels justified punching him in the face.

"We'll be in touch before first shift tomorrow," Lorn says.

He stays in the booth, opens his comm, pours himself another cup of rancid coffee as though settling in to do some work. Gia pushes through the door and into relatively fresh air as fast as she can, walking past the toughs like they're furniture.

Back out in the corridor, far from the deli, Gia checks her comm and doesn't see a message from Starla asking where she's at. Which means Starla is probably also late for their date at the gym.

You skipping training? she messages.

The screen blinks, message read.

Be there in 5.

That means fifteen, Gia knows from experience. Add to that a few minutes for Starla to get changed and warm up on her own, and Gia still has plenty of time to get her own ass to the gym.

Be here in 2. Had any luck?

The screen blinks as the message is read; Starla doesn't answer.

Panic spikes Gia's gut, but she takes a deep breath.

They're not in Bulari, where for the last years danger has lurked around every corner. Starla's fine. Gia will head to the gym, only a few minutes late, and by the time she gets there the girl will be gearing up to practice.

She has to be.

———————————————————

3

Starla

———————————————————

Mona's signing is rusty, like her fingers need a drop of oil in the joints or her brain needs some dust brushed out of years-old neural pathways so the words flash through rather than catch and snag on the barbs.

"I can't believe you found me," Mona signs.

And Starla gives her a *Wait, what?* look. "You just found me," she signs.

"I've been watching. Those Alliance assholes just got here," Mona signs, and if Starla has had any doubts that this woman is her cousin they're dashed aside by the nonsense sign Mona uses for the Indiran Alliance, the rude one she and Starla made up when they were kids.

Mona's hair still grows long and coarse, curls still tangled and frizzy even though they're now a magenta that practically glows in the neon hologram lights from the brothel behind them. Her girlish freckles are still there, only intensified, constellations scattered across her nose and cheeks. She's still thin, with that tall grace that comes from being raised off-planet, though it's entirely more common here than on New Sarjun. Starla doesn't realize how much she missed not standing out for her own height.

But Mona's changed, too. An old scar cuts across her chin, and another slashes at the same angle across her cheek and the bridge of her nose, the thin line of Durga's Belt slicing through a backdrop of stars. She wears makeup, done like she's well practiced, but Starla's seen makeup cover scars like that easily, and Mona isn't trying.

Starla's fortunate that the Alliance assumes she's dead; there's no bounty on her head to tempt one of Jaantzen's associates into giving up the location of a girl no one has really deemed a threat in the end. Not like there had been on some of her family members who've been captured and murdered in the past five years.

Even so, she looks different, just like Mona does. Keeps her hair cut close and spiky, and lately she's been taking to thick black eyeliner to see if Jaantzen says anything. He gives it a second look sometimes when he thinks she won't notice, but she's pushed enough buttons by this point to know he'll never bring it up.

Not like Raj Dusai would have.

But now's not the time to think about that.

"You and I need to stay out of sight," Mona signs. "I'm glad I found you in time."

"You knew I was here? Where have you been?"

"Watching. I heard someone was asking about me. Wanted to be sure." Mona jerks her chin at the door to the terminal beyond, where the Alliance squadron is still working the crowd. "Can't be too careful."

"The Alliance; I thought they didn't come here." It was one of the reasons Jaantzen had agreed to let her come, that Maribi Station was, well, not hostile to the Alliance. But unwelcoming. And he certainly wouldn't have sent Gia — shit. Starla dug out her comm, held up a finger to Mona.

Ran into trouble, am fine. Found

Mona snatches the comm out of her hands before she can finish the message.

"Who?" Mona asks.

"A friend." Starla holds out her hand for the comm, but Mona slips it into her pocket.

"We need to talk first."

A thread of unease has been winding itself around Starla's gut, tickling faintly at first. Now it's cinching tighter, more insistent. This woman is her cousin, there's no doubt about that. But it's been almost six years. Who has her cousin become?

"The comm," Starla signs sharply. "Give it to me."

But Mona just crooks a finger at her and spins like a dancer, magenta curls whirling out from her shoulders as she darts back into the crowd.

Starla doesn't hesitate.

Whatever's going on, she didn't come all this way just for Mona to flash in and out of her vision like a mirage. And anyway, she's got a few more minutes at least before Gia completely freaks out.

She follows the bobbing magenta curls.

Mona doesn't slow, only gives a quick glance over her shoulder to see if Starla's following her. She's weaving through the throng of people with subtle side steps and bobs like she's been navigating these crowds for years. Starla pushes, less gracefully, always just missing threading the eye of the needle behind her cousin.

Once, Mona checks her own comm, then reaches back to pull Starla into a souvenir shop. They stay there until the pair of Alliance troopers has passed.

"How did you — "

But Mona just winks and continues on.

Who is this woman? Starla knows people change, and she expected Mona to have shifted and grown like anyone else. Starla knows she's done her fair share of changing herself since coming to live with Jaantzen on New Sarjun.

But this woman is confident and unapologetic, decisive. Not the cousin Starla remembers always looking over her shoulder for authorities while Starla dragged them into trouble. The vivid hair looks amazing, warming her cool olive skin, but it's not a color the Mona of Starla's memories would have chosen. That Mona wore grays and blacks, painting herself in the invisible tones of her surroundings in an effort not to be noticed among the throngs of family members. As a result, she was always missing, even when she was in the room — people asking Starla where she'd gone while Starla frowned, puzzled, and pointed to where Mona was curled on a cushion in the corner with her book.

This Mona stands out in a crowd. And that scar . . .

Mona leads her down a staircase past the platform for Maribi's one rickety orbital tram, down three levels to where the rooms have been partially carved from the heart of the asteroid. This floor is part of an entertainment district, but at once seedier and more relaxed than the casinos and bars lining the terminal. Fewer flashing lights, no callers gesticulating in the doorway. Just guttering electric signs announcing Live Dancers, Cold Drinks, Hot Noodles, Cheap Rooms.

Starla's only been on this rock for a few days, but she's starting to know her way around — much better than Gia. Maribi Station is a mining resupply hub built into an asteroid, a transient place built in layers spreading out and down from the docks: entertainment, supply shops, medical bays. Gia's used to navigating cities spread flat, not ones that burrow and cling and climb, passageways winding in on themselves like tangles of cable.

Starla's sense of direction was honed on an asteroid station, though. The Alliance may have destroyed her home, but they can't take that from her.

Mona slips through a doorway edged by a projected hologram that gives Starla the stomach-clenching feeling that she's standing at the edge of an open airlock, staring into the glittering void, ready to let go. Beyond the doorway is only black, illuminated by a scattering of stars and the words *The Nebula* drifting, pulsing neon pink, across the entrance.

Starla pushes through the words; her feet appear to be stepping on nothing.

She takes another step, feeling a giddy rush in the pit of her stomach as the floor seems to drop into oblivion, a startled lurch of confusion when her foot connects with the floor. A few patrons near the door glance up with bored disinterest. They must watch a lot of newbies walk through that door.

Holographic space scenes are projected over gleaming black lacquer walls and floors; for a moment, Starla feels like she's floating, remembers her one stolen space walk years ago, as a teenager when her family was still alive, drifting among the stars while Mona watched timid behind the airlock doors.

Mona's watching her from the bar, grinning.

Starla's soul soars, her heart thrumming with giddiness — and the rhythm of whatever music is playing.

It must be loud; patrons are shouting conversations to each other with gaping jaws while only two feet away. The bartender's bobbing her head just slightly in time to whatever music is playing, black braids wound in an intricate crown, silver-and-turquoise rings outlining both eyebrows.

Mona leans in to ask something — she's angled away from Starla, and Starla's heads-up doesn't bother trying to transcribe over the racket in the bar.

The bartender just shrugs and shakes her head, chin still bobbing to the music. Another question gets an affirmative, and the bartender hands them two weak, over-carbonated local brews, served in sipping bulbs as though they're really in zero G. Mona hands one to Starla and leads her to a low table in the corner of the room. It looks like a glowing asteroid, slowly spinning through the cosmos beneath their glasses.

"Here's a place we can talk," she signs as soon as she's set her drink down.

The effect of this place is so good, Starla almost expects the bulb to drift back up. But, no. They're still on Maribi. Gravity holds.

A thousand questions crowd Starla's mind. Where has Mona been this whole time? What happened to her face? Did anyone else survive?

But there's something she needs to take care of first. Gia needs to know about the Alliance.

"The comm," she signs. "I need it."

Mona nods, but doesn't pull it out of her pocket.

"Your friend, who is she?"

"She works for — " Starla's hands hesitate at *godfather*. "My boss." She fingerspells his name, Willem Jaantzen, and Mona just shrugs like she's never heard of him. Probably true, out here — back home, everybody knows who Jaantzen is.

"Do you trust her?"

"I do. I need to warn her about the Alliance."

"If she's smart she'll be fine."

Starla just holds out her hand for the comm.

"I need to know I can trust you."

Starla doesn't have a response to that. Her own cousin? The years they've spent together, the trouble they've gotten into. The years Starla has spent trying to find Mona, trying to pull her back into the fold. What has she gotten into?

Mona must see the look of shock on her face, because she pushes her palms out. "Calm down. I mean I just need to know." She leans back in her chair like she's relaxed, like the last five years hadn't happened.

Like she isn't holding Starla hostage.

Starla shrugs, stands. "I'll find you later," she signs.

She's halfway to the door when Mona catches her: fingernails light above her right elbow, Starla would recognize the touch anywhere.

Mona presses the comm into Starla's palm. "I'm sorry. I'm sorry. Sit. I trust you."

People are watching, surreptitious glances that prick Starla's skin with heat, but she doesn't sit, not yet.

I'M FINE, she types, hits send. Then: *WATCH OUT FOR ALLIANCE, PATROLS HERE. I FOUND MONA. WE'RE SAFE.*

The reply comes before she even gets back to her seat.

HOTEL. NOW.

SOON, WERE SAFE. AT THE NEBULA LEVEL 15 DONT COME. SEE YOU SOON.

Starla expects another sharp command in answer, but her comm stays dark. She slides it into her pocket, then leans back in her own seat and looks at her cousin, evaluating where they might go from here.

"Okay. Let's talk."

"This place, I love it," Mona signs, fingers making

fluttering motions at the twinkling, floating stars. One drifts past her nose, glittering in her hazel eyes. "And it's safe. I just want to talk."

"Me too."

"What are you doing here?"

"Looking for you." What does Mona think she's doing? "Did you know I was on New Sarjun?"

Starla doesn't want to ask it — a yes, and it means her cousin didn't care. Or couldn't get there, but didn't bother to send a message. But she has to know if Mona knew.

There's nothing but pain in Mona's face.

"I thought you were dead, at first. Everyone thought you escaped from Redrock Prison and died in the desert."

That's the story told, that a fifteen-year-old Starla Dusai, daughter of the notorious Raj and Lasadi Dusai, ran from Redrock and perished in the Jupari Desert. But Starla assumes that most of those in the Durga System's criminal underbelly have put two and two together since a deaf teenaged girl showed up in the home of a Dusai family ally, soon after the destruction of Silk Station. Maybe that just means Mona's not a part of those gossip grapevines. A prodigal cousin of the Dusais now gone straight and narrow and out of the loop.

Though that scar says there's more to the story than straight and narrow.

"You thought I was dead at first," Starla signs.

A look of deep sadness creeps over Mona's face. "I heard, eventually. Sounded like you found a good place, like you were safe. And it's not exactly cheap to travel out here."

She could have sent a message, she could have — Starla lets it go. For now.

"Someone could recognize us here," Starla signs.

Mona wrinkles her nose. "No one who cares."

That doesn't make Starla feel any better, and she doesn't bother to keep it from her face.

"Relax." Mona grabs her drink, taps the bulb against Starla's. Sips. "I missed you," she signs when she sets the bulb back down.

Starla doesn't drink — it's never been her vice. Beads of condensation slide down the sides of her bulb, pooling in patterns that lie just out of sync with the hologrammed surface of the asteroid the table's pretending to be. The liquid seems to hover in a glossy, impossible ring.

"I missed you, too. I thought I would never find you."

"Yet you did." Mona's expression becomes cagey. "How?"

"I've been asking around Jaantzen's connections. One of them recognized you. Why are you on Maribi?"

"What kind of connections?"

Starla shrugs, rotates her wrists in midair as she tries to think of the right words. "Smugglers. People like family. No one to worry about." A thought hits her. "Are you in trouble?"

Mona shakes her head. "More the opposite."

She reaches past her own glass to take Starla's gingerly by the tip of the bulb, holds it to the minimal light. She pulls a thin tube from her pocket, telescopes it with her teeth and wands the faintly glowing internal scanner over Starla's prints.

"What are you doing?"

Mona only grins at her, hands full. After a moment, she secrets away the device and watches her comm until an ident card pops up on the screen.

"Starla Deyva," she says out loud after a moment, hands still full; the lens garbles the transcription, but Starla recognizes her alias on her cousin's expressive lips. Mona gives Starla a sad smile at the name, the first gesture that seems to jive with the sweet, timid Mona Starla used to know. "Relax," she signs. "It's slaved to my comm only."

"Do you know what happened to Deyva?" Starla asks, her fingers forming her mentor's namesign with easy memory even after so many years. But Mona only shakes her head and looks back down, absorbed by whatever she's typing into her comm.

Starla watches her, a familiar chain of thoughts slipping link by link through her mind. If Deyva had survived the attack — and that still seems less than likely, with how close to the core of Silk Station his workshop was — he would've slipped away and remade himself in a new place, as easily as he did when he moved to Silk Station from whatever life he'd left behind that time.

And he'd tell her now to do the same.

She'd asked him once where he'd come from, and gotten nothing but a closed door in response. "The past doesn't do shit for you but tie you down," he'd told her. She'd been twelve, maybe, elbows deep in some generator he was trying to teach her to repair, so she hadn't responded. Deyva had barely understood her USL anyway.

Mona's tapping her fingers on the table beside her comm, which she's slid across the table face up. Starla's fake ident card is displayed there, along with an in-depth analysis, some of which Starla understands, most of which is coded with numbers and acronyms.

She looks up at Mona.

"Your ident card is pretty good, but there are gaps,"

Mona signs. "Like schooling — if someone went digging they'd see that you don't have graduation records."

Starla raises her eyebrows, thoughts of Deyva forgotten. "Just that fast?" Though she can't possibly be wanted, here in this club, the place makes her nervous. The corners are blurred, masked in holograms and dazzled by stars. There are too many things to pay attention to at once.

"No. I wrote a program to crawl for gaps. It's not standard. But I could fix them for you." Mona's expression turns mischievous. "Or I could make you a new name. It's so easy. We could disappear together. It's what I do."

"You forge identities?"

Mona shrugs. "It's just numbers in space. No looking forward. No looking backward."

Starla trails an idle thumb along her jaw, thinking. Mona's always been good at numbers, and at hiding in plain sight. Is it any surprise she might learn to hide other people, too?

Mona leans over her knees, long, thin wrists arched amid drifting constellations. Starla's caught by the intensity of her hazel eyes: they've always been flecked with gold but now the sparks are catching the neons of the strange light from the bar, like Mona's originating stars of her own, like the holograms of the bar are actually dancing lazily forth from Mona's irises.

"I don't need a new name," Starla signs. "I've already got two."

"It's not about having a new name. It's about doing it right."

"Is that how you ended up here?" Starla asks.

"I was invited," Mona signs. "People asking for help. Out here in space, it's not like if you get in trouble, you can just run until you hit a border or get off the grid. There's no way to disappear except to come see somebody like me." She smiles. "I am the border."

"Are there a lot of people looking for border crossings on Maribi?"

"Lately, it's the opposite. I was invited here by a group that plans to work against the cartel. They needed reinforcements, but most of the people they needed were on a watch list — they couldn't just waltz onto the station. And if things go badly, a lot of people on the station are going to need to get off fast. I've got them set up to do it."

A sense of unease grips Starla's stomach. What Mona is telling her is dangerous, much more dangerous than running across Alliance troops.

"Are you saying there's going to be war?"

"The goal is for things to end cleanly," Mona signs. "But, yeah. Things could get ugly. That's why I came to find you, once I knew you were here." She leans forward. "You and me? Let's get out of here. We can go anywhere, be anyone, just like that." Mona snaps both her middle fingers, then bursts fists into stars like a magician. Glittering holograms swim in her irises.

"I can't just leave," signs Starla. "I'm here for a reason."

"On a mission for your boss?" Mona raises a skeptical eyebrow; it's clear what she thinks of the concept of bosses.

"Not just my boss, my godfather. Family."

"They're not your real family. I am."

Her words are technically true, but nothing feels farther from the truth at this moment.

"Then why didn't you try to get in touch, if you

knew where I was? If you knew I was on New Sarjun — "

Mona's fingers flex, stalling for an answer. And Starla can tell she doesn't have a good one.

Starla waves a hand. "Never mind, that's not important. But you can come back home with me now, if you're tired of running."

This gets a laugh. "Running?" Mona arches an eyebrow. "I'm not running, I'm free. Be whoever I want to be, go wherever I want to go. You remember wanting that feeling? I remember you telling me how badly you wanted to leave, to go travel and see the stars. Well, that's what I'm doing. That life you always wanted? I have it, and you can have it too."

For a few seconds, Starla is transported to the past. She remembers that dream for freedom like a terrible, haunting ache deep inside. Like growing bones, period cramps. No way to ease it, impossible to ignore for long.

Mona squeezes the rest of her beer from the bulb; Starla's sits, mostly untouched. "We have a lot of catching up to do," Starla signs. "Let's not start off by fighting."

Mona's expression softens, and for a moment, behind the scar, behind the makeup, beneath the magenta hair, she looks like the timid, uncertain cousin Starla remembers.

"Come back to our hotel. I'd like you to meet Gia."

Starla almost expects her to say no, but after a brief hesitation she nods.

"I'd like that."

They begin to walk, and for a moment it almost feels like old times, elbow to elbow in the corridor, fingers flying and laughing as they catch up. It feels so much like old times that Starla nearly forgets where she is, nearly forgets the years of vigilance and training that have been drummed into her since the last time she saw her cousin.

And so the rough hand on her arm as they pass a trinket and souvenir booth catches her off guard. She tries to spin, but her attacker is stronger, and he gets his arms around her from behind.

Starla wrenches in his grasp, trying to see Mona — she's clawing at an assailant of her own.

"Run," she seems to be shouting.

But there's no way Starla is going to run.

4

Gia

Level 15.

The Nebula.

Gia's going to find Starla there chatting, and she's going to have a calm conversation, going to be the chill big sister, not the overbearing twenty-years-older matron, the house mother.

Gia had mothers and fathers back in the commune, of course, but the authority figures she remembers the most are the brothers and sisters at Sulila, the women and men — Gia's age now — who had learned medicine well enough to teach but not to serve out their indenture in a good Sulila hospital. The most skilled were the professors. The others were house parents, eyes peeled to ensure that each new wave of incoming Sulila students adhered to the moral code: not a sip of alcohol, not a breath of smoke, not a second glance at another student's test — or body. Bots in the blood to check for intoxication. Sensors in the beds to check for . . . well.

But Gia's desire to be the chill not-a-chaperone is in a knock-out-drag-down fistfight with the painfully dangerous reality she's lived in during the last few years of civil war.

And the panic is definitely winning.

Besides a short text an hour ago saying she was fine and not to worry, Starla has gone dark.

Gia isn't worrying, not quite. Instead, she's deflecting it into a balance of fury and barely controlled flashbacks of every time in the last three years that someone disappeared only to show up days later broken or eviscerated, like their enemies were sending her personally intricately designed puzzles to test her skills. She's counting the ones she saved and the many, many more she couldn't.

She rounds the corner of the stairwell to Level 12 — three more to go — and picks up her pace. Their enemies back home are done with. And they have no influence out here in Durga's Belt, Gia tells herself.

It doesn't help.

Level 15.

Fucking finally.

She's trying not to sprint down the corridor when she sees the commotion up ahead. Slows to reassess. She doesn't recognize three of the scrappy fighters in the mix, but she's sparred with the fourth.

Starla.

The rising panic in her chest smooths to confident assurance.

This, she can handle.

Gia wasn't looking to get in a fight, but there one is, right in front of her. Two dudes after Starla and a second girl, and Gia doesn't need to know why or how the fight got started, she just knows they look like they need a beatdown.

And that Starla needs to stop skipping her training

sessions and get her ass fit. But she'll save the I-told-you-sos for later.

The first guy has Starla from behind, pinning her arms, though his stance is off. All it would take is for Starla to drop into horse, destabilize him, jam her sharp-ass elbows into his groin.

For fuck's sake, girl. Think!

The second guy is struggling with a magenta-haired waif just about Starla's age and with the facial structure that says they share blood somewhere down the line, even if her coloring is darker, her bones finer. She's not doing any better than Starla is, though her attacker has a vicious-looking scratch down his cheek.

Girl's been fighting with her fingernails. It's not efficient, but it'll do.

The two thugs are so wrapped in their own fights that they don't see Gia until she's on them. She aims a side kick square into the knee of the man holding Starla, and is rewarded by a satisfying crunch. He goes down with a yowl, and Starla's apparently been paying enough attention to Gia's lessons that she breaks his grip and spins, driving the toe of her boot into his belly.

The other guy spots Gia, sees his buddy fall, and is fast enough to pull a knife from his belt and press it to the magenta-haired girl's throat. He edges back towards the door, footwork pulled off-balance by the squirming young woman in his grip.

"I ain't got no fight with you," he says. "Just looking for this one."

"Yeah, us too," Gia says. She hears a moan behind her, snaps in Starla's field of vision to catch her eye, points at the man on the ground. Starla may not listen to Gia normally, but at least she can take orders in a fight.

She steps back to let Gia deal with the problem, her expression half determination, half terror for her cousin.

But whatever this guy's got planned for Mona, it's not killing her. Way he's holding the knife is for show — this one's got plans that need her alive.

"Stay back or I'll kill her," he bluffs, and Mona catches Gia's eye. There's only anger there, no fear. She knows he's bluffing, too.

Some of Jaantzen's crew are known for their smart talk and negotiation skills. Like Manu, he's got these quips, these little verbal pirouettes he likes to spin around before the fighting actually starts, or to head off the fighting entirely. Even Jaantzen, for all his reticence, can be a smooth talker when he wants to be.

Gia, though, is known for not dealing with assholes.

She gives Mona the faintest of nods, then strolls forward. The guy takes a step back, but Mona's dead weight and he's lost his good stance, shuffles when he realizes he's putting his back against a wall.

"Stop — "

And Gia rushes the guy. He shoves Mona out of the way to face her, but it's clear in seconds that he's not here to make a stand. He slashes wildly and Gia ducks, gets a punch to his kidney before pain lances through her upper arm.

He's gone, shoving his way past her.

Gia calms her breath, turns to make sure Starla and her cousin are all right, and finds a small crowd of gawking bystanders sprinkled along the edges of the row of shops. Knife guy may have gotten away, but the other won't be running anywhere anytime soon. He's lying in the corridor, panting and clutching the knee Gia kicked in.

"Did you enjoy the show?" Gia barks at the crowd.

"Call the cops or something." Though she's not certain what passes for law enforcement on Maribi Station, and she suspects things could go just as well her way as theirs. She won't be sticking around to find out.

Her arm is throbbing, soaked with blood. She lifts her chin at the magenta-haired girl. "You better be who we've been looking for."

"I am."

"Good. Let's get the fuck out of here, then you two can tell me why you're out here getting into trouble."

Starla signs something with a roll of her eyes, and though Gia's USL is shit, she's plenty fluent in twentysomething girl.

"I don't care whose fault it is. But you're not going anywhere but the gym until we get off this rock."

"You're bleeding." This from Mona, who's grabbed a towel from somewhere and hands it to Gia. It says Maribi Station in big blue letters and has a picture of a tourist couple with cocktails in hand against a backdrop of embroidered stars.

"I noticed."

"I know this clinic, it's just a couple floors away. Noncorp clinic, non-cartel; they've fixed up a bunch of my friends for free."

"Sounds like you need better friends. And I've got plenty of credits."

Mona ignores the barb. "They're discreet," she says.

Discretion is probably a good idea at this point. People are staring, and a larger crowd is starting to gather. Someone has helped the man with the crushed knee into a chair, and Gia can't tell if it's a kindness or they're holding him for the authorities. Could go either way, on this rock, and Gia isn't going to wait to find out if she's just come down on the wrong side of a fight in a neighborhood she doesn't know.

Gia's not keen on going to a doctor she doesn't know, but she follows Mona down one corridor, then another, keeping a sharp eye behind them. No one seems to be trailing them.

"Who were those guys?" she asks. "What did they want with you?"

That flash of a look on the girl's face, she's got a lie cooking up.

"I've never seen them before in my life." She's speaking and signing as they walk, including Starla in the conversation.

"I'm sure that's true. But I bet you know what you did to piss them off."

Mona just glances over her shoulder. "We can talk about it later. We're here."

"Here" is an unassuming glass door with a snake-wrapped staff stenciled in the glass. Maribi Free Clinic is stenciled below.

There are a few others in the waiting room. Gia scans them all out of habit, but no one looks outwardly injured or sick. She's the one with blood soaking into her shirt — and it's getting looks.

"Oh my!" The woman behind the receptionist's desk looks up in alarm, then presses a button in the corner. She stands up, businesslike, and ushers Gia to a bank of seats near the door.

"It's fine," Gia tells her. "Didn't hit an artery, just needs a couple of stitches and I'll be good."

The woman makes an unconvinced noise and points at the chair again. "The doctor will be right out."

Mona and Starla are engaged in conversation, and Gia can only catch a fraction of what they're saying.

She's relied too much on Starla's heads-up translator and text over the past few years rather than making the effort to learn her language. She's known that, academically. Now it's starting to sink in.

The clinic door opens and Gia looks up expecting to see a Sulila sister, maybe, or some grizzled asteroid doc. Instead she's looking straight into familiar golden eyes. Her heart stops.

For a moment, neither of them says a word. Then: "Giaconda?"

Tevi Sharaf says her name like he doesn't quite trust his eyes, a look on his face like he's seen a ghost. And maybe he has, maybe he thought she was out of his life for good, washed his hands of her and moved on.

He doesn't much look like he's changed. A complicated cocktail of feelings swells up: regret, joy, anger.

Mostly anger.

The way he's looking to her, he doesn't seem to remember being such a shit boyfriend.

"Let's go," she says to Starla. "I've got a med kit back at the hotel."

But Tevi's already calling for a nurse like Gia's been brought in on a stretcher. Brushing away the receptionist like Gia's on death's door.

Taking her elbow to lead her back to his office like it hasn't been over twenty years since graduation day from Sulila, since he walked out of her life for good.

He's aged, but hasn't lost his good looks. Dark curls cut close and showing the first hints of salt-and-pepper, square jaw dusted with a bit of stubble, the time away from the sun — and the bad lighting in the clinic — taking a bit of the bronze out of his light-brown skin but not the spark from his golden eyes. She's staring despite herself — and despite the audience.

Starla and Mona are watching all wide-eyed like they're going to get a show.

"You and you," Gia says, stabbing a finger at each of them. "Let's go."

Starla juts her chin at Gia's bloody arm, eyebrow raised in an obvious question.

"Now."

Starla gives her a conspiratorial smile, then raises a fist to fingerspell. Gia squints in concentration, her blood-drained, Tevi-addled mind wrapping itself around the letters. *H-O* — shit, is that a *T?* — *E-L.* God, this girl must think she's daft.

"Yes," she says. "Let's go."

She realizes Tevi's still trying to get her back through the door to the examination rooms, that he's asked her the same question more than once, that he's got his scanner out and is starting to check her for a concussion, and she pulls herself together.

"Tevi, I'm fine," she snaps. She waves a hand vaguely at her arm. "Just a scratch."

He frowns at her. "There's a lot of blood for a scratch. Let me take a look."

He touches her arm, hands like they're still sharing a bed, and every fiber of her body doesn't want to stop him.

But.

No. This isn't happening.

Gia catches his wrist with her good hand, pulls him into an wristlock not hard enough to be painful but hard enough that he yelps. The scanner clatters to the floor. She forces him to his knees before releasing his hand.

"Don't touch me," she says. And in his face she sees not the anger she expected, but pain. Grief, even.

"Gia, wait."

"Fuck you," she says. She turns to leave, and when Tevi reaches to stop her, Gia doesn't bother with the ladylike slap she owes him. She decks him with a right hook and walks right back out the clinic door, ignoring the whispers, dripping blood as she goes.

5

Starla

Gɪᴀ's ʜᴏᴛᴇʟ ʀᴏᴏᴍ ʟᴏᴏᴋs ᴊᴜsᴛ ʟɪᴋᴇ Sᴛᴀʀʟᴀ's ɴᴇxᴛ door. There's a single bed and a cot that folds out, a nightstand, a single dressing bench that used to pull out of the wall but is now permanently stuck open. The bathroom is down the hall, which Starla expected from the places she'd stayed with her parents out in Durga's Belt but Gia has been complaining about.

Gia slumps onto the foot of her bed with a sigh; Starla rummages through Gia's duffel for the med kit. A thousand questions are running through her mind, but she knows better than to ask. Gia's not going to say a damn thing if she doesn't want to — their weeks together have hardly been full of heart-to-hearts, and that's even less likely now that Mona is sitting in the corner of the room.

Mona, though, has no such reservations.

"Who was the guy?" Mona asks, signing and speaking.

It earns her an expected knife-edged glare from Gia. "None of your business."

"Looked like an old boyfriend."

"Well, he wasn't a very good one."

"I've had some of those. What'd he do?"

The glare doesn't soften. Mona just lifts her hands: *All right, all right.* She pulls out her comm, entertaining herself while Starla works.

Starla sets the med kit on the edge of the bed and helps Gia out of her shirt. Gia grimaces; the fabric is already glued to her arm with a thin layer of blood. Whatever she's saying shows up in Starla's display as gibberish. Starla's really going to have to look at the language censorship setting on this thing.

The bleeding has slowed considerably and the wound doesn't look deep. Starla's honestly surprised the woman *can* bleed — sparring with her feels like punching carved obsidian. Gia lets Starla clean the wound, then takes the suture machine herself.

"Hold it there," Gia says, guiding Starla's fingers to hold the lips of the wound shut. Starla moves just ahead of the machine as Gia applies the sutures; Gia lets out another string of profanity.

"Who were those men?" Gia asks Mona. "Your own shitty old boyfriends?"

Mona doesn't look up right away, but she does stiffen, fingers still over the screen of her comm. Finally she presses a button and the screen goes dark. She slips the comm into a jacket pocket, zips it shut.

"Nothing like that," Mona says and signs.

"Seems like they had it out for you in particular."

"Not everyone on this station likes me."

"You wanna tell me why?"

Starla's trying too hard to follow the conversation and not paying enough attention to what she's doing — Gia flinches as her finger slips.

"One more," she says.

One last flash from the suture machine and the gash is a puckered caterpillar with perfectly spaced segments, an aberration in the hard topography of Gia's dark bicep. A clinic would have the tech to seal the wound in a way that would nearly eliminate the scarring, but even so, Gia's work with the suture machine is precise. Gia holds out her hand for the swab, gets to work mopping up the blood while Starla settles the suture machine into its self-sterilizer.

"I haven't been on this rock long," Gia says, dabbing at her arm. "But I get the sense it's ruled with an iron fist. Everyone says it's one of the safest places in Durga's Belt since all the crime's regulated and monopolized by one group." She drops the bloody swab into the trash chute and fixes Mona with a look. "Seems to me if someone had the gall to snatch a couple of girls in broad daylight, they weren't worried about it getting back to the cartel."

Mona shifts in her seat, crosses her arms, lower jaw jutting forward just slightly. Five years later, and she's still got the same tell Starla remembers from their childhood: she's been sniffed out.

"They were with the cartel," Starla signs, as simply as she can, and with fingerspelling for Gia's sake. "Are you in trouble?"

Mona just laughs. "In trouble?" She says the words as she's signing. "I'm the one causing trouble. But don't worry about me — I'll be fine."

"I'm not worried about you, kid," Gia says. "I'm worried about us. Gauze?"

Starla had been about to say something, but she takes the bandage and begins to wrap Gia's arm.

"What are you mixed up with?" Gia asks.

"Why should I trust you?" Mona says and signs.

"Because your cousin does."

Mona flashes Starla a look. "Is that true?" she signs only; she's caught on that Gia's shit at USL.

Starla smooths the self-sealing end of the gauze in place. "With my life," she responds. "And with yours."

Mona finally sighs, draws her feet up onto the narrow bench to cross at the ankles, rests shoulder blades back against the metal wall behind her.

Gia shrugs on a clean shirt with a grimace of pain.

"So the cartel owns this place, right?" Mona says, fingers flying as she signs along. "And they own the crime. They set the prices for everything here: food, wages, data, oxygen, you name it."

"And tariffs and dock fees," Gia says.

"Absolutely. Workers here aren't indentured, but they might as well be — they can't negotiate their salaries, they work shitty hours and like it, they don't get any medical care. You saw that charity clinic where your old boyfriend works."

Mona winks at Gia, and to Starla's astonishment, Gia doesn't look pissed at her for the needling.

"You want a better job, what can you do?" Mona says and signs. "Work for someone else? There is no one else. You complain, you try to organize for your rights, and you get tossed out an airlock." Mona gives Gia a pointed look. "The cartel doesn't allow collective bargaining — unless it's coming from rich trading part-ners like your boss. And even then, we'll see how far you get."

It's an odd way of phrasing it, but it is what Jaantzen and Julieta Yang and all the others are doing with this meeting, isn't it? Collective bargaining.

"What does this all have to do with you?" Gia asks.

"People are tired of it," Mona says. "The dock-workers and some of the other workers on the station, they've formed an underground union to organize themselves, and they're going to force the cartel to listen." She smiles, and there's a spark of danger in it that Starla doesn't recognize. "Even if it means forcing them out."

"When."

"I don't know." Mona shrugs, and Starla can't tell if she truly doesn't. This new creature in front of her is so close to the cousin she remembers, yet so foreign. "That's not my part in it," Mona says.

"Your part is to forge identities," Starla signs.

"Yes, my part is making false identities." Mona's seen Gia's look of fierce concentration at Starla's USL and is falling back into her childhood role of interpreter. "I did up the ident cards that got the mercenaries they need onto this station, and the ones that will help the organizers escape if they need to when everything goes down. And I plan to be long gone before that happens."

"Then you better get out of here soon," Gia says.

"What do you mean?" Starla asks.

"I mean I was approached today by someone claiming to represent a group planning to overthrow the cartel," Gia says. "He wanted to offer Jaantzen a better deal, and said we needed to act before tomorrow's meeting."

Mona takes a long, slow breath. "I would take that offer. I've seen the firepower these guys have built up. There's no way the cartel knows it's coming." Mona unfolds herself from the narrow dressing bench and stands. "I have one last bit of work to do before I'm free to go. Sounds like I should probably take care of that." She pulls out her comm and opens a new message, begins to type.

"I'll go too," Starla signs.

Gia's eyebrows shoot up. "Over my dead body are you two heading back out there alone. First there's Alliance troops, now you get jumped in broad daylight — or whatever you call this — and you think I'll just let you go?"

"I'll be careful," Starla signs, but Gia doesn't seem to understand, so she pulls out her comm and begins to type.

I'll be careful, Starla types. *We were talking. We'll pay better attention.*

"Damn right you'll pay better attention," says Gia.

And maybe her paranoia is justified, but there's no way Starla's going to sit in her dingy little hotel room while her newly found cousin disappears again.

Gia's said something Starla missed, the words blinking on and off the heads-up display. Starla holds up a finger. *Listen*, she types. *And don't say anything yet.*

She shows the screen to Gia, gets a nod of agreement.

I trust Mona not to harm me. I don't know who her friends are, but we need information, don't we?

Gia's lips quirk to the side; it's reluctant assent. Starla holds up her finger again before she can answer.

I'll go ask questions, I'll come right back. Mona will tell me more with you not around.

But Gia just shakes her head.

You're not my babysitter.

"You try telling Jaantzen that."

Starla has no doubts that Jaantzen gave Gia strict orders to keep her out of trouble, but what? She's going to tie her up? Knock her out? Lock her in her room?

I'm going with my cousin. I'm sorry.

Gia holds her gaze for three breaths, then sighs

deeply. "Fine," she says. "Just keep in touch so I know where you are, and don't stay long. And watch your back."

I DON'T NEED YOU TO TELL ME TO WATCH MY BACK.

"I don't care what you think you need. What do you think your godfather does to me if I come home without you?"

Starla starts to type, Nothing, he's not a monster — Gia's being ridiculous and Jaantzen certainly wouldn't blame her for Starla's choices. But Gia just waves a hand.

"Forget him. I would never forgive myself. And he would never forgive himself for not coming with us." For a moment, something raw and emotional slips through the cracks of Gia's fierce expression. She tamps it back down before Starla can guess at what it means. "Just promise me you won't do anything stupid."

"Fine," Starla signs. "I promise."

"That had better mean what I hope it meant," Gia says. "I know you're an adult and I'm not a babysitter, but I am your friend. And we're both in an unfamiliar place. Just do me a favor, okay?"

Starla nods. *DON'T PUNCH ANY OTHER DOCTORS WHILE I'M GONE*, she types, testing a little joke and emboldened by the way Mona seems to have escaped unscathed from Gia's prickly lack of humor.

It gets her a wry little smile, then Gia claps her shoulder.

"Go be safe," she signs — or tries to sign.

Starla understands her anyway.

6

Gia

THE BEST CURE FOR THE BURNING ACHE OF A KNIFE
wound is probably sleep, but Gia still has work to do
tonight. Fortunately, there's a run-down little watering
hole just down the corridor from the hotel, and a drink
could just be the next best thing.

Gia settles into a spot at the far end of the bar where
her back's to the wall and she can see the door, then
scrolls through her messages. One from Calanthe Yang
finalizing details for the meeting tomorrow. One from the
medtech she left in charge back in Bulari, updating her
on the status of the human rubble left in the wake of the
war. She scrolls through until she finds the name she
wants.

MANU JURIC: NO SIGNIFICANT IMPROVEMENT.

A hot stab of disappointment pierces her gut. She
downs the rest of her beer, orders another. Opens a
message to tell Jaantzen about Lorn's offer, and that Starla's made contact with Mona.

She doesn't tell him the more worrisome bits of this
trip — he's got enough on his plate at the moment

without hearing about knife fights, or that Starla's currently out adventuring.

Gia's trying not to worry about her. The first argument that surfaces in favor of not worrying is that Gia was Starla's age when she was shipped off to prison — and she survived just fine. It's an argument that would be more compelling if not immediately followed by memories of just how naive young Gia was at the time, how little prepared to handle what had been about to happen.

It's been almost twenty years since she ended up in Redrock Prison, Gia realizes. She's reached the point where more than half her life has happened on the other side of ruin. There's no tipping *that* scale back. No going back to the girl she remembers being: sunny and hopeful, a newly minted doctor ready to make a real difference in the world.

She'd been born in the New Sarjunian desert to a commune of religious types who believed in everything and nothing, two parts superstition and one part mysticism. A lot of "seize your destiny" talk, but she'd bridled at the way they closed themselves off from people who actually needed their help. We could be doing more, she would say — only to be told, We can't save everyone, so why try?

She signed up for Sulila in an act of rebellion. It was a corporate university. It was religious, but offered a profession she could actually use to do good in the world, even if it meant indenturing herself to get that education.

She and Tevi Sharaf had graduated together and had both gotten indenture offers at a Sulila hospital in the Fingers — the slums in the ravines east of Bulari. It was even more run-down then than it is today, with more bodies showing up on the street than even in the past few years of civil war. The culprit in those days and in the war was one and the same: a young and vicious woman who called herself Blackheart and was dedicated to shredding her way to the top of the streets.

Gia had stitched wounds, set bones, pulled out bullets, but none of it made a difference. She was mopping blood out of an arterial wound, and no one was doing anything to stop the bleeding at the source.

There's nothing we can do about it, that was Tevi's argument during those long nights when she'd rail to him about the injustice of it all. We're doctors, not the police, he would say. We're doing all we can.

But one day, when Gia couldn't save one too many kids, she found herself holding a child's mother as she wept. And she learned that it was common knowledge who the killer was, even though the police were telling her over and over they couldn't find the perpetrators.

She coaxed evidence from the mother and took it to a detective she thought she could trust, and was relieved when they actually arrested the guy.

Tevi warned her she was playing with fire, but Gia became obsessed with learning everything she could about Blackheart's crew, gathering evidence from her patients, passing it along to the police. Information was her power: making connections, gaining trust, making a difference.

At least, until Blackheart identified the star confidential informant who was testifying against some of her most powerful lieutenants and turned the tables, framing Gia so perfectly that even her closest friends — even her lover — shook their heads like *We can't believe we never knew her* as she was shipped off to Redrock.

Fuck them, anyway.

Gia is nearly finished with her second glass of the

diesel-fumed local buzz when the door to the watering hole swings open and the last person she wanted to find on this station steps inside.

Tevi's changed out of his scrubs and is wearing a simple pair of gray slacks that fit him very well and a ribbed black sweater with sleeves pushed up his toned forearms. A delicate gold Sulila ID bracelet circles his right wrist like a shackle. He's shaved off the afternoon's stubble, and outside the harsh light of the clinic waiting room, she can't see the salting of silver in his curls.

He looks exactly like she remembers.

Gia's light-headed from blood loss and booze, but she's off her stool with her hand on her weapon before he steps another foot towards the bar.

The bartender glances between them, remembers some more pressing matter in the back room.

"Giaconda." Tevi's voice is soft, melodic. "Can we talk?"

"Rather not."

"C'mon." He takes a slow step towards her, then another, and when she doesn't react to that, he closes the distance between them and slips onto the bar stool beside her. Slowly, like he's sidling up to a stray he's not sure won't bite.

Won't bite again, at least. He's cleaned himself up, but a lump mars his fine jawline, flushed dark under his golden-brown skin.

Gia wants to feel satisfied by that. She doesn't.

But she sits back down and thumbs her comm back on to finish the message to Jaantzen. Buying herself time.

Apparently reassured by the lack of an all-out fight in his bar, the bartender warily returns from the back room and comes over to greet his new guest. Tevi orders two of something Gia's never heard of; it sounds healthy, not intoxicating, and when it shows up she sniffs it suspiciously. It smells like vinegar and lavender. It reminds her of rancid bath soap.

Tevi taps his glass against her untouched one and sips a bit of the froth off the top, his tongue darting out to catch the smudge of foam that remains on his upper lip.

"I hope I'm not intruding," he says.

"Hope springs eternal."

"I just wanted to apologize."

Even in her light-headedness, Gia remembers to bite her tongue. The best way to scuttle a well-meant apology is to be a bitch about it. She reaches for the new drink in front of her for something to do with her hands. It tastes astringent and faintly sweet — way better than it smells.

"I deserved that punch," Tevi says. "If you want to know the truth, I've been wanting somebody to punch me for what I did to you for years."

Gia spares him a glance; he's staring at his drink. "I'll do it again if you need me to," she says. She's rewarded by the twitch of a smile on the corner of his lips.

"I couldn't believe my eyes when you walked in today," he says. "It was like, all these years I've been wanting to apologize, and I haven't even known how to get started finding you."

Gia doesn't trust herself to answer. She takes another sip of the vinegar-soap drink instead.

"'You could save a lot more lives with a gun than with a med kit,'" Tevi quotes, and the skin between Gia's shoulder blades prickles with memory. "Do you remember saying that?"

She does. In her mind's eye they're hiking, one of their rare days off together, an early morning hike before the sun's blasting down. Gia used to love hiking — the loneliness, the empty sky, the birds, the fauna and flora, everything that used to be within arm's length growing up. These days, the desert just reminds her of Redrock, of days battling thirst and heat and exhaustion, hard labor, sand everywhere and nowhere to wash it off, scorpions lurking in her boots and in the corners of her cell.

Now she hates leaving the city. But that day, they'd stopped at a vantage point in the bluffs above Bulari. They were to the north of the city, the valley below them a glittering mess of skyscrapers in the downtown core that flattened out in all directions to sprawl into the plains. The bluff they were standing on wraps around to the southeast, the five ravine slums of Bulari clawing into the hills like fingers. From so high up, you couldn't see the carnage happening where the second and third finger joined, where Blackheart's territory disputes were filling their hospital with bodies.

When Gia remembers that day, she remembers wishing she could enjoy the scenery, but only being able to stare in rage at the spot she'd left, knowing that when she returned that afternoon, more would be dead.

It was one of the last times they had truly spent together. After all those nights staying up smoking and drinking while she fumed about the indenture system, growing increasingly obsessed with the kids in the emergency rooms, in hunting down the monsters who were doing this to them — they'd grown apart. Gia was finding solace in her quest, and Tevi cautioned that she was going outside the bounds of her oath with all this talk of vengeance.

This talk of saving more lives with a gun than with a med kit.

"Yeah, I remember saying that."

She's not sure if she believes it now, or if now she just understands that there are always more killers hiding behind the ones you take out.

Maybe some force brings more order. Maybe the Maribi Cartel, for example, has a low body count because they run a tight ship. Maybe a Bulari with her boss Jaantzen in charge and Blackheart gone is a safer place, or maybe it's just become unsafe for a different set of people — she doesn't know.

She's not a philosopher, she's a fighter.

"What are you doing on this rock?" she asks. She juts a chin at the chain on his wrist. "You still working for Sulila?"

"Yeah. This clinic isn't a Sulila one, it's run by a local charity. Some of the people coming into Maribi haven't seen a doctor in years. They come in, get fixed up, ship back out into the black. The clinic's model's good, though — they train locals in Durga's Belt for free in exchange for a commitment to work for two years at the clinic before finding other work."

She frowns. "Still sounds like an indenture."

He shakes his head. "No contracts, just the honor system. We've got some doctors who've been there over a decade. Others go back to their home stations and start their own practices. Others go get good jobs on one of the planets, or take on with a ship's crew. It's providing well-paying jobs and much-needed medical personnel out here."

"We could use something like that on New Sarjun."

"I've been thinking about that," he says. He's starting to relax, that spark glinting in his eye as he shares his dream. "I'm here on loan from Sulila to help with training, but I also needed to get away and think about what's next for me. I earned out my indenture five years ago and I don't have family tying me down, so I think it's time for a change."

Gia makes a noncommittal noise, realizing too late that it sounds dismissive. The truth is, listening to Tevi's optimism and plans to make a difference in the future is putting an uncomfortable twist in her gut.

Or maybe it's the vinegar-soap drink, which she pushes away.

Or maybe it's annoyance at the giddy flip in her stomach when he said "no family tying me down."

"You look good," Tevi finally says, and instantly a flush creeps into his cheeks. "Fit. I mean, you obviously are fit." He rubs a palm over his jaw where she hit him with a rueful smile. "You train?"

"As much as I can."

"And how's life? Still on New Sarjun? Kids? Married?" He gives her a too-casual smile at that last question, then clears his throat.

"Just to my job."

"And what is it you do?"

"Right now? Manage shipping logistics for a small Bulari importer." It's true enough this week; what she does for Jaantzen changes day by day.

"That sounds uneventful." Another look, this time pointedly, at the bulk of bandage visible under the thin silhouette of her sleeve. "Did you get in a fight with a shipping AI?"

"Muggers." Gia takes a long drink of her beer.

"That doesn't happen on Maribi. The people in charge — "

"Keep it safe. I've heard the propaganda."

He glances around, but she didn't say it loud.

"Well, it sounds interesting," he says, though it clearly

doesn't. Gia's fully aware of how gamely he's trying to engage her in conversation, and how difficult she's making it. She just hasn't decided yet if she's ready to play along.

This trip to Maribi Station was supposed to be a cakewalk to help take her mind off what's been going on back home — not a meet-and-greet with old ghosts.

She tips back the rest of her beer, shakes her head when the bartender catches her eye. Having another tonight isn't going to make anything better. The only thing that will is heading back to her hotel room and burying herself in work until she falls asleep.

"Giaconda."

She's breathing shallow. Nobody says her name like that. Not anymore.

"Gia, what happened to you?"

Gia shifts in her stool to look at him full, considering. What happened to her? It's written on her body in tattoos any asshole can see.

"Prison," she says.

"I can see where you've been," he says. "I asked what happened to you."

Coming out of any other mouth, Gia would've left right then and there. Coming out of Tevi's, the question's filled with genuine curiosity and compassion. He always did have that way of making you want to bare your soul, tell him your truths because no one else in the world seemed to actually care when they asked. She's seen complete strangers open up to Tevi, tears streaming down their faces as they answer his question, "Tell me how you're doing," with more honesty than they've answered anything in years.

It's a heady feeling, being seen, and for a moment all Gia feels is lightness, yearning, an overwhelming desire to share her story with the one person who will truly listen.

What happened to her?

"Long story," she says, and because old habits die hard, because her old instinct is still to derail his intense emotional gaze into safer, less vulnerable territory, she finds herself saying, "But I got a few tattoos in more interesting places I could show you."

She sees the way his pulse quickens, the Adam's apple jump in his throat. And maybe she'd only meant that as a joke, but heat is blooming in her belly now.

His smooth fingers find hers, his golden brown against her midnight black. Stars are born in the places their skin touches, scattering deliciously through her nervous system.

"Gia," Tevi says softly. "I'm so sorry I didn't believe you."

There's a flood of pain hiding behind the barrier that will fall if she allows herself to contemplate the sincerity of his apology.

So she doesn't. She leans against the back of the bar stool, fingers still laced in his, and lifts an eyebrow. "Then why don't we go someplace where you make it up to me?" she asks.

And she doesn't even regret it.

7

Starla

Starla's been feeling like she has a handle on
Maribi Station's layout, but Mona slips through it like
she grew up here. She leads them through secret corridors and service entrances, and twice she gives a subtle
sign to a rough-looking worker who lets them through an
entrance he's casually pretending not to guard.

The longer Starla's on Maribi, the less it's starting to
feel like home. Nothing on Silk Station was really off-
limits other than someone else's quarters. Nothing
needed to be guarded because there were no secrets —
there was only the wild, tangled nest of the extended
Dusai clan.

Their destination is a door, half-hidden behind the
slumped husk of a forklift suit. The suit is missing an
arm, and it looks like most of the wiring has been
salvaged — nobody's going to come looking for it
anytime soon. Mona raps on the door in a precise
pattern, and after a moment the handle turns and juts
forward an inch. Mona pulls the door open and motions
Starla through.

The room beyond is cramped and hot, shot through with the vibrating hum of servers, glowing with monitors, and draped with a spider's web of wiring and cables. A guy about their age is absorbed in a screen — he glances up long enough to see Mona beside Starla, then holds up a finger and goes back to what he's doing. His skin is a rich dark brown, his cloud of black hair cut short and teased into a sea of spikes, concentration held in his pointed chin. He's wearing what looks like a dockworker's jumpsuit, with a prosthetic glove encasing his right hand.

Starla leans in for a closer look. The prosthetic's a cage of tendons and pulleys designed to compensate for his partially missing middle three fingers. The exoskeleton fits snugly over the back of his hand, but the ring finger seems to be off — the boy taps it against the table every few keystrokes in an attempt to straighten it back out, but it doesn't seem to be slowing his typing any. He's got a rhythm.

"This is Ahmed," Mona signs, speaking aloud to include Ahmed; he doesn't get a namesign. "Ahmed, this is Starla."

Ahmed lifts his chin but doesn't look away from his work. "Hey, Starla," he says, the words scrolling across her lens. "Gimme a second."

Mona pushes a stool towards her and finds her own perch on the open corner of a table. Starla watches Ahmed's screen, but she can't tell what he's doing. She's always had an intuitive sense of how machines work mechanically, but the intangible flow of numbers and information within a computer is not her thing.

Ahmed's back is to them, so Starla figures they can talk without disrupting his concentration.

"Who is Ahmed?" Starla signs, and the twinkle in

Mona's eye tells her before her cousin's hands can make the sign.

"A friend," she signs, though the mischievous dimple in her cheek says he's clearly more. "He works for the Dockworkers Union."

"What's he working on?" Starla asks.

"The last few false identities for union workers. They're pretty confident they can win if the cartel tries to break their strike, but they need an out in case something goes wrong."

Mona looks over Ahmed's shoulder, cheek brushing cheek, and says something to him that comes through as technical garbage on Starla's heads-up display; he nods and goes back a few lines of code, replaces a few characters.

"I've been doing this for longer, but he's almost as good as me now," Mona signs in explanation. She winks. "Almost."

"How'd you learn?"

"Do you have all night?" Mona asks with an expression that says, *It's a long story.*

"I have all the time you want."

"Well . . ."

All the rust has shaken off Mona's USL since their first few moments in the Nebula. Now her hands are fluid as mercury, her expression shifting from guarded to open, even silly at times, as she launches into a story about bouncing around the Belt with the few cousins she'd escaped with, reuniting briefly with her older brother Amit before he wandered on to his next big adventure. About ending up in a public boarding school for orphans and children of deep space crew members on one of Indira's moons before she learned the intricacies of creating new fingerprints, new names, new lives.

About slipping out of the boarding school with no money, just a clutch of stolen ident cards which helped her open bank accounts, about the years of learning the subtle ways to dance through the back webs of financial institutions without getting caught, about starting to make a name for herself as the person to go to if you needed to disappear.

"And that's just your life, now?" Starla asks. "Disappearing?"

"It's worked this long, hasn't it?" Mona glances over Ahmed's shoulder again; he's still busily typing. "Tell me about New Sarjun. Do you like it?"

And so Starla tells her about the planet she's started to think of as home. At first it's benign things, about the heat, the incessant grit, the sandstorms that blacken the horizon and clog the air filters, what it's like to see a moon through atmosphere, to see Indira on the horizon, to have Durga so bright.

She stays light and Mona doesn't probe. Starla's still not sure how to talk about the things that have truly passed since she last saw her cousin. Her parents' deaths, what it was like in the Alliance prison before Jaantzen broke her out, how lonely she is even among friends.

"I'm done," Ahmed says, and Starla breaks away from the small talk with relief. Ahmed spins the chair around to face them, rolling his neck and taking the prosthetic glove off with a sigh — she can see places where calluses have built up on his knuckles, the scarring around his wrist where the harness clamps on awkwardly.

"Can I look at it?" Starla signs, glad for another topic besides the one which was starting to hit too close for comfort. "I might be able to fix the finger."

"Yeah, let Starla look at it!" Mona's speaking as she

signs again; she holds out her hands to take it from Ahmed and pass it to Starla. "She's amazing with machines."

Starla holds up a hand, raises an eyebrow, like *Don't oversell me.* But the problem is apparent instantly. One of the pins in the fingertip's hinge is too short and worn round by use, allowing the bracket to shift off the pin and bind up. It needs a new pin — or, maybe she can fix it with the length of wire coiled on the table beside her.

"Do you have a tool kit?" she asks Mona, who rummages for one on the crowded table behind her.

A few moments later, Starla hands the prosthetic back. Ahmed flips the cage back over his hand. He flexes his fingers, turns back to the terminal and types. His face lights up with a grin.

"That's perfect, thanks!" He runs through his fingers a few more times, then undoes the prosthetic again. "Work accident," he says. "I managed to cobble this thing together with the help of some friends and some free printer plans I found on the net, but the cartel doesn't really pay out wages if you hurt yourself and can't work. Meant I had plenty of time to learn skills that don't involve being on the wrong end of a ten-ton shipping crate being pushed through zero G. You may float like nothing else, but a shipping crate still feels like ten tons when it hits your fingers."

Mona's watching her to see how much she's caught, and Starla gives her a thumbs up. The heads-up unit's transcription software doesn't always work with strange accents, but either Ahmed's is pretty close to standard New Sarjunian or he's speaking clearly enough for the tech to catch almost everything.

"Did you finish what we needed to?" Mona asks him.

Ahmed nods. "You should check it over, but I think

we're good to go." He gets up, stretching carefully in the cramped space so he doesn't hit anyone. Mona takes his chair and leans into the screen, scrolling through the lines of text.

"Mona tells me you're here as part of that group that's trying to negotiate better terms with the cartel," Ahmed says. He's half turned away from her now, one eye on what Mona's doing, making it harder for Starla to verify what the display's telling her with what his lips seem to be saying.

You know about that? Stella types on her comm. She shows him the screen and he laughs.

"Of course. Everyone in the union thinks it's hilarious to see a bunch of off-worlders thinking they can come and negotiate with the cartel. Clearly none of you have tried to before." His expression grows darker. "It doesn't work."

But they allow unions? Starla types. I didn't think they did.

"Of course not. If they get even a whiff of what we're up to, we're all out an airlock. And they're starting to get suspicious, which is why it's time to act. They're getting close to figuring out who we are. Especially — " He gives Mona a concerned look, and whatever he says next is too muffled, his face turned away.

"It'll be fine. Did you get the stuff I asked you for?" Mona says.

He answers and she turns back to the screen. They're both turned away from Starla now, and Starla can feel the electric hum of the room in her chest. It must be dampening their voices, because only a few scant words push through to fracture in her heads-up display. She switches it off and entertains herself tracing wires from machine to machine, matching what she sees with systems configurations she's been studying lately.

Mona scritches her nails above Starla's elbow to get her attention, a gesture unchanged by the years. On the screen behind her, data is streaming from one server to another.

"We're good to go," she signs. Then, speaking to Ahmed: "Tell Berzac the file's encrypted and I'll send him the code as soon as I'm off this rock."

Starla doesn't miss the glance shared between them. There's something deeper behind it on Ahmed's end: pain, resolve, reluctance, disappointment.

Mona stands, breaking eye contact with him sharply; Ahmed's gaze lingers a moment longer before he picks up his prosthetic and begins to test the finger, as though trying to distract himself.

Mona turns to Starla with a smile. "I hope you're as good with scissors as you are with a screwdriver," she signs.

Starla raises her eyebrows. If Mona is looking for a craft partner, she's going to be disappointed. "That's a solid no."

But Mona just flicks a wrist dismissively. "You'll do just fine."

THE APARTMENT AHMED and Mona are sharing is little bigger than the hotel rooms Gia and Starla are in. The bed's a little wider, and there's room for a chair as well as a dressing bench, along with a tiny pull-down counter in the kitchenette and a rehydrator that looks barely big enough to fit a single ration box.

Mona goes immediately to the bed, roots through the

shopping bag sitting there. "This is perfect, baby," she says to Ahmed; he's drifted in the door behind them. She pulls out a pair of scissors, a comb, a couple of bottles labeled things like Creme Developer and (Into The) Black.

While Mona's busy setting out bottles, Starla takes the opportunity to text Gia: AT MONA'S PLACE I'M FINE. BE HOME SOON.

After a moment she gets the reply.

I'M OUT. MESSAGE ME WHEN YOU'RE HOME.

Out? Grabbing a drink? Starla doesn't think Gia has any friends here, unless . . .

Mona's gentle nails on Starla's arm get her attention. "What's up?" Mona signs.

Starla shows her the comm. "I wonder who she's out with."

Mona claps her hands in delight. "That doctor! God, he was hot." It's a sign Starla hasn't seen in years, their own personal slang for the dreamy vid stars they used to fawn over as girls. It brings with it a stab of longing; Starla shoves the feeling aside.

Starla throws up her eyebrows in mock horror. "He was ancient!"

"Oh, honey." Mona gives her a secret smile. "Old and experienced is a good thing. Here."

Mona hands Starla the scissors, then shucks off her chunky knit sweater. Beneath the bulky garment she's scrawny, shoulder blades jutting like knives.

"I'm thinking short in the back and long in the front," Mona signs; she's voicing again, too. Starla glances over to where Ahmed has been watching them sign, curious. "But we can just play with it until we come up with something that seems to work. I've never had short hair, it's probably going to be a mess with my curls." She frowns at Starla. "Do you think I should just straighten it? I hadn't thought about that."

Starla shrugs, shares a look with Ahmed. Fashion isn't her strong point, and she's never cut anyone's hair before. She sets the scissors down. "I don't know what will look good," she signs. "What are you going for?"

"Different," Mona says and signs; Starla catches Ahmed's wince. Mona hands Starla her comm, with an ident card displayed. Rania Jacovsin, it reads. There's a list of demographic stats, but no photo. "Make me look like somebody who has this name, whoever she is."

Tentatively at first, then with gusto at the sharp, tactile feel of the blades through Mona's thick hair, Starla starts to cut. Swaths of magenta curls coil on the floor at her feet.

She catches Ahmed's expression in the mirror; he looks physically pained, though he hasn't said a word. After the first few cuts, he leaves, with a comment about the room being too crowded, and Mona's shoulders finally relax when he's gone. She breathes out, slow.

Stella catches her eye in the mirror and lifts an eyebrow: *You gonna tell me or what?*

"He doesn't want me to go," Mona signs. "But what will I do here? Sure, I think his union can win, especially given what I've seen of the cartel. But I'm not gonna risk being here if they don't. And even if they do, I'm done with this place. Time for something new."

Starla takes the opportunity to set the scissors down and fluff Mona's hair before she answers. "He doesn't want to go with you?"

Mona shakes her head. "He keeps saying he'll come maybe later, but we both know he's not really going to. He's invested in this place, in this fight. That's just not me."

"And who are you?"

"Rania Jacovsin," Mona fingerspells. "Or whoever."

"Come back to New Sarjun. You can be whoever you want to be there."

"No I can't. There I'm your cousin."

"You're my cousin no matter where you are."

Mona gives an annoyed little shake of her head. "You know what I mean. This looks good." She rakes her fingers through her new bob.

Starla manages to keep the conversation away from heated topics while they pull the magenta dye from Mona's curls, rinsing her hair in the tiny bathroom sink before daubing (Into The) Black in its place.

But she can't help thinking she should have been there when Mona dyed the magenta in the first place, that she should have been there through whatever gave her that scar down her cheek. That they never should have been separated.

"What is it?" Mona asks, when they've got her dye-soaked hair safely wrapped and have rinsed most of the traces of purplish-black from their hands.

Starla flexes her hands, thinking how to phrase it. "I'm just thinking about how much we missed," she signs finally.

She's said the wrong thing; Mona's face closes down.

"Why do you spend so much time thinking about the past," Mona signs. "Here's a tip: Don't obsess about it, and you'll be happier."

Starla frowns at her. "What's so wrong with thinking about happy times?"

"Don't you get it?" Mona says out loud; Starla's touched a nerve to get Mona to forget to sign. Mona glances at the door as though she'd been louder than she intended, then switches back to sign. "Silk Station is gone," she continues. "Your parents are dead. My mother is dead. Everyone we know is dead and gone."

"Not everyone."

"Does it matter?" Mona pauses, and a muscle twitches and sets in her jaw. Starla can see her resolve stiffen, her spine straighten. "I don't think about the past," Mona signs. "I learned not to at the boarding school. You think about the good times and you just get sad. You think about how your family's all dead, and you start to cry. You think about the last thing you ever said to your brother, and it's devastating because you don't know if you'll ever see him again."

And the resolve softens, just a touch, just enough for Starla to rub a tentative thumb across Mona's knee.

"I know," Starla signs. "Of course I know."

"How did you deal with it?" Mona asks.

Starla shrugs. "I was angry. But I decided I needed to find everyone. I had a goal."

Mona stiffens again as though rebuked.

Shit. "I didn't mean — "

"I thought you were dead." Mona voices the words as she signs, snarls it, teeth bared and defensive.

"I didn't mean you weren't looking for me."

"I thought you were dead," Mona signs again, but this time it's not an excuse, it's grief.

Starla pulls her into her arms. She can feel the vibrations of Mona's vocal cords humming against her shoulder, feel her soft, hot breath on her neck, but she can't see Mona's lips, and if her heads-up display transcribes whatever it is Mona is saying, Starla can't tell — it's fogged from tears that have appeared from nowhere.

Mona stinks of sharp, astringent hair chemicals and old cigarette smoke.

Starla circles *sorry* over her heart, in front of Mona's

nose, and Mona nods into her collarbone, hands clawed into the back of Starla's shirt.

Eventually Starla breaks the embrace, releasing Mona and feeling her cousin's hands go slack, the muscles which had been like iron bands melting back into flesh, and fall to her side. Mona rubs the back of her hand across her eyes — they're red-rimmed now, her makeup has smeared, and she suddenly seems so much younger. The gangly teenager Starla remembers, not this poised and angry young woman Starla doesn't know what to do with.

Mona turns back to the mirror and daubs at her face with a towel, blotting away streaks of eyeliner, though not the signs of her grief. Her shoulders finally slump into stillness, and her body relaxes, leaning to rest against Starla's comfortably.

"I should leave this in another hour," she finally signs, wafting open hands at her wrapped hair. "And you should probably go home before your bodyguard gets done with her booty call."

Starla lets herself laugh at that.

"How do I get in touch with you?" she asks, seriously.

Mona grabs Starla's comm and types her number in, followed by another, more complicated address. "That's my local comm, I'll have it while I'm on Maribi. But you can always call me at that other address. No one knows that one and I can check it anywhere."

They hug again, and this time it's fierce.

"I'll see you before you or I go," Mona signs. "I promise."

8

Gia

A chime from her comm — the "it's the boss" chime — wakes her.

It takes her a moment to realize that she was dreaming, because she never sleeps deeply enough to dream; it takes a moment longer to realize she's not in her Bulari apartment — or in her hotel bed on Maribi. Or alone.

She blinks herself awake with heart racing to find Tevi. Okay. She checks the time on her comm: it's still plenty early. Good.

A new message from Jaantzen blinks on the screen. Gia rolls away from Tevi's gentle snores, then plays the message with the volume almost all the way down.

A trick of the camera is painting Jaantzen's dark-brown skin ashen, and he's thinner than she's ever seen him. Not gaunt — the big man will never be gaunt. But . . . haunted.

She glances over her shoulder as the message begins to play, but Tevi doesn't wake. Twenty years later and the man can still sleep through anything, bolstered by a babe-like innocence and trust.

It continues to be maddening.

"Thank you for letting me know about the potential counteroffer," Jaantzen says. "I find it compelling, but I trust your judgment on the ground. Ah, so to speak." He rubs a palm absently over the back of his neck, thinking; he looks exhausted. Gia finds herself simultaneously wishing she was there to help and guiltily grateful to be far from it all.

"My gut says yes," he finally says. "But talk with Ms. Yang before making a final decision. Follow her lead."

It's what Gia would've done if she hadn't been able to reach Jaantzen. Calanthe Yang and her mother have more experience with international shipping matters than Jaantzen does — and certainly more than Gia does.

Jaantzen clears his throat. "I'll make the funds available to you if you need them. And give my . . . regards to Starla." He leans forward to switch off the screen.

"Do whatever the Yangs do, tell Starla you love her," Gia mutters, translating.

Beside her, Tevi stirs. "Who was that?" He yawns.

"My boss."

Gia switches the screen off; Jaantzen's face and name gets around New Sarjun, especially lately, but there's no reason Tevi should recognize his voice. She feels another twinge of guilt at wanting to hide who she works for. Everyone she knows now in Bulari is aware she works for one of the more notorious crime bosses in the city, and for years, being one of Willem Jaantzen's people has been a badge of honor.

But the thought of telling Tevi gives her pause, and that pause fills her with shame.

Though what does it matter? She'll be off this rock and never see him again after this.

She tosses her comm onto her balled-up pile of clothes and rolls back to face him. Tevi's all pecs and sleep-tousled curls in a tangle of sheets. He gives her a smile that erases twenty years and makes her heart stop beating.

"I gotta work," she says. She doesn't have a lot of experience ending these sorts of things. "Thanks."

"And I should get back to the clinic," he says, but his smile doesn't fade. She'd meant it as a farewell, but apparently he isn't taking it that way. "Maybe we can meet for dinner tonight?"

"Maybe," she says, managing to make her tone sharp even though her words betrayed her. Tevi's smile fades.

"Let me take a look at your arm before you go, at least," he says. The sheets slide down as he sits up; she cuts her gaze quickly away.

But she stays a moment longer, lets him unwind the bandage and reapply the dressing in silence. He doesn't tell her she should come into the clinic and have him fix it up so it doesn't scar; he knows she knows.

He finishes and she shrugs her shirt on, grateful for the thin layer of clothing between her skin and his touch. She busies herself finding the rest of her scattered garments and putting herself back together.

"How do I find you again?" he asks. When she looks back, he's pulled on his scrubs; she relaxes a fraction more.

"Give me your number," she says, a slip of the tongue — what is wrong with her? She tells herself to mistype it, to forget it, but her fingers ignore her and type the correct number into her comm as he speaks.

"My post ends in three months," he says. "Then I'll be back on New Sarjun. I'd like to see you again."

"I'll call you," she says before she means to. For fuck's sake.

She can't call him. Their paths diverged decades ago, and she can't see a way to bridge that gap back into his world.

No. This has to be it.

She realizes she's lingering awkwardly, waiting. That he is, too. A couple of hours ago, being tangled together in sheets and nothing else had felt like the most natural thing in the world; now, she won't be comfortable around him unless they're both chastely zipped into vac suits.

She takes a step towards the door before she realizes he's still holding her hand. Or is she holding his?

For a moment she thinks he'll kiss her, but he doesn't try. Tevi just squeezes her hand and steps back.

SHE ALMOST MANAGES to sneak into the shower cubicle in the hallway outside her hotel room, but Starla's door opens just as Gia is keying in. It might look like a regular morning trip to shower, or it might look like Gia's still wearing yesterday's clothes and didn't make it to her own bed last night.

From the conspiratorial look Starla gives her, Gia's pretty sure it looks like the latter.

Nice job, chaperone.

"Be ready in fifteen," she snaps by way of greeting. Starla gives her a thumbs up and a grin.

Inside the shower room, Gia sinks onto the bench with a sigh. Pulls out her comm, where Tevi's new contact card still blinks on the screen. She almost opens a message to him, but swipes it into her comm's archives instead; she's got more important matters to attend to than her rebellious libido.

She's not sure if communication within the station is monitored — fortunately, Calanthe Yang is a master of corporate espionage and information brokering, and on the weeks-long trip out to Durga's Belt, she had coached Gia through various scenarios they were likely to encounter and came up with a code for them to use just in case.

One that now makes Gia very uncomfortable.

She shakes the cobwebs from her mind and begins to type, cursing Calanthe's whimsy.

THINKING OF HOOKING UP WITH A GUY I MET YESTER-DAY. INCREDIBLY ATTRACTIVE, BUT SEEMS A BIT YOUNG. LOTS OF CONFIDENCE, THOUGH. WHAT DO YOU THINK? I CAN SEND PICS IF YOU HAVEN'T MET HIM.

Gia reads it through a couple of times to make sure the meaning is clear enough, then hits the shower, scrubbing her skin raw and scalding. She's getting dressed when the comm chimes again.

It's Calanthe:

I SAW HIM YESTERDAY, TOO, AND I SAY GET THAT SUGAR! YOUNG MAY BE RISKY, BUT A GIRL'S GOTTA LIVE! AND ANYWAY I'VE BEEN NOSING AROUND THE SCENE FOR US BOTH AND I BELIEVE HE'S THE MUCH SMARTER CHOICE. SEE YOU IN A FEW!

Gia takes a deep breath, parsing past the exclamation points to Calanthe's true meaning: Calanthe got the same offer Gia did, and the Yangs are putting their money on the union beating the cartel. Which means Jaantzen wants Gia to, too.

She scrolls through her past messages and finds one from Lorn that came in during the night. It looks like a junk invoice, the sort of thing designed to get the unwary to enter their account numbers so scammers can siphon out funds. But at a closer look, it's clearly from him. Gia fills out the form with the account numbers Jaantzen sent her, checks everything twice more before hitting send.

There's a sharp *tat-a-tat, tat-a-tat* on the door. Starla's knock.

"It's time," the girl signs.

I HEARD FROM JAANTZEN, Gia types, then shows the words on her screen to Starla. Her USL is way too bad to communicate this, and she won't risk saying it aloud. All this subterfuge has her paranoid, but it's certainly founded. She wouldn't be surprised if they're being bugged. *HE SAID THROW OUR WEIGHT BEHIND THE UNION. YANGS ARE TOO.*

Starla nods seriously, then takes Gia's comm to type her reply.

She hands the comm back.

HOW'S THE DOCTOR?

Starla winks.

"None of your goddamn business," Gia says. "Now let's go."

IN BULARI the rich build their meeting spaces high in skyscrapers, perched like kings surveying their glittering city. But here on Maribi Station, the cartel buries deep. Intellectually, Gia knows this is safer — the deeper they go, the more protected from radiation they are. But in her gut she can feel the weight of the rock around them. It's like being buried alive.

Calanthe Yang meets them at the lift. Gia has met Calanthe's mother on more than one occasion, and she'd expected Calanthe to be as serious and austere as the old lady. But Julieta Yang's eldest daughter is ferociously energetic and unexpectedly bubbly, more like a successful businesswoman than the heiress to the empire of a smuggler extraordinaire.

Calanthe greets them both with exclamations of delight and air-kisses on the cheek that keep her dark purple lipstick firmly on her full lips. She's slim and poised, wearing an impeccable suit of dusty gray-blue wool so fine it shines and a soft peach silk blouse that matches the rose gold and mother-of-pearl combs in her glossy black hair.

Even during their weeks on the shuttle, Calanthe made Gia feel underdressed — and today is no exception. Starla's wearing something that says she belongs on the station, though Gia doesn't know enough about fashion to put her finger on how. Gia's wearing a simple, loose-fitting suit Manu picked out for her when she was worrying about what to wear before she left. It's one part comforting and one part heart-wrenching to be wearing something that reminds her of her best friend, still paralyzed from the waist down back home.

Not for the first time does she wish he was here in her place, as he should be. But since Gia isn't Manu the Silver-Tongued, she recognizes that she's here in part as muscle for Calanthe, a reminder that the Yangs have powerful allies who win wars. Her job is to look tough and let Calanthe, the lawyer, do the talking.

"All good to go?" Calanthe says to Gia, and she's not just talking about whether or not she's ready for the meeting. Gia nods. "Us, too," Calanthe says. "Fantastic." She pushes the button to call the lift, and they don't say much after the doors close around them, just Calanthe exchanging the few pleasantries she's learned to sign with Starla.

When the doors open again, they're in the biggest room Gia has seen on the station. It's three times her height, and could easily fit a regulation boxing arena with seating for several hundred. It's done up in what she assumes is space station chic, all gold inlaid wire in geometric patterns across the walls, with black enamel accents and recessed lighting fixtures that wash sprays of light up onto the walls.

The room is big enough to host a sizable gathering, but right now their small group barely makes a dent in the space. Aiax Demosga, whose family owns a string of glitzy casinos in orbit around New Sarjun, is already sitting at the big round table. Beside him is a middle-aged man with smooth black skin wearing a suit of the type Gia associates with Indiran businessmen — something about the narrowness of the lapel, the flipped-up collar.

The name's Chevalier, she recalls from the briefing. If she remembers correctly, he deals mostly in weapons and has made most of his fortune supplying both sides of the civil wars on Indira.

Just because he sells guns doesn't mean he knows how to use one, though, so she hasn't yet slotted him into the category of useful friend or viable threat.

Not that anyone has guns on the station. There's far too much potential of accidentally hitting something that could explode and destroy them all, or of puncturing an outer wall and sucking them all out into the vacuum of space through a hole the size of a fist. Or whatever terrifying shit happens out here in the black.

Some of the cartel soldiers carry stun carbines, and she's sure she seen at least one electric barb on a security guard's belt. But otherwise it's probably knife fighting if things happen to get out of hand. Not Gia's favorite, but she's not bad at it, either.

Aiax Demosga stands to greet her, his glittering smile, his loud shirt, even his sun-baked leather tan aggressive in this gray metal place. He shakes her hand; it's predictably finger-breaking.

"Giaconda, it's nice to meet you in person," he says. He shakes Starla's hand and trades air-kisses with Calanthe, then turns to his companion. "Calanthe, you've met Absolon Chevalier? Absolon, Giaconda Áte and Starla Dusai, Willem's representatives."

Chevalier's hand is slim and warm. "It's a pleasure," he says in a light Arquellian drawl. And to Starla, "I was very sorry to hear about your parents."

The slight wrinkle in Starla's brow tells Gia she's reading the transcription on her heads-up, and Chevalier notices the device at the same time. "My apologies," he says, and then signs something to her instead. Gia catches the signs for *parents*, *sorry*, but his hands are too fluid for her to follow with her limited USL.

He and Starla converse a moment longer before they all take their seats at the big circular table. It could fit another ten; like the enormous room, the table dwarfs their small group. It's almost as though it's by design, and it's starting to bother Gia.

"We're still missing a few," she says to Calanthe, who nods slowly, eyes narrowed as she scans the room.

"I didn't know you spoke USL," Demosga says, clapping Chevalier on the shoulder.

Chevalier shrugs. "Indira is a planet of many countries and many languages," he says simply. "I have endeavored to be fluent in all that I can."

Thankfully, before Chevalier can expound any more on how cosmopolitan and advanced Arquellians are, the door opens. Gia has done her homework, and although she doesn't recognize the knot of soldiers standing guard at the door, the head honcho of the Maribi Cartel is hard to miss.

Malcolm Saint would have stood out immediately for his swagger, even if she hadn't already recognized his face from her briefings: copper skin, round cheeks, a full head of thick hair, and a salt-and-pepper beard close-trimmed and neat. "I see we're all here," Saint says.

"We're waiting for a few more," Demosga answers.

A smile tugs at the corner of Saint's mouth, and unease churns in Gia's gut.

"It will just be us for the moment," Saint says. He sits at the far end of the table, a swath of seats between himself and his guests, then plants his elbows and interlaces his fingers, leaning forward so his chin rests on his knuckles. He gives them all a look in turn.

"I appreciate you all making the effort," he says. "And I've heard your complaints about our variable tariffs and service fees."

"Glad to hear it," Demosga says. He flashes his movie-star smile. "I've been going over the last decade's worth of records for our family's shipping expenditures, and I have some suggestions. Let's take a look at — "

"I wasn't quite finished," Saint says. His eyes glitter with malice. Gia can feel the mood go cold — this is not the posture of a man who's planning to negotiate. "The cartel will be standardizing the rates and service fees. Forty percent across the board."

Demosga lets out a shocked curse, but Calanthe just leans forward, smooth fingers steepled. "I think that's a bold opening position, Malcolm," she says.

"It's not a starting bid, Ms. Yang," Saint says. "It's

our company's new standardized rate. You're welcome to find somewhere else to ship your goods."

Gia glances at Calanthe, who's wearing the slightly amused expression she and her mother both wield to devastating effect. "Believe me, my family is always looking for the best option. Unfortunately, the cartel has quite a monopoly out here."

"I would think you would be more interested in working with those who share your interests," says Chevalier calmly. "Without any legal recourse, it's best if we all work together."

"It wasn't a small journey to get here," Demosga snaps. "If you had no intention of negotiating with us, why the hell invite us out here?"

"Oh, I had the intention of negotiating," Saint says slowly. He leans back in his chair, imperious. "I just thought I would be having this conversation with honorable business partners."

This time, Gia doesn't risk a glance at Calanthe. They've been found out. Which means Demosga and Chevalier were probably also approached by Lorn and his union of dockworkers. She feels a shift around the room, an atmospheric hush, clouds gathering before storm.

She catches Starla's eye. "Be ready," she signs.

Starla nods, shifting herself in her chair in a way that looks casual, though Gia can see alertness, readiness in the lines of her legs. There's no way she can let this come to a fight, though. They are outnumbered, members of the cartel stationed at the doors and fully armed.

"If you're not interested in negotiating, I have calls to make," Demosga says. He stands, and the cartel soldiers around the room reach for their weapons. Demosga looks around him with the steely-eyed glare of a man well seasoned by business negotiations in Bulari's underworld. "Unless of course, you're taking representatives from four of the biggest crime organizations on two planets hostage?" he asks.

"Sit down," Saint says. "We're not done talking." Demosga remains standing, his hands on the back of his chair.

Gia's running the odds. She doesn't have much hope in any of the others to have her back. Starla is scrappy but still new, and Calanthe and Demosga are much better known for their sharp business tongues than their knife skills, though Demosga has a reputation for bar brawls. And Chevalier? There was nothing in the briefings she read about physical fighting.

Negotiation isn't her strong point, but they're all goners if this thing comes to violence.

"Have a seat, Demosga," she says. "The man just wants to talk."

Demosga turns his glare on her, then finally relents, settling back into his chair with his chin raised.

"We're all good," she says to Saint. "Let's chat."

Saint looks at her, and his lips move in what could be considered a smile, though there's nothing of warmth or camaraderie in it. "Who would've known the only person here with a cool head would be from Willem Jaantzen's crew?"

He clasps his hands together in front of him and leans forward like a teacher lecturing a group of disobedient schoolchildren. "You have all committed incredible trespass by speaking to somebody working against the cartel, let alone giving them money," he says. "If you were one of mine, you'd be dead. But, as Aiax pointed out, that would most likely lead to war with four of my best customers, who have powerful allies on both New Sarjun and Indira. So even though I would be completely justified — because it was you who first made aggressions against me — I will be the generous one."

Saint spreads his hands as though granting them a gift. "Tell me everything you know about this group, and I will happily continue doing business with you and with everyone else who has come here to negotiate today. At a flat forty percent rate to help remind you all that you do yourself no favors when you cross the Maribi Cartel." He smiles darkly. "If any of your colleagues in the other families have a problem with that, I'll let them know to take it up with you directly."

"And you'll let us walk out of here," Demosga says.

"Of course. Provided your families see twice as much value in you as they were willing to give to my enemies."

"Ransom," says Chevalier.

Saint's smile is vicious. "Reparations." He shoves back his chair; it screeches on the polished floor. "I'll have you all escorted back to — "

Around the rooms, comms chime. Calanthe brushes a fingertip against her rose gold cuff; the corners of her lips tug down at the words displayed there. Starla's eyebrows arch as she reads the message on her heads-up. One of the cartel soldiers near the door swears loudly.

Saint's glare sweeps the room before he pulls his comm out.

Gia thumbs her own on.

Citizens, this is a message from the United Dockworkers of Maribi. Be advised that all traffic and supplies going in or out of the station will stop until the Maribi Cartel agrees to our terms. We are a movement of many, supported by other secretly unionized worker groups throughout the station. Do

NOT TRY TO ENTER THE DOCKS. WE WILL SEND FURTHER COMMUNICATIONS.

Beside her, Calanthe swears under her breath.

Whatever Lorn and his group were planning, it's beginning.

9

Starla

THE MESSAGE FROM THE UNION FADES, AND THE SCREEN of Starla's heads-up unit flickers. A yellow dot pulses in the upper left corner to tell her it's looking for signal, then goes solid green once more.

The strike has begun.

The room's energy has shifted abruptly from tensely crumbling negotiations to something even more uncertain. Calanthe is furiously conferring with Aiax; Gia's watching Saint, poised for action. Across the table, Absolon Chevalier catches Starla's eye and gives her a slight nod, but she's not certain what he's trying to convey.

A man comes in to whisper something in Saint's ear, and Saint sends two of his guards out the door with the messenger. Apparently whatever's going on out there is more threatening than the family representatives sitting at his conference table.

Saint turns back to the group with a smile.

"How fortunate," he says, his words scrolling across the bottom of Starla's display. "I'm about to get a chance to demonstrate just why it was so unwise to bet against me."

He's a man who likes to talk, Starla thinks. She's used to being among people who choose their words carefully and without much fanfare. In her experience people who like to talk tend to overestimate their situations.

"Throwing your lot in with the dockworkers may have seemed like a good idea at the time," Saint says. "They told you we wouldn't see them coming, that they had the element of surprise. But believe me, they did not. I've known about their plans for months, and it's only been a matter of waiting for them to tip their hands." He smiles maliciously. "And, apparently, yours."

He glances at his comm as though judging the time. "Give us a few minutes and these traitors will be out an airlock."

Icy fear stabs through Starla's chest: Mona. She had been planning on escaping before all this went down, but there's no way she could have gotten off in time. Especially since she promised to at least say goodbye before leaving.

He's a man who likes to talk, Starla reminds herself. What he says has no bearing on what's actually happening.

"We have plenty of experience dealing with this sort of thing," Saint says. He stands. "Whatever little coup you all expected to happen is dead already. Let's put you somewhere for safekeeping. I'll — "

Starla feels the concussion in her chest, shivering through the station. The room goes dark, the pure, awful dark of Durga's Belt with not a scrap of sunlight to seep through the edge of a curtain or catch in a pane of glass. Here, the pressure of the black has physical weight, pressing like fingertips against Starla's eyes.

But only for a moment.

Emergency lights flicker on, transforming the gleaming gold threads in the wall into bloody, metallic streaks as the red light hits them.

"Get them out of here," someone says, the transcription crawling across her heads-up. Starla feels a hand on her arm, shrugs it off as she stands. In her pocket, her comm vibrates, and another message appears. From Mona.

Where are you, shit's going down.

Starla doesn't dare take her comm from her pocket to respond, not with all of these guards and guns surrounding her. And a moment later her chance is gone, anyway.

A second concussion, and the pulsing yellow light is back in her display. Only this time it flashes to red. They've done something to the network.

A guard grabs her arm, pulling her from her chair, and she shakes him off. Gia catches her arm before she can do anything, though, and motions in the dim light for Starla to follow her, with Calanthe in between them.

At the elevator, a guard is pressing the button without response. Once, twice, before he punches the wall beside the door. Starla can only assume the power has been cut to the elevators, too.

He turns to yell something at them, but without the network, Starla's heads-up isn't transcribing anymore. The useless thing is a mess of flashing red lights and error messages, so she unclips it and folds it into her pocket. She doesn't need the distraction.

Someone touches her shoulder and she glances back to see Aiax Demosga. He taps his temple, right where her heads-up had been. "Is everything all right?" she thinks he asks.

She pulls her comm from her pocket, taps it and shrugs. He frowns at her, then looks at his own comm. She sees the realization spread over his face as he notices the lack of connection. He says something else to her but she can't make it out — and then the guards are prodding them to another corner of the meeting room.

They're led to a cramped maintenance stairwell that looks like it doesn't get much use; Starla remembers similar stairs from Silk Station, lit only by dim strips of emergency lighting, the perfect place to get away for long heart-to-hearts with Mona where they wouldn't be underfoot — or found. These are cramped and narrow, almost as much climbing a spiral ladder as mounting stairs. They climb in single file, the stairs disappearing into gloom high above them; looking up she sees only the back of Calanthe's suit and Gia's legs beyond.

Aiax follows her, and the stranger with the dark skin and Indiran cut to his suit, Absolon Chevalier, takes up the rear. They climb for a few minutes before the group comes to a stop for no reason Starla can understand. She glances down, and Absolon catches her eye.

"Sounds like we stopped at a landing," he signs. His signs are slightly different from what she's become accustomed to on New Sarjun, but not so much so she can't understand him. He looks past her as though listening, then meets her gaze again. "We're going to climb on a few more floors. Can you fight?"

Starla nods, and Absolon gives her the ghost of a smile.

"Tell your friend," he signs. "Act when we get to the next landing."

They've started moving again, and Gia seems to be arguing with the guard above her, who Starla can't see.

Starla grabs Calanthe's calf as they climb, and the woman looks down at her.

"Be ready," Starla signs, and seeing the V that forms between Calanthe's brows, she's not sure if the other woman understands. But Calanthe touches Gia's leg, and motions back down at Starla.

"Attack when you get just past the next landing," Starla signs, and she's one hundred percent sure Gia doesn't understand that. She sighs in irritation, mimes a gun, and points at the stairs. "2-0," she signs as she takes one step, then another. "1-9. 1-8. 1-7."

Gia gives her a nod and Starla takes a deep breath. The countdown has begun.

Hopefully.

She reaches the landing just as she feels the whole staircase shudder. She pulls Calanthe back down onto the narrow landing with her as Gia attacks the man above her and the Indiran begins to grapple with the guard below him. Starla tries the door handle, but although it's not locked, it's stiff with disuse. Aiax Demosga motions her out of the way, then uses his broad shoulder like a battering ram to burst through.

They spill out into another emergency-lit hallway. It's empty — for now — and Starla stands guard, the only thing she can do while Gia and Absolon finish off the guards inside the narrow staircase. The station shudders again, like a skipped heartbeat. Is this what Mona felt when Silk Station was being bombed apart by the Alliance? Starla had been on her parents' ship, the *Nanshe*, and there the attack had felt more immediate, more violent, flesh bruising against restraint belts as the ship lurched. Here the bombs feel more like a distant nightclub.

The fight is over as quickly as it began, and Absolon

steps out of the stairwell, followed by Gia. She's got one of the guards' stun carbines slung over her shoulder. Absolon is bleeding from a gash on his temple and Gia has a split lip, but otherwise both seem fine.

"We need to get to safety," Gia says, and even without transcription, Starla has enough experience with Gia to feel confident in her lipreading.

Aiax Demosga, though? Not so much. He and Gia start arguing, and Calanthe cuts in. "We need to get to a ship," she says, as calm and easy to read as always.

"The docks are where all the fighting is happening," Gia says. "And we don't even know where we are."

Starla snaps her fingers for their attention. "I know," she signs. At least, she has a vague idea where they are, after all those hours spent studying the station maps trying to find Mona. And it doesn't hurt that she was born into the labyrinth of an asteroid station. She still has a map of the station downloaded onto her comm, and though they won't be able to see where they are without the network, she should be able to figure that out. She opens the map and hands her comm over to Gia.

"We climbed nine flights," she signs, catching Absolon's eye in the hopes that he understands her.

Absolon nods. "Yes," he says clearly, signing slowly as he speaks. "I counted nine flights, too."

"But where are we," Gia asks. "That big-ass meeting room isn't anywhere on the map."

It wasn't, but Starla's been working out where it must be ever since they arrived in it. She scrolls through the station map in Gia's hand. Points to a spot. "We're here," she signs. "Here is the elevator shaft, and the stairwell doesn't seem to be marked."

"That seems right," Calanthe says after Absolon's

finished interpreting. "Which means to get to the docks, we need to get to this stairway. Here."

Aiax grumbles something that looks like it could be about guards.

The stairway Calanthe is pointing at would deposit them in the passenger terminal outside the docks, but if the unionists are holed up in the docks like they said, the passenger terminal is probably teeming with cartel fighters trying to get in. That staircase is going to be suicide. Starla's not sure how to get into the docks, but she thinks she knows where Mona will be.

"We need to get into the docks, past the cartel," Starla signs. She points to the far end of the station map. "My cousin will probably be there, she'll get them to let us in. There's a secret stairway over here."

"A secret stairway?" Absolon says and signs. He doesn't seem to have much practice at it, and his USL is slower and clumsier than usual. "How do you know about it?"

"My cousin took me. It was being guarded by the dockworkers."

"Her cousin. It seemed like it was guarded by dock-workers," Absolon says to the others.

"Her cousin is who we need to get to," Gia says. "It doesn't matter if we get to a ship if they won't let us off the station."

Aiax seems to be objecting to the idea, but Calanthe holds up a hand. "After this, I doubt propriety matters to Saint," is what Starla thinks she says. "We are dead if we don't get off the station, and we certainly don't get off the station unless the dockworkers win. I may not be much of a fighter, but I know where to throw my lot."

Absolon nods. "The only sensible thing is to go find the leaders of this little rebellion and see what we can do to turn it in our favor," he says and signs. "Because we certainly know what will happen if the cartel wins."

"Unless anyone else has a secret private way off this rock," Gia says.

Finally, Aiax nods assent.

"Lead the way," Absolon signs to Starla.

IT'S smooth sailing for a few hundred meters, Gia and her stolen stun carbine taking lead while Starla points her in the right direction, Aiax and Absolon taking up the rear. Smooth sailing, that is, until a small knot of cartel soldiers catches sight of them when they round a corner about two-thirds of the way to the elevator.

Gia hits one in the chest right off the bat; he slumps to the ground, twitching. Another grabs for Starla, but Aiax is there beside her in a heartbeat. He pulls the cartel soldier off and knees him in the gut, then finishes him with a punch to the throat. It's not elegant, and it's certainly not what Gia has been teaching her. Aiax Demosga fights like a street brawler, and the way he cracks his knuckles and goes after the other guy, it looks like he enjoys cracking heads.

Gia takes out the third soldier, then turns to watch Aiax headbutt the last one. Although it doesn't look necessary to Starla, he does it again for good measure. Calanthe is watching him with a raised eyebrow.

"Come on, Aiax," says Calanthe. "You enjoyed that far too much."

Aiax opens his mouth to answer, but there's a flash of movement down the hall behind him, and before anyone can react a fifth cartel soldier steps from a doorway and flings a knife into Aiax's back.

And then the soldier goes down in a limp tangle of limbs, the result of a brilliant flash from some small device Absolon Chevalier is holding in the palm of his hand. Stella catches only a glimpse of it before he flips it back into his pocket: it's shiny, all chrome and inlaid lapis lazuli. She would mistake it for a cigarette case if she saw it lying on a table.

Whatever it did, her skin is crawling from the residual effects. Beside her, Calanthe runs her hands over her forearms with a suppressed shudder.

Absolon is a weapons dealer, Starla reminds herself — and apparently he has access to some pretty interesting stuff. She'll have to ask him about it later, because right now, Aiax Demosga is slumped on the floor, breath coming shallow and lips forming unintelligible shapes that might or might not be words.

"We're not far from that clinic your friend works at," Starla signs to Gia. "We have to get him there."

Gia frowns at her. "We're not where?"

"Apparently there is a medical center nearby," Absolon says to her. He turns to Starla. "On this level?" he signs.

She shakes her head. Points up at the ceiling and holds up two fingers for Gia's benefit.

She sees realization dawn on Gia's face. "The clinic," Gia says. "We can't all go. Demosga, can you walk?" She slips her arm underneath and helps him to his feet. His knees buckle once, then he braces himself and nods.

"Stay with them," he says — Starla thinks he says.

"No one else is strong enough to help you," Gia says. She helps him lean against the wall, then turns to Starla. "You'll be all right," she signs to Starla, and whether it's a command or a reassurance, Starla can't tell from Gia's usual fierce expression. "Get them to Mona and safety. I'll get Demosga to help."

Starla fights back a thrill of fear and adrenaline. Gia will be fine. She'll be fine. Mona will be fine — so long as she steps it up and acts right now. Absolon and Calanthe both look to her for guidance, and she tamps down any fear she might feel.

"Stay behind me," she signs, pointing to Calanthe. She turns to Absolon. "And you, take up the rear." Absolon nods his assent, and they head off down the hallway.

As they pass the cartel soldier Absolon took out, Starla can't help but stare. He's not bonelessly slumped like the men Gia shot with the stun carbine. This one's all frozen limbs and sharp angles, like a dead spider curled in on itself. Calanthe's eyes widen. But when Starla meets Absolon's gaze, he only smiles.

10

Gia

DEMOSGA IS HEAVY, BUT ONE BENEFIT OF THE LIGHTER gravity on Maribi Station is that he's not as much of a burden as he would be back on New Sarjun. Even so, by the second flight up he's stumbling more than ever, and he slips from her grasp entirely in the stairwell. Gia curses. If any enemy comes across them now, they're both dead.

The network seems to still be out station-wide, and beyond emergency lighting, all of the electrical system seems to be down, too. Except for the intercom, and a pleasant male voice has been talking to them on repeat, telling everyone to return to their quarters or risk detainment, as they'll be assumed to be a member of the striking forces.

The people they do see seem to either be obeying the command or actively seeking to join in the fight, though Gia can't tell for which side.

And she's not the only one helping someone with an injury.

The scene at the clinic is just as chaotic as Gia had

anticipated. The waiting room is even more filled with people than it was yesterday, but fewer of them are patients. Instead it's become a staging area of equipment and supplies, medics in uniform rushing to get everything prepared.

Tevi Sharaf is directing traffic in the middle of the room, wearing the formal white Sulila jacket that means he's prepared to assert his status if need be. "We'll need another set of those," he says to a nurse. "And the mobile burn unit — get it ready and meet us there. We need to — Gia?"

Other faces turn to them, and a nurse — a man closer to Demosga's size — hurries over to help her. Gia straightens in relief as the big man's weight lifts off her shoulders. Demosga's been losing a steady stream of blood and is starting to lose consciousness, too.

That burden's gone, but Gia steels herself for her next task: ignoring the wide-eyed look Tevi is giving her and telling herself he's just another guy in scrubs at just another triage scene that she needs to deal with.

"He got stabbed in the back," she says to the nurse. "The knife's still there, but he's losing blood fast." The sleeve of her suit jacket is heavy with blood, but it's not hers; she ignores it. The nurse helps Demosga onto a gurney — it was probably waiting to be wheeled down to the scene of the fighting — and Demosga's eyes flutter open.

He blinks at her, gaze focusing on her face. Beneath his coppery tan, his face is bloodless.

"Sir? Sir, we're going to get you into surgery right away," the nurse says.

Demosga winces as the nurse begins to wheel the gurney away, then reaches to catch Gia's hand. The nurse stops, glancing between them.

"I owe you for this one," Demosga says, his normally booming voice quiet.

"I'll let the man know," Gia says. She doesn't know what kind of tally sheet Demosga and her boss have, but right now doesn't seem like a good time to start caring. She's got bigger things to worry about. "Now let these guys take care of you."

"Not Jaantzen," Demosga says. "I meant you."

"Just don't die," Gia says, extricating her hand. She's not sure what favors one can ask from a man like Aiax Demosga, but she hopes she's never in a position to need one.

She watches as he's wheeled through the doorway, then turns back to Tevi, who — she realizes too late — has been standing silent behind her through this entire exchange. The look he's giving her could make the deserts of New Sarjun feel arctic.

He heard the name. And of course he will recognize it.

"Tevi — "

"I don't disagree that you can save a lot more lives with a gun then a med kit sometimes," he says quietly. "But I know the names of some of those who have put bodies in my emergency room. Especially lately."

"Tevi."

"Who you work for now, that's your choice," he says bitterly. "Just tell me the rest of it wasn't true, all those things they said about you when you were on trial." The look in his eyes is both pleading fund despairing, like he wants desperately to believe what she's about to tell him, but is afraid he can't.

"It wasn't true," Gia says quietly.

"But now — " He doesn't seem quite ready to say it. "You work for Willem Jaantzen."

"I'm making the right choice." She can't explain it, what sets this one man apart from the woman who sent her to prison. And she shouldn't need to explain it. She made the decisions she needed to when she left Redrock, and Tevi has made decisions of his own. There's no reason either of them should have to explain anything to each other.

Gia looks around the room, at the med kits and people in disarray. They're all trying to pretend they're not watching the scene in front of them.

"It looks like you're going into a war," she says finally. "Do you need someone who knows how to hold both a scalpel and a gun, or not?"

11

Starla

DESPITE HER MAP, THE STATION IS LIKE A MAZE, AND more than once Starla leads Calanthe and Absolon into a dead end before figuring out the right turn and finally arriving at the room Mona had led her to last night. The forklift suit is still leaning in the hallway, slumped in on itself in an eerie mimicry of the cartel solder Absolon zapped.

Starla tries the handle. Locked. She knocks, the same *tat-a-tat, tat-a-tat* she used to use to get Mona's attention when she was supposed to be studying in her room, but nothing happens. She frowns at Absolon, jerking her chin at the door.

"I don't hear anyone inside," he says.

Starla tries the handle again, then Calanthe Yang taps her on the shoulder and produces a tab the size of her thumbnail, which she affixes to the lock. It begins to glow a pearly, opalescent orange. Calanthe types a code into her comm, and the device blinks three times, then shifts to a cheerful green.

The handle turns under Starla's palm.

Calanthe just smiles and uses one lacquered thumb-nail to peel the device back off, pocketing it. "A very useful bit of tech," she says clearly, so Starla can lipread. "I'll show you how to use it on the flight back home."

If they get a flight back home, Starla thinks, then dashes the thought away. They certainly won't if she starts down that path.

Starla pushes through the door with a rush of anticipation and dread as to what she'll find inside.

And — nothing.

The monitors, the terminals, the swags of wires — everything but the tables has been cleared out. Starla groans in frustration. She could lead them to Mona's room, but if she's pulled up roots here, what's to make Starla think she'll be there?

"What is this place?" Calanthe asks.

"Used to be my cousin's lab," Starla signs.

"Your cousin's lab," repeats Absolon, signing and speaking. "Where is she now?"

Starla shrugs, exasperated and embarrassed at having brought these two — business partners of her godfa-ther's — to a dead end. She turns in frustration to scan the room. If nothing else, at least they'll be safe here for the time being. Then maybe she can head out on her own to try to find Mona.

"We'll be safe here until we can contact her, or another member of the union," she signs.

"If it's safe, we should stay here for now," Calanthe says, and Starla's not sure if she understood her signs and is agreeing with her, or if she's making her own suggestion.

"I'm not interested in sitting around," Absolon says

and signs gamely. "We should find the head of the union and offer our help."

"But how do we find them without running into the cartel?" Starla asks.

Before Absolon can answer, a flash of movement at the door behind him catches Starla's eye. Absolon spins with his palm outstretched, the same silvery cigarette-box-shaped weapon in his hand.

Starla shouts at him before he fires, grabbing his arm.

Ahmed stands in the doorway, clutching a black duffel to his chest like a shield.

He looks wide-eyed between Calanthe and Absolon before settling on Starla.

"What are you doing here?" he asks.

Starla nudges Absolon. "This is a friend of my cousin. Explain to him that we need to find her."

Absolon's explanation is longer than Starla thinks it needs to be, but judging by Calanthe's expression it doesn't seem to be going off base.

When Absolon finishes speaking, Ahmed nods. "I can get you to see her, but there's one problem. She's in the docking bay. It's the heart of all the fighting."

"That's where we need to be, too," Starla signs.

Ahmed nods. "Let's go."

***

AHMED LEADS them to a back passageway. No one seems to be guarding the entrance, but when they slip through the hatch they get a face full of plasma carbine barrel. To Starla, the thought of what might happen if someone fired one of those things on a space station is almost as gut-clenching as the thought of being its target.

But the guard lowers his weapon when he sees Ahmed.

Starla's heart rate drops back to normal. For a second, at least, until a man stalks over to them and begins yelling unintelligibly.

Starla may have navigated them here; now it's Calanthe Yang's turn to be in her element. She steps forward, all polished lawyer. Starla can only catch snatches of what Calanthe is saying, and she can't read the burly man's lips at all, but the way the conversation goes is evident by their body language. The station-born man towers above Calanthe, and he uses his height to intimidate, standing a little too close and bowed forward, forcing Calanthe to arch her back to see him. If it makes her uncomfortable, though, she's far too poised to let it show.

He's fighting a battle of aggression; Calanthe is all about the smooth, calm persuasion. Her expression, her mannerisms, everything is polite yet strong, and when she refuses to budge, he finally acquiesces, takes a step back. She straightens, chin lifted and smile professional.

This entire trip, Starla has thought that Calanthe was the weak link when compared to Gia. Now she revises her estimation of the woman. Where Gia uses her muscles and weapons skills, Calanthe does battle in a way that can be just as effective. Maybe Starla has something to learn from her after all.

Calanthe motions Starla forward. "We're looking for her cousin," she says.

Ahmed says something that Starla doesn't catch, and the man finally looks at Starla, assessing her.

"She told me about you," he says finally — at least, she thinks he says. "Come with me."

Starla hasn't been back to the docking bay since the

day they arrived — access is restricted to dockworkers and passengers who are actively embarking or disembarking. It's three times as wide as the busy passenger terminal on the other side of the long wall, with smaller ships clamped into neat rows and materials handling equipment parked around them. She doesn't see the shuttle they came in on; presumably it's already left, packed with people on their way back to the inner planets.

People who got off this rock just in the nick of time.

Instead of the hustle and bustle Starla remembers from their first day here, there's now a different sort of energy. One area, near the center, seems to be set up as a support station, with people putting out food and handing out weapons. The four sets of bay doors that lead to the passenger terminal are shut tight, but it doesn't look like the dockworkers think that will keep the cartel out for long. They're parking machinery in a barricade, arranging stacks of cargo crates to use for cover if it comes to a fight.

Mona had told her that they'd been hiring mercenaries, but their supply of weapons still looks meager, especially compared to what little Starla has seen of the cartel. A small squadron of men and women are running through drills in an open space at the far end of the docks. It looks like they've drilled before, but none of them move like they've fought together.

Starla's heart sinks. The union is going to need much more than a few extra fighters if they're not all going to be crushed into dust.

Starla scans the crush of people before remembering that the Mona she was getting used to yesterday has already shifted like a chameleon. Right — she's looking for a short black bob, not the magenta mane.

She spots her about fifty meters away, hunched over a makeshift web of monitors and terminals, her newly black curls wrenched into a tangled knot on top of her head. Relief washes over Starla. She heads that way with Calanthe and Ahmed at her side, only to realize she's lost track of Absolon. She knows no one else here is her responsibility, but she feels a sense of obligation to her godfather's name to make sure they all get through this all right.

She spins, scanning the room, and spots the dark Indiran man examining the barricade of machinery the dockworkers have put up.

He glances over as she walks up. "I saw one of these over by the room where we met your friend," he signs. "Do you know what it is?"

"It's a forklift suit," Starla signs. It's a newer-looking model than the ones she's familiar with, and it looks much more comfortable and maneuverable then the ones she remembers in her parents' docking bay. It even has a chestplate and clear safety shield over the face to protect the user against crushing injuries.

"The dockworkers might outnumber the cartel, but they're certainly outgunned," Absolon signs. "Unfortunately, my entire inventory is ship and station weapons systems — far too powerful to use inside the station, even if a human could lift the artillery."

"An unaided human," Starla signs, and Absolon nods thoughtfully, tilting his head to consider the suit.

Starla runs her hands over the forklift suit, examining the attachment system and auxiliary clamps. They look proprietary, designed to be used only with branded add-ons, but the dockworkers could always weld something directly to the arm. And one of the suits has a dexterous-looking drum-handling clamp that just might be useful.

"Show me what you have. We could modify weapons to mount on these suits."

"But the firing interface?" Absolon signs. "Ah. You said your cousin is a hacker." He smiles. "Then let's go find her. And see if someone will let me onto my ship."

12

Gia

Someone gave her a medical tunic emblazoned with
the clinic's logo to replace her bloody suit jacket, and the
surgical cap she found in a closet should be making her
look a lot less like an escaped prisoner you should shoot
at and more like a doctor you shouldn't. She lays her
stolen stun carbine on top of other supplies in a duffel
bag and leaves the seam unsealed when she shoulders it
so she can grab the gun quick if she needs to.

Tevi doesn't say a word to her, doesn't look her way.
But he doesn't send her away, either, and Gia joins the
rest in the trek to the passenger terminal.

Last time she was here it was all souvenir shops and
tourist-trap restaurants. Now the storefronts are all shut
tight and the wide promenade in front of them is
teeming with cartel soldiers. The bay doors along the
longest wall, that lead to the docking bay, are all shut
tight, and by the frustrated way one soldier is mashing at
a control panel, the union has them locked out.

Tevi pauses briefly and scans the scene; when his eyes
meet hers it seems like an accident, and he looks quickly

ahead. "Everyone stay back," he says. "I'm going to go find out who's in charge."

"Everyone" clearly means her, too, but Gia ignores him. She walks a few paces behind, duffel bag open and over her shoulder, trying her best to look like a nurse in generic scrubs and not like she's going to kill anyone who puts a hand on him.

There'd been fighting here before those doors closed, and recently. A few bodies are slumped along the wall, but there are also injured people — cartel members and dockworker prisoners — who need immediate attention.

Gia ducks her head. Few of the cartel members should know her by sight, and if she's lucky they'll simply ignore her. She's seen it happen often enough in the past, her uniform blending in with the chaos of the scene, no one taking time to stop and look at a face.

A rangy man with tattoos scrawled up his cheeks stops Tevi with a scarred hand on his chest. "What the hell you want?" he asks.

"I'm here to speak with whoever's in charge," Tevi says. "We're here to help anyone who needs it."

The rangy man curls his lip. "No one is injured, and even if they were, these people don't need your help."

Tevi looks pointedly to the right, where a man in a dockworker's uniform is shackled and huddled against the wall, cradling a broken arm, blood streaming from a cut on his forehead.

"He looks like he needs help," Tevi says.

"He's going out an airlock," the soldier says.

"Absolutely not. The Sulila charter states that in wartime — "

"Who says we're at war?"

It's a new voice joining the conversation, coming low and lethal over Gia's left shoulder. She turns towards it, right hand dropping into the open duffel at her side, but the man the voice belongs to — a cartel lieutenant whose picture Gia remembers seeing in a dossier — walks past her to confront Tevi.

Tevi stands his ground, every bit as cool under the murderous attention of well-armed cartel soldiers as he ever has been in an emergency room. If Gia hadn't already screwed this one up, she'd let herself be proud.

The lieutenant — Baxir, his name finally comes to her in a flash — glares at Tevi. "Who says we're at war?" he asks again.

"I misspoke," Tevi says calmly. "There are hostilities between two parties, and I brought my team to tend to the injured." He motions to the shackled dockworker with the broken arm, then turns to a cartel member who's still got a gun in his hand, even with the bloody knife slash across his thigh. "You have to let us help these people."

Baxir gives him an impatient look. "I don't have to do anything. Your little clinic is here because we let you be here, but the cartel says what goes. You're welcome to help Maribi citizens, but none of the prisoners."

Tevi shakes his head. "Sulila code is to treat all, no matter their background or status."

"Cartel code is to fuck those who try to fuck us," Baxir snarls. "Don't get on that list." He turns to acknowledge a woman who's appeared at the edge of the group. "Are you ready?" he asks.

"Yessir," she says. "The dock is fully sealed for breach."

"Where is Saint?"

"On his way."

"Good. He'll give the order."

Gia's mouth goes dry, and she turns to look at the

bay doors. If Starla and Calanthe made it, they'd be just on the other side of that wall, no way to get out. She'd misunderstood what the cartel soldier was doing to the door panel when they first came in. He wasn't trying to get in — he was making sure the people inside couldn't get out.

"There are innocent people in there," Tevi says. "You can't just open the airlocks."

"If they were innocent, they wouldn't be in there," Baxir says. "Although, come to think of it, your team is welcome to go into the docking bay and tend to anyone injured inside. Be our guests."

"Murdering Sulila staff is a war crime," Tevi says, venom in his voice.

"Then it's a good thing we're not at war," Baxir says with a grin.

"Tevi," Gia says softly. They need to get a message to Starla, and standing around arguing with this asshole isn't going to get them anywhere. He doesn't hear her or he's still ignoring her, and she reaches to touch his arm.

Someone grabs Gia's shoulder, wrenching her back around.

"Hey!" shouts Tevi. "Leave my people alone."

Gia drops the duffel as she pulls the stun carbine free. She's too close range to use it on the man who grabbed her, but she slams the stock into his knuckles to break his grip and punches the butt into his sternum.

It thuds against his armor, and before she can strike again the man pushes her back with a roar. She stumbles. Meaty hands close around her upper arms before Gia can catch her footing; a torso like a wall of muscle is at her back.

Malcolm Saint steps towards her, rubbing the

knuckles she split with the stun carbine. He wrenches it from her hands, all bared teeth and ferocious grin.

"She isn't one of yours," he says to Tevi. He turns back to Gia. "Where are the rest of the traitors?"

"None of your goddamn business," Gia spits. She's not afraid for herself; that ice-cold stab of guilt is for what she may have brought on Tevi and his team. Her biceps ache where the goon behind her is squeezing, thick fingers digging into muscle.

She can't see him, but his bulk feels impressive, and even if she could take him and Saint and Baxir down, this whole passenger terminal is packed with well-armed cartel members.

And even if she were willing to go out in her own blaze of glory, she couldn't risk what would happen to Tevi and the others if she tried.

"Let me go," Gia snarls. "Or forget doing business with anyone back on New Sarjun."

Saint grabs her throat, face close to hers. His breath is hot, sharp; somewhere outside her field of immediate attention, she hears Tevi yelling.

"What risk?" Saint asks. "Doing business with some thugs from Bulari? Losing a couple of your boss's friends as my customers? Sweetheart, I don't give a shit what your boss thinks of me."

13

Starla

ABSOLON'S SHIP IS PARKED AT THE FAR END OF THE
docking bay.

It's nothing much to look at from the outside, all
unpainted metal plating and unbuffed rivets. But the
complicated set of biolocks Absolon has to activate to
gain access says there's something interesting inside.

It reminds Starla of her parents' ship. Starla grew up
on the *Nanshe* — at least, when it was in dock. Then,
she'd spend long hours feeding wires with skinny fingers
through narrow spaces for her mother or holding metal
sheeting in place for her father while he patched up the
holes that got punched through their bow with startling
regularity. She hadn't been allowed to go with them on
any of their raids.

Except for the last one, which was the only reason
she'd ended up in Alliance custody rather than blown to
shrapnel or scattered to the wind like the rest of the
inhabitants of Silk Station.

At the thought, she glances involuntarily over her

shoulder to where Mona is hunched about twenty paces away, staring at her hand terminal, which is plugged into a port in the forklift suit. She's frowning at whatever she sees, but looks up as though sensing Starla's attention.

"Is everything good?" Mona signs, a little flick of her gaze indicating Absolon.

"Don't worry about him," Starla signs back. He may be Arquellian, but Absolon definitely isn't tied to the Alliance. She knows that's not the only qualification for being trustworthy, but he seems all right to her.

Absolon types in a complicated code and a ladder descends from the belly of the ship. "Welcome, welcome," he signs, beckoning for Starla to follow him up the ladder; he's pretending not to have noticed the exchange between her and Mona.

The ladder leads directly into the cramped cabin, where there's barely room for the two of them to stand. Starla wonders if Absolon runs with a crew, or if it's just him piloting alone through the vacuum for weeks on end. Although, if this ship is anything like the *Nanshe*, it took him a lot less time to get here — even from Indira — than it took Starla and Gia to get here on the slow shuttle from New Sarjun.

Absolon's scanning the cabin as if out of habit, as if looking for anything out of place rather than looking for something specific. A little nod of satisfaction to himself and he motions for Starla to go through the small hatch behind her.

Much like the *Nanshe*, Absolon's ship is designed with a preference towards zero-G navigation. The passageway Starla's clambering through would be a simple shaft to float down when weightless, but in dock it's a cramped corridor, and Starla ducks low to navigate it. Fortunately, it's not very long.

Though Absolon's ship looks reasonably roomy from the outside, inside it's compactly designed. A pair of open bunks are built into the corridor walls; beyond them, a series of roll-up panels are labeled things like Rehydrator and Sanitizer and Waste. The labels are all situated to be read right-way-up if you're floating up the shaft with your head aimed at the cabin — instead of a real kitchenette and crew quarters like the *Nanshe* had, you're meant to float in the corridor while taking care of your food input and waste output needs.

It's not the most comfortable setup Starla has ever seen, but it's impressively utilitarian.

And once Starla reaches the end of the corridor, she sees just why the designers cut down on space for the humans operating the ship. The corridor opens into a room five times Starla's height wide and ten times as long. At least two-thirds of the ship is dedicated to cargo space.

She climbs down the ladder to what is currently the floor, though there are crates strapped to scaffolding on all the surfaces around her. Elastic webbing suspends a cube of shelving units packed with crates in the middle of the room, and there's just enough space for her and Absolon to stand on the operations platform at the bottom of the ladder. If she cranes her neck, she can see cargo packed in crawlspaces back around the central corridor, too.

When he joins her, Absolon calls up a screen and begins scanning through what looks like a manifest. Light streams around his dark fingers as he finds what he's looking for. "This is it," he signs, pinching open a line item that reads: T53N01 Flamethrower LX-4 Med

He types in a command and Starla feels the shiver around her of the ship coming to life, looks around the room until she sees the robotic arm swiveling on a gimbal to pick a crate and deposit it near the stern of the ship.

Absolon's scanning through the manifest again. Starla stops him. "This. What is it?"

Absolon shakes his head. "Those cannons would tear a hole through the side of the station."

"Right." Starla points at another item in the manifest. "But what if we modified it to shoot this, instead?"

A slow grin spreads over Absolon's face. "That might just work." His finger reaches to touch the line item, but they stop just short, flexing as though he's contemplating saying something else to her. He takes a deep breath, then he activates the picking arm and turns to her with a sad smile.

"I knew your parents," he signs. "In fact I worked with them a time or two, before you were born. Maybe I'll tell you some stories once we're through the other side of this." He stops, considering his next words. Starla is still; one breath will ruin the moment.

"If I know anything about them, they'd be proud of you," Absolon signs, and the moment is past, anyway. As it should be, considering the circumstances; a bitterness rises in the back of her throat.

"We should get these crates to the rest," signs Absolon. He steps off the platform, drops to the catwalk graceful as a dancer.

Starla's heart is racing, but she climbs down after him, batting the sudden flurry of questions she wants to ask out of her mind.

Now isn't the time.

Absolon palms the cargo ramp, and the one part of the ship designed to be more functional while docked than not descends into Maribi Station's docking bay. He's already slaved a pair of pallet jacks to his comm, and they scurry up the ramp to retrieve his cargo, then zip with the crates down the ramp and over to where Mona, Ahmed, and a crew of dockworkers have assembled a squadron, a yellow-and-black army of forklift suits.

The suits are slumped in rest, like an army already defeated.

Or one about to rise.

A woman's yelling at Starla as she pries open the crate of flamethrowers, jaw wide and hands gesticulating in nonsense. Starla frowns, then recognizes her: the woman driving the forklift suit who had been shouting at her shortly before she found Mona, or Mona found her. Was that only yesterday?

"I'm deaf," Starla signs, and the woman mouths something back. Starla points to both ears, shakes her head, does the flat-hand *null* handsign, and after a confused blink, the woman points at her own ears and yells something. Starla shakes her head with an expression like *I'm afraid not*, assuming they're having a conversation.

The woman nods slowly, then points at the flamethrower, then the forklift suit. She wraps gloved hands around the far end of one of the heavy weapons and pretends to heft it, then lifts her eyebrows. That, at least, is clear: *Can I help carry?*

It's short work, and the attachment clamps aren't as difficult to modify as Starla expected. The yelling woman catches on quick, grabbing another pair of forklift operators and explaining the process to them so that the work can go twice as fast. Mona's hack to the firing systems is easily replicated from machine to machine, and soon a half-dozen forklift suits are outfitted and ready to go. The yelling woman climbs into the first one and straps herself into the controls, grinning. Beyond her, another team have mounted the modified cannons to pallet jacks and are running them through maneuvers.

Starla's about to sign for the yelling woman to test the flamethrower when she feels a hand on her upper arm, the friendly squeeze and trailing downward brush that can only be Calanthe. Starla turns with a triumphant smile. Calanthe's face says, *We have a problem.*

She hands Starla a comm; a feed is already running. "We need to get out there," Calanthe says; it's directed to someone just beyond Starla.

Starla turns to see the burly station-born commander of the dockworkers. He's scowling at the forklift suits with something that might be approval, but he shakes his head at Calanthe's request, barks some kind of command.

Mona slips up beside Starla, bicep warm against hers. "He says we need more time," Mona signs, then cranes her neck to look at the comm Calanthe handed Starla. Starla feels her stiffen, then looks herself.

It's blurry, but Starla would know that bullheaded surgeon anywhere.

Gia is in the center of the passenger terminal. She's wearing a medic's jacket, standing near her doctor friend in his white Sulila uniform. A half-dozen others in the same white uniform are huddled a bit farther back — and for good reason. Gia and her doctor are surrounded by a squadron of cartel soldiers, and it doesn't look like things are going well.

Starla squints at the screen.

Is that Saint?

She's shouting in her head at the screen but Gia can't hear. Almost too late, Gia grabs a stun carbine from the duffel over her shoulder and whips around to face Saint — but she's too close to use the weapon and he pushes her back into a mountain of a man, whose hands close around her arms like steel clamps.

Starla shoves the comm back at Calanthe. "We don't have any more time," she signs to Mona. She waves an arm at the forklift operator woman, points her towards the door. The woman grins and the ground shakes as she and the other operators take their first thudding steps towards the door.

And the shaking stops.

Starla turns back, confused.

The commander's waving his arms to stop the forklift operators. He rounds on Starla, clearly unhappy that she's taken control of his — dammit, *her* — fleet of forklift suits.

"What's your problem?" Starla signs, exasperated. "We have to get out there."

"We have enough to do without saving some Sulila doctors," the commander says; Mona's slipped into Starla's line of sight, interpreting. "If they want to get themselves into this mess, they can get themselves back out."

"They're not just doctors, they're my friends," Starla signs. "Though that shouldn't matter one goddamn bit." She sweeps an arm over her tiny army. "Because how many of you have been fixed up at that clinic?"

The commander turns to glare at Mona as she says it, but some of the forklift operators straighten.

"That's what I thought," Starla continues, and whatever the commander snarls at her, she ignores it before Mona has a chance to interpret. She's not looking at him anymore, anyway. "Are your weapons working?" she signs, and a half second after Mona repeats it there's an answering chorus of flame and heat.

Starla shares a grin with the yelling woman, then sprints to the nearest bay door. It's closed — she lifts her hands to it, gives the man at the control panel a *What the fuck* look.

"I couldn't get it open if I wanted to," the man answers — Mona's sprinted ahead with Starla to interpret, though her dusky face is ashen with fear. "They've locked it from the outside."

"They've sealed it?"

Mona nods in affirmation, and Starla's mouth goes dry. "They're not going to — "

Just then, the lights in the docking bay dim once, twice, three times. Everyone around Starla stills and turns their gazes to the ceiling, listening to whatever alarm is sounding.

Mona's wide eyes meet hers, but Starla doesn't have to ask to know what the alarm means.

Those doors aren't just locked, they're sealed.

For vacuum.

Starla grabs Mona's arm and runs to the control panel — her cousin's the hacker, but maybe her knowledge of mechanics and engineering will help. She's so focused on the red blinking screen beside the bay door that she doesn't even notice Absolon standing next to it, not until a flash of silver in her peripheral vision catches her attention.

He's holding a weapon she's never seen before, but if she had to guess it's a mix between a plasma carbine and a laser, with a splash of concussion shot thrown in for good measure.

He proffers it with a small smile — it's far lighter

than she expected, but of course that's the gravity here. The chrome feels like silk in her palms.

Absolon points at the center of the door.

"I'll need that back when you're done," he signs.

Starla grins.

She fires.

14

Gia

"Let her go," Tevi is saying, and it's that same calm, well-reasoned voice he uses on patients who come in way too high on some street drug. Or on mothers who are clinging catatonically to the bodies of their children. "She's a Sulila doctor. She's with my team."

"She try to pull one over on you, too?" Saint says to him. He tugs the surgical cap off Gia's head, turns her chin to look at the tattoos behind her ears. "This one's nothing but a double-crossing criminal." His grip tightens around Gia's throat; her lungs buck in her chest, burning for breath.

"Please take your hands off my doctor," Tevi says, voice an edge of steel.

Saint smiles at Gia, eyes glittering points as the margins of her vision darken. "Okay," he says.

His grip loosens and she gasps for air. Then he spins, punches Tevi in the gut, driving his knee into Tevi's chin when he doubles over. Tevi drops to his hands and knees.

Gia doesn't realize she's screamed until Saint looks back at her, the corner of his mouth quirking up. She's made the oldest mistake in the book — she's let him know that Tevi is a way to hurt her.

Saint kicks Tevi once in the ribs then hauls back for another. And Gia shoots out a quick, frantic prayer to the gods of reduced gravity that the muscle behind her doesn't drop her. She drives her knees up to her chest and kicks out as hard as she can, putting the full force of her boots into Saint's hip. The goon behind her grunts and staggers back, but his iron claws in her biceps continue to hold her weight. They pierce like spikes.

Saint's already off-balance, about to kick; he crashes to one knee, but then he's up on his feet again with a speed driven by fury. He turns on her with a hiss of pain, a limping step to close the distance between them.

If she lets him see old age, that joint's gonna give him troubles.

"I'm done with you," he snarls, grabbing her throat once more. His free hand pats at her hips, then worms into the front pocket of Gia's slacks, slipping back out with her comm. He lets go of her throat, then forces her thumb onto the pad to unlock it.

"Contacts, contacts. There we are," he says. "Recording a message for Willem Jaantzen."

He clears his throat. "Jaantzen, you piece of shit," he says. "You think you can send your people to my house and throw me out my own airlock? You think the Maribi Cartel is a bunch of weak-ass punks just waiting to roll over for you? I've got your woman, and I'll find your little girl. And you send anyone else close to Durga's Belt, they'll get a bullet in the head, too."

He turns the comm back to face Gia, then pulls his pistol from his waistband and shoves the barrel under her chin. The small part of her that's still paying attention to the world outside of Saint and that gun notices the muscle behind her flinch and try to distance himself. The iron grip loosens just a fraction.

Out of the corner of her eye she can see the recording image: her dark face shining with sweat, brown eyes wide. She forces her attention away, doesn't let it distract her.

"Any last words for your boss?" Saint asks with a mocking grin.

"No!"

Saint's attention wavers for a split second as Tevi rushes him, and Gia shoves her weight to one side, slamming a forearm into Saint's to push the gun in the opposite direction. She feels the concussion in her eardrum like a sharp silver spike, and all sound is replaced by a high, tinny whine.

The grip on her biceps goes slack and the muscle behind her slumps to the ground.

Tevi has Saint locked in an awkward hug, but Saint is quickly getting the upper hand. Baxir rushes in to pull Tevi off, and Gia elbows him in the throat, kicks him in the groin, and he goes down. Another bullet whizzes by Gia to bury itself in the wall. Saint, his aim going wild as Tevi wrestles for control. Another shot, and Tevi yowls in pain and falls to the floor, blood blooming from his thigh.

Gia tackles Saint from behind as he levels his gun at Tevi's head, sending the weapon skittering across the floor.

She punches him once at the base of his skull and he flips her — he's stronger, even if his technique is sloppy and his hip is injured. She breaks his grasp and notices his fingers straining towards his boot. There — a flash of a knife. With all of her strength, Gia throws him off-balance and back into a crate, spine against edge with a sickening crack. She snatches the knife from his boot and some part of her mind is shouting to keep him as a hostage, use him as a bargaining chip, but she buries the knife in his throat.

His eyes widen, then go glassy; his body slips down the crate, legs sprawled, arms limp.

Through the scream of adrenaline and ringing in her ears, Gia's focus expands out to the room. She turns slowly, Saint's blood on her hands, to see Tevi watching her with a shocked look on his face.

And behind him, a semicircle of well-armed cartel members. Every weapon is aimed at her head.

Just then, the world explodes.

15

Starla

OKAY, SO THIS IS FUN.

The forklift operators led the first charge into the passenger terminal — and through a thoroughly surprised pack of cartel soldiers. Starla commandeered one of the pallet-jack-mounted cannons and grabbed Mona's arm; they staked out a spot and started shooting.

While she'd been outfitting the forklift suits with flamethrowers, Absolon had been modifying the cannons to shoot the bungee-type nets dockworkers use to hold down cargo. Starla's first shot goes wide and sends the pallet jack careening back into the wall — she didn't think to set the brake — but Mona reloads it and Starla fires again, the weights on the net flaring wide before colliding with a group of cartel gunmen, tangling them together in a lumpy knot that would be more amusing if the walls around her weren't being scorched black by energy blasts and the air didn't stink with blood.

The passenger terminal is chaos.

Farther down the promenade, dockworkers have blasted open another of the bay doors and are heading off the cartel soldiers who are on the run from the flamethrowers and flinging nets that poured out the door Starla blasted open. Amid the chaos, Starla finally spots Gia and her doctor. Saint is on the ground with blood running from his throat, but the doctor looks badly injured and Gia won't last long fighting off five soldiers. Starla takes aim and snares two of Gia's opponents just as they're about to shoot her, but now she can't use the net cannon anymore without snaring Gia, too. She shoves the controls into Mona's hands and breaks into a run.

Fighting in real life is nothing like in the gym sparring with Gia.

It's at once easier and more incredibly complicated. For one, despite the constant crossfire, nobody is paying specific attention to her. One man turns to fire an electric barb at her as if an afterthought, but before he finishes pressing the button he's hit by a blast of flame from the yelling woman in her modified forklift suit. The barbs flail widely off target. Starla gives the woman a thumbs up. The woman grins and aims her flamethrower elsewhere.

The man who is about to sink his knife into Gia's kidney doesn't see Starla coming, and she stomps as hard as she can on the side of his ankle. It crunches beneath her boot and he drops to his knees, face contorted. She kicks the knife out of his reach, then ducks out of the way as Gia shoves her other assailant off, sending him flying past Starla. Gia yells something that Starla misses, then grabs the man Starla kicked by the back of the neck and slams his head against the wall. He goes down cold. Gia grabs the pistol from his holster and fires it into the third soldier's chest, then aims it at the man Starla disabled.

He lifts his hands and Starla binds them with the disposable cuffs a dockworker tosses her way; Gia slumps down the wall, exhausted, the pistol dangling from her hand.

The room reeks of scorched metal and burnt hair and blood, emergency lights flash red and angry. The surge of union workers has pushed the bulk of the fighting farther down the terminal and into the main station, and almost as suddenly as the fighting started, it's calm. At least where they're standing.

Starla scans the scene. One of her forklift operators is crumpled in his suit, a white-coated nurse bending over him. Three others are sprinting towards the far end of the passenger terminal to help with the fighting there, and she can't see the other two. Presumably they've already spread with the tide of the battle through the corridors leading to the rest of the station as the union sweeps over the cartel.

People are moving slowly through the aftermath of the battle. The medics, helping wounded union and cartel soldiers alike. Dockworkers apprehending prisoners — mostly wads of cartel soldiers tangled up in bungee netting.

It's over.

Starla's mouth is dry and tastes of metal. Her hands are shaking.

It's over.

She spins, looking for Mona, and sees her ducked behind a pile of crates. Good, she didn't rush out to do anything stupid and get herself killed. Starla motions her over.

Gia is at her doctor's side, but she looks calm, not worried. In the last two years Starla has learned to discern how someone is doing based on Gia's expression: this man is going to make it through.

Gia catches her looking and holds out a pair of scissors. "Give me a hand," she says.

Starla looks from Gia to the retreating battle. She'd sent people armed into that fray. She should be there for them. She should be helping.

Gia waving in the corner of her vision pulls her back. "You can't do anything more out there," she says. "This isn't our fight."

Finally Starla drops to her knees beside the doctor and takes Gia's scissors.

"Finish wrapping his leg, nice and tight," Gia says, miming tying the bandage. She turns away from Starla to say something to the doctor, and whatever it is makes him laugh.

"Go, help somebody else," he says — Starla thinks he says — with a smile. "I'll live." Gia leans in suddenly, unexpectedly, and for a second Starla's heart stops: Gia's collapsing, hit by a bullet, maybe.

But, no. She's darting in for a kiss.

Starla looks away quickly, meeting Mona's delighted gaze. They've definitely solved the mystery of where Gia stayed last night.

Gia stands and glares at them both, then points at Mona. "You're with me," she says. "Grab that med bag."

Starla leans over the doctor's leg, wrapping and cutting the bandage, then tucking the end tight, proud of the skill she's acquired over the last couple of years, even if she feels a small pang at having learned it through such awful repetition. She sits back and looks at the man, who's clearly been saying something to her. Oops.

Starla taps her ear. "I'm deaf," she signs.

His lips part in surprise, and he gives her a small nod

of understanding. He taps his chest. "My name is — " and he fingerspells it, *T-E-V-I*. It's clear he's pulling the letters screaming from the recesses of his memory, but they're right. Or at least they spell a name.

Starla smiles in encouragement and fingerspells her own name.

"Nice to meet you, Starla," he says.

Across the room, Gia and another of the medics are conferring. Gia looks oddly relaxed — more so than Starla has seen her in years. It strikes Starla that maybe this is her element, consulting with others on the team about more serious injuries, handing out orders and coordinating supplies.

She feels a politely tentative touch on her shoulder and turns back to Tevi. He taps his chest and points across the room.

"Help me walk?" he says, relatively clearly. "I need to help them."

She nods and pulls Tevi to his feet, supports his weight across the room and helps him sit on a stool someone else pulls up for him.

She catches his "thank you" but not the rest as he turns his head to talk to someone else — presumably the rest wasn't meant for her.

She goes to find Mona.

<hr>

EVEN WITH THE strike and battle over nearly as soon as it had begun, it's nearly a week before the docks are repaired enough for anyone to leave Maribi Station. That's the official word, anyway. The hole Starla blasted in the bay door was repaired within the first few days, but Starla's heard from Mona that the new bosses are holding things up, not wanting to let a bunch of cartel members or sympathizers escape until they're sure of everyone's identity.

Mona's escape plan hasn't changed, even with the new bosses. "The union's not any different — just a different name," she signs, speaking aloud for Gia's benefit.

Starla glances around, but no one seems to have heard. Then again, it's probably plenty loud here. They're in the Nebula once more, having managed to drag Gia out of the clinic for a drink at long last. Starla has barely seen Gia these last few days; she's spent most of her time at the medical center filling Tevi's role while he heals. He was the only real surgeon on the staff, and the glut of new injuries from all the fighting has kept Gia busy.

She promised she'd relax if she came out with Starla and Mona, but she looks as tense as ever. It's the Nebula's dark corners, maybe, the hologram asteroid tables, the way your brain keeps insisting that you're floating even though you're sitting firmly in gravity — Starla loves it, but Gia doesn't exactly look like she's enjoying herself.

"At least the union will probably treat the people at the bottom better," Starla signs.

Mona's shrug is liquid, her eye roll vivid.

"Maybe. But they still won't let anyone have a real choice around here. Anyway, I'm not sticking around to find out."

"Come with us," Starla signs. "You don't need to stay on New Sarjun, but you can at least ride with us a while."

"I already have a ticket to Toro Station on the *Four Silver*," Mona signs.

"Sell it. Trade it. I'll pay your way with us."

Starla can see Mona thinking about it, see her about to cave, and she knows from experience it's not even a matter of coming up with the right argument — she just needs to ask enough times.

At least, that's what always worked when she was trying to talk Mona into some scheme when they were kids.

"Come on," she signs with a wink. "It'll be fun."

Mona's shoulders rise with breath, lower, and she finally nods. "I hear your planet's ridiculously hot," she signs.

Starla grins. "It's terrible," she signs, but in the joke she realizes just how much she misses it: the way the stars look through atmosphere, the way the sun beats down. Misses them: her family.

"You'll love it," she tells Mona. "We can share a room on the ship. They're cramped, but it'll only be for a few weeks."

Gia shifts forward then, suddenly, fingers steepled and mouth set in a serious line. "You can have my ticket," she says to Mona.

Starla stares at her in surprise. "You're not coming back?"

"No, I am. But." Gia takes a long sip from her cocktail bulb, then sets it awkwardly back on the hologram asteroid table. "I've already talked with Jaantzen about it. It'll only be until Tevi can take over his shifts again. I can't let them work shorthanded with so much going on."

Starla raises an eyebrow with a smile. "Just until he can take over his shifts, hmm?" She lifts her hands in surrender at Gia's glare. "But seriously. You are coming back?"

Gia's nod is slow to come. "To New Sarjun, yes. We'll see what happens after that."

Starla stares at her a moment, slowly letting it sink in. Gia, the fearsome lioness protector of their little crew, is moving on.

It seems . . . right.

Hugging Gia is surprisingly comfortable, her mentor's rock-hard muscles melting around Starla's shoulders after a few hesitant seconds. She smells like sweat and honey and mint, and her vocal chords vibrate as she murmurs something Starla can't see.

Finally, Gia releases her, holding her at arm's length. "Make sure Manu's keeping up his therapy? And that Jaantzen is sleeping?"

"I promise."

"And don't you dare skip your training," Gia says. "If I'm not there, you've got to have their backs, all right?"

Starla nods solemnly, but it didn't need to be said. Nothing is getting past her to her family. Not anymore.

Gia's expression is serious. "You can handle this," she says. "And if you need anything from me, just call."

"Thank you for everything," Starla signs, and Gia smiles and tips back the rest of her drink.

"Of course, kid," she says, getting to her feet. "Now you two get out of here — I have work to do."

$$\overline{}$$

Epilogue

IT'S A THIRTY-SECOND CLIP, AND GIA'S WATCHED IT A
dozen times since she came back from her shower and
found the alert blinking on her comm. By now, she's not
even bothering to hold back the tears.

The clip starts shaky: blurs of blue and tan furniture
and a blinding flash of sun through window before the
lighting levels auto-adjust and the camera focuses on
Oriol. He's standing in the living room of Manu's apartment, filming himself at a bad angle, his pale face backlit
against the window.

He can't keep away the grin as he greets her.

"Hey, G, hope you're doing well. I figured you'd want
to see this." His grin widens, eyes sparking gold as he
pans away in another blur of furniture and sunlight.

Manu is standing — *standing* — his legs strapped into
braces, one of Oriol's crutches under his good arm as he
takes his first steps.

And every time she watches this part, Gia forgets to
breathe. Manu walks the length of the couch, then looks

at the camera and smiles, pain etched into every line of his face.

"You probably thought I'd be slacking off without you here to yell at me," he says. "But I want you to know I've been doing all those goddamn exercises you told me to. Every single day."

"Not every day." Oriol's voice from offscreen.

"You said you wouldn't rat me out, babe," Manu calls back. "He's a liar, Gia. Anyway, I just wanted to say thank you. Come on home safe, okay?"

The clip cuts off again, and again Gia's finger hovers over the icon to replay it, and then she realizes she's not alone. Tevi clears his throat, and she twists on the couch to find him standing in the doorway. She turns away, dashes a hand over her wet cheeks. They're heating with embarrassment at her display of emotion.

"A patient?" Tevi asks, coming to sit beside her. He lowers himself carefully on his good leg and his hand slips comfortably onto her thigh. The sharp, medicinal odor of the clinic still clings to him, but beneath it she catches hints of cedar and honey, and she fights a sudden impulse to bury her face in the crook of that brown neck and let him wrap his arms around her. Let him comfort her like a little girl.

She slides the comm away from her as though it'll erase the fact that he saw what she was watching.

"He's . . . a friend."

The hesitation is because she might have called him a co-worker to anyone else, but using that word here just reminds Tevi who she works for. And lets him paint Manu with the same dark brush he's painted Jaantzen with before the two of them even meet.

The half truth ties itself in a knot and settles in her

gut — and trust is a rope only so long, even the tiniest lie knots it just a touch shorter.

"Just a friend?" Tevi asks, misinterpreting her hesitation.

She nods. Maybe she'd had thoughts on him when they first met, but she'd been too bitter and Oriol so sweet, and in the end she knows it wasn't even a contest. And if it had been, Manu made the smarter choice for the long run.

"What happened to him?"

Same bitch that happened to me, Gia thinks. Thala Coeur may have torn Gia's life apart metaphorically, piece by piece, but with Manu she got physical.

"Moto accident," Gia says. "What do you want to do tonight?"

They both have the night off, the first time in the weeks she's been here that they're not slipping past each other in their off hours. Yet while they might not have had much time together, those stolen moments have been well spent. And if they're both showing up to their shifts a little sleep deprived and giddy, nobody has commented.

Gia hasn't minded the work itself one bit. She'd forgotten what it can be like at a normal job, where the life-and-death scenarios are limited to the imagination of human cells, the animal malice of viruses, some unfortunate accidental contests between flesh and machine, and the occasional bar fight. She's treating wounds that weren't made maliciously, getting to the root of her patients' maladies by prescribing antibiotics and rest rather than assassinations.

She still finds herself stunned by it on occasion — how wonderfully boring it is.

And the best part of all is that when she stitches up a

dockworker's hand or sets the broken arm of a child who fell from the kitchen counter while trying to grab sweets from a high shelf, she won't be seeing them again. She's not fixing them up to send them back out into the fray, so they can return to her with an even worse injury.

Tevi is still on crutches, but just barely, the bullet wound in his thigh healing up nicely. She insisted on being the one to treat it because — Lord knows — she has the experience, but also because she feels responsible. She said that, once, and he responded that he'd known the risks when he brought his team out to the docks. He hadn't quite known the risks of bringing *her* along, though, had he?

Because she was — and still is — Jaantzen's woman on Maribi. She hasn't been asked to do much since the first flutter of messages and meetings, but the expectation is still there — hanging over her head — that she'll help out as needed for as long as she's here.

It's continued to be a sticking point for Tevi, though she tries not to talk about it. A naive part of her wonders if they can just leave this topic be forever. Wonders if there's any universe where building a life together can happen without ever having to talk about the past.

They go back home together, they're gonna have to figure this out.

"Did you get your ticket today?" Tevi asks, like he's reading her mind.

She blinks at the suddenness of the question, then shakes her head. It was the only task on her list today, besides going to the gym, but somehow she hadn't quite managed to find the time.

"You said you were getting stir-crazy," he says, surprised. "Not that I'm trying to push you out."

"You want your bed back?" Gia teases.

"Not at all. But I might want a bigger one, if you're going to stick around."

Tevi's apartment wasn't meant for two people to share for the long term, and the bed is no exception. It wears off quickly, the ability to share a single bed with another person, no matter how much you want to press your body against theirs. In that way, their opposite shifts have been a blessing, giving them enough time together without spending too many nights trying to actually sleep in the same bed.

"You could," Tevi says. "If you wanted. Stick around, I mean."

Gia's mouth tightens, and he squeezes her thigh.

"I'm only going to be here another few months," he says. He's watching her, and he doesn't seem comforted by whatever he sees on her face. "If that's what you want," he finishes. "Because that's what I want."

"Let's play it by ear, okay?" She doesn't know what else to tell him, but she takes his hand in hers.

"I was thinking today," he says. "About when I get back. I have enough money saved up that I could live for a few years without a salary. And I, or we," — he gives her a sideways look — "could get the training center started without too much extra cash. I just heard back from the operations director at the Sulila hospital; she said corporate would help with an equipment donation."

Gia gives him a skeptical look. "Just like that?"

"Not just like that," he says. "There's a vetting process I'd have to go through. They'd need to approve my business plan to make sure they're not funding a competitor."

"So it comes with strings attached."

"Everything comes with strings attached."

"It matters if those strings get in the way of what you're trying to do."

He looks down at their hands, interlaced on her thigh.

"Tevi, I thought your whole point was to be a competitor for Sulila. Training doctors who don't come with built-in corporate indentures."

Tevi takes a sharp breath. "I think I can still manage that."

"Even with Sulila's oversight?"

"Do you have a better idea?"

"Private donors."

"And you know a bunch of rich people we could ask?" Tevi asks.

She doesn't speak, and his expression darkens as he remembers the answer. "I'm not taking money from your boss. Imagine what kinds of strings would come attached with that."

"Not the kind you'd think," Gia says. "But it doesn't have to be from him. We can get introductions. There are plenty of people with money in Bulari who would be willing to support a project like this."

"People whose money I wouldn't mind taking?"

"Probably not. Nobody with the kind of money to make a difference got it clean. Not Jaantzen, not Demosga, not the Yangs, and definitely not Sulila Corp." Gia lets out a sharp, frustrated breath. "Sorry. This isn't what I wanted to talk about tonight." She squeezes his hand. "What do you want to do?"

"I'm sorry, too," Tevi says. His fingers tighten around hers, and he slouches lower on the couch, nuzzling his cheek into her shoulder. "And what do I want to do tonight? I'm doing it."

"You got any good restaurants on this rock?"

She feels him smile, the muscles of his cheek rasping rough stubble against her bare shoulder, the exhale of his laugh warming her collarbone. "Like a date?" he asks. "You never liked those."

"I'm willing to try new things."

"Mmm. There's a place I've been hearing good things about, actually. I've just been waiting for the right reason to splurge."

"Splurge? Does that mean I have to dress up?"

"Don't worry," he says, and he shifts beside her, his lips following his breath to brush her collarbone. The strap of her camisole slips off her shoulder. "Nobody has formalwear on this rock. You can wear whatever you want."

"Even my scrubs?"

"I know you can do better than that, Giaconda." His hand releases hers, and he pushes himself off the couch, kneeling in front of her with a wince.

"Get up, you're going to hurt yourself," she says.

He looks up at her, a mischievous grin tugging at his lips. "That was a pretty half-hearted protest."

"Gotta say I tried."

"Duly noted, Dr. Áte." His palms slide slowly up the outside of her thighs until his thumbs can trace her hipbones above the drawstring house trousers she's wearing. "You're not starving, are you?" he asks.

"Not for dinner," she answers.

EVERYTHING SHIFTS in an instant as New Sarjun takes hold of Starla.

At first it's a faint tug in the pit of her stomach — *home* — but then the shuttle bucks and the passengers strapped down around her react with eyes pressed closed, hands clenched tight.

A reassuring message crawls across the screen at the front of the shuttle.

The way Starla's stomach drops is at once euphoric and terrifying. With every pitch and roll, a part of her mind says, This is it, this is the end, be stoic, say goodbye with grace.

She remembers the first time she felt this sensation. The only other time she's felt this sensation. When she was strapped into restraints meant not just to keep her safe, but to reassure her Alliance captors that the teenaged daughter of notorious space pirates wasn't going to do them any harm.

And that time, she hadn't been worried about whether or not she was going to die. Back then, strapped to a seat in an Alliance shuttle, she had been buoyed by rage.

What a difference five years has made — and Gia's training reshaping her from a gangly, scrappy teenager to someone who, though she could still use some work, at least isn't going to collapse into a pile of dry bones the instant she hits gravity.

Of course, terminal staff will be waiting with wheel-chairs for anyone who needs extra help. Last time, Starla hadn't been given the option to walk out of the shuttle, even if she could have — she'd been half dragged, half carried by a pair of Alliance guards. And she hadn't landed in the fascinating bustle of Geordi Jimenez Space Terminal, either. She'd been dropped behind barbed wire and bars and concrete walls in isolation.

A lot of things are different this time. This time she's coming home to family.

And she's bringing family home.

Mona will feel the gravity, of course, even after the drug regimen she's been on and the physical training she complained about. It wasn't enough to truly prepare her, but at least she won't go into her first few days on New Sarjun as brittle-boned and frail as Starla had felt. Starla's seen to that.

Her stomach drops again with the shuttle, and she fights down her body's panic response. People do this all the time, she tells herself. Ten times a day, and when's the last time you heard about a shuttle going down? She can't think of one.

She rolls her head to see Mona in the chair next to her; her cousin's eyes are wide, her lips bloodless. She swallows, hard.

Starla waves a hand for attention. "Are you going to throw up?" she asks. She signs it with a smile, like she's teasing, but she'd also really like to know the answer before Mona loses it all over the shuttle.

"I'm fine," Mona signs back, but she has a bio bag tucked under her thigh, close to hand.

A safety notice scrolls across the screen at the front of the shuttle, reminding everyone to prepare for the descent, in case they hadn't noticed what was going on.

Mona squeezes Starla's knee to get her attention. Her far hand is digging into her pocket. "I have something I wanted to give you," she signs.

"Now?" Starla asks. "We're not gonna die. People do this all the time."

Mona doesn't respond to that. Instead, she pulls free a delicate chain, the links chattering against each other, spilling out of her hand and dancing a ragged jig in time to the movements of the shuttle. A particularly violent thrust slams both girls into their seats, and Mona's grip tightens on the necklace.

She takes advantage of the following lull to place the necklace in Starla's hand. It's stone, a smooth oval that nestles perfectly into the heart of her palm, and Starla knows — without looking, she knows — what's carved on the other side.

For a moment, Starla's stomach plunges in a way that has nothing to do with the descent.

She turns the pendant over to see the carving: a stylized winged figure coiling upwards, more emblem than artwork.

She feels the cold stone pulling the heat from her body, and for a moment her feeling of being two people at once — now-Starla and then-Starla — is amplified. A girl who thinks she knows what the world has to offer and desperately wants it all, and a woman who now knows enough to be wary, to be prepared. A girl torn free and set adrift, and a woman who's gotten herself a paddle and the will to learn to use it.

All that from a simple stone necklace.

Her mother's necklace.

"Where did you get this?" Starla asks. The shuttle jostles again and the stone leaps from her palm. Starla clutches her fist, fingers snarling in the chain before it can get away. She takes the necklace in both hands, holding it to her chest until the turbulence smooths once more, then she puts the chain over her head, tucking the pendant safely down her collar. She can feel it cold on her sternum and refusing to warm, like it has drunk in five years of grief and locked it deep inside its heart.

"Where did you get this?" she signs again when Mona opens her eyes.

"My mom had it," Mona signs. "I guess the chain had broke? She was going to repair it for your parents, for when they returned to the station, but . . ."

Starla nods; she doesn't want Mona to continue. All her most painful memories are held in that gesture, that trailing off of the fingers. She doesn't need Mona to spell it out for her.

"Thank you," she says, reaching to take Mona's hand. The two girls hold on as long as they can, until the shudders of the shuttle returning to gravity make it impossible and they plummet toward home.

Free stories!

Want more of the Durga System?

Check out my short story, "Rogue."

"Rogue" takes place many, many years before Starfall, when Jaantzen is just getting his feet underneath him.

A tricky job is starting to go south — and it only gets worse when he comes face-to-face with the most notorious space pirates in the Durga System.

Rogue is an exclusive Durga System short available to newsletter subscribers — newsletter subscribers also get occasional other free short stories, early access to books, and other perks.

I'll see you there!

Get "Rogue":

WWW.JESSIEKWAK.COM/ROGUE

DOUBLE EDGED:
BOOK 1 OF THE BULARI SAGA

Thala Coeur—Blackheart—is dead. Willem Jaantzen has been waiting to hear those words for almost twenty years. But he was also hoping they'd hold more satisfaction. Because it turns out his arch enemy has died as she lived—sowing chaos and destruction—and when a mysterious package arrives on his doorstep, he realizes she's sent him one last puzzle from beyond the grave.

As Jaantzen and his crew are plunged back into a game he thought they'd left far behind, one thing becomes painfully clear: Solving Coeur's puzzle could be key to preventing the city from crumbling back into another civil war—or it could be the thing that destroys them all.

Because this secret isn't just worth killing for. It's worth coming back from the dead for.

Continue the adventure:
JESSIEKWAK.COM/BULARI-SAGA

About the Author

Jessie Kwak is a freelance writer and novelist living in Portland, Oregon. When she's not working with B2B marketers, you can find her scribbling away on her latest novel, riding her bike to the brewpub, or sewing something fun.

Connect with me:
www.jessiekwak.com
jessie@jessiekwak.com

www.ingramcontent.com/pod-product-compliance
Lightning Source LLC
Chambersburg PA
CBHW031611180726
48284CB00005B/1497